Walking a Tightrope

Emma Gilman

Copyright © 2021 Emma Gilman

All rights reserved. No part of this book may be reproduced or transmitted in any form or by any means, electronic or mechanical, including photocopying, recording or by any information storage and retrieval system without permission in writing from the publisher.

Venture Press—Colorado Springs, CA
ISBN: 978-1-7378599-0-1
Library of Congress Control Number: 2021919726
Title: Walking a Tightrope
Author: Emma Gilman
Digital distribution | 2021
Paperback | 2021

This is a work of fiction. The characters, names, incidents, places, and dialogue are products of the author's imagination, and are not to be construed as real.

Dedication

For Olivia, my sister, friend, and first reader.

Chapter 1

It was an era of wandering souls, horse-drawn carriages, and gloved hands yearning to escape modesty—the only virtue mothers consistently taught their privileged daughters. Church bells rang atop steeples all across the city, and shouts arose as paperboys flew through the streets, informing well-to-do citizens of the daily news. They were a band of misfits, really, but performing their unique role in society. And the news was that of the circus.

Everyone in Axminster was deeply devoted to Jesus, and anyone who deviated from that was deemed a messenger of the devil. Otherwise, life was average but strangely exciting there. Children ran around in search of the perfect dandelion to pick among the hundreds blowing in the fields. Smoke wafted from sweet-smelling shops filled with cinnamon bread, banana cream pies, and tiny raspberry tarts. Husbands in top hats, fine fitted suits, and shiny black boots buckled at the ankles clipped along on their way to work, while their wives, dressed in silk, lace, and ruffles waited idly by for them to return each day. And on Sundays, paupers lined the street corners begging for money, while these rich men hung jewelry on their wives and attempted to contain their disobedient children as they made their way to church. The air was always warm and smelled of honey and roses, and the constant commotion was wonderful.

Such was the general atmosphere in Axminster, but on this particular day, amid the clacking of carriages rolling by on the cobblestone streets, there was a disruption in that wonderful commotion.

"Watch it, pumpernickel!" I shouted, while a man in a plum-colored top hat hit his horse with a crop as his carriage rolled quickly by, practically taking off my brand-new lavender saddle shoes. My mother always taught me not to swear at strangers, and I listened for twenty-one years. But today, the urge to lash out overtook me.

My name is Juniper Rose, and those who know me describe me as a quirky girl with curly black hair resting on her small shoulders, a sweetheart smile with the rarest red lips, and green eyes always searching for amusement.

I carry myself with purpose, despite the ache in my heart for a different reality—something other than the old buildings pelted by rain and my flashy-but-lonely house on the outskirts of town. I have even grown tired of Mr. Marbury's poor dog hunting for scraps, starting every morning at precisely eight o'clock. I believe I've seen it all. The time of lace gloves, simple sun hats adorned with flowers, and pastel gowns is a time of beauty, but one that cannot hold my affection.

The town of Axminster is where my family lives, where all of my friends and I attend baking classes, and where my older sister is currently struggling to find a husband. But I'm certain this city does not want to keep me any more than I want to stay. After years of repeating the same routine over and over, my feet have begun to drag and my eyes have lost their luster.

Today I found myself lazily walking by shop windows to pass the time in this unadventurous life of mine. I noticed ladies floating past me with fake smiles, trying harder than they ought to find a suitor. If only they knew there was more to life than silly men. I rounded the corner on Chicopee Street, familiar with the path to the esteemed chapel. Where other towns' most prized possession would be the city square or the town hall, in Axminster it was the church. My mother always insisted that I go there to show my respect for God as often as I had the chance to do so. And despite not feeling the same conviction, I remained an obedient daughter and followed her wishes. At least I tried to.

Without even recognizing my rebellion, I turned down a side alley, away from the proverbial light of heaven. I had no idea where my feet were carrying me, but I knew it would be far more interesting than my original destination. Suddenly, a glint caught my eye. My saddle shoes, with their short heels, stopped me in my tracks as a cloud of dust formed around me where I stood. There was a wall of glass to my left, and in the glass I saw an image of a girl with bouncy curls and charisma staring back at me. But this version of me looked different. I saw a crown of black feathers sitting atop my head, bejeweled wristbands snaking up my thin arms, and tight scarlet elastic stretching across my thighs, which had finally been allowed to see the light of day. The image broadened as I gazed dreamily at silver horseshoes on snow-colored stags and fire-breathing humans. I saw a future of enigmatic and energized people before being awakened from this strange allusion by a man rushing past with a small suitcase in his grasp. He bumped me on the shoulder in his hasty endeavor.

"Sorry, Miss!" The man said in an English accent that matched mine. As he swung his arms, I saw what seemed to be a flyer clamped securely in his hand. "I'm going to be late!" he exclaimed.

I stepped aside and he began to hustle again. "Late for what?" I shouted, but he was too far away. I shouldn't have been so interested. After all, Mother taught me not to put my nose where it didn't belong. But this man seemed so carefree, I felt I could ask.

To my surprise, he stopped briefly, turning to look me in the eyes. "The circus!" he exclaimed with wild enthusiasm.

I blinked once and he was gone. And maybe it was just the wind that forced the crumpled piece of parchment to bounce at my feet, revealing that fateful invitation to the circus. But then again, maybe it was not.

I opened the brass doorknob to my house, built of tan brick with bay windows on almost every side. I was greeted by my sister when I walked through the door, my dress brushing on either side of the wooden frame. She sat in the floral armchair by the front window with a porcelain plate and what was left of a tea cake. Her name is Colette, and she is beautiful. Her dark hair matches mine, but it is curled to perfection, whereas mine is frizzy and wild. Her skin is clean of blemishes, and her lips are perfectly round.

I watched our servant, Kathryn, present Colette with a tray of milk and sugar for her tea. My sister brushed her away rudely with a flick of her hand, and Kathryn bowed her head and walked away, wiping her stained hands on the yellow apron pinned to her simple black uniform. There are no ruffles, lace, or shiny pendants on her dress, but I can say more of Kathryn's loyalty than that of my own family.

"Oh, my little prune," my mother said as she gallivanted into the room, patting my cheek lightly. I took a seat next to my sister and shivered at the nickname. My mother loved to garden and we had a particularly large plum tree in our backyard. Mother dried the plums herself to make prunes for cakes and jams. When I was five, I ate an entire jar of prunes without asking. I had the worst stomachache for days, but I loved the taste so much that I kept eating them, and to my dismay, that became my nickname. "How was the chapel?" Mother asked with fake interest.

"It was just fine," I lied, and then quickly approached the question on my mind. "Have either of you heard of the circus coming to town?"

"Filthy ragamuffins. They don't know how to make a legitimate life for themselves. Almost worse than beggars," my mother said with a distasteful frown.

My mother wasn't the only one who disagreed with the circus. All the wealthy people in Axminster, and throughout the land, thought the circus was for lazy people who didn't want to work hard at a normal job. They thought of them as homeless bottom feeders, who attracted too much attention to the odd and disorderly.

My sister piped up, noticing the change in my face. That's what I admired about my sister. She matched me. She didn't comment rudely like our mother, but rather inquired about my interest. "Why do you ask?"

"Just curious. I saw signs posted around town today. Seems quite the exciting life on the road," I remarked.

"You know not to talk like that," Mother added as she whipped her dark hair toward me with a deliberate glare in her eyes. Mother doesn't like it when I botch my English. She'd rather I talk like a proper lady, in full sentences and finishing each phrase with an elegant smile. "A filthy life, I'm sure you mean. I do hope you are not creating a fanciful dream of chasing along after the train to join the circus. I'd disown you faster than I could recall the name of my favorite pastry," she laughed haughtily. The sound was hard and strained.

"Of course not, Mother." I cupped my cheek to hide my nervousness. I could not fathom how she would disown me so easily, as if I was never her daughter at all. "Could you imagine the back pain from sleeping on such a hard surface?" I added to hide my interest.

Mother and Colette laughed jubilantly. I sighed and smiled, feigning interest while they spoke of the new prime minister and his son, *the one worthy of her daughters,* according to my mother. Colette has always gone along with my mother's desires, just as I have, but I know she would never accept his hand in marriage, even if he did summon the courage to ask. That's the last thing on her mind. She pretends to please Mother, though, which is something I intend to stop doing.

I laid awake that night, with the unbearable thought of returning to the chapel early in the morning. I was so weary of stopping by the bakery for a loaf of bread and a slice of cheese. So weary of passing the bookshop on Clarenster Street. So weary of seeing the same old dandelions that mark the path up to my home. Nothing changed in Axminster. Every day was the same, and I was bored with it.

Overwhelmed by the burning desire in my heart to flee, I jumped out of bed and grabbed my leather duffel. I threw in my undergarments, several shirts, a few pairs of worn pants I used to wear for riding practice when I was young, a sweater, and the chocolate-colored leather boots in the back of my closet. They may be a little tight, but they are the sturdiest pair of shoes I have. I creeped down the stairs, holding my boots in my hand to avoid the usual *click-clack* they make, packed a loaf of bread and an apple, and grabbed one of my mother's cakes on the way out the door. I made it down the road about ten feet before stopping in my tracks to take one last look at the house behind me. I remembered the cream-colored curtains and matching rugs, the dark oak floors and the clear glass windows too perfect for grubby hands to touch. It would always be the house I grew up in, the place where my memories were made.

I held back the tears, and my nose burned as I thought of my sister there. She will most likely be there until the end of her days. My mother will have her stay even when she has a husband and a family of her own. I only hope someday she can be brave enough to make the same decision I've made.

I trekked through dark and musty alleyways on the edge of Axminster, searching for the train that runs through our town every night at midnight. The train usually carries necessities like oil and grain. But tonight, it carried something else—something unusual—ruffians with odd talents who felt perfectly natural sleeping on mold-ridden floors and drinking booze into the wee hours of the morning. For a week, the tabloids had touted the circus's arrival, but in a million years, I didn't expect to spring out of bed and escape there, leaving everything I had known. But since that's exactly what I'd decided to do, the circus felt like the only place to go. I'd have a place to eat and sleep, and no harm would come to me. A cat whined in the dark as I approached the train, and I scuttled back and slid across the rainy cobblestones. The poor live in the outer banks of Axminster, where scraps of food and random boxes and beggars are scattered in the dark streets. I wanted to stop and help the hungry, but if I was delayed, I might miss the train. And this was my only chance at a new start in life. There was a roar in the distance and I ran, turning left and right along the oily dirt roads, emerging from the city and into a small meadow of golden grain. As I ran through the grain, I hoisted my bag higher on my shoulder, worried I wouldn't make the train. Finally I saw the glare of the white light and heard the sound of the blaring horn. I waved my arms wildly, stopping just feet away from the tracks. The train moved quickly, and for a moment, I was unsure it would stop for me. I imagined it leaving me behind, confirming my worst fear—that I was a girl who would never escape her privileged life. Then the train's speed finally decreased until it stopped completely, and as its wheels scraped against the track, sparks flew. The circus had made one more stop.

The side of the main cart on the train read CIRCUS in fanciful red letters that had been worn by the sun. A man in a top hat extended a leather glove to me, and I grabbed it with great enthusiasm. I found my footing on a rail in the dark, and he wouldn't let go of my hand as he led me inside. Doing something so daring had caused a great deal of adrenaline to rush through me. I had never done anything like this… because of my mother's wishes.

I followed the man through narrow aisles to the back of the train where barrels of rum were stored. I heard someone call him Wilman, and he seemed like he was in charge here. My nose burned with the acrid smell of alcohol, and I silently thanked my mother for never allowing me to have any. That brought back to my mind memories of the life I had just left behind. And for once I felt uncertain about my future. I shoved the thought out of my head, fighting the urge to turn around and run for the sunflower hills surrounding my home, where life was comfortable and certain.

Suddenly a man with a graying beard opened a barn door and a sea of people came into view, laughing with drunken smiles, talking too loudly for the middle of the night, wearing tattered clothing loosely on their shoulders. I watched in amazement as they laughed heartily and exchanged jokes.

"You should've seen the old pimp that came to the tents last night." The man's accent was rich, although I couldn't tell where he was from.

"What'd she look like? Your mum?" Another man spit out, and everyone roared in laughter.

My eyes squinted at their vulgar comments.

Wilman appeared again and spoke up, "These a' most of da performers, 'cept for a few stragglers in da other carts." He didn't fully pronounce his syllables, so it was a little hard to understand him, but I nodded along. "I'll show ya dem now." He walked slowly, holding out a lamp, alight with a flame. It must have been around midnight, and I couldn't believe all of the circus performers were still awake and so lively. To see them in their raw and unhinged state was exciting. I couldn't imagine acting like that, but maybe in time I would get used to it.

That is if you stay, a voice in my head said.

"We been on da rails for a week now. Just got done wit' a performance in Beckinsdale across da sea." His dark eyes caught the firelight when he looked back at me.

I had heard of Beckinsdale, but I had no idea where it was. I figured after a few months, I'd know every city within a thousand-mile radius.

"Now," he stopped abruptly, making me bump into him. "Here is da main performer. He don't like visitors too much." Wilman opened a door similar to the last, and inside I saw about ten more performers, laughing and talking quietly. It reminded me of my neighbors' charming laughter when they came over for supper back home. *Back home.* It seems weird to think of it that way. My eyes flicked around the small room as the trainman introduced me as the recruit. My ears betrayed me and his words turned to molasses when I caught a boy's eyes boring into mine from across the room. Others had welcomed me, but his laconic presence almost seemed disrespectful. His sickly smile made it so I couldn't take my eyes off of him. The boy's hand was resting on the hip of a woman with curly blond hair and a loose silver silk dress. His hair was as black as a raven's wings, relatively contained except for the one piece that betrayed him and hung over his eyebrow in a soft curl. His eyes were like dazzling caramel and dripped with seductiveness.

I had heard of those who could trick others...put people under their spell. They're called witches, and for a moment I considered him one. I wondered why I couldn't look away when a woman's loud voice spoke up, drawing me from my fascination.

"Don't mind Cassius. He's always fascina'ed with new lots like ya, especially one so pretty," a girl in a revealing skirt said. I had the urge to offer her my trousers.

Just then, he looked away. *Cassius*, I thought. That name made him seem even more dangerous.

"This is da wild bunch. Be careful 'round dem." Wilman winked at me.

"Come on Wilman, you know you love us." A girl wrapped her arms around his neck, and he laughed as if to say, *you're funny*. She had piercing ice-blue eyes and straight, white hair, and she looked at me and said, "Whatcha got?"

It was the first time anyone had spoken to me directly. My throat caught and I whispered, "What?"

"What talent do ya got?" She repeated slowly and loudly, as if I was hard of hearing.

No one had ever asked me that before. I guess I should have thought about that before jumping onto a train with a bunch of hooligans. I thought for a moment. I was always good at balancing, and I was the best dancer in my ballet class before I quit four years ago. I remember that I could hold a relevé for ten minutes when evaluated by my teacher. I relayed all this to them shyly and watched as smiles took over their faces.

"Well, my friends," the white-haired girl said as she looked to her fellow ruffians. "It looks like we've got ourselves a tightrope walker."

Chapter 2

The reflection of a young girl gazed proudly at me. Dark hair and cheeks as red as the raspberry tarts in the corner bakery. Small hands with bony fingers on a slim wooden bar, too high for a slowly growing girl. A plastered smile and jealous blue eyes. Young ladies with blonde hair and straight smiles also appeared in the mirror, pirouetting and stretching their perfectly long legs for all the world to see. This image is burned in my memory. They were the image of perfection, and I was a grey stone amid the glittering gems. I wore a simple pink bodice and white sheer skirt that bounced slightly as I spun around the room, pointing my feet in perfect form. Upon reaching the other side of the room and finishing my lovely dance, I could hear the beauties talking quietly while waving their long fingers delicately. I was never part of their glory, but I felt as though I was accomplishing something great, springing across that floor. Black tendrils of hair prickling my cheeks, toes pointed, and fingers curled. I felt like I was flying, but no one noticed. That was when I began to dream of escaping.

"Wake up, Miss! Day's a crackin'." Wilman rustled my shoulder.

I woke groggily, rubbing my swollen eyes. I had slept on a bed of hay all night and my back was so tight, it felt like it had been molded like a hard piece of candy.

I spoke incoherently for the next few minutes while I laced up my boots. The sun shone brightly outside and I had the urge to take all my clothes off and warm my skin in the rays that poked delightfully through the splinters in the wooden train cars. A smile took over my face as I remembered the events of last night. The glistening smiles, not feigned, but made of pure bliss. Different people living together in celebration, no matter the size or color—no one left behind.

It took me a moment to get my bearings. The train had rocked steadily for hours the night before, and I had the sensation that I was still moving back and forth. Wilman led me down the narrow passages where people still laid, barely awake, eyes roaming lazily. Up ahead, a group of people hurriedly unpacked boxes and bags full of miscellaneous things.

"Here we are," Wilman announced in response to my confused expression. "We settle in Dangarnon but travel 'round da world. We'll train here for two months 'fore we get back on da road again." He quickly marched forward to where one of the train walls had been lowered onto the dirt floor outside, creating a ramp.

I covered my eyes with a pale arm as I walked outside into the disarray. A girl in a brown dress made of scraps flew by brashly with a peacock resting on her arm, and a boy followed her shouting, "Get back here, Poppy! You know Hemper don't like to be separated from Harper!" I assumed he was talking about the bird, but I had no idea.

"Those a' da twins. Specialize in animal speech." Wilman spoke of the circus as if he knew it like the back of his hand—as if he wasn't in some fantastical place of energy and mystery. It was hard to believe I would ever become accustomed to this place. "Animals are in da lower bunkers." He pointed to the last carts on the long train. "In da middle are da eating quarters, and on da opposite end are da sleepin' quarters. Pretty easy, eh?" He shrugged his shoulders and led me inside to meet the animals.

We ventured past so many different animals it was hard to keep track. There were sugar gliders in a small cage next to a colossal one where a giraffe stood tall, its head reaching the top of the metal bars, and the lions and horses and buzzing bees seemed to welcome me. I wanted to acquaint myself with each one, but Wilman pulled me away. He led me a little farther down the corridor, stopping abruptly beside a door stained cherry red.

"This is all yours," he said ominously, pushing open the door.

I peered inside to find props ornamenting every wall. Ruby red hoops like the one I saw atop my head in the glass windowpane in Axminster, embossed with a golden circus emblem, and countless leashes and balls littering the floor. I began to think this was a room for another circus animal until I saw the outfits hanging on a brass rack to my left—pea-green petticoats, linens lined in gold, lavender waistcoats, camel-colored skirts that rippled in the wind, bright blue stars speckled on black bodysuits, and netted stockings embedded with diamonds. There were so many colors to choose from.

"These are da uniforms you'll wear when you perform," Wilman said.

I was taken aback by his offer. These pieces of fabric looked more like undergarments than articles of clothing. I would have to wear these in front of hundreds of people? After a troubled moment, I gulped and nodded. I was still the girl from Axminster who was modest and innocent, despite her adventurous soul. For years, I'd been angry with my mother for forcing me to do things I didn't want to do, like wearing impossibly high collars and long skirts. Life in Axminster was scheduled and controlled. My mother criticized everything I did, and I resented her for it. Wearing these costumes seemed frightening to me, but maybe it would help me forgive my mother for being so rigged.

Wilman closed the door behind him and led me back to my room. On the way, I noticed a soft *pitter-patter* echoing outside as small droplets of water disturbed the dirt where the animals roamed. Clouds formed and the sky grew dark as a heavy rain began to fall. The train got dim, but within moments, the crew had lit the candelabras hanging on the walls and a warm glow illuminated the hallways. The pulsing of the flames made the small train feel warm and comfortable. When I got back to my room, I was surprised to see a dress lying on my bed.

"You're in for a treat." Wilman laughed.

"What do you mean?" I said and realized these were the first words I had spoken to him since arriving here. My voice sounded too soft and polite for such a wild place. I took the fabric in my hands to explore the soft texture.

Wilman didn't answer my question, but rather instructed me to put on the dress. There were so many different pieces that I couldn't figure out where my arms were supposed to go. After several tries, I pulled the thing over my head, and the small mirror in the corner confirmed that I looked ridiculous. The dress was long and had slits travelling from the floor to my hips, revealing my bare legs every time I stepped. And there was a large slit down the front where my chest spilled out. The dress was really just a heap of straps. I hated the modesty back home, but I felt a little too free in this.

I peeked my head outside the door, and Wilman turned to look at me.

"Is there anything else I can wear?" I asked.

"No," he said abruptly, sauntering toward the dining hall.

"Wait! I can't wear this!" I argued.

"Yes, you can. And you will if you want to fit in here." His arms waved back and forth coolly as he walked. I suspected he was over forty, even though he fit right in with this group of ruffians. Surely, he didn't understand the reason I had such trepidation.

I followed obediently behind him with my skin crawling. I felt terribly uncomfortable, and I had the scary sense that my mother would come around the next corner and reprimand me. I wasn't overweight or anything even close, I just wasn't used to showing my body to everyone. And now that I was, I worried they wouldn't like it. And their rejection would be worse than hiding it away forever.

We reached a crowd of people standing in the middle of the floor, talking amongst themselves. The tables had been pushed back into the corner and the chairs stacked. I assumed this would be the dining room when not transformed into a dance hall. Beyond ballet lessons and recitals, I'd only danced a few times in my life at family gatherings, and always respectfully. My mother taught Colette and me that it was not lady-like to dance unless we were at a wedding.

My boots slid precariously on a sticky mess coating the floor. People were jumping up and down in jubilation, thanking the storm brewing outside for interfering with their practice plans. The room was small and there was a merry band playing in the corner with soft candles flickering lightly overhead. Wilman had left the room to manage the animals and make sure they were safe during the storm, and now I truly knew no one. I stood there awkwardly in my new dress, feeling all eyes on me, and wrapped my arms around my stomach to cover a morsel of myself.

"What is your name?" A young girl had appeared at my side without my notice. She was small, with beady brown eyes and wiry hair.

"Juniper Rose," I declared as if my name held value here as it had in Axminster.

"Good to meet ya! My name is Olive!" The young girl must have been nine or so. Her skin was a deep shade of olive, just like her name. I wondered if she received the name upon joining the crew or if that was her original title. "What got ya here?"

I raised my eyebrows in a questioning way.

"Your talent?" She added, speaking up.

"Oh." My eyes sank to the floor. I really must get better at understanding their way of speaking. "I'm good on my toes. I'm to be one of the new tightrope walkers." I said, unsure of myself.

"One of? Darlin', you are the *only* tightrope walker," she said to me, as if I was the younger one. At that moment, I felt as much. I had no idea what I was doing here. "Mr. Monte has been looking for one for almost five years now."

"Mr. Monte? I thought Wilman was in charge of all of this?"

"It's okay to say its name." Olive frowned at me. "You're in the *circus*. It took me a bit to get used to it too." She winked and looked at the crowd. "Wilman is the footman. He recruits new members, but they only stay if Mr. Monte approves of them. Be glad you're in his good graces."

I looked at the girl curiously, and the warmth of her skin surprised me when she grabbed my hand suddenly. "Come meet everyone."

I tried to retreat but she was stronger than I expected, and I yelped when she tugged me to a table in a dark corner so we wouldn't be overheard. She was like a little schoolgirl, filling me in on all of the latest gossip. Rather than introducing me to the performers, she pointed her finger and began to describe each one.

"Those are the twins." I traced Olive's finger to the same boy and girl from earlier, completely bedecked in animal skins. Then her finger moved to the right, where a large group of girls stood, their hair teased a mile above their heads. With them was a girl who had such large earlobes they dropped down to her shoulders, a girl with red hair who had her lips sewed shut, and an older woman with graying hair who had six fingers on each hand. They were odd indeed.

"Those are the dancers."

I counted thirteen before she moved to the back of the room. "And those are the flamethrowers." Men with scraggly beards and giant golden gages in their ears stood in a circle, hands shoved in their tattered pockets. They looked frightening.

One of the men caught us staring and approached us, his low voice matching his appearance. "Hey O, who's this?" He pointed at me with a smile. He didn't seem so frightening when he smiled.

"This is Juniper Rose. She's the tightrope walker everyone's been gushing about." Olive smiled happily, showing her small crooked teeth.

"Everyone?" I asked. "Who has been talking about me? I barely know anyone here, and I doubt anyone knows me."

"Everyone," she clarified. "Mr. Monte will explain later," she said, and waved away the issue carelessly.

"Juniper Rose." The man let my name settle on his tongue, as if trying to discover if it tasted good or if it had gone bad. "That's a nice name. It's got a ring to it. That's important for pleasing a crowd." He winked at me, then turned and left abruptly.

What was with people winking here?

Olive continued in a rush. I couldn't retain all the information she gave me, but I was sure it would just take time to get to know everyone. "Those are the horse riders."

The group was made up of only boys, the most attractive and lean I had ever seen.

"The jugglers."

These were small men with long arms parading around the room with large bottles of wine.

"The cyclists."

A few young teenagers mingled with one another with what I hoped was grape juice in their goblets.

"The magicians."

Two men sat at the only table in the room, dressed in fine fashion, complete with top hats on their heads. The top hats reminded me of the kind of formality common to Axminster, and I wished they would take them off.

"And lastly, the lion tamer." Olive's tone darkened at the mention of this performer.

I followed her arm to where a man sat with women flanking his sides, although he didn't appear interested in them at all. It seemed as though they were the last thing on his mind as he downed the contents in his glass. I recognized him. I had met him the previous night. I hadn't spoken to him, but I remembered his face. Cassius. I stared for far too long, watching the bob of his throat, before his head turned. His caramel eyes were fixed on me, and I turned my head away quickly, uncomfortable with his attention.

"The lion tamer?" I questioned. Cassius appeared intimidating. He had that look in his eyes that made it seem like he hated everyone around him. He must have thought this life was dreadful.

"He tames all of the big scary animals. A real crowd-pleaser, that one!" She looked him up and down greedily.

I kept my eye on all of the performers as the rain fell. A roaring thunderstorm shook the train as the animals kicked in the holding pens. It was a wild night full of drinking and hollering, one which I didn't feel right about joining. I was not familiar with the life these people lived. Nonetheless, I knew I'd rather be here than back home listening to my mother and sister go on about the fine gentlemen in town.

Colette...

"Where is your sister?" Mother yelled from across the kitchen.

"I don't know, Mum! Juniper told me nothing!" I screamed back at her. I was worried about my sister. I had always known she was unhappy here, and it was my mother that had driven her away. But to where? She was on her own in the world, doing God only knows what. I cursed myself for using the Lord's name in vain. "I'm sure she's just gone on an early morning stroll, and she'll be back this afternoon. Let's not worry." I tried to convince my mother as well as myself, but deep down I knew she wasn't coming back. A part of me was terrified for her, and the other part was grateful that she'd escaped. And all of me was lonely.

"She is my daughter. The only one with a hope of providing for this family. Of course, I will worry." My mother ruffled her black hair woefully.

Her words stung. Juniper was younger than I, and more likely to marry into a fortune that would provide for our family. I was too late to find a husband or the charmed life my mother intended for me. I prayed my sister would return, but I hoped simultaneously that she was too far gone to even consider it.

16

The sun had just come up and I was eager to get started, but only once the ground had dried and the animals had calmed, did I begin. With two months to prepare, I would have to work hard to give the audience what they wanted.

That afternoon, I was beckoned to see Mr. Monte. I was eager to see him, eager to know more about every aspect of the circus. I should have known before I boarded the train, leaving everything behind, but there was no turning back now. Wilman rapped on Mr. Monte's door and I was instructed to enter. Wilman didn't follow me inside, but left me with a total stranger instead.

I figured being polite and introducing myself was the right thing to do. "It's nice to meet you. My name is Juniper Rose."

"And you shall be our next tightrope walker, I hear." His words were as smooth as honey but full of doubt. "What makes you think you can be a tightrope walker for my circus?"

The question was one I had been turning over and over in my head. Why was I special? How would I, above anyone else, be good enough to be one of the circus's most famous attractions? My mind then transitioned to my childhood ballet studio where I trained for seventeen years, and my confidence was restored. "When I was six, I looked into a mirror and saw myself in jewels and wristbands and tight leather clothing. And two days ago, I saw the same image in the window of a store. I've been trained in ballet since I was four years old, and I may be a bit rusty, but I imagine myself do greater things than I once thought possible."

Mr. Monte leaned back in his old wooden desk chair, folded his arms across the ivy green peacoat he wore, and sat up to look me in the eyes. He stared for a long time, and then finally stood to circle me and observe my form. "In good shape. Good height. Long legs that will please the crowd."

I could not discern whether his comments were inappropriate or if I should simply take them as a compliment.

He continued, "Your hair is perfect. You can tan your skin if you'd like, but it's not required. After all, what is more typical of the circus than odd features and colors?" His full cheeks bloomed with freckles, and he pushed back his auburn hair into a top hat and turned to go.

I liked the idea of not having to be fixed, of not having to change to fit in. I wasn't required to wear bulging skirts to hide my feminine features. Here they were praised. And I wouldn't have to hide my face under a bonnet to keep the sun off of my cheeks. Here freckles and rosy cheeks were put on pedestals.

"You will be our rose." He immediately plucked a rose from the opal vase on his desk and handed it to me. "Juniper Rose, the blooming tightrope walker from Axminster."

I took the rose from his hand in acceptance. I knew that from this day on, I would be free to be who I was born to be.

Chapter 3

Mr. Monte walked me personally to the tents on the premises beyond the train. Four big red and white canopies rippled gently in the wind. A multitude of tents were available so that performers with different talents could practice at the same time, ensuring their privacy. I could envision opening night so clearly, with stars shining brightly in the sky and a raucous of cheering, a stage big enough for all of us, the arenas lit by flame, and footprints of every size in the sand telling of the acts that happened there. Colors dancing on the walls, reflected off the performers' dazzling costumes—if amusement could be a color, I was sure it would be bright magenta!

"This is where you will practice for the next two months. Six hours a day. Dinner is at six o'clock sharp and you can eat your other meals whenever you please. Do spend as much time here as you can to familiarize yourself with the equipment before our next show," Mr. Monte said, without even stopping for a breath.

He sauntered off before I could say a word. Entering the tent, it was just like I might have expected. The floor was covered with giant circular rings full of sand. There were thick, wooden beams stretched as high as I could see, and at the very top, the tent came to a point. There were no spectacular colors though. No golden hues or magentas. This was the circus in its restful state. I knew the magic would happen when the excited crowds arrived, when the flames were lit, and when the dazzling performers took center stage. The place could hold hundreds of guests, but today it was just for me. And I had no idea where to begin.

The nostalgia from my childhood dance class had been replaced with fear. Above me hung what should be the main attraction at the

19

circus—what should be my talent. But there was a world of difference between the old days, spinning on a dance floor, and this! How could I be the main attraction on a three-inch piece of rope, forty feet above the ground?

I stared at the tightrope for an hour, trying to convince myself to just take the leap and try it. I wasn't going to get anywhere just staring at it, but I couldn't move. It was impossible to imagine myself on that thing, in a tiny uniform, in front of all those eyes. It's not who I was. But it's who I wanted to be.

I walked back to the train and up the ramp to grab a plate of dinner—grain salad and a slab of pork, which I salted and ate grudgingly. Before I had a chance to feel alone, Olive plopped herself down next to me, bringing an entourage of people with her. She introduced the other members to me—something I wouldn't have done myself. I wish I had the courage she had.

I recognized a few faces from when she pointed them out last night at dinner, but I wouldn't have remembered their names without her help.

The same flamethrower I spoke to last night took a seat across from me. His head was bald, and tattoos snaked up every inch of his arms. I'd never seen such things drawn on a body before. It was quite fascinating.

"My name is Hugh." He held out a thick and scarred hand for me to shake.

I smiled and grabbed his hand. "It's very nice to meet you." I wanted to ask him about his hands. I wondered how long it took to stop getting burned by the flames, but that would be a talk for another time I suppose. I met so many people that day, but a kind girl named Hazel was the most memorable. Her eyes were hazel, so maybe that's where she got her name, but her pupils were more oval than round. If you squinted, her eyes looked more like a snake's. Her skin was pale—paler than mine—which was saying something. Hazel was quiet, but whenever she spoke, she made me giggle. I hoped to speak with her more.

The tent continued flapping in the distance, the blood-red leather contrasting with the snow-white strips. I felt inspired after meeting performers who had found the circus to be their only hope, an escape from their sad lives. I was fortunate enough to have been given a life of comfort, but I was here for a reason. Inside this world, something was waiting for me. Not a pirouette or a pointed toe, but my true self. The real me, the free one, maybe even the immodest and rebellious one. I decided then and there that not trying was my worst mistake, so I ran to the tent and flung myself inside. I was ready to spin.

I'd been practicing for hours with simple pirouettes, pliés, and double turns. It had been far too long since I'd danced, and before jumping onto a tightrope, I'd better remember the foundations. I placed my hand on the beam in the big tent, bent my knees up and down, and moved my arms in rhythmic synchronization. Forward, side, down, side, forward. I repeated those motions while my left leg pointed forward, to the left, back, and then into relevé. I bent my upper body forward and lifted my right leg this time, toes pointed at the sky. The warm-up was familiar, but the hours were long, and when my tight pants began to cling to my clammy legs uncomfortably, I decided to call it a night. My feet pattered on the dirt as I returned to the train. The night air was warmer than I expected and when I breathed in, fresh air filled my lungs for what felt like the first time since I had arrived. I tilted my head up to the sky to see the stars welcoming me overhead.

"You know," a voice spoke from close by. The sound was low and smooth, almost calming.

I snapped my head to the right.

"People are beginning to think you will never be anything but a modest little girl." Cassius. His eyes were golden in the dull candlelight illuminating the path back to the train, but his hair blended into the midnight sky.

"I think it's a little too early to tell," I told him honestly. My voice sounded too high and proper to convince either of us.

"Not for me," he said so surely, I almost believed him. He tucked a hand into the loose breeches that hung on his torso, walking away without another word. His boots scraped on the dirt, and it was almost as if he meant to make my ears ring.

Cassius didn't agree with my being here, that was clear. I stood there, waiting for the sound to fade, or rather for the fear that I may always be that little girl to relinquish. But it never did.

"You've got it! Just take one more step." Mr. Monte watched me as I placed both feet on the small tightrope that was only ten feet above the ground. This was the training tightrope and I had only managed to take one step. He clasped both hands to his heart, yearning to see me excel.

"What if I fall?" I yelled. He encouraged me and I took a deep breath, but my legs wobbled so violently that I knew it was only a matter of time before I fell. I positioned my arms out at my side as if I was preparing to take flight, but my right leg turned sharply on the tightrope when I tried to step forward. My stomach lurched into my throat and suddenly I hit a heavy pad. When I caught my breath, I sat up to look at Mr. Monte.

He was not disappointed, not in the slightest. "One step. That is a fine start, young lady. Tomorrow it will be two."

Chapter 4

A week had passed and every day held the same routine. I woke up, ate breakfast among the performers I hadn't begun to understand, practiced for two hours, ate lunch, practiced another four hours until dinner, and then practiced some more. But no matter how much I practiced, I was not improving. Mr. Monte was disappointed with my lack of progress. He didn't say it, and he even watched me every other day to see if he could help, but I saw it in his eyes. It seemed that after the last tightrope walker, the circus and everyone watching was expecting something spectacular. Something I couldn't give.

That night after dinner, instead of returning to the tent to practice, I ventured to the magicians' quarters at the far end of the train. I walked past dilapidated candelabras with wax dripping onto the worn wooden walls. I sneered at the pints of ale that littered the floor and marveled at how much time the other performers spent together. I hadn't made any close friends yet. No one could believe that a girl from the privileged city of Axminster would join their unprivileged ranks to walk on a piece of rope just for fun. They expected me to fail and return to my wealthy life without batting an eye because that's all I'd ever known.

That was the last thing I wanted to do though. I struggled every day to produce something spectacular for the circus, and I would never go back to Axminster or to my mother and her selfish ways. She and everyone else there was consumed with money and status. They had no real interests besides being well known and being able to buy anything they desired. I missed my sister dearly, but I could not tolerate that dreary destiny just to be in her presence.

I'd reached the last train car, and there were two doors for the two magicians—one in front of me and one to my right. The first magician performed magic tricks with top hats, flames, flowers, and cards, while the other specialized in reading fortunes and predicting the future. I figured the latter was the man to go to for answers about what had happened with the circus over the years. I could have asked Olive but she seemed too young to remember the former tightrope walker, and I didn't intend to intrude on Mr. Monte after my less-than-stellar performance on the tightrope.

I rapped my knuckles on the door looming in front of me, and after a few moments of silence, heavy footsteps echoed on the other side. The brass doorknob turned slowly and the door opened to reveal a hulky man staring back at me. His eyes were such a vibrant color green, it looked like his eye sockets had been replaced with emeralds. He had straight brown hair, hanging just past his ears, and a thick beard on his burly chin. And he was a big man, to the point that his stature took up the entire frame of the door.

"My name is-"

"Juniper," he answered for me, tilting his head to the right. He smiled genuinely and seemed very kind, which was odd in contrast to his looming eyes and authoritative stance. "Come in, come in." He beckoned me inside with his long arm.

I entered the small space that was furnished sporadically. A small sofa sat square in the middle of the room with a large zebra print duvet hanging over the side. Pillows cluttered the room and a small bed was positioned in the corner with scraps of paper littering the rough, yellowed sheets. A cart of tea was hidden in the corner, and a silver tea set sat on the floor next to some of the random pillows. The room was a mess, but a mahogany undertone made it warm and comfortable.

"What can I help you with?" The magician took a seat on the sofa, stretching his long legs out in front of him. The candles placed on the mantel cast odd shadows on his face, causing me to look away.

I didn't intend to continue calling him The Magician, so I requested his name.

He answered politely, "My name is Gus." The innocence of that name was fitting.

I nodded curtly. "I've come to inquire about the previous tightrope walker who seems like a ghost rather than an actual person." I laughed lightly, hoping not to interrupt the calm atmosphere of the room. The air seemed to hold a spirit, like someone was listening.

Gus echoed the same light laugh. "I'm surprised you've come to ask me, but I'm glad, nonetheless. 'Twas a wise decision." He looked at the wall adjacent to him, covered in random articles about the circus and some tabloids mentioning his own involvement. "Five years ago a woman boarded the train. Her name was Penelope Plume. She was beautiful and talented—the most talented any circus had ever seen, with a body that moved like a stream of molasses. Penelope was famous for the plume she wore on her back when she performed, and Mr. Monte was quite proud of depicting her as a peacock—the finest woman of the era. She represented wealth in the midst of poverty, and the connection between the two classes attracted many watchers." He paused, smiling as he recalled the beautiful woman.

It was not hard to envision how beautiful she must have been.

"But she's gone."

Something in his tone told me that he was leaving out an important part of the story, perhaps because it was too personal.

"The fame she received made her anxious and fearful, mostly because her privacy was jeopardized by those who became too enamored with her. Mr. Monte was distraught at losing his biggest star, and he's been looking for a tightrope walker for five years now. And here you are." He bowed his head in my direction.

I wanted to laugh. No pressure at all. Penelope Plume—the famous tightrope walker—had abandoned the circus five years ago and *I* was to be her replacement? There was no way I would please the crowd as she had. But it was intriguing to me that Penelope had used her last name as a platform to become famous, and I wondered if I could create a design for myself to be as grand as Miss Plume one day.

While I listened to his ostentatious story, Gus's voice surprised me. He sounded noble almost. His speech was eloquent and graceful, instead of the chopped words most of the other circus members used.

"Where are you from?" I questioned. "It sounds as though you've known privilege." My assumption was rude. I should have allowed Gus the time to answer willingly, rather than because of my nosiness. My action reminded me of my mother. She liked to think she was polite, but the first question she would ask when meeting someone or inviting them into her home was about their status. It was terribly rude. Someone shouldn't assume a higher position just because of the coin in their pocket. I always believed a more important quality was the condition of someone's heart.

Gus snickered, easing my worry. "Eanverness is where I grew up."

Eanverness was another wealthy city, one that was much larger and more populated than anything I had ever known. I had never traveled beyond Axminster in my life, but I had heard great things about Eanverness.

If Gus was privileged before joining the circus like me, then how was he so accepted among the other performers? "How did you show them that you were more than the money in your father's pocket?" I inquired.

He thought for a moment and a smile took over his face. It was easily discernible that Gus loved the circus and every performer in it. "Many of the performers are ruffians. They are wild and careless and daring. That's not what you're used to, I'm sure." Gus looked at me from under his heavy brows. "It was certainly not what I was used to. I was terrified to jump on this train, and I doubted my decision every day for a long time. But you'll see that this is all the other performers have. You and I may have a life to go back to, but they don't. Try doing the things the other performers enjoy—dancing, drinking, and having fun. Try walking in their shoes to gain their trust, and it won't take long for everyone to welcome you with open arms."

It was easy speaking to Gus. He was friendly, warm, and encouraging. He didn't threaten me with his differences or doubt my allegiance. I thanked him quietly and slipped out of his confines to walk along the thin corridor of the train. A shadow depicting my figure flickered along the wall, and I pondered the idea of the shadows belonging to previous members of the circus. A large head turned sharply with jagged teeth pointing out whenever its jaw opened. Animals of different shapes and sizes bounced on the wall. A tall figure slowly walked across the mahogany wall, a cane moving back and forth at his side, before he leaped and bounded out of sight. A thin figure pointed her legs and spun around and around, a silhouette of long hair flowing around her. I blinked multiple times to make sure I wasn't dreaming, but when I opened my eyes, the same figures were dancing on the wall. Lions were roaring, men were blowing fire out of their mouths, and delicate women were dancing. The oil lamp above my head flickered softly, and when I looked again at the converging walls of the train, the images were gone.

But a real figure stood at the end of the hall, right in front of my room. "You've gone to speak to the magician, haven't you? I'm surprised." The figure moved slightly and I caught a glimpse of his dull chocolate eyes. "Usually most new members speak to me when they have questions, but I'm glad you've inquired about our past walker." Mr. Monte came into view and the suspicion in my heart lifted. "Come with me child. I must show you something."

I followed him obediently to the back of the train where the animals had been herded into their pens. I didn't have to wonder where we were going for long because Mr. Monte quickly pulled a key from inside his fitted suit to unlock a faded gray door. I'd never ventured this far down the train before.

"Where are we?" I stepped over the threshold into an abandoned, moldy room. It was incredibly dark, except for the white sheets hanging over small night tables and jewelry stands. I ran my fingers across the dusty platforms that once belonged to someone long forgotten. There was a small bed and a vanity, which I imagine was once decorated with glittering gems.

"This is where Penelope Plume resided." Mr. Monte's voice was melancholy. I wondered how often he came here to mourn his lost performer.

I gasped audibly. Penelope Plume. The woman I aspired to be. It felt as though this room was inhabited by a ghost. "Why has no one taken her place?" It was odd for such a room to remain empty when any number of performers could have used it. Surely the circus was cramped for space.

"I didn't want to give away the room of a performer who impacted our circus so greatly. I tried to, but it didn't feel right. I wanted to keep a piece of her with us, and this is all we have left of her." Mr. Monte walked to the closet in the far corner and slid open the double doors. His fingertips turned gray with dust. "These are for you," he said soberly, and led me into a large closet full of splendid costumes. "I wouldn't want them to go to waste."

I ran my hands over the soft fabrics, studded with jewels and covered in lace. Bright lavender, glistening pomegranate, and iridescent ballet pink. A periwinkle so light it almost looked like snow, a dark blue corset studded with stars, and a deep green dress with ivy strands attached to it. Vibrant colors like sunflower yellow, tangerine, and cinnamon. There were too many beautiful costumes to count, and all of them belonged to her.

"I wouldn't want to disrespect Penelope by wearing her old uniforms." I pulled my hand away, despite how I longed to feel their detail. "I'm sure it would offend many people."

"You will not offend anyone unless you flail around on that tightrope. If you can show everyone that a new star has made her appearance, then no one will care whose costumes you're wearing. They'll be too busy lavishing you with praise." Mr. Monte grabbed an extravagant leotard made of deep purple silk. It was stained purposefully with graphite, which created the image of falling rain, with diamonds dropping off the end of the thin skirt.

Mr. Monte's words made me think of Gus's story of Penelope's fate. *They'll be too busy lavishing you with praise.* Isn't that what caused Penelope to flee? Too much fame could be unhealthy, no matter how good it might feel. At some point, that good feeling fades because the honor and glory is never enough to truly satisfy. I learned that from the rich noblemen in Axminster who paraded around in their silk gloves and velvet top hats like they held something over society. But deep down they were more unhappy than the poorest beggar because they could never get enough of their hearts' desires.

"Juniper?" Mr. Monte questioned softly.

I shook my head. "I love them all. I just hope I can please the crowd enough."

"That's exactly my point in bringing you here. Put on this uniform and meet me in the tent," he instructed brashly. The tail of his coat swayed as he walked out of Penelope's sacred room.

I put on the leotard, struggling with the tight fabric, and thought about one thing that didn't add up. Why would the master of the circus keep one performer's bedroom a shrine if she had fled? Wouldn't it be more reasonable to use this space for those who had chosen to stay? So why was she being treated like royalty if she had deserted her own people?

I plodded my way across the deserted field lined with tents and cages full of animals. It took a moment for my eyes to adjust in the dark, but finally I reached the main tent. I secured white tape around my feet for extra padding so I could walk comfortably on the tightrope. I was determined as I still hadn't made it to the opposite side of the rope.

"You will not need those tonight." Mr. Monte emerged from behind a podium where a phonograph rested idly with dust coating the maple wood. It had a beautiful golden bell speaker. "You did ballet, correct?"

"Yes-" I answered tentatively, unaware of what he was planning.

"Then I want you to dance." Mr. Monte wound the handle and soft, slow music poured out. It was beautiful music—so beautiful that my body yearned to sing along with it.

"I have no choreography," I sputtered. "And it's been a long time since I've danced."

Mr. Monte shook his brown hair. "You don't need choreography. All you need is music. Do whatever you will with it. Just move."

I skipped to the center of the ring where a large circle of sand had been disturbed by footprints from last night's practice. I closed my eyes and listened to the violin and cello mixing together, and a harp being plucked lightly in the background. And almost involuntarily, I pointed my foot and kicked softly into the air.

"Walking on a tightrope is just like dancing, but in a much smaller space." Mr. Monte spoke over the music. "You must be one with the rope as you are with the music. You must learn to know the rope's rhythm so you know when to bounce and spring and when to turn and glide. You must learn how the rope reacts to your movements. If you spin right-"

In obedience to his words, I pointed my right toe against my knee, and spun to the right.

"Which way will the rope bend? And if you spin left-"

I relevéd, steadied my balance, and spun a double turn on the course sand below my feet. Remembering my dance training, I whipped my head around, searching for one point on the wall to come back to so I wouldn't lose my focus.

"If you are one with the rope, every single step you take will align with its gravitational center, just as the strings in a quartet will resonate with each other if they are playing the correct chords. If they feign to do so, their beautiful song will fail. And if you do not follow the rope's instructions, then you will surely fail. You cannot lead in this dance." Mr. Monte held out a hand for me to stop, and I looked at him, breathing hard, with sweat forming on my brow. "You must follow."

Chapter 5

"You have to kick higher! People do not pay to see your knees. They pay to see your ankles high in the air! If you do not continue to stretch yourself then you will not accomplish your other tricks." Mr. Monte lashed out, rubbing a hand across his temple. "I'm sorry." He walked away but stopped short, and a sliver of his dirty brown eyes shot me a glance. "I'm counting on you." Mr. Monte pulled away the tent flaps and exited furiously.

I walked around the large tent and circled the ring of sand in the middle. I was more disappointed in myself than I had ever been, even considering the Axminster version of myself. Despite my monotonous life, I had been confident in everything I did. And upon boarding the train to the circus, I thought I knew what I was doing, but I really had no clue what I was getting myself into. Maybe everyone was right. Maybe I was too different. Maybe I couldn't exceed my past life. But Christ, I wanted to!

I sighed and took a seat on the ledge around the pit of sand, shoving my head in my hands. Before I had time to breathe, a group of women walked into the tent, and before they could witness my hollow face, I quickly sat up and pretended to get back to work.

"Juniper, right?" A woman with tight yellow ringlets on her head looked at me kindly.

I recognized her from the first night I boarded the train as the one latching onto Cassius and laughing wildly with the other performers. She was beautiful. Looking again, I caught something odd. Her eyes were different colors. One was a light green, the other one dark brown. She was very intriguing.

"I didn't mean to invade your privacy, but my girls and I couldn't help but overhear Mr. Monte's fury." The woman motioned to the other girls around her, most of them young, but one that was grey and weathered.

Olive showed me these women that night when it stormed. The dancers, she called them.

"It's no big deal." I tried to wave it off.

She pressed further, "Being dancers, we were all trained to be especially flexible. Would you like us to help you?"

Her offer took me by surprise. Most everyone here thought I was a wealthy snot. I considered refusing her kindness, hoping I could learn on my own. The others wouldn't truly know how much I was struggling if I didn't show them. But realizing this was a chance to make friends, I accepted. "I would appreciate that very much." I nodded my head and smiled.

The small blonde dancer bounced over, followed by her companions.

Each dancer introduced herself, shaking my hand and offering delightful smiles. There were thirteen altogether. Charlotte was spritely and blonde, and she was the one who had been kind enough to help me. Olive was the youngest, and Piper, who was close to her in age, stuck to her side like a thorn to a rose. Evelyn had six fingers on each hand and was considerably older than the rest. Always together were Mila, Scarlett, and Finley, the girl with fire red hair and lips sewn shut. And Emma, Autumn, and Josephine—the girl with earlobes so long they touched her shoulders—were similarly joined at the hips. Raelynn and Raegan were sisters, and last was Daisy who was as pretty as her name suggested.

I came to know every single dancer that day. The words, *this is your place*, rang in my head. These women were kind. They were free and wild and immodest, but they worked hard. They were everything I wanted to become.

"What are you struggling with?" Charlotte asked me brightly.

"There's a kick I must perform on the tightrope. I can't seem to get my leg high enough, and I end up falling because my balance is off," I explained.

The dancers nodded along with me, acknowledging their past struggles, and I was glad to know it wasn't just me.

"Try this exercise." Charlotte led me to a wooden bar and grabbed my waist to guide me. "Keep your waist as straight as possible. If it twists to one side, so will your balance." She poked me in the stomach and I swatted her hand away. "Keep your core tight. If you exercise to strengthen your core, it will be easier," she added. "Now rise into a relevé."

I followed her command and rose, my right foot coming to my left in the fifth position.

"Lift one leg into the air and balance on the other. If you can do this, then you'll be able to walk one foot at a time across that rope. After a bit of practice, take yourself off the bar and walk across the room, shifting from the right to the left leg." Charlotte's voice was silky, and her words strung together beautifully.

My gaze flicked between her different colored eyes, and I was entranced by their brightness.

"Juniper?" Charlotte asked.

"Ye-yes, okay," I replied quickly, looking down at my feet.

"Never do that." She flicked my chin up. "If you look down, you will also lose your balance. Head to the sky."

I looked up and focused on the tightrope while I practiced my walk. I pointed my left foot and balanced on my right foot for as long as I could before switching. I did this for what seemed like hours before I was ready to climb the ladder to the tightrope with thirteen sets of eyes watching me expectantly. The floor seemed miles away, but this was nothing compared to the highest rope I would be expected to perform on.

"You got this, J!" Charlotte yelled, clasping her hands in front of her heart.

I closed my eyes and took a deep breath. The rope was still and I felt as though it was inviting me to destroy that stillness. I took one step, clenching my core and pointing my leg in front of me. When I stepped onto the rope, it wavered slightly and my leg buckled from side to side, but when I looked down in fear, I reminded myself to keep looking forward. I found that lifting my head up caused the shaking to stop almost immediately, but when I eased into another step, and the entire rope bounced beneath my weight, I gasped.

"Remember to relevé while you walk so all of your balance is not dependent on the rope!" Charlotte yelled up to me.

I raised my right heel so that my toes were the only thing touching the rope. It scared me to not feel my whole foot on the rope, but when it stopped quivering, I smiled in relief and took a few more steps. The end was getting closer and closer, and I was determined to make it across and not fall. I leveled my arms out to my sides, curled my toes around the rope, and when I made it to the end, I bent my knees and hopped onto the adjacent platform. I clutched my heart in relief, finally feeling something solid underneath me.

High-pitched cheers echoed in the large tent. I tried to envision what it would sound like when I first performed for the crowd—how people would react seeing a tightrope walker for the first time in five years.

I looked down to the dancers who smiled and laughed at my success. Even Finley, unable to laugh with her lips sewn together, clapped wildly. For the first time, I was convinced that I could really do this, and I was eager to do more...even perform leaps and flips on the rope.

Charlotte, afraid I was being overzealous, moved to offer me her hand to help me off the platform. "It's going to feel amazing for the next few days, but it will not always be easy. These next few weeks will be very demanding. So let's not overdo it and just celebrate your success tonight!"

I tried to refuse, wanting to stay and practice for another hour, but I was practically dragged to the train where the other performers had gathered for a drink. Barrels full of ale with a musty aroma filled every inch of the room. Evelyn hobbled through the crowd ambitiously, hauling me behind her. I laughed and tripped over my own feet, apologizing to the performers who spilled their drinks because of my clumsiness. Evelyn and I filled eleven cups and carried them back to our table, doing our best not to spill them, but the brown mixture sloshed around, pouring out onto our hands and arms. The dancers cheered when we arrived, but Olive and Piper frowned, noticing we were two cups short.

"Sorry girls, you are too little yet." Mila, a girl with deep gray eyes, patted the children on their heads. They weren't having it and crossed their arms defiantly, which made me snicker.

"You haven't taken a drink." Charlotte noticed my full glass, while most of the group was either half finished or going back for seconds. "It's not as bad as you think." She winked and returned her attention to Raelynn, who was downing a whole glass after losing a bet.

My mother had taught me three things: 1. Never swear. Ladies should never disagree so much as to prove others wrong with naughty words. 2. Cover up. No man should see what is under your pinafore until he is devoted to you completely; in other words, until you are married. 3. *Never* drink. Alcohol makes you far more vulnerable than is respectable for a woman.

Memories of my mother flooded back to me, so I brought the brown mug to my lips and guzzled it down. The taste was sour, and it stung when it traveled down my throat. I worried it might sear a hole in my stomach, and the aftertaste was absolutely repulsive, but the feeling was wonderful. After gulping down two more drinks, I felt as light as a feather. It must have been one-hundred degrees in that room, and the clothing on my arms itched terribly and the back of my throat burned. I took Josephine's cup along with mine to the back where the barrels of ale were to refill them, and as I prepared to return to my table, I turned to find Gus right in front of me.

"You scared me!" I yelled, slightly amused.

"I'm sorry." He laughed at me, then turned his attention to the group of dancers swaying wildly and screaming. "I see you've taken my advice."

"I have," I surveyed the room. "The idea of doing what the performers enjoy terrified me at first, but it's-"

"Fun?" He concluded for me, raising his eyebrows in surprise.

"Yes, fun." I nodded my head in agreement.

"Who would've guessed?" He shook his head playfully before walking away.

When I returned, I spotted Olive sipping out of a mug, with foam curling at the peach fuzz on her lip. Emma, the woman whose drink Olive had borrowed, had her back turned when I snatched the cup out of the little girl's hands and shook a finger at her.

She pursed her lips and pouted with her arms crossed, which made me laugh. She could really be dramatic.

I felt more comfortable with the members of the circus after indulging with them in their activities. As I clapped along to the music and watched Charlotte rise to dance with a fine gentleman, I realized for the first time, I was truly enjoying myself.

<hr>

Mr. Monte had assigned me a new task, and I woke hurriedly as soon as the sun rose to get started on it. There was no time to delay or doddle. My first performance was in one month, and I finally felt comfortable on the tightrope, although my tricks were still lacking. Mr. Monte had instructed me to practice a front walkover, so I pulled on my mustard-colored leotard and began to warm up on the rope with easy things like walking across and adding a few high kicks. My toes were permanently calloused from gripping the rope so tightly, so I consistently kept them covered with white tape. The tightrope was laborious, but I felt stronger every day, even though the muscles in my torso and legs ached.

"You're going to point your foot and prep like always, and when you do, you will push yourself into a handstand," Mr. Monte informed me.

"Where shall I place my hands?" I ran through the image in my head, and it didn't look good.

"One in front of the other. Grip the rope tightly and then let go as you fold your legs over your head. It will take a lot of strength and balance to bring your body back up, but let's give it a try." He waved his hands toward the rope.

I stepped out on the rope and kicked my foot out, but when I lifted into a handstand, my body twisted to the right and I spun off sideways, landing hard on my back on the mat below. I didn't have enough strength to balance with just my hands quite yet, but I groaned, got up quickly, and tried again. And I fell again. I must have fallen twenty times before Mr. Monte ordered me to stop.

He held his thick hand up in the air, thinking through his choice of words. "Take a break. We'll try again tomorrow."

I grabbed my things in a bit of a fit. Charlotte was right. Success comes with failure, and for me, the failure was just a little harder to take. After successfully walking across the rope, I was tempted to push my limits, but it wasn't fair to expect so much of myself. So, I slung a bag of equipment over my shoulder and marched out of the tent, but I was whipped back when the flaps of the tent got stuck on the corner of my bag.

"You piece of garbage!" I cursed at the fabric and tore it away.

"Someone's angry," Cassius snickered, but I only caught a glimpse of his pearly white teeth before he disappeared behind a slightly smaller tent in the distance.

I squinted in his direction, noticing his fine attire. Usually he wore loose shirts that cuffed around the wrists, loose breeches, and a vest when he was feeling spritely. But today he wore the entire ensemble—a clean white shirt, a plum vest, a black velvet waistcoat, and a top hat with a thin gold line across the brim. He looked like a gentleman.

I followed him through the tent and a new world came into view. This tent didn't hold tightropes and large sandboxes with hoops and miscellaneous instruments. This tent held cages made of gold, copper, and steel. Some were small, some large, and all oxidized. *Cackaw!* A rainbow-colored bird twirled above my head from a swinging ladder, poking at my hair. I hurried away from the creature and witnessed a baby bear sliding its inky nose across the dirt floor to itch its snout. Just then, a tall giraffe poked his head out from his compartment, looking around curiously and giving an odd *snort*. Just then, heavy footfalls shook the ground and my legs trembled. A *roar* echoed loudly, filling every inch of the room and making the fabric of the tent quiver.

I stepped back in fear, wondering if I should retreat. Where had Cassius gone? I was sure I saw him enter this tent, but he was nowhere to be found. My voice was stuck in my throat, but I was drawn to the energy floating in the musty air. It was dangerous and mysterious, and I didn't know what would happen, which made the situation even more enticing. The smell of dung and urine was drowning, but the animals were amazing. Just then, I took a step forward and a voice startled me.

"I thought they'd teach a newcomer not to enter this tent alone." Cassius emerged from a dark pen in the back, looping a rope around his elbow and through his hand. The muscles in his jaw flinched thoughtfully as he focused on the motion.

"I'm not alone," I tried to answer confidently, but the shake in my voice betrayed me. Cassius was not friendly, and he didn't like me. That much was clear. I could barely have a conversation with him. He was mysterious, dark, and secretive, and I wanted to know why.

"You are no safer with me," he said, raking a hand through his black curls.

Cassius and I looked similar with the exception of my breasts, round hips, and long hair. We could be brother and sister, which prompted my next question. "Do you have a family? Any brothers or sisters?"

He ignored my question, and his laconicism made me want to step on his toes with my pumps. He disappeared again, and when he emerged for the second time, he was not alone. A hulking lion stalked by his side, its footsteps labored and heavy. The golden animal's claws dug into the dirt, removing clumps with each step. The muscles rippled in the predator's arms, and a mane of sunlight engulfed its head. The lion bucked his head wildly, but Cassius was calm and almost loving to the animal, and he continued to hold on fearlessly.

I felt like running. And screaming, as a matter of fact. I stood near the back, like a small child sent to time-out to think about their actions. I watched silently as Cassius guided the animal into the cage and trapped himself inside as well. I wanted to tell him to get out of there, that it was too dangerous, but I remained quiet, assuming he knew what he was doing. How could anyone put themselves in that kind of danger? On *purpose*?

Cassius slowly circled the inside of the cage, and the lion's eyes followed him wherever he went. He pulled out a large piece of meat and waved it in front of the lion's face. The animal's pupils widened as it reared up on its hind legs, preparing to fight Cassius for the meat.

Get out of there, the voice in my head urged.

The lion sprang forward, snapping its jaw at Cassius's outstretched arm, and I jumped.

And Cassius jumped—all the way to the top of the cage. He squeezed his slim body through the metal bars and stood far out of the lion's reach, with a cocky smile that made the right side of his face scrunch together. He hopped off the tall cage and landed effortlessly on his feet, and shrugging his coat off, he pressed his back to the cage. The lion's mouth was inching closer and closer to his head, and as soon as its teeth touched Cassius's curls, he unlocked the cage and threw the piece of meat as far as he could across the room. Then the lion sprinted in my direction and a scream rose in my throat, and I closed my eyes tightly, wishing I had never come here. Suddenly the pounding stopped as the lion came to a halt, and I cracked one of my eyes open to watch him tear the meat apart in a matter of seconds. The sound of its teeth slamming together made me shiver.

Cassius stood a foot in front of me with his back turned, and I wished I could see his face to determine if he was as frightened as I was. Of course he wasn't.

Cassius led the lion back into the cage and shouted a series of commands in a low, demanding voice. Subserviently, the lion backed up slowly, licking its lips. Cassius grabbed a wooden chair from the corner of the cage and straddled it, wrapping his arms around the back. He waited patiently for the lion to approach, not flinching once as it got closer and closer. Just as the lion lashed its claws at the chair, Cassius sprang back and held the chair up into the air. The golden creature tried to focus on all four legs of the chair at once, not noticing as Cassius snapped a rope around its neck.

The lion whipped his head harshly, attempting to get out of the restraint, but Cassius gently reached out to grip its face. He quieted the beast with surprising gentleness, and then all motion stopped abruptly and before I knew it, the lion was led away.

I stood there in shock. Only minutes had passed, but it felt like hours.

Cassius gathered his things and prepared to leave as if I hadn't been standing there watching the whole thing. He was composed and confident in his actions, which made me extremely jealous.

"Teach me!" I shouted in desperation before he left.

"Excuse me?" Cassius turned, and his deep eyes caught mine.

"Teach me how to not be afraid." If I continued to fear the tightrope, I'd never learn how to do a front walkover or any of the tricks Mr. Monte required that I perform. I wouldn't be able to impress the crowd without becoming as confident as Cassius.

Cassius's tongue flicked over his smooth, defined lips, as he dropped his equipment and it landed with a hollow *thud* in the sand. Then he stalked over to me, stroking a hand down the stubble on his chin.

I pushed my back against the wall instinctively and continued to study him.

"If there is one thing I will teach you, let it be this." He dipped his head lower so he could look me in the eyes. "Our pasts are very different. I did not have the choice to *learn* how to not be afraid. I was forced to." He was only a foot away from me, and I could feel his breath on my collarbone.

My chest heaved up and down at his closeness. Forced? What had happened to him? I had the desire to ask him hundreds of questions, just to know him a little more. He was so intriguing to me, and I didn't know why.

"You don't belong here. You will *never* belong here. I'd run back to the city before you embarrass yourself if I were you." Cassius took one lasting look into my eyes and glared before walking away. His waistcoat swished from right to left, and his shoulders matched his movements as he disappeared from view.

I stared blankly ahead of me, processing his words. This had been my fear since arriving. I was not like the others. I knew this, but at least I was willing to try. I had no desire to return to Axminster.

Golden eyes pierced through the darkness of my dreams that night, and a large tongue flicked over sharp teeth. Cassius had learned to tame his lion. Now I had to tame mine.

Chapter 6

I ventured down the dark corridor toward Penelope Plume's previous dwelling place. My steps were light and quick as I passed sleepy animals, softly purring as they drifted off to dreamland. I turned the rusted door handle and the door creaked, making me wince as I entered the dark room. There was no time to light a candle. I was too worried about getting to the wardrobe. As I sifted through the linens, a soft fabric entangled itself in my hand, and I stopped abruptly, caught by the texture. This irresistible costume was made of velvet with golden stars embedded on the collar, and I snatched it from the closet and dressed quickly.

I sprinted to the tent with the wind whipping through my hair, skipped stretching, grabbed a hoop, and climbed the ladder. The rough tan rope wobbled, so I bent my knees and curled my toes around it. Gripping the top of the metal hoop, I twisted my wrist and threw it into the air, causing it to rotate three times before landing in my palm.

Don't look down.

I hooked the hoop around my toes and lifted my leg high, then bowed my head and let my gaze fall to the ground while the veins in my forehead pulsed, making my eyes water. I pointed my toes toward the top of the tent and the hoop fell down over my waist. Upon lifting my head, I saw stars dance in my vision, and I grasped the hoop with my hands and bounced it from hip to hip. As I swayed from side to side, attempting to turn around on the rope, I lost my balance and had to let go of the hoop. I was able to steady myself not long after, but I groaned in anger.

Grabbing the rope below me, I threw my legs off the side and sprung down onto the ground. If this was all I had to offer on show night, the crowd would be sorely disappointed, and so would Mr. Monte.

"I think you're ready," a low voice spoke. Mr. Monte was gilded in moonlight at the entrance to the tent.

"Ready?" I exclaimed in exasperation. "Did you just see what I did? I can barely walk and hold a hoop at the same time."

"Not ready for show night, but ready for the high rope," he clarified.

My eyes traveled to the rope on the opposite side of the tent, reaching twenty feet higher than the one I had spent an entire month practicing on. I couldn't do it. I had put on a performer's costume, hoping to build my confidence—to tame my lion—but I was far from ready for this. I was still struggling to understand what I was even doing here.

"Not a single one of my performers was any good upon arriving at the circus. They struggled just like you." Mr. Monte looked up to the ceiling as he explained.

Then why does everyone treat me differently? I wanted to scream. It wasn't as if I was doing any worse than they had. Feeling especially defeated, I shrugged on a silk robe and tied the strings tightly around my waist.

"It comes with time. Your first performance may not meet your standards. And that's tough to accept because it is your first, and you want it to be memorable, but it will be after more practice." Mr. Monte guided me toward the high rope.

My stomach churned when I came to stand beneath the high rope, my eyes ranging in and out of focus.

Mr. Monte pushed me forward and I grabbed the ladder with trembling hands. I prayed that I would be to make it to the top safely, but when I reached the platform, I was not as relieved as I had hoped. The world spun below me, and Mr. Monte looked like an ant. I choked down the bile in my throat and longed to crawl into a warm bed where I knew I would be safe. Finally, I understood my lion. It was safety. Or the absence of it. In the circus, everything was unknown, including success, income, and a family to hold close. I was not guaranteed anything here except a life of adventure, so I had to forget knowing safety and comfort and welcome all that was unknown and *frightening*.

I stepped forward, approaching the ledge. A figure materialized at the entrance to the big tent, but I couldn't make out who it was from that high up. Strangely, there was a bright glow surrounding him that reminded me of turmeric and pink Himalayan salt. When the figure took one more step forward, I could see him clearly. Cassius leaned with indifference on the edge of the tent, nodding his head, as if to say *please continue.*

I thought of him trapped in that steel cage. The lion's golden hair billowed, its canines snapped, and its paws stomped into the sand, and not once did Cassius flinch. Not once did he back down.

You will never belong here. His haunting words came back to me.

I turned my eyes to the rope before me and let the silk robe fall off my shoulders and into a heap at my feet. Out of my peripheral vision, I saw Cassius looking me up and down before abruptly walking away.

Part of me wished he would stay in case I completed a trick that was worthy of his time. But if I failed again, I would be terribly embarrassed, and for that reason, I was glad he was gone when I stepped onto the rope. I needed to prove him wrong, not for his acceptance, but for my own. I belonged here. So, placing my hands on my hips, I walked forward, reached up, and then to the left in a rhythmic motion. I tightened my core and rotated my feet to spin on my axis, and then with my knees bent, I took a breath and folded forward. My right hand gripped the rope in front of my left, and I leapt into a handstand, making sure not to push too hard and fall over. I balanced there for a moment, feeling all of the blood rush to my head. My legs tipped forward and I arched my back, remembering to reach my chest toward the sky once my feet touched the rope. Finally, I extended my arms out in front of me.

I had done a front walkover! Without even thinking, I had just gone for it! Mr. Monte smiled, clapping his hands proudly, and I swung off the rope and landed hard on my back on a landing pad, unable to contain my laughter.

"You can come out now!" Mr. Monte yelled over his shoulder, and the dancers burst out from behind the tent.

Running over to me, Raelynn and Raegan offered me their hands. "Let us help you!" Each of them grabbed one of my hands and pulled me up off the floor.

Charlotte clutched my arms like a schoolgirl talking about her latest crush during lunch. "That was impressive! I'm amazed at how you were able to balance on that rope after such a short time here."

"Would you like to join us for dinner? You can tell us all about how you did it." Josephine nodded and her long earlobes swung wildly.

I looked to Mr. Monte for approval, and he waved a hand at me and said, "Go."

I said my thanks, and then sprinted out into the field of dandelions and blooming green grass, letting the summer air brush across my cheeks and listening to the crickets chirping. As I felt the grass tickle my ankles, I clung onto the girls around me for dear life. This was wonderful! I was never allowed to go out at night back home, and now being able to look up at the stars and feel the cold wind on my face made me feel so alive. I breathed in deeply, until my lungs couldn't take anymore.

I had so much work to do, but I wasn't frightened anymore. I had finally begun to tame my lion.

Chapter 7

"Winston, your mother is as big as a cow. There is no way you can criticize Mr. Berny, here." A fire breather by the name of Temple with golden hoops hanging out of his ears, laughed at Winston—a fellow fire breather who was quite drunk.

Winston stood and raised a mug of ale in the air. "I won't even disagree with you, Temple."

Temple clapped him on the back. "Here's to fat women with nice hips!"

The two men clinked glasses, and I scoffed.

"Brutes, the lot of em'," Charlotte complained, untying the ringlets on her head and letting tight curls fall onto her shoulders. She gulped down the last of her ale and grabbed my hand. "Come on, we'll be late."

Late? I had almost forgotten. We headed to the large stadium which had been built in the middle of the works for the horse riders. The pounding of hoofbeats could be heard from a mile away. Today, I would get to watch their practice and understand better what the other performers contributed to the show. This would give me a good feel for the program before show night.

I took a seat on a wooden bench. Golden drapes hung from the ceiling and dust filled the air, and I thought how strange it was that I had become accustomed to the smell of manure in such a short time.

Ten riders exited dark cages and rode into a single-file line.

Charlotte hollered loudly, and I had the urge to silence her in anticipation of the performance about to begin. What if she spooked the horses?

But the man leading the line of horses tipped his head at her with a smirk on his face. I had assumed Charlotte was associated with Cassius, seeing her position in his lap the night I arrived, but it seemed more gentlemen caught her eye with every passing day. I didn't know whether to be disturbed or impressed by that fact. In

45

Axminster, a woman was loyal to her husband or to the man she was planning to wed in the future, and no one else. Women did not hop around or show their affection for whomever they pleased. But in the circus, everyone was friendly with everyone else. A little too friendly, if you asked me.

The horses trotted synchronously. Right, left, right, left. Halfway down the dirt arena, the first rider turned right, the second left, and the line of horses dispersed to each side of the arena, one after the other in an opposite formation.

"Halt!" Mr. Monte instructed from the podium.

The horses stopped abruptly and dust rose in the air like powdered sugar in a mixing bowl. The riders looked dead ahead, not flinching an inch.

"Board!" Mr. Monte stood with his eyes flicking back and forth between the riders.

The first horse—an auburn-colored stag with a golden collar around its burly neck—galloped forward slowly. The slim boy riding the horse, who looked like he was six feet tall, unhooked his foot from the holster and lifted it onto the horse's back.

No way, I thought. *There is no possible way this man could balance on top of a moving animal.*

The leader gripped the reins so tightly his knuckles turned white, and with one foot behind the other, he stood slowly into the air with his arms held out steadily in front of him. His horse gained speed, causing its head to dip up and down, its dark nostrils to flare, and its white mane to billow in the wind. The steed came to a full stop and the man remained standing, raising his arms in the air to finish. The other riders followed him, but in less difficult positions on their horses. Some of them balanced in their foot straps, level with the horse's body, and others rode with only one foot in the strap.

"No! Stop!" A voice shouted angrily.

I turned my head to Mr. Monte, but his face didn't resemble the angry tone.

From the top of the stands, Cassius stomped down to the ground level. His black boots scuffed the chipped wood loudly. "Do you think our customers come to see half of you fall off your horses and the other half wobble from last night's drink?" Cassius sounded absolutely furious, which was a drastic contrast to his usual indifference.

The riders remained silent with their heads bowed in shame.

"I didn't think so. Do it again." When Cassius sat down, he brought his pointer finger and thumb together to pinch his dark pink bottom lip, and his eyes were glowing with intent.

I leaned forward slightly and watched his breath grow more ragged as the riders completed the sequence for a second time. His knuckles tightened and his cheeks bloomed with red fury. He was all that a man should be—strong, commanding, and furious at times, but passionate. And for some reason it scared me. He didn't seem kind or funny. He was just mean. Why was he even here to begin with? He was a lion tamer, not a rider.

I looked at Charlotte and before I even had the chance to ask, she answered my question.

"Cassius used to be a rider. When he came to the circus, he was rather young. He was given a pony and was practically raised by horses, which explains his animalistic behaviors." Charlotte rolled her eyes and tucked a strand of blond hair behind her ear. "He became the captain of the riding team, but some time later he was recruited to be the lion tamer. He gave up being a rider to take on an individual act, at Mr. Monte's request. But due to his knowledge in the field, he has been an apprentice to Mr. Monte in training the horseback riders. He's always been very passionate." She smiled when she said this, which led me to wonder how deep their relationship was.

"He seems very devoted," I remarked politely, gently folding my hands in my lap. I never knew Cassius was a rider, and I still wondered why he had to speak to people in such a demeaning manner.

"You're in the circus. It smells like shit all year round and you have the audacity to fold your hands like a princess being courted. You will always amuse me," Olive said, as she appeared out of thin air by my side and popped a peanut into her mouth.

"Come on O, give the girl a break," Charlotte said, in my defense.

I wasn't even listening to their brawl, because from across the arena, Cassius's eyes had met mine. The amber color burned a hole in me as he looked me up and down, and then laughed lightly to himself and raised his eyebrow.

Was he judging me? Ugh, he made my blood boil!

With one more sly grin, he returned his attention to the men in the ring.

"Run it again." He circled his finger in the air. "I need to see a cleaner cut from William. And Tom, you have to keep the flag straight. Riley, don't make me mention the spin off again, do you hear me?" He pointed to a ginger boy who immediately dismounted his horse and ran to the edge to run the routine again.

It was wondrous experiencing another group's performance. It was easy to be consumed in my own act, but the greater purpose of the circus was togetherness. Acting as one, in all of the absurdity, was what made the circus grand.

Hugh's thick fingers danced over the black and white keys on the grand piano in the dining area. As I scanned the room, I saw that silk robes hung loosely around women's bodies and strings of pearls draped their necks. The men's top hats and overcoats were strewn into empty seats, and the cuffs on their wrists were unbuttoned while their blouses hung wide open to reveal dark hair curling on their chiseled chests. Steam hung in the air and bodies moved too quickly to discern who was who, but it didn't matter. Dancers, flamethrowers, jesters, and palm readers alike let go and felt the music down to the soles of their feet. Their backgrounds were different, but their purpose the same.

I laughed drunkenly as the unicyclists bounced on their feet and clicked their ankles together. And when the group of jugglers threw red and orange balls into the air, I tapped my hand against the table in chorus with their movements. I remained in the back, seated at a dilapidated table with a half-finished mug of ale.

"Your mother taught you to sip, I assume?" Cassius held out his pinky, pretending to hold a saucer and sip politely from a teacup.

I took a large gulp of the alcohol and tried to ignore the sting in my throat to prove him wrong. I avoided his eyes for as long as I could, but he continued to prod at me.

"Little princess, are you just going to watch?" Cassius took the seat next to me without asking.

The endearment rolled off his tongue, sounding sickly and insulting, but his voice was sweet like honey.

I rolled my eyes, deciding not to give him the satisfaction of answering.

"The maiden fair is mute as well. I wonder what else her prestigious mother taught her to keep her tongue from saying." He smiled and the right side of his mouth lifted toward his eyes. His smile almost seemed honest when his eyes crinkled. It was clear he was very good at fooling others and was impressed with himself.

"My mother taught me many things, one of them being not to talk to scoundrels like yourself."

"A scoundrel? No. Charming, though." He flicked his head to remove the dark hair on his forehead and the stray piece that was caught in his long eyelashes.

I almost choked on my spit. "You? Charming? Never," I laughed.

"I'm sure you have high expectations with all of the rich courtiers in your district." He looked at the dancing women in the crowd and bit the edge of his lip. His canines were pointed, making him look like he had fangs.

"What are you hoping to achieve by insulting me?" I asked, while swirling my drink back and forth.

"I only wish you'd go back to where you belong. Back to your loving family and your house in the countryside. Back to the church where Father Almighty taught you to keep closed those lean legs of yours."

I bit the inside of my cheek to keep myself from slapping him across the face.

You must not ever act in anger, my mother's voice rung in my head. *Keep your shoulders back and your head high and take it! Take whatever is said to you, no matter how it angers you. Men do not listen. There is no use in fussing over the fact.*

"You know nothing of where I belong." I tried to keep my voice even. He had no idea what it was like to live in Axminster. My family was not loving, but rather forceful, and my house was lonely. And I hated church! I hated every minute of it!

I thanked the Lord in heaven when Olive ran over to me and grabbed me with a sweaty palm. I had the urge to grab the handkerchief tucked into my corset and wipe away the grime from her touch, but instead I listened to her frantic voice filled with glee.

"Come dance, Miss," she huffed, short of breath.

"I would be honored!" I laughed with her and jumped into the throng. Cassius was not worth my time, but I couldn't help wanting him to know how much I wanted to be here and that I would never belong in Axminster. I wanted to convince him that being wealthy wasn't so great. I wanted him to understand me, which was probably the stupidest idea I'd ever had.

As soon as I was in the midst of the heat, I let go of everything I knew, everything I once was, and I danced. I danced until my feet throbbed, and I didn't do it to prove Cassius wrong. I did it for myself. I ripped the leather slippers off my feet and stripped off my tight overcoat. My scarlet poet blouse dangled loosely from my thin arms, with the black corset overtop pushing up my breasts.

Temple, the flamethrower, beat on a white leather drum, his tattooed hands vibrating the instrument. The dancers pulled me into the circle and pushed me from side to side, grabbing at my waist and my hair. Before meeting such free people, I would have thought this was inappropriate, but my mind was changed by the circus. I laughed so hard my lungs hurt, and when the room finally stopped spinning, I saw Cassius put his peacock-colored top hat back on his head. His eyes were covered in shadow, and from the disdain on his face, I understood that our disagreement would not be over anytime soon.

Colette...

"She's my daughter. And I need your men to find her," my mother screamed at three men dressed in black with golden ropes strung across the brims of their top hats.

Axminster security guards patrolled the streets and dealt with any minor incidents, whereas the Axminster Investigators, clad with shiny boots and walking canes, dealt with more serious investigations.

"Ma'am, how long has your daughter been missing?" A tall man with a rather large belly brought out a notepad and waited for my mother's response.

"One week," she declared, almost proudly.

"And you didn't think to report this earlier?" Another man spoke derogatorily.

"You know young girls, getting into trouble." My mother laughed her negligence off. "I thought it was one of her escapades and that she would be back in a few days, but she hasn't returned."

I rolled my eyes when my mother tried to feign sorrow for Juniper. I knew in her heart she was worried, but for all the wrong reasons. *How would Juniper be wed? Would she have children on the road like some vagabond? And what of her service at the church?* She wanted my sister to be safe, living the life she had always planned for her, instead of the life *Juniper* desired.

"We will bring this to the attention of our captain and begin searching. You no longer need to worry, Ma'am."

My mother nodded her head, and the three guards exited the room respectfully, closing the door behind them.

I snatched the basket off the kitchen table and hustled out the front. "I'm going to pick some flowers for the spread tonight!" I was referring to the lavish dinner we were serving tonight in the presence of one of the wealthiest families in Axminster, which my mother had begun preparing for weeks ago.

Mother waved me off and I leapt down the walkway of our home, bustling towards the retreating officers. I lifted the skirt of my lace dress to keep the grime off, just like she taught me.

"Gentlemen!" I said, hopefully not loud enough for Mother to hear across the meadow.

All three men turned at once.

I brushed the pollen off my floral corset. "My sister is not missing. She *ran away*. It was her desire to experience a new life, away from my mother and away from Axminster."

"And how do you know this?" A tall, young officer asked as he stepped forward.

I hadn't gotten a look at him before, but he was handsome, tall and lean, and his lips were soft and round. His jaw clenched when I didn't answer, but he wasn't impatient, just curious. His eyes were a kind, soft green, with crashing waves inside them. His hair was dark orange, like cinnamon cookies at Christmastime, and it shimmered in the sun.

"Because she wrote my family a letter, bidding us goodbye. If my mother had it her way, she would have you search across the globe for my sister, despite the fact that she doesn't want to be found. Please, do not look for her," I pleaded, while searching his eyes.

The other officers waited for him to respond, feeling that it was a conversation between the two of us.

"If you say so, Ma'am." He tipped his head and smiled.

I smiled and said, "Please, Sir, don't call me ma'am. It makes me feel old."

"Alright, Miss, but only if you don't call me Sir. It exceeds my rank." He said humbly.

I curtsied before him, and when he walked away I realized I had missed his name.

In the days following my successful walk across the high rope, Mr. Monte assigned me many more tricks to learn, including a front handspring, a dip-swing, a split, and a carry. The handspring was the hardest to maneuver, because when I flipped, it created a lot of bounce in the rope that was hard to counteract. Steadying myself was extremely difficult. My feet slipped, and I burned the skin on my thighs sliding on the rope too many times to count.

"Miss Juniper, I'm turnin' off da lights. Why don't ya get some rest?" Wilman carried a flickering lantern above his head.

"Go ahead with the other tents, Wilman. I have to keep practicing." I raised my hands above my head and attempted a front handspring for the twentieth time.

"You've been at it for hours!" He exclaimed, noticing the bags under my eyes.

"My first performance is in three days. I can't waste any time!"

"Alright, alright, Miss. Ya get to bed soon. The zebras are out grazin' tonight so be mindful when you approach da cart." The light from his lantern followed him into the night.

The tent was mostly dark except for the large chandelier hanging overhead, likely to blow out with the breeze moving in. I raised my hands above my head, bent my knees, and kept my feet steady. I leapt forward into the air and grasped the thin rope with my palms, then pushed off with all of my strength and arched my back. The ceiling spun, but when my feet landed on the rope, I remembered to bend my knees to lessen the impact.

It was only the fifth time I had successfully landed the move, but I intended to perfect it in the coming days.

Gus appeared out of nowhere and said, "You have really improved," as he tucked a card into the pocket inside his vest.

"Yes." I was relieved to finally admit this. "And it is getting easier to understand the life the circus members lead every day."

"And what about the life you lead? Is it similar to theirs or do you regret coming here?" He stepped closer, and I was reminded how his height would never cease to surprise me.

"Are you doubting my commitment?" I questioned. First Cassius, and now Gus—one of the few people that had helped me feel like I belonged. I needed him to continue believing in me.

"Never. I only wonder if there's more you could do to prove to everyone that you're here to stay."

I climbed down the ladder eagerly and took a seat on a dusty bench while I hastily unstrapped the tape from my feet. "What else can I do?"

"I've spoken with Charlotte. She has agreed to help you," he said mysteriously, backing toward the entrance to the tent.

"What does that mean, Gus?"

"You'll see in the morning," he said with a wink.

I grabbed my clothes and began the walk back to my room. Forgetting the zebras, I almost ran right into a mother and her calf. The mother bucked wildly to protect her young, which scared the life out of me.

The space in my room was tight, and sometimes the walls closed in uncomfortably. I wasn't sure why tight spaces made me feel like I couldn't breathe, but they did. I fell asleep and descended into a strange dream about a pretty ginger-haired woman, floating in a black sea, with a white dress billowing around her. The hours passed quickly, and before I knew it, the sun was rising and the birds were chirping. I could recall bits of my dream and I wondered if there was some connection between it and my current situation.

"Good morning, Sunshine!" Charlotte's high-pitched voice filled my chamber as she shuffled around my bed in her robe. It seemed to be common to find performers in their robes whenever they weren't in costume.

I rubbed my eyes groggily. "What are you doing here?" I suddenly remembered Gus's words from last night, and my heart dropped.

She looked me up and down greedily. "You need a makeover. I know your mother taught you innocence and modesty, but it's time to show the world that you're one of us. No more questions."

Charlotte pulled me out of bed to push me in front of the mirror, and I huffed when she slammed me into the chair. She didn't pin up my hair as I always had, but left it in wild ringlets around my face, teasing the roots for volume, and then she grabbed a garment off the back of the door and demanded that I undress.

I raised my eyebrows and asked her to turn her eyes away.

"Listen here, Rose," Charlotte commanded as she plucked my cheeks. "All of the men will see your skinny waist in a matter of weeks anyway. Showing another girl is nothing."

I wanted to protest—to tell her that I wouldn't easily fall for any of the men here. And I wouldn't let them see a fraction of the skin she was in the habit of showing. But if I were to say that she might be offended, so I told myself to forget my mother's instructions and consider the possibility of showing off my body. My waist was rather slim, and one of my best features. My hips were a little large, but to make up for it, my breasts were full, which I was thankful for. If I was to truly belong, maybe this was the first step. A little skin wasn't so bad, was it? I carefully stripped myself of the loose blouse covering my chest, trying to ignore how Charlotte's eyes scanned up and down my body. Then I took off my pants while trying to cover my breasts with my discarded shirt.

Charlotte handed me a fine, white silk robe, laced with transparent flowers. The end of the robe was trimmed in soft fur and touched the floor. She helped me slip it on and tied a snow white choker around my neck.

"Beautiful." Her small figure appeared behind me in the mirror.

I gazed at myself, utterly amazed at what I saw—a suddenly older and more mature version of myself. My collar bones protruded and the silk clung to my hips wonderfully, making me appear more like a woman than a child. Not even a month ago, I witnessed a woman in the glass of a dilapidated antique shop, and she was covered in rubies and black feathers and looked like a queen. I got the same feeling looking at the girl in the mirror now. But she wasn't the same one I left in Axminster—the girl who thought frequently of what the Lord must think of her. The one that dressed to conceal her hips instead of accentuate them. This one was all grown up, and I liked her better. She seemed...pretty. Sexy, dare I say?

"There she is," Charlotte mused while looking at my figure in the mirror. "We're going to be late for breakfast."

The thought of everyone seeing me in this attire made my stomach drop, but it excited me at the same time. When I entered the dining hall, all eyes traveled to me at once. I felt like I was in school and everyone had just heard my deepest secret. I felt naked. In a sense I was. When I walked, the slit in the side of my robe opened to reveal my long leg. Surveying the room, all of the girls were giddy with approval, and the men blinked through blank stares, with their jaws practically on the floor. One's back was turned to me, but I recognized the heap of curly hair atop his head without seeing his face. Turning around to view the spectacle everyone had begun to gossip about, Cassius choked on his drink. His eyes were wide open and ale dribbled down his chin. And my cheeks warmed when he looked me up and down.

A man whistled before being slapped across the head by Evelyn, and he rubbed his temple while criticizing the woman for her incessant violence. The dancers clapped and welcomed me to their table, and the room returned to its buzz, but I felt eyes on me for the duration of the meal. It was a foreign feeling, but now I understood why Charlotte wore all those fancy clothes and took the time to make her hair a beautiful work of art. The attention was exhilarating.

For the rest of the afternoon, Mr. Monte detailed the schedule for our next performance. I could hardly believe that in two days, the world would see my face and know my name, as the tightrope walker returns after five long years.

"First up will be the horse riders. They will make an entrance from the south. Next will come the flamethrowers, followed by our lion tamer." Mr. Monte had this down to a science.

I tried not to envision Cassius in his performance attire, with a fitted suit defining his muscular arms, but the image was too tempting.

Mr. Monte snapped me back to attention, "After that will come the magicians, the jesters, and all the puppeteers. The cyclists will introduce the dancers. And finally, the tightrope walker. And a lasting impression you will leave with the crowd, I am sure." He smiled warmly at me from across the room, but I felt like I was going to vomit. I was performing last? Would the crowd love me or hate me? What if I ruined the circus's image forever?

If I messed this up, the crowd would be horrified and wouldn't ever want to come back! I opened my mouth to protest, but Mr. Monte spoke before I could. "I've discussed your costume and theme with the designer. You'll find her three doors down from my own."

I sat despairingly, wringing my sweaty hands together.

"Off you go!" Mr. Monte prodded, pushing everyone out of their seats.

The hallway buzzed with energy while performers passed in heated conversation. As bodies flashed by me, my eyes went blurry. The sound in the room decreased, and a quiet hum filled my ears. *And finally, the tightrope walker. I've discussed your costume and theme with the designer.* Mr. Monte's voice played over and over again in my head, so much that my ears rang. My vision focused in and out until I noticed Mila, the dancer, emerging from around the corner, wrapping a fur scarf around her pasty neck.

"Are you alright, Juniper? You look sickly!"

Mila grabbed my arm, which I was grateful for. I was not able to process her question. "I need to see the designer."

She led me down the cramped hall. I passed one door, then two, and then we stopped. I grappled for the rusted door knob. "I'll be alright from here. I was just lightheaded," I assured Mila.

Mila smiled kindly and turned to leave beside a cute boy with long hair.

I entered the room filled with scarlet rugs and drapes hanging over every inch of it. The ambiance in the room made me want to fall asleep. Watermelon pink hues glowed in the small lanterns strewn around the room. A woman with silver glasses sliding down her nose sat in a large leather chair that seemed to consume her whole body. She had unruly grey hair framing her face.

"Juniper, it's nice to meet you. My name is Valetta, and I am the circus's fashion designer. Mr. Monte and I have a grand surprise for you." The woman spoke resolutely.

What had I gotten myself into?

Chapter 8

The ground trembled with the heavy footfalls of an elephant. A lion roared and dust rose into the air and settled on crowded stadium benches. On one side of the arena, ruffians with dirt-stained breeches clapped wildly. And on the opposite side, men in fine, strapping suits and women with a superfluous amount of pins in their hair, clapped politely, barely touching their fingertips to their palms.

How could I have ever associated myself with such pomp and circumstance? It looked as though the rich men and women were afraid to have fun. The rich were only concerned with what others thought of them. A despised place such as this would raise many questions about their status, and if it meant that much to them, then why show up here at all? Because it was odd. The circus was different from anything in the normal world. It was *weird*. The rich were drawn here by a fascination for the unnatural, to escape the realities of their mundane lives. The ruffians from the less privileged side of life may be dirty and loud, but they weren't afraid to celebrate their uniqueness.

At the back of the tent, performers were getting dressed and preparing for their acts. Watching the eyes of small children become wide with wonder was magical. My mother always spoke of the circus as a grimy, corrupt place, but I had come to know it as much more than that. The circus was full of friendship, family, and a passion unlike I had seen anywhere else. I just wished my family could see it from my point of view. Of course, they would never stoop so low as to watch me perform with such a rambunctious crowd.

"Juniper, Mr. Monte requests you upstairs." A woman with a schedule in hand directed me to a wobbly wooden staircase which led to his office. The performers were stationed behind the tent, in an adjoining layer that held all of our equipment but kept us out of the crowd's view.

Valetta dressed me quickly while Mr. Monte briefed me on the routine. For my first performance, he had created quite the spectacle.

"Time to shine, my little walker." Mr. Monte tucked a tight curl behind my ear. "The crowd will love you." He looked me up and down and made sure my appearance was perfect.

Before I descended the stairs, Mr. Monte grabbed my arm as he wiped his forehead with a handkerchief from his breast pocket. "Remember, if you fall, make it look spectacular." He breathed out nervously before bounding down the stairs to help the other performers prepare.

Mr. Monte was just as nervous as I was. He owned this establishment, and if he were to disappoint his customers with an unprepared tightrope walker, he would lose his business.

I took my place beside the dancers, and a cold shiver ran down my spine. So many things could go wrong during my performance. But then again, so many things could go right.

The applause of the crowd went silent, and I could hear peanut shells falling to the floor and the tiny cry of a baby. I was surrounded by lush red fabric, and the outside world had disappeared. A vision came to me while I waited for the curtains to open. I closed my eyes and drank in the smell of manure, popped corn, and peanut shells.

The room was dark and the dancers dressed in scarlet robes gathered around me, each one carrying a giant red petal. I remained hidden under this collection of petals which together formed the image of a rose. The lights slowly came up and the dancers began to pull away at the canopy that covered me. And as the last four dancers pulled away their petals, light began to pour through the fabric. I had been hunched over as if withered by the winter, but now I bloomed as a beautiful rose does in the spring. Until that moment, all I could see was red, and now I saw a multitude of people—an African man smiling with bright white teeth, a baby sucking on a lollipop, and a fine woman clapping, with white gloves up to her elbows. The bodies in the audience leaned forward, struck by my appearance, and there was a collective gasp.

I wore a lavish crimson gown with a tight corseted bodice and a sweetheart neckline. Under the corset was an off-the-shoulder blouse with blooming sleeves. The skirt was magnificently large with a long train behind it, and the entire thing was made of tulle. It was something a woman of mystery would wear.

Next to the strewn petals in the sand, orbs of glass as big as our heads surrounded us. The dancers collected the orbs and leaped as though they were afraid to drop them. I picked up a large orb to mesmerize the audience as Gus read a beautiful crystal ball. The audience leaned in closer, and all of a sudden, the dancers threw the orbs onto the ground. Glass shattered and the room erupted with a high-pitched cacophony. I dropped my orb last and black smoke filled the air, blanketing the room in darkness.

Small children screamed and their parents gasped. Peering into the mysterious fog, the crowd searched for the dancers and their rose. But when the fog settled, they found that we had all vanished into thin air. And bemused whispers filled the room.

I hustled to the back of the tent, up the stairs through a secret entrance in Mr. Monte's office, and onto the tightrope. A large curtain hung in front of the rope so no one could see me. Filling my lungs with air, I took a step onto the tightrope with my large gown weighing me down. The ground felt miles away, and when the veil dropped to reveal me standing there, fifty feet in the air, the audience erupted into cheers. I smiled and grabbed at the waist of my dress unlocking the clip in the back, so the giant skirt fell to the floor below. What remained was a crimson leotard with a sweetheart neckline, billowing sleeves, and a tight waist. And to top it off, my neck was sprayed with silver powder, so that I glowed in the candlelight.

I began my routine by walking halfway across the rope, leaping up, and turning one-hundred eighty degrees to face the other side of the audience. The could faintly see the crowd craning their necks to see me. I bent my knees and arched my back before I had time to think about the move I was completing. Looking for the rope, I placed my hands down and flipped my legs over my head, landing safely with my hands up high to finish. I spun once more to face the other side of the crowd and spotted a young girl in a pea coat waving at me. I winked at her, placed my hands on the rope, and clenched my core and buttocks to remain parallel in a handstand. But my arms shivered under the weight of my body, and suddenly I tipped to the left and I fell.

The crowd gasped.

With every intention of tricking them, at the last second, I grasped the rope and swung my stomach over to pull myself back up. The crowd clapped wildly and laughed when they realized I had intended to fall the whole time.

I raised into relevé and brought the tips of my fingers together while I did a pirouette, focusing on a point in the distance to keep my balance. Bending my knees, I jumped into the air and split my legs into a line as straight as the tightrope I walked on. When I landed, my knees shook and I lost my balance for a moment, but I managed to appear composed while I regained my balance.

When I finished walking to the other end of the rope, I saw someone in the crowd I didn't expect to see. Cassius sat in the first row with his legs spread wide as if he owned the place. When his caramel eyes met mine, he leaned forward to watch closer. And in response to the weight of his stare, I pushed my chest forward and shook my breasts. All the men in the crowd hollered while the women covered their children's eyes in an attempt to maintain their innocence. And I raised my leg into the air and grabbed my ankle to complete a high kick.

Cassius furrowed his eyebrows in defeat.

The dancers sashayed and kicked their legs into the air synchronously, while they grabbed at their hearts dramatically and slinked back to the pool of fabric in the middle of the tent. Their movements were hypnotizing. The crowd realized too late when I leaped from the tightrope and fell, my loose shirt rippling in the wind and my hair billowing about my face. The dancers looked up to me in terror, and four things happened in the next five seconds:

1. Around the pile of giant rose petals, the dancers all fell to the ground, closing their eyes.

2. I crashed down in the middle of the rose petals, and dust raised around my body.

3. The room went dark. I coughed and crouched low while making my way to the back of the tent.

4. Cheers resounded off the walls like a heartbeat.

After the fog darkened the room, I secretly retreated to the back of the tent where I was greeted by all the performers. The dancers hopped around me eagerly, and the flamethrowers congratulated me. The horsemen couldn't wait to announce an idea for our next show, although I was too dazed by the fact that I had just accomplished my first performance to even listen.

"Now boys, give the girl some space." Hugh separated the crowd that surrounded me, and tiny Olive trailed behind him in a scarlet dress.

I thanked him for his interference.

Gus spotted me from across the room and walked over with an appreciative smile. "You did very well, Miss Rose." He nodded in congratulations, with his hands folded behind his back.

"Please, call me Juniper," I said.

He smiled but I was unable to return the favor as I spotted Cassius glowering at me from across the room, his eyes dark under his manicured eyebrows.

All of the sound in the room diminished. He stood by the horses with a canteen of some god-forbidden alcohol in his hand, and when he took a gulp, honey-colored rum ran down his clean jaw. He did not congratulate me on my first performance, but instead looked at me as if I had failed. Cassius was the most disrespectful boy I'd ever met.

Mr. Monte beckoned me over to him, "Come, my rose. You have pleased me greatly, but we are not finished yet. I want you front and center for the closing ceremony."

The flaps on the tent reopened before I had the chance to disagree. The glass had been cleared and the candles relit, and the crowd stood and clapped as Mr. Monte shuffled to the front. Taking off his plum-colored top hat and extending it to the crowd, he bowed deeply.

Children jumped up and down. This was true happiness, a place where money and status didn't matter. We might be a spectacle of odd ruffians among wealthy landholders, but the attraction could not be mistaken. People would continue to watch what fascinated them as long as we were daring enough to give it to them.

Mr. Monte grabbed my hand by surprise and pulled me to his side. The applause made my head feel light and airy, and I smiled exuberantly, looking to my left and right. I instinctively waved politely, like my mother taught me to, and held my stomach to keep from laughing. The men in waistcoats and expensive cravats noticed my gesture and bowed deeply out of respect, as if they understood I was one of them.

I looked around nervously and dropped my hands, worried that my new friends might think differently of me. I was surprised to see Cassius sitting on a gallant horse, and my throat tightened when he shook his head slightly, not to be seen by the crowd, and raised his eyebrow at me.

Look at them. They want you back. He might as well have said it out loud, because I knew that was what he was thinking.

I was no longer part of the wealthy world, and I couldn't have people continue to see me that way, but I knew Cassius would try to prove I belonged with them until the day I died.

Despite the judgement in his eyes, I put on a smile.

"Excellent work. I have a proposition that I would like to speak to you about tomorrow morning," Mr. Monte whispered in my ear, while the other performers waved and smiled. To conclude our performance, the flamethrowers took in a mouthful of gasoline, placed a stick of fire to their mouth, and blew out a stream of golden fire. And the crowd went wild. It was the perfect ending to a perfect night.

I changed out of my tight leotard, slinging a dark blue robe over my shoulders, and fingered the string of pearls at my throat as I watched the crowd file out of the tent. A few of the performers stayed back to groom the horses, but most had gone to return to the train. I could still hear the audience's chants. Hours after my performance, I still felt like I was high in the air. I looked at the now empty tent and tried to envision myself on the tightrope. What must I have looked like? I giggled before grabbing my suitcase and marching back to the train. I might never understand how I came to be part of this world.

Chapter 9

"Good morning, Rose." Piper bounced up to greet me in the morning as I made my way to Mr. Monte's office.

"Morning Piper." I bopped her on the head before she ran to the dining hall in search of Olive.

Charlotte brushed by me, hanging onto the arm of a boy named Finley who specialized in horse riding. I smiled at the pair, wondering if she'd be with someone new the following morning. The dancers are known to drift between men, sometimes visiting more than one each night.

All the activity made the small hallway shrink something fierce as I approached Mr. Monte's office. I stood outside and listened as voices spoke softly within.

"She will prove very useful in the future, Monroe. She can be a connection to the wealthy. Imagine the shows we'll book!" Mr. Monte's voice was no longer low and commanding, but light and playful.

"I don't know, Edward. It may cause unrest between the performers," the other man proclaimed, seeming to take up my defense.

Who was speaking to Mr. Monte? Was Edward Mr. Monte's first name?

"Just consider it. That's all I ask."

Feet shuffled behind the door and I immediately scurried around to make it seem as though I hadn't been eavesdropping.

Mr. Monte bid his acquaintance farewell, and as the man came out of his office, he gave me a sidelong glance. He didn't say anything to me before he shuffled away awkwardly. He seemed odd but nice enough.

I wanted to ask Mr. Monte about the stranger, but he was eager to get to business.

"I was sincerely pleased with your performance last night. After years of searching, I have finally found a worthy tightrope walker.

You have much to learn, but I have a proposition." Mr. Monte sat with his feet crossed on his creaky desk.

"A proposition?" My voice cracked when I tried to sound indifferent.

"You were raised in Axminster," he began cautiously. "Your mother is a rather wealthy woman, courted by the fine gentleman of the Rose family, although he is absent from your life, correct?"

I felt as though my knees may buckle. I could just see my mother sitting at the kitchen table, her peach-colored lipstick staining the rim of her teacup, her legs folded politely, and my sister sitting beside her waiting dutifully for my mother to speak first. The memory of the tidiness of our home made me want to vomit; it made me want to tear the pristine curtains to shreds and take the place setting at the head of the table. That place was reserved for my father, and no one had ever sat there.

I had not come there to be interrogated or to have my life spread out to dissect.

"I would like you to be my associate in organizing our performances. Specifically, I desire to expand the circus. I want to perform for the ruffians who appreciate our odd talents as well as for the rich who will pay top dollar. And to accomplish this, I need someone who understands the ways of proper men and women. That person is you." Mr. Monte pointed at me.

I tried to be as respectful as I could. "Sir, I do not intend to overstep my bounds, but isn't performing for those who can actually enjoy our show without criticizing it enough?" I didn't want to do what he was asking of me. The other performers would surely be convinced that I wasn't one of them. I wanted to move on from my past, not dive deeper into it. And that meant distancing myself from the wealthy as much as physically possible.

"It is. But without the support of the rich, the circus will die. If we cannot afford to pay the veterinarians for our animals, or for food to be shipped in for the performers, or for land to rent for our shows, there will be no circus at all." Mr. Monte placed his hands on the desk, waiting impatiently for my answer.

His eyes twinkled pleadingly. His intentions were honest—honorable even. But by welcoming the past I had tried so hard to escape, I worried I would lose the trust of my new friends. They had welcomed me, but it was well known that we came from two different worlds, and I was doing my best to fit in.

Cassius's low voice began to echo distantly in my head. *People are beginning to think you will never change from the modest...*

I stopped the thought before it set in. I would prove Cassius wrong by rejecting this proposition.

Just then, a harsh laughter bounced off the walls in the hallway, waking me from my thoughts. The dancers, the jesters, the magicians, the twin animal experts, the men who swallowed flames, the horse riders. Even the lion tamer. They all meant a lot to me. How could I risk their joy by letting the circus fall to ruins?

I was being selfish because I didn't want their opinion of me to change, but I had to put my friends first. "What would you have me do?" I took a seat and looked Mr. Monte in the eyes with determination.

He smiled. "I have a few ideas."

***

Colette:
"May I present to you, my son, Joseph Young." A man with receding gray hair and hard blue eyes pushed his son in my direction. Mr. Young's son was a fine fellow. He had sunshine for hair and the strands were pushed back gently with musky gel. His eyes were such a pure blue, like the soft waves off the coast of Islebury where the waters were warm and translucent. There was not a single blemish on his hands. He was clean...too clean.

"It's nice to meet you, Mr. Young." I greeted the boy by extending my hand to him.

He took my palm softly and touched his smooth lips to the tips of my knuckles.

My mother glared at me for forgetting to curtsey.

I sank into a quick bow before my mother beckoned all of us to the table to speak about the latest spring dresses with Mrs. Young. Crisp, white china plates were set out, and not a single piece of cutlery was out of place. The white linen tablecloth was washed and pure of any stains, and crocheted placemats were tucked beneath the glistening plates. Tall crystal glasses decorated each place setting, while a chilled bottle of champagne rested in the center of the table.

I instinctively folded my napkin over my lap while the Young men tucked theirs into their vests under their overcoats. My mother made small talk with the two adults, and I sat silently, hoping the boy would not start a conversation with me. I'd been in this situation before. Fine gentlemen would have dinner at our house, barely speak to me, and then ask to see me again at the end of the night. These invitations were always easy for me to forego. Even so, I would rather the silence at the table than talk of boring things like the ups and downs of the economy. All we ever talked about were new fashions, current affairs, and the new Baptists joining us in church on Sunday mornings. And to think that this dinner was something my mother had prepared for and fawned over for months. It wasn't any different than all the other dinners.

Our plates were filled with juicy pork, potatoes lightly seasoned with garlic, and sprigs of asparagus. After our plates were licked clean, the servants collected our dishes. Kathryn emerged from the kitchen with flower and powdered sugar on her apron and laid a tray of cinnamon croissants filled with custard in the center of the table.

I picked at the dessert, feigning interest in Mr. Young's conversation over his business alliance in Wimborne. Mr. Young was a wealthy businessman who bought and sold land, and all he ever talked about was trade and the prices in the market.

My mother spoke up, "I must confess. I enjoy your company more than most, but I do have a proposal to offer before your family leaves. Or rather, one for your son." My mother turned to the Young boy.

Oh no. This boy had said maybe two words to me all night. There was no way I could marry him. He was handsome, but too reserved for me. With him, I feared I would live a life of solitude, devoted to my husband and only him. I would give away my independence as a woman and serve him alone.

"My daughter Juniper is one of great beauty and intelligence. She tends to embark on little adventures, but she is extremely devoted to the church. Upon her return, I hope that you would consider taking her hand. It would give me great solace to know my daughter is in loving hands, protected by such a fine gentleman." My mother tipped her head forward.

My eyes widened. Juniper? Of all the charades my mother pulled, this was by far the most egregious. For the past few years, my mother had worked to find me a suitor, and every time I had found an excuse to refuse their hand. But handing off my sister who had finally escaped Axminster, to a boy she had never met, just to return her to the life my mother expected her to live was...well, it was cruel!

I searched my mother's face but she didn't meet my eyes. *Look at me!* I wanted to scream. *Please!*

"What an honor." Mr. Young spoke up for the dumbfounded boy. "My family will earnestly consider your offer and be in touch."

I looked regretfully at Joseph. It seemed he was just as controlled as the rest of us.

In the dining hall, everyone picked at their dinner while talking merrily. I enjoyed watching Olive and Piper attempt to sing a ballade on stage and I tried not to giggle. Hugh grabbed under Olive's armpits and lifted her onto his shoulders, while she laughed and grasped his bald head. A waltz began and Hugh quickly launched her to the ground and spun her around like she was his own daughter. And in typical fashion, the dancers all grabbed partners and kicked their legs freely into the air.

I went to the bar to snag another ale. By now, I had become accustomed to the acrid drink. I smiled and listened to the music, wishing I could be as loose as the dancers. All I knew was ballet, which was a tight, structured dance. I had no idea how to let my limbs go and just...wiggle.

"Ah, the muse of the circus...Juniper Rose! All the way from Axminster!" Cassius pretended to read from a billboard. His eyes drooped and his skin was sickly pale. I'd seen Cassius drink three ales every night. His tolerance was unheard of, so he must have had a lot to drink tonight to be in such a vulnerable state.

"Is that jealousy I smell?" I retorted while looking into his golden eyes.

He bent his head awkwardly to look at me before pinching his thumb and pointer finger together. "Only a pinch." He shook his head and downed the rest of his drink.

I watched his Adam's apple bob up and down smoothly while his eyes closed, relishing the taste.

"More so bitter amusement." He leaned back on his forearm and looked to the throng of people dancing.

"I thought you'd be tired by now," I admitted, but by the crease between his eyebrows, I knew he may need more of an explanation. "Of criticizing me. If there's anything I proved last night, it's that I'm here to stay."

"And because of that, I am less angry at you than I was yesterday." He looked me up and down.

His honesty made me gulp. Cassius was drunk. Tomorrow he would return to detesting me.

"I may have mistaken your talent."

"That you have," I said with a nod. Noticing the boyish gleam in his eye, I clutched the stylish ruby overcoat that hung over my shoulders. Underneath, I wore a glittering champagne dress that dipped low to reveal my cleavage. It only reached halfway down my thighs, its glittering tassels waving every time I took a step. I shed my coat and threw it into his grasp, which made him stumble and spill his ale.

"Juniper!" Gus grabbed my hands and twirled me around quickly.

I allowed him to lead me by trying to be light on my toes, and as I hopped through the crowd, Piper grabbed me and pulled me close so she could whisper in my ear.

"He's looking at you, Miss," she giggled.

I followed her hand and found that she was pointing at Cassius. He watched me carefully, trying to decide whether to join the dance and have *fun* or to maintain his always-serious demeanor.

I wished he would join us, although I wasn't sure why. Instead, he took one more swig from the wooden cup, brushed his long arm across his shining lips, and left the room with a scowl on his face.

I wrapped my tools in leather pouches and tucked them safely into a metal chest to protect them. The circus was packing up and moving to Penketh, which was a day's ride from Dangarnon. I wound up the tightropes and organized them by size in their divided bins, covering each rope with a protective cloth. The flamethrowers helped me take down the poles that held up the ropes and place them in the metal carts.

"Mr. Monte, the giraffes are spooked! They won't settle down!" Charlotte yelled from the stables.

Mr. Monte ran over to the jumpy animals, trying to get a hold of the straps around their necks. Their legs were impossibly long, which made it difficult to tame them without being crushed to death.

Cassius sprinted out from the cages where he was taming one of the tigers and ran for the biggest giraffe. There was an intense fear in his eyes as he reached for the lead giraffe's neck, trying to soothe her, to no avail. There was no way Mr. Monte and Cassius could help all five giraffes on their own. Without thinking twice, I leaped into the stables and ran for one of the calves that was screaming in terror.

It stomped its hoof and I scrambled back in fear.

"Juniper get away! It's too dangerous!" Cassius screamed, finally grabbing ahold of the reins and tugging the animal's head down so he could stroke its jaw.

I didn't listen to him but instead followed his lead and grabbed onto the calf's reins and forcefully pulled its neck. When its head met mine, its breathing slowed, and its big brown irises starred right at me. I gently ran my fingers through its coarse fur and the beautiful animal dipped its head toward my touch.

As I looked to Cassius for direction, his face was frozen.

Mr. Monte gazed oddly at me.

Had I done something wrong?

Cassius regained his composure and strode toward me while pulling the animal behind him with care. He stopped before me, nostrils flared, and demanded, "Do not ever step in front of an animal again." He kept his head forward, and that signature black curl fell in his eyes.

I was only trying to help. Why was he so upset? At least I had decided to do something instead of standing around foolishly like all of the other performers!

He took the calf from my hands and secured both the giraffes in their stables.

"What's wrong?" I spit out. I was frustrated with his silent, rude demeanor.

"Don't invade my space as if you know what you're doing. This is my job and these animals are my priority," he shouted at me.

Everyone had gone back to doing their own tasks, which I was grateful for. I didn't want anyone to see our disagreement. "I was just trying to help!"

"Then stop. I'm sure it's a struggle for you, anyway, having been served every day of your life."

"Would you stop already! Why do you hate me? I've tried so hard to learn your ways and accept all of you for who you are. I've changed a great deal and I love it here! And I'm not leaving." I stepped towards him angrily.

He seemed frightened by me, and he opened his mouth to speak, but then closed it and walked away with his hands curled into fists at his side.

I thought Cassius was beginning to trust my intentions with the circus. From what he said last night, I thought we were becoming better acquainted. But Cassius was drunk, and I was a fool to think we could be anything close to friends.

That afternoon, after the tents had been folded up, we set course for Penketh. I remained in my room, reading over the schedule for our next performance, while the train rocked my body back and forth. After arriving in the next kingdom, we would only have a week to prepare for the show, before setting out on the road again. In Penketh, I would be the opening act instead of the closing act, but the other details would be a surprise.

Suddenly a knock sounded on my door, and I rose from the chair and opened the door to find two different colored eyes staring at me.

"Are you ready?" Charlotte asked ambitiously.

"Yeah," I said and grabbed the bag next to my dresser. The dancers and I were spending the night together, and I was certainly ready for a night with the girls. I'd only been to a few sleepovers in Axminster, where caviar served with cucumber water and silk nightgowns were all the rage, and makeovers were things proper young girls looked forward to. I was interested to see how this night would differ from the ones back home.

Wild laughter filled the small room. Empty champagne glasses littered the floor, and dresses were strewn onto Charlotte's bed so that all the girls were left in their lacey silk robes. I strapped a baby blue robe around my waist and tied the string tight. One of the girls had been dared to shed her robe completely, so she sat on the floor in only her undergarments.

This was not how I expected the night to go, although there was something freeing about these girls. They were not ashamed of their bodies or of the pleasures that come from them. For years, my mother told me how to act. *Tie up that corset, pull up your stockings, shine your heels, pull back your hair.* I didn't know who I really was after being taught who I *needed* to be for so long. So being surrounded by women who were completely and uncontrollably themselves made me want to become that way too.

"Drink this." Charlotte handed me another glass of champagne.

I gulped it down and my skin started to tingle.

"Let's go entertain the boys!" Charlotte said, as she led the group down the hall.

I let go of reason and ran down the hall with them, toward the men's quarters.

When we arrived, a tall boy scooped Charlotte into his arms and swung her around, and then kissed all over her face, making her shriek. Meanwhile, the other girls latched their skinny arms around the necks of random boys.

I was not sure what to do with myself. I stood with my hands in front of me and gazed around the room, feeling really insecure. I had never been with a boy before, and everyone here seemed to know what they were doing. And despite my loneliness, I didn't know how to engage with a boy in that way.

I felt like someone was watching me, and when I turned around, I spotted a tall gentleman with sharp cheekbones. A small smile played on his lips, and before I knew it, he was walking toward me.

Maybe this would be easier than I thought.

When he reached me, he pulled me close. His abruptness surprised me, but I was thankful not to have to worry about proper introductions. We drank heartily and he made me laugh by explaining his many adventures with the circus. His name was Flint Rye, and he was very easy to talk to. He had straight brown hair that was carelessly pushed back out of his gleaming blue eyes. He was rather tall, which pleased me, and he was a horse rider, which intrigued me. I wanted to know how they did such amazing tricks on moving animals, and certainly he could tell me.

In the throng of people, I saw Cassius's eyes beaming like a lighthouse. He sat in a chair with his legs spread open and two thin girls strapped to his waist. God, I hated that boy. He was impossible to relate to, never said nice things to anyone, and always had a demeaning look on his face. I don't think I would ever understand why he despised me so much, but I *could* decide not to put up with it.

I turned to Flint and rose to my tiptoes so that our faces were inches apart. I loved how kind his eyes were. "I have no idea what I'm doing," I whispered in his ear, and I thought I felt him shiver beneath me. I kept my eyes on Cassius the whole time by poking my head over Flint's tall shoulder.

"Neither did I when I first arrived, but it seems like you're a quick learner," he whispered back in a raspy voice.

The compliment made me giggle. I'd never kissed a boy before, but for some reason I wanted to know how it would feel to kiss Flint.

Do not get ahead of yourself, Juniper, I thought to myself.

Just then, a figure rushed past me, interrupting my euphoria. I recognized the pretty blond to be Charlotte, and she was determined to kindly ask the other women on Cassius's lap to leave before dramatically laying across him.

He looked at her as if she was the only girl in the room.

She played with his unbuttoned shirt and smiled lightly. Time suddenly slowed and all I could see were Cassius's eyes, deep set and round. He looked up at me, then down at her, before crashing his lips onto hers. It was strange. His eyes were fixed on me while he kissed her, and isn't it customary to close your eyes when you kiss someone? His stare made me really uncomfortable, but if his intent was to make me jealous, it wasn't working. I felt bad for Charlotte. Although she might not admit it, I knew she cared for him. And Cassius was unable to care for anyone other than himself.

I looked up to Flint, and his eyes were bouncing between my lips and my eyes. His lips were full and pink, which prompted me to give in to my curiosity. I brought my lips to his a little harder than I intended, and despite my inexperience, the feeling was wonderful. My stomach fluttered, and my heart beat so fast I thought it would burst right out of my chest. His mouth was wet and tasted bright, like alcohol and mint combined.

I pulled away and he opened his eyes to look up and down my body.

Before I had time to comprehend what had just happened, Autumn grasped my arm and pulled me away from him. I tried to protest. I wanted to kiss him again. I wanted to feel that lightheadedness and touch his warm skin again. It wasn't something I could explain, but he was strong and tall and kind, and I longed for him to hold me tight. I looked back at him and smiled as she dragged me along with the other girls fleeing the room.

He just shook his head and laughed.

What an interesting night...

Chapter 10

The next morning we arrived in Penketh. My limbs were sore from being on a moving train all day, and my head throbbed. We all got busy tying up the tents in preparation for the next show. The harsh sun beat down and my forehead was dripping with sweat by the end of the day, causing my black curls to stick to my face.

"One, two, three!" Hugh yelled.

All at once, we pulled on the ropes and the red and white striped tent rose into the air. After we had pulled it up, the men circled around the perimeter and pounded the stakes into the ground to keep the tent in place. I tried not to notice the muscles moving in Cassius's back or how the sweat made his tan skin show through his loose shirt.

After hours of working in the hot sun, the tents were up, the tightrope was set in place, and all of the animals had been put out to graze. I attended a fitting for my costume and Valetta lectured me on the importance of oiling my legs before a performance and powdering my hips to keep my leotard in place.

For three days, I practiced on the tightrope and my feet were blistered and bleeding. I kept to myself and avoided most everyone because I wanted to concentrate on making this performance impressionable. I had failed to accomplish a front flip, and every time I attempted it, I missed the rope entirely when I tried to land. I also couldn't procure a split dip, which is accomplished by lowering into a split on the rope, twisting off the side, and grasping the rope before falling. And to add to this list of failures, I hadn't been able to successfully finish a double handspring. With only a week to practice, I was becoming frantic.

I shut the doors to my tent intentionally so I could practice without interruption. I attempted the double handspring again, bouncing on the rope and reaching with my hands to throw my weight over my head. When my feet touched the rope, it jerked violently to the right, but I grabbed the rope instead of falling onto the landing pad below. My arms stung and tears threatened to spill from my eyes, but I knew that all this practice would be worth it when I could dazzle the crowd with all these difficult tricks.

"You seem to be making great progress," Cassius said as he pushed through the entrance of the tent. His hair got caught in the large flaps, causing him to curse and whip his head back.

"So now you're illiterate? You didn't see the sign I posted out there?" I jumped down onto the landing pad and marched over to point out the piece of paper on the front of the tent that read *no interruptions*.

"Sorry, I don't read privileged handwriting," he said, and then laughed at his own joke.

I was fuming and I clenched my jaw to hold my tongue. He laughed harder to provoke me, and in response, I pushed his shoulders back as hard as I could. They were hard and strong, and it felt strangely nice to be that close to him.

He didn't falter as much as I imagined he would, although he looked at me dangerously. "That's what I was looking for. I was starting to think you might fold your hands and take my rude comments forever like the proper lady you are."

"So you admit they're rude?" I raised my eyebrows.

He tilted his head from side to side, thinking over his decision. "Possibly just a bit demeaning."

I shook my head, unable to form a response. I wanted to hit him. Hard. And I wanted him to feel it. I wanted to punch that pretty smile right off his face, and then sock him in the groin where I knew it would hurt.

But instead of being violent I rolled my eyes. "Possibly," I said, referring to his previous comment. I walked back over to the rope and wrapped my ankles with white tape to cover the dark purple bruises.

"You're afraid." Cassius looked at me confidently, not caring if his opinion offended me.

"What?"

He cut me off. "You're afraid. Every time you fall, it's because you're afraid of not landing your move. I may not know the techniques of a ballerina, but I do know the art of balance." Cassius hadn't explained the story of how he used to be a horse rider, but somehow, he knew I understood.

I didn't try to cut his speech short or disagree with him, because he was right. But it was more the fact that I enjoyed hearing him speak about his knowledge. And as much as I hated admitting it, Cassius was talented, and I needed all the help I could get.

He continued, using his arms as a visual, "When you leap into the air, you think about falling off the rope instead of landing the trick. As much as skill is involved, there is an equal amount of mental preparation."

"I try to think about nailing the flip. I think about where my hands should go and when I should arch my back," I said.

"Then you're thinking too much. It's simple. Don't think so much."

I scoffed, as if to say *easier said than done.*

He nodded his head for me to give it another try.

I walked over to the high rope as he watched carefully. His hands remained patiently behind his back while I climbed the everlasting ladder to the top. For the next few minutes, I stood on the platform before the rope, thinking about my next move. A double handspring. No problem.

"You're thinking, Juniper!" Cassius yelled from down below.

He rarely said my name. He usually went with something like privileged queen, princess, or that one. But I had to admit, my name sounded lovely rolling off his lips.

"Step onto the rope and jump."

"And if I fall?" Not being able to process my moves ahead of time terrified me. What if I forgot to arch my back or tuck? I'd plummet to the ground. If I thought through my moves, at least I'd be able to plan for a fall. But why would I want to plan for a fall? Maybe Cassius was right.

"Then you try again," he encouraged me.

Breathe in. Breathe out. I placed my right foot in front of my left and bent my knees quickly. I sprung into the air and tucked my knees into my chest, but it was too late. I knew because when I tucked, my vision was on the ground instead of on the ceiling where it should have been. I spun over myself and attempted to grab the rope, but I missed. My stomach dropped and my lungs flew into my throat, and I let out a short scream before falling on my side on the landing pad.

Not expecting to fall made it hurt more. I was so tired of falling over and over again.

I figured Cassius would make fun of me, but instead he stood patiently without saying a word and then flicked his head toward the rope.

I stood to do it all over again and fell three more times. Cassius's footprints hadn't moved an inch in the sand.

Step onto the rope and jump, I repeated in my head. I bent my knees and leveled my arms so they were parallel in front of me, then arched my back and propelled my weight over my head. I didn't think about falling, but rather how it would feel to land on the coarse rope. I tried to imagine the twisting fibers of the rope and how it would bounce under my weight. And when my feet hit the rope, I looked around, dumbfounded, thinking I might have imagined it. The rope settled quickly and I stood to my full height, and I could feel the smile on my face making my eyes crinkle and my cheeks bunch up.

Cassius clapped his hands and beamed with pride. He stayed with me for the next hour before I finally convinced him to dish about his experiences on the riding team.

I listened intently as his lips moved quickly, rambling through story after story. It was possibly the first time I had seen him really smile. He helped me oil the threads of the tightrope as we talked, and he got quiet many times throughout the night, which made me realize that he often seemed rude or standoffish because he didn't feel comfortable talking to people.

"I thought you didn't want to help me?" The memory of his refusal many weeks ago still pained me to think about. I was so lost then, so afraid I would never belong here. But I had grown because I had to teach myself, which was something I wasn't used to.

"I am a gentleman." Cassius straightened his black coat over his shoulders when the brisk air hit our bodies as we stepped outside. He buckled the golden buttons over his strapping chest and said, "I help damsels in distress."

I burst out laughing harder than I had in months. "It brings me the utmost amusement to listen to you speak so highly of yourself."

He punched my shoulder lightly and I faltered to the side.

Before he could see me smile too brightly, I retreated to my bedroom. It took me almost an hour to finally fall asleep, because I couldn't shake the sensation of flipping through the air.

Colette:

I pushed back the midnight curls from my forehead. I was dripping with sweat, dressed in a pea green gown with white ruffles cascading down the front, walking along the cobblestone streets of Axminster. The sweet smell of bread and butter wafted from a storefront, as always. And a man with dirt-stained cheeks and a sad look on his face dropped his coins on the street, and I leaned down to help him pick them up.

He looked up at me with a smile. His teeth were crooked and dirty, but the appreciation in his eyes made my heart warm. I couldn't imagine being on the streets like this man. Was he cold or hungry...or both? I rummaged in my pocket and pulled out a handful of coins. "Buy yourself something to eat today, okay, Sir?"

Something in his eyes shifted when I called him sir, perhaps because he'd seldom been treated with respect.

"Thank you. Thank you." He bowed gently and smiled as he plodded toward the bakery on the corner.

I received nothing but glares from the other women in town. How dare they judge me for being kind.

It had been a week since the Young family visited our humble abode; a week since my mother sold off my sister's independence. To think that Juniper would have to give her virtue to someone she didn't love made me sick. There was nothing wrong with Joseph Young. He was kind and handsome enough. He was everything fine and proper and, knowing my sister, it would kill her to be attached to such a moral man. I had to stop this marriage. No matter how far away or how reluctant Juniper was in accepting his offer, my mother would travel to the ends of the earth to bring her back home and see her married.

Across the village square I spotted a tall man dressed in black attire with a matching top hat on his head.

"Sir!" I yelled with all my might as I waved my arms wildly.

He turned his head left and right, trying to find the source of urgency. I shouldn't have screamed because he probably thought someone was hurt. When his eyes landed on me, and his determination was replaced by a smile.

"Ma'am." The guard tipped his body forward out of respect when I approached him.

I smiled, remembering our previous promise to one another not to use these titles.

The officer took off his hat solemnly and placed it on his chest. "The name is William Lloyd."

William Lloyd. It sounded very official. I smiled and said in response, "Colette Rose."

"It's nice to finally meet you." William gave the homeless man in front of the well one last look, warning him to stay out of trouble. And then he popped out his elbow and said, "Care to take a stroll?"

I wrapped my arm through his and thought for a moment. I had declined so many prestigious men because I hadn't found one worthy of my hand. But William had something no one else had. Maybe it was honor in upholding the law. I wasn't sure, but I liked him. We walked through the square and to maintain conversation, he asked me about the status of my sister.

I briefed him on my mother's plan to marry her to Mr. Young. "In a way I'm grateful it's my sister. Every month there's a different suitor at our door that my mother tries to pair me with. It's tiring." I rubbed my forehead.

"Don't you want to be married to a fine gentleman?" William asked, looking down at me in confusion. I was struck by how the sun cast his hair aglow.

It was hard to maintain eye contact with William's bright eyes. I felt he knew every one of my secrets without asking. So instead, I looked to the gray cobblestone below my lavender heels. "A fine gentleman, yes, but one of my own choosing."

"Ah." William looked away. "You don't like the men your mother fancies for you." He seemed relieved by my answer, although his shoulders hung lower. Something was weighing on him.

"No, I don't like them," I scoffed. "They're rich men who care more about attending parties and making business deals than actually loving their wives."

William remained silent, thinking over my words. Did he think of himself as less when compared to these rich men that sought my hand? I would never want him to think of himself that way.

I wanted to know the things that occupied his mind, the things that made his heart ache, and the things that made him smile, no matter how small they might be. I only wished it was that easy. My mother would never allow me to be courted by someone of his ranking, and he knew that. If she were to find out about my interest in him, she would lock me in my room. Suddenly I was jealous of Juniper's choice to run away. Maybe if I had the gumption to take responsibility for myself, I could be with William. But I was foolish and tried to appease my mother, and now I was paying for that choice.

"And that would work?" Mr. Monte questioned me in his dimly lit office.

"I know it will. Advertising is the most effective way to spread word. If we can print an ad about our show on every billboard, storefront, and newspaper throughout the kingdoms, everyone will come to know about us!"

"The cost is great." Mr. Monte rubbed his temple, going over a list of the prices he had gathered for all of this.

"Do what you can. Use any extra money to pay for advertisements in the newspapers instead of ale for Hugh. We all know he could do without it," I snickered.

Mr. Monte laughed gruffly. "Thank you for agreeing to help me. I'll see what I can do."

I nodded my head, but before leaving the room, I turned to him and said, "If we put an article in the newspapers about our performances ahead of time, instead of showing up unannounced in each kingdom, I just know that more people will come to see our show." I shut the door behind me and left him to mull over the idea.

It was a nice feeling, knowing that I'd done something important, something that would make a difference.

"That sounded 'portant. What was it all about?" Olive asked.

The slang of this ten year old girl would never cease to amuse me. "Just talk of our next performance. Which reminds me, I have to practice."

"Have fun," she said as she saluted me seriously, like she was captain of the guard.

I returned the gesture, and as I left she held her finger up in the air to stop me. "Oh, there's a boy outside your tent. Thought I'd let you know." She winked before marching away like a soldier. I watched her try to snag a small cup of ale from the dining cart as Wilman smacked her palm away.

Why would Cassius be outside my tent? Although he offered to help me last night, it didn't mean that we were the best of friends. Unless he was there because he wanted to continue to help me. I wondered what had changed his mind about my problem with privilege. But as I walked briskly across the field, I found someone I didn't expect.

"Flint?" I exclaimed. I had thought about Flint frequently after I kissed him only a few nights ago, but both of us had been too busy preparing our acts to do anything else. It was a surprise to see him there, and I don't know why my first thought was of Cassius.

The tall boy turned abruptly at the sound of my voice. He pushed back his hair with a large, bony hand, and the ends curled around his ears to accent his sharp cheekbones. I wanted to touch the dip in his cheeks to determine if they could cut me as I suspected.

"I thought I might check out your scene," Flint said as he stepped closer.

"Well, what do you think?" I pushed back the heavy flaps of the tent, and my world full of high places came into view. Tall rods of steel connected a long rope, a ring of sand laid in the center, and on the far wall, hoops, slings, and ropes were piled in a large bin.

Flint's head moved around the room to gaze at every tiny morsel of space. My reaction must have been similar to his when I first arrived. It seemed like my first day was only yesterday and years ago at the same time. I hoped I would never get used to this place but that it would always remain magical to me.

"I can't imagine doing what you do," he admitted.

"As I cannot imagine doing what you do," I agreed.

He smiled suddenly, and I had the urge to stroke his cheeks but didn't know why. Often I found myself wanting to touch him. If

Cassius were here, he would say something cruel about how I stood around all day and walked on a string. But Flint made me feel like what I did was special, and we all deserve to feel like that.

One day, every kingdom would realize that the circus was worth remembering, but it had to start with us. When we recognized and respected each other's talents, only then would we be able to convince the rest of the world.

Chapter 11

Workmen in dirty overalls stood on wobbly scaffolding to glue posters depicting the circus onto the sides of every building. The posters were enormous and were outlined in gold trim, with pictures of jesters in blue and white striped uniforms riding unicycles, lions and tigers roaring in front of a lion tamer, women spinning in long golden dresses, and a woman flipping in midair above a wire-thin rope.

Newspapers gushed about the latest acts. Penketh was one of many to announce their enthusiasm for the circus.

> **Ladies and gentlemen, ministers and bishops, kings and queens...**
>
> **Come witness the finest performance of the era! Do you want to see magic tricks? Do you want to see a lion tamed by a mere man? Do you want to watch a woman levitate? Then join us at the circus where all things are possible! A new tightrope walker has joined our ranks, and her unique talent is something you will never forget. But don't take our word for it—come watch the performance and determine its greatness for yourself! We promise you the night of your life!**
>
> **--The Articles of Penketh--**

The streets of Penketh were flooded with anticipation about the performance coming to town. People scurried about and the cobblestone streets rattled with passing carriages. The newspapers fluttered along the pavement, with the front-page article depicting a man with a daring smile and a trimmed beard.

It was a picture of Mr. Monte, the esteemed leader of the circus. The ink on the page mirrored his facial features perfectly, but a cold breeze flipped the page, and the ringmaster disappeared. The town would eagerly await the show to find him again.

The stands were packed to capacity, and the crowd was overwhelmed with joy that night. There were a few kinks in my performance, which I would work out for next time, but overall, the night was a huge success. The total revenue was sure to be more than the two previous performances combined.

After our final bow, Charlotte took my arm quickly. "We're going to the pub in town. You wanna come?"

I nodded eagerly and dressed in a simple grey dress with a tight corset, which always accentuated my best features. Walking through the town rejuvenated me. I'd been with the circus for almost two months now, and not once had I left its confines. I had enjoyed my time there, really, but I wanted to experience the world more. All I had ever known was Axminster, and given this chance to travel, I was eager to explore each of these new cities.

Olive grabbed my hand and her eyes beamed at the chance to roam the streets and explore life in Penketh. Being so young, she was rarely allowed to enjoy the splendors beyond circus life, so this would be one of her first excursions too. People on the streets recognized us, having seen us only hours ago. They shouted their appreciation, and some of them asked for autographs. One kind gentleman even kissed my knuckles, which meant so much to me. Instead of belittling us, the wealthy were now praising us. I wondered if my connection with the wealthy could be working to change people's minds about the circus. We approached a pub called the Stout Monk, where a sign hung outside showing a small man bowing before a bottle of ale, which I thought was ironic. Wouldn't the consumption of alcohol be contrary to a monk's beliefs?

Nonetheless, I entered the busy room. The candlelight was low, creating a comfortable feeling, and green and brown bottles of miscellaneous wines and ales were stacked behind a counter where a man in a dirty apron stood taking orders. Most of the tables were full of men with bellies spilling over their trousers. Top hats were strewn on the tables, vests were undone, and sleeve cuffs were unbuttoned. This was freedom—the ability to forget yourself and your status and enjoy the city with people from all walks of life. A group of drunk girls stood to offer us their two tables, and we thanked them kindly as we spread out, just in time for our glasses of ale to arrive.

"Penketh is known for its ale. Drink up, Missy!" Charlotte pushed me a brown mug, and I downed its contents.

After twenty minutes I was as loose as a woman of the night. I jumped around the table with Piper and Olive, dancing to the soft music. The room was so hot, and my chest was sticky with sweat. The god-awful corset I wore was too tight, so I began to unbutton the top of my dress, attempting to assuage the discomfort.

Flint abruptly stopped my endeavor before I had abandoned all modesty. His hands were cool which made me sigh, and I was grateful for the interference.

"Come on Flint, don't stop her there. She was jus' gettin' to da good part!" One of the jesters—an overweight man with receding hair—shouted.

Even in my delirium, I spotted Cassius laughing from his secluded spot in the back. I laughed, realizing my embarrassment, and then looked up at Flint in appreciation. To my surprise, he leaned down and pecked me quickly on the cheek to ease my shame, and my cheeks bloomed with color.

Henny, a wild magician, began to sing a small tune. "Ho, hey, the circus has arrived. It's late now, come and play outside." His voice was gentle in the chaotic room.

Gus, his partner in magic, continued the verse, "You'll never know...how far you'll go." His voice was beautiful and melodic.

I looked around the room in amazement to find the circus members listening intently to the chorus. The quiet medley gave me goosebumps, and I watched the candles flicker as smiles spread across the performers' faces. This was their song...

The entire circus erupted at that moment. "Take a chance! Beat your fate! Kick the dust! Clap your hands! Say your name out loud! Here comes the crowd!" Everyone linked their arms and hung onto the last note, and when the chorus came to an end, they clinked their glasses together and shouted, "The circus has arrived!"

Chapter 12

I took a cup of blueberry tea from Mr. Monte in an antique china cup. The steam rolled off the glassy top and curled up into my nostrils, and the smell was earthy and fresh, but the taste was sweet. I sipped at it, being careful not to burn my tongue. Tea was a far more expensive tonic than alcohol, which was why Mr. Monte only possessed a small selection of it. If we had more money, maybe we would drink tea and lemonade, but we couldn't afford such luxuries, so we drank ale.

"There were two hundred guests at our revel last night, and I'm thrilled to say that your idea worked. I don't know why we haven't promoted our establishment before now!" Mr. Monte exclaimed.

"I'm only glad that we have begun to do so. Better late than never."

"Mmm." He nodded his head and took a long draw of tea. The delicate cup in his large, calloused hand looked out of place.

I set down the saucer and the dark purple liquid sloshed around the sides of the cup. "I have another idea," I announced out of the blue.

"Do tell," Mr. Monte said as he cleared his throat.

I inched to the edge of my seat with eagerness. I had been thinking for a while now about how the business side of the show was lacking. "We've begun advertising about the circus, so people have come to know *what* we do, but not *when* we do it," I began.

Mr. Monte furrowed his eyebrows. "Go on."

"Usually we show up in town a few days before our performance. Word gets around as people see us setting up, but people living further away still don't know about us. I suggest we print our schedule in the newspaper so people all over will know of our shows in advance."

Mr. Monte's eyes darted around the room. I couldn't tell if he was confused or just thinking my proposal through. I worried I had overstepped my bounds this time for sure. But he surprised me by saying, "That's an excellent idea. Why hadn't I thought of that before?" And then he leapt from his chair and proclaimed, "We must tell the crew!"

These were simple ideas I was offering, and I was happy to do it because it meant I could be part of making our show great.

Mr. Monte bounded from the room, headed toward the dining hall, and because of the commotion, the performers bustled out of their rooms to follow him. I struggled to keep up and by the time I arrived, the dining hall was full, but I pushed my way to the front as Mr. Monte hopped onto the wooden stage.

"My muses, we have a grand idea to help our establishment!" When he announced all that I had shared with him mere seconds ago, the crowd was silent. That was not the reaction he was expecting, I was sure.

"Sir, the circus is not known for being scheduled. That's something everyone loves about us. We show up at random." Gretta said, and her twin brother agreed.

"I understand that, Gretta, but if people know we're coming in advance, think about the crowds we might draw!" Mr. Monte exclaimed.

I'd never seen him this excited before. Surveying the room, I spotted the dancers looking skeptical, the tight-knit group of flamethrowers weighing the option suspiciously, and Cassius in the back corner with his arms folded across his chest. One of his eyebrows was furrowed and he looked angry, and I couldn't imagine why. This was a good decision. This would help the circus. How could they not understand that? After years of doing something the same way, I guess it might be hard to change.

In an attempt to convince them, I spoke up. "If more people come to our shows, then we have more money to buy props and costumes. And ale," I added, turning to Hugh to punch him in the shoulder. I was proud of myself for adding that last bit.

He grabbed my neck and ruffled my hair like a brother would.

I pushed at his arms until he let go, leaving my hair looking like a messy bird's nest.

Finally, the crowd laughed wildly and toasted to Mr. Monte's idea.

"To more people at our shows!" Josephine yelled.

"And to more ale in our bellies!" Hugh added, as he lifted his cup.

I guess they weren't all that opposed to change after all. Or maybe I was just learning to speak their language.

Cassius...

From across the room, Juniper clapped her small hands together and grinned from ear to ear. What was she so happy about? She looked up to Mr. Monte like he was a god. Maybe it was because he rescued her from her treacherously boring, pompous life. Maybe it was because she'd convinced him to shine her shoes and offered him four shillings an hour. Maybe it was because she was just having a good time. But that will only last until she realizes there's more wealth and security for her in Axminster, where her mother coddles her and fine gentlemen worship the ground she walks on. I can't wait for the day she decides to leave this life behind like one of her silly schoolgirl adventures. Then I can say, *I told you so.*

But aside from my annoyance over her constant need to dress like a widowed mother obsessed with worthless charities and her annoyingly affluent speech, something felt different. Why did she so fervently support Mr. Monte all of a sudden? What had he offered her?

The very next morning, the press printed another article on the esteemed circus.

Don't miss the chance to be stupefied at our upcoming performances!
1. Dangarnon- August 17th (Black Hollow Ranch, South Spuk)
2. Penketh- September 21st (Upper East Gumag)
3. Culchester- October 1st (Queestrap Circle)
4. Hewe- October 30th (Sprionnamp District)
5. Turnstead- November 13th (Wrentstoll Forest)
6. Eanverness- December 19th (L'Acre du Grand Ours)
7. Axminster- February 3rd (Upper North Rafad)
8. Wimborne- March 18th (Neollaird Hills)
9. Islebury- April 28th (Blue Moon Grange, Skirruk Corner)

Our trip to the next show in Culchester would be a quick one. And from what I know, Queestrap Circle is one of the most renowned entertainment centers in the world, surpassed only by Blue Moon Grange in Islebury, and Sprionnamp District in Hewe. It happens that Hewe is the most profitable kingdom, famous for luxurious silks that are imported from across the sea. It is also where Horton Perrot, Viscount of the Northern Kingdoms, resides with his wife, Viscountess Lottie Perrot. Our performance in Eanverness was sure to be on the calendars of the most esteemed designers and entertainment managers, as well as the Viscount himself.

Packing up our equipment the next morning was difficult because we drank too much the night before. My head throbbed painfully, and I barely felt like myself. Some of the others drank far too much, but all of them had been drinking for years, so alcohol didn't affect them like it did me. Where it would take me two drinks to feel lightheaded, it would take them about five. Nonetheless, we got everything packed into the train and set out for our voyage before the sun was at its highest point. It would be just over a day's journey to Culchester.

I spent the long night in Penelope Plume's quarters, trying to center myself before my next performance. I trailed my fingers along her dresser which was still covered in dust. In the dark silence of Penelope's room, I was able to breathe. I could think.

As much as I felt good about helping Mr. Monte advertise the circus, I also felt like I was betraying my friends. I worried that if they knew I was trying to get more of the wealthy crowd to come to our performances, they would be angry with me. Especially Cassius. I groaned just thinking about him. He was so caught up in the way things had always been, and so opposed to change. It infuriated me. What was so wrong with a wealthy woman joining the circus anyway?

But every time I went down this road, I wondered if he was right. Could a wealthy woman possess as much talent as one who had to fight for her dreams? Penelope Plume had no other option than to join the circus. And because of her hard work, she earned a great reputation. She was exquisite. Devine. Talented. And me? Would I be remembered the same way she was? In Axminster, people knew me because of my name, but here I was nothing. Maybe that was the point. I had a fresh start. And if I worked hard enough, I could create a great reputation for myself too.

Upon returning to my room, I was surprised to find someone already inside. Flint's long body was sprawled across my bed.

"What are you doing here?" I asked. I'd never had a boy in my room before. It was something that frightened me because I didn't know the slightest thing about romantic interactions. Flint had been my first kiss, and it was electrifying, but beyond kissing, I knew nothing.

"I was terribly bored." He smiled innocently, leaning against the frame of my bed. "You should really lock your door."

"And you should learn to knock," I joked. "Who's going to bother me anyway? Are you worried the twins will come in here late at night to show me their new animal pelts?"

He laughed at that. "I guess you're right."

I took a seat on my bed next to him, and for the first hour we made small talk, laughing and joking about the other performers.

Flint wrote out the circus anthem for me, although he refused to sing it, and I laughed at his horrible handwriting as he scrawled the words on a piece of parchment. And in the next ten minutes I had it memorized, which made me feel like I belonged just a little more. Flint did a very good job at making me feel welcome.

After a period of silence, I asked something I had been wanting to ask since I met him. "Flint Rye...where does that name originate?"

Flint wrung his hands together nervously. "Turnstead," he answered briefly.

"What was it like there?" I'd never been to Turnstead before, so I was really curious.

Flint shrugged and continued, "My family didn't have much money growing up, and what money we did have, we spent on meaningless trinkets. When it came time for me to pay for my education in the city, we were bankrupt. Instead of putting savings into the bank like every other wise family, my parents refused, fearing the government would steal our money. And then the small business we had was sold off to a wealthy landowner who intended to convert it into a tavern. I had the good fortune of being offered a scholarship at Turnstead College, but the cost was still too high. And after my parents declined to send me to school, I left for the circus."

I began to see Flint with a new perspective. If I were to ask the other performers, they would probably answer with similar stories. No matter how smart or talented they may have been, they would not have been offered the same opportunities as a wealthy person, and it saddened me greatly. I determined to do better at taking into account other people's struggles from then on.

"You would have made a fine student. One of the highest in the class, I'm sure." I didn't want to make him sad by dwelling on the fact that he never got to go to school, so I changed the subject. "Tell me, what did you wish to study?"

He looked at me curiously, like he was trying to determine my intent.

I would rather focus on his dreams than speak of the poor decisions of his parents.

"Mathematics." Flint said, pronouncing each syllable clearly.

I smiled thinking about him in a pair of eyeglasses, eagerly scrawling out the solution to a difficult math problem. "I could never. Numbers and equations are too hard for me to understand," I laughed. In school in Axminster, I always had trouble with math. My mom hired a tutor because she didn't have the time to help me, but I still didn't understand it.

"I'm sure that's not the case," he encouraged me. "It only takes practice. Anyone can excel in the subject if they put their mind to it."

His words reminded me of why I was here. I didn't know much about how to succeed in the circus, but I was determined to figure it out. And if I put my mind to it, I could become great like Penelope Plume, maybe greater.

"Please, show me one of your equations."

Flint and I burned the candelabra late that night, working into the wee hours of the morning. He taught me how to solve simple problems, and already I had learned more math than I would have in a year of schooling in Axminster. I was looking forward to learning many things from Flint Rye.

For the performance in Culchester, we would act out a drama. All members of the circus had been asked to gather in the riding arena after we set up camp. Because it was so hot there, I dressed in a flowy white shirt and loose riding pants with black boots. I followed the crowd into an open field where a ring of wooden planks had been set up as a barrier for the animals.

We were welcomed by Mr. Monte's enthusiastic voice. "I know most of you are tired after the long journey, but it's important that we begin practicing immediately since we'll be performing in one of the kingdoms famous for their art and entertainment. I want teams to practice together as follows: the horse riders and our tightrope walker; the dancers, flamethrowers, and the lion tamer; and lastly, the jesters, twins, and magicians. The performance will begin with a kidnapping…"

I assembled my things in the ring of dirt where the riders were stationed. Mr. Monte walked briskly to our group after he had dismissed everyone. "Alright everyone," Mr. Monte clapped his hands together. "Juniper will be the prize possession of a group of five burglars. I will select the five burglars later this afternoon, but I want all of you to practice getting into character while I teach Miss Rose some stunts."

Mr. Monte led me to a small tightrope set up in the middle of the riding area, but all the groups were busy talking about their separate acts, which made it difficult to focus on what I was being told.

He grabbed my shoulders and turned me so I would look him in the eyes. "Listen closely, my rose. The next performance is all about you," he whispered, tucking a stray strand of curly hair behind my ear. "I need you to look scared. I need you to pretend. You can do that for me, can't you?"

"I've been pretending to be someone I'm not my whole life. I think I can manage."

Mr. Monte laughed off my degrading comment and continued, "I have set up a contraption that should be really fun." He smiled wickedly and pointed to a large rope netting laying on the floor.

After briefing me on the plan, he gathered some of the most fit performers in the circus—Hugh, Gus, Flint, and Cassius. I avoided

Cassius's eyes as the four of them grabbed one edge of the netting and lifted it. The strands were extremely flexible, not like the tough rope I usually walked on.

I stood on a platform twenty feet above the group with my heart beating rapidly. "I don't know about this, Mr. Monte!" I yelled to him down below.

He looked up at me from the ground. "Please trust me. They will not drop you."

The men nodded their heads reassuringly, but their knuckles were white from holding the rope so tightly. I closed my eyes for a moment and when I opened them, my sight shifted to Cassius immediately. His brow was furrowed again, most likely doubting that I would go through with the trick. If anyone were to let go, it would be Cassius. Maybe that would be the way he'd finally get rid of me. To shake that thought, I turned my attention to Flint, and he nodded his head and smiled with certainty.

With his reassurance, I took a breath and then stepped and jumped straight back, folding my arms across my chest. I closed my eyes and when my back connected with the flexible rope, bouncing me high into the air, my body jolted.

The performers bent their knees to absorb my weight before lifting the netting above their heads. I hadn't kept my arms folded over my chest as Mr. Monte instructed, and when I fell, my stomach dropped. My vision turned blurry, like I was looking through foggy glass, and I felt as though I might vomit. My friends lowered the netting to stop my momentum, and when all motion had stopped, I was left lying there, unable to move my frozen limbs. That was by far the most terrifying thing I'd ever done.

"Are you alright?" A voice spoke from somewhere beside me.

When I opened my eyes, Mr. Monte's face was close to mine and his eyes were wide. The wooden arena shifted around him and before it was too late, I leapt up and ran to the edge of the arena, while my vision focused in and out of clarity. Acid burned my stomach and my mouth tasted salty and moist with mucus. My throat heaved and I leaned over to grab the wall as my stomach contents emptied onto the ground. It was difficult to breathe, the smell was putrid, and I was terribly embarrassed by everyone watching me.

Just then a warm hand touched my back, and when my stomach finally settled, I realized it was Flint standing behind me, rubbing slow, soothing circles on my lower back. His eyes were filled with concern. It was probably my exhaustion that made me crash into him and grab tightly onto his shirt. He was so caring, and I wanted to feel his warmth over every inch of my body. I wanted him to crush me.

Flint looked around, contemplating what the others might think of us, but then he grabbed my waist to bring me closer. "Do you want to take a break?"

My breathing calmed after a few moments in Flint's arms. And peeking over his broad shoulders, I spotted Josephine and Scarlett looking worried, Gus and Hugh still holding onto the rope, and Cassius's golden eyes penetrating the air between us. A devious smile played on his lips.

I could hear his voice inside my head, *I told you. You weren't meant for this. You're just a scared little girl.*

He was provoking me.

I was tired of his constant pestering! Two could play this game. I cleared my throat and rubbed Flint's chest, feeling his heart beat a little faster beneath my palm. And this gave me the courage to turn to the group and say, "Let's try again. I promise I won't throw up this time."

The others laughed, and when I looked at Cassius, he was biting the inside of his cheek and glaring angrily. He would have to try much harder to put me down.

The next time I fell, I ignored the sinking feeling in my lungs and enjoyed the freedom of my body crashing against the bouncy rope.

Chapter 13

The sun was falling, casting a warm glow into the large tent, and the sand was still, not a speck of dust rising. All week the performers had practiced together to form a wondrous drama for the audience to get lost in. And finally it was showtime.

"Welcome, welcome!" Mr. Monte proclaimed in a strapping, midnight blue tailored coat. "I'm enthralled that you all have come, and I assure you that you won't regret it. Welcome to the circus." He bowed deeply and exited the stage, walking with certainty.

The room dimmed and the crowd went silent as I focused on the stage and took a deep breath. It was my turn to introduce myself.

The lights remained off and I stepped out from behind the curtain into the darkness. I climbed onto the tightrope and placed one hand dramatically on my forehead and the other on my hip, popping my elbow out. The lights turned on all at once and a spotlight shone down on me from the ceiling, nearly blinding me. My oiled skin glowed and the diamonds on my neck shimmered. I was dressed in a periwinkle blue leotard with diamonds covering the bodice, and silver tassels hanging from my arms that swayed every time I moved.

At this moment, the crowd saw me, and me alone. I didn't have any dancers to hide behind or any dark fog to shield me. It was finally time to show the world what I could do. Without delay, I kicked my leg into the air and balanced one foot on the tightrope, and then swiveled, holding onto my ankle and spinning three-hundred and sixty degrees. Then I lowered my foot and leapt into the air, and tucked my knees to my chest to complete a backflip. Upon landing steadily, I bent forward and placed my hands on the rope, while kicking my feet into the air into a handstand. I clenched my buttocks to remain upside down for as long as I could muster, and I realized in that moment that I was off to a great start…

The crowd seemed to be holding their breath.

The veins in my forehead pulsed harshly, and I lowered my arms so that my chest would touch the rope. My biceps were shaking, but I didn't have to hold up my weight for too long. Just in time, I let go and spun off to the left, swinging under the rope and pulling myself back up. I couldn't believe how well it was going.

The crowd erupted in applause.

Suddenly five bandits emerged from behind the tent in a full sprint and grabbed the levers on the poles that held up my rope. They cranked with all their might and the rope began to rise. The steel poles quivered under my weight, and for a moment, fear made me shiver in my core. If I fell, my act would crumble to pieces. When the poles finally reached their full height, I was the highest I'd ever been and my head was almost at the top of the tent. With no other place to go, I pointed my toes and took one step after another until I reached the other side of the rope.

Way down below, I could see the crowd straining their necks to watch me. They looked so small from up in the air.

The bandits were dressed in black from head to toe with masks covering their faces to portray themselves as bandits. Four men climbed the pole nearest where I started my routine, as I covered my mouth with my hand to feign surprise and then performed a double handspring in an attempt to get away. Near the other end of the rope, I performed a triple pirouette, and as soon as I turned, there was a man standing on the platform just behind me.

The crowd gasped. No one had seen him climb behind me as they were preoccupied with the other four men approaching. I breathed hard and tried to maintain my balance this high in the air. The man on my platform took a tentative step forward, as if he could walk across the tightrope to reach me. I backed away, and after a minute of apprehension, I retreated to the other end of the rope where the four men were nearing the top of the pole. As the men emerged onto the platform, I tried to calm my racing heart as I spotted the netted contraption far below. I was also well aware that above the rope, a ring was hooked to the top of the tent, just out of reach.

One of the bandits reached his long arm out to grab my ankle, and I screamed and leapt as far as I could, out of the reach of all four men. I grasped the ring firmly, and threw the full weight of my body up through the ring. Finally, my hips were balanced on the steel.

Defeated, the bandits retreated to the ground, and the crowd relaxed momentarily.

I slipped my legs through the ring so I was hanging on my knees, before dropping my arms to let my body hang limp. I swung back and forth, reaching my hands toward the crowd, but I gained so much momentum that I slipped off the ring.

I began to fall with my arms and legs flailing, and I could see the women grabbing at their chests as they anticipated my fate. The ground came closer and closer, and at the last moment I twisted so I would fall on my back into the net.

The bandits held each corner of the net and flung their arms above their heads, making my body spring up and down, closer and then further from the top of the tent. I had worked so hard that week to perfect my position, so I could create the most dramatic effect in the air. And to add to that drama, I reached my arms up high, as if trying to escape the trap I was ensnared in.

The crowd leaned forward in apprehension, and when I sprung into the air again, I spun to the side and caught Flint's green eyes under his mask. I didn't know he had been assigned as one of the bandits.

Slowly the men stopped throwing me, and when my body was still, they lowered the net to the ground and crawled across the floor toward me.

The women in the crowd screeched in terror, still very much enthralled by the suspense.

Flint grabbed me by the waist, and I kicked and pulled away from him, pretending to fight. But something happened when he touched me this time. It must be that I had feelings for Flint—otherwise, why would I have thrilled to his touch? Meanwhile, the other four men grabbed me and lifted me into the air.

"Sorry princess," Flint whispered in the middle of the group, drowned out by the roaring of the crowd.

I giggled, finding it hard to maintain the facade, but I continued to thrash until the lights had diminished and the burglars had lowered me behind the curtain. I hustled into the back of the tent before the next act continued, and Hugh grabbed my hands while Flint and Gus slapped each other on the backs as we rejoiced about the success of our performance. The crowd had been on the edge of their seats the whole time!

The other performers bustled around us, trying to get into their positions, and the next group surged into the tent. We watched through a gap in the curtain as Cassius pulled the lion out of its cage on a thick leather leash, while keeping it from the dancers standing helplessly behind him. When he flung a piece of meat in front of its face, the lion snapped its jaw and the children in the crowd clapped in awe. The theme of the play had shifted to a heroic man saving a group of women from a monstrous beast. Cassius leapt onto the metal cage after detaining the animal, and the lion snapped at his feet, gaining the whole crowd's applause this time. While Cassius was consumed by the praise of the crowd, the flamethrowers brought orange and yellow syrupy flames to their lips to blow colossal bursts of fire from their mouths. And before Cassius could save the women, they were taken by the hulking men—the moral of this act being that praise is sometimes enjoyed at the expense of others.

The twin acrobats rolled into the tent on their stomachs with their legs hung over their shoulders grotesquely, and the magicians sat them down at a table to predict their future. I laughed when Gus pushed forth a rather risqué card to the female twin, and Gus wiggled his eyebrows provokingly, making the adults in the crowd giggle. Meanwhile, the jesters rode around the tent on unicycles, their faces painted white with blue tears down their cheeks.

While the others performed, I began preparing myself for my concluding act. I sat in front of a mirror and pulled my hair back in a bun and decorated it with a pin.

"You did well." Cassius's figure reflected behind me in the mirror, but the room was rather dark, making his eyes appear dangerous.

"I had a good teacher." My face was neutral as I continued to apply powder to my skin.

He didn't react to my statement as I expected he would, but simply placed a hand on the back of my chair and tapped his fingers lightly against the wood, while he watched me in silence.

The skin on the back of my neck began to tingle under his gaze.

Finally, he opened his mouth to say, "You didn't need me." And before I could respond, he walked away.

Was that kindness? From Cassius? I smiled as I thought over his words. Could he have really meant that? A few days ago, he had scoffed when I fell onto the net for the first time, doubting that I would go through with the act Mr. Monte had given me, and now he was supporting me? The back and forth with Cassius was exhausting. I hadn't been able to gather how he really felt about me, and he was the hardest person to convince that I was here to stay, but I think I'd just done it.

When it was time for the final bow, I joined hands with Josephine and smiled at the crowd. Guests threw flowers and coins onto the sand, and above the raucous of noise, an adamant, strong chant began to echo.

"Ju-ni-per! Ju-ni-per! Ju-ni-per!" The crowd shouted.

It had been five years since the world had seen a tightrope walker, and I never imagined being the one to replace the famous Penelope Plume. My name—they were chanting my name! I was elated that people of all ages were clapping and singing for *me*.

"I have a...connection."

Mr. Monte's eyebrows perked at my confession.

"If we really want the circus to explode with fame, I think we have to perform for the wealthiest family." I paused to think through what I was about to say. This family was directly associated with my family, so I would know the people we were performing for personally. Could I do it? Could I risk my place in the circus to perform for people who'd always seen me as Axminster's little rose? "My mother is a friend of the wealthiest couple in the kingdom of Hewe," I said, as I placed a folded newspaper on Mr. Monte's desk.

His eyes scanned line over line, searching for the purpose of the article.

I pointed to a bolded section below a black and white picture of a beautiful woman and her beau, standing behind her with his arms wrapped around her. "This is Gisèle Janvier. Her father is the most recognized businessman in all of the kingdoms. He's able to obtain the most expensive jewels and fabrics from overseas, and he's made his family famous in the world of trade. And in two weeks' time, Gisèle will marry the dashing Lionel Perrault, the most esteemed designer of all time. The joining of these two families will be envied by all--"

"Are you thinking we could somehow perform at the engagement?" Mr. Monte interrupted me.

I nodded my head and continued, "The Janvier family is extremely welcoming and jovial. I'm sure they would love to be given a performance in their honor. I could write to them to ask."

"Yes, yes," Mr. Monte answered hurriedly.

At first, I was wary of helping Mr. Monte. I didn't want my new friends to know that I was still in contact with the people back home. I wanted to show them I was completely devoted to this new life. But seeing Mr. Monte's love and enthusiasm for the circus made me want to do anything I could to help.

Mr. Monte pulled out a pot of ink and a quill. "I'll help you formulate the letter."

We spent the next hour devising the perfect letter to send to the Janvier family—an impeccably formal one. I was afraid they might look down on the circus as my mother did, but perhaps we could change our style for this one performance in order to please this esteemed couple.

In the middle of our conversation, a man entered the room without knocking. "Oh, forgive me. I presumed you were alone."

I recognized him immediately. He was the man talking to Mr. Monte before, the one who called him Edward, which I still had not been able to figure out. What was this man's name? Merlin? Moore?

"Monroe! My friend, take a seat!" Mr. Monte exclaimed.

Monroe. Twice now I had seen this man, but I didn't know a thing about him.

Feeling remiss, Mr. Monte cleared his throat and said, "Monroe, this is Juniper Rose, our tightrope walker. Juniper, this is Monroe Béringer!"

At this, Monroe's clean-shaven face twisted oddly, and his head tilted slightly to the right, as if he was considering something.

I shifted my weight between my feet nervously, before stepping forward and offering my hand. "It's nice to meet you."

He didn't even blink, but tipped his head forward and kissed the top of my hand. His lips lingered far too long, but finally he said, "I have heard many great things about you. I hope to witness your work soon."

Monroe's eyes were a dull grey with a dark black ring around the iris. His face was clean, and his hair was medium brown and curled around his ears. He was a rather tall man and surprisingly strong for his age. I would have guessed he was fifty years old. There were no tattoos or rings piercing his body either. He looked...normal. Nothing like the performers I was surrounded by every day.

"Monroe is our financier. He distributes pay to the performers, ensures we have enough money to rent our arenas, and makes sure everything goes according to plan." Mr. Monte wrapped his arm around Monroe's shoulder, and I could tell they were very close.

I was unnerved that Monroe's eyes still had not left me. "I'm sure the circus wouldn't survive without you. Gentlemen." I tipped my head and exited the room as quickly as I could to avoid any more awkwardness.

The way Monroe looked at me...he seemed suspicious. Had he heard rumors about my background? The last thing I needed was another person making me feel like an outcast. I needed to see Flint. I needed him to remind me that I belonged.

I walked briskly down the cramped hall and brushed past Charlotte without a word. The men's and women's quarters were combined, but each performer's name was written on a small plaque hanging on their door.

Esmeralda. Billow. Chad. Josephine. Flint. *Flint.*

I sighed in relief, but when I reached Flint's room, I noticed a figure emerging a few doors down. Cassius's hair was ruffled and he looked younger, standing before me with his wrinkled shirt untucked from his breeches. His eyes were glazed over, his lips swollen, and his cheeks were bright with color. Annoyed, he brushed by me and asked, "Attempting to sleep your way around the circus to get us to like you?"

My jaw quivered and my fist shook at my side. I hated him. I hated him. I hated him. I had gone crazy trying to determine whether Cassius would ever accept me. He was kind last night at our performance, and now he was being cruel again. And I would be lying if I said it didn't hurt.

"Trust me, nothing will change their minds, not even an expensive flower," he continued.

I rushed at him and pushed him against the wall. His eyes were wide in surprise, but his frown turned into a slick smile, and that stupid dimple formed on his right cheek. His smug attitude made me sick.

"I didn't think you had it in you." Cassius lifted one eyebrow.

Our faces were inches apart, and for a second I imagined what it would be like if he just accepted me like the others. I wouldn't have to try so hard if it weren't for him. I wouldn't have to kill myself every day, attempting to impress him. I might even be able to enjoy my progress for once. My nose was stinging and my jaw trembled. I was tired of being treated this way, but I refused to cry in front of Cassius.

Hearing the ruckus, Flint barged from his room to see me inches away from Cassius, my cheeks red and my eyes swollen. Flint grabbed my waist and I struggled against him until he spoke softly in my ear.

His voice was so soothing. "Juniper?" He phrased it almost like a question.

I turned around then and saw that his eyes were full of concern, and I sank into his chest, not caring who was watching.

Flint shuffled backward, not daring to let go of me, and glared at Cassius dangerously. Cassius straightened himself and glared back at Flint, and after what felt like ten minutes, the door finally closed.

I buried my head in Flint's chest and cried, and my whole body shook when I finally let myself breathe out.

For a moment Flint stood as still as a statue. He didn't move or speak for fear of disrupting me, but when I looked up at him with swollen eyes, he grabbed my head in his large hands and held me tight. His body was firm against mine and I grabbed at his shirt, wrinkling it in between my fingers.

"Tell me I'm enough," I whispered in a hoarse voice. My lungs were so dry, it hurt to speak.

He pulled away to look at me, and his thick brows were furrowed in confusion.

"Please," I begged. "Tell me I belong."

"You belong," he said quickly to reassure me. Seeing the worry still on my face, he repeated these words over and over again. "You belong. You belong."

I closed my eyes and listened to his voice and then wiped my face and tried to forget about the embarrassment I'd just felt. I didn't want to think about Cassius's rudeness anymore. I also didn't want to think about the weird look on Monroe's face when Mr. Monte told him I was the tightrope walker. So instead of thinking, I ran my hand down Flint's warm chest.

Looking up at him longingly, I saw that his eyes were lingering on my lips. Was he thinking what I was thinking? Did he want to kiss me as badly as I wanted to kiss him? I didn't want to rush this, but I couldn't help but crash my lips against his. The warm, sweet texture of his mouth made my stomach flip, and I grabbed his shoulders and pulled him closer to me.

He grabbed my cheeks and pulled my face away to look me in the eyes, and I saw that he understood. "You are more than enough," Flint whispered.

Neither of us spoke. The barrier between us was gone, and we both realized we felt something worth pursuing. I wanted to be with Flint. Through all the stress with Cassius and my worry about the world's approval, he was my rock—my steady place.

He linked his arms around my back, and we swayed from side to side.

"We're going to perform twice in Hewe," I blurted out. I had to tell someone. I couldn't let this information be only mine.

"What?" He asked, startled.

I nodded my head to confirm. "I'm helping Mr. Monte organize and publicize more shows. With my connections, we're hoping to draw in more of the wealthy parts of the kingdoms so we can increase our revenue." I hoped Flint would understand. I hoped he wouldn't think of me as a traitor, because that would do me in for good.

"Anyone would come see us if the richest landowners supported us. That's actually quite smart," he said, to my surprise.

"You aren't upset with me?" I asked.

His biceps clenched as he kept hold of me. "Why would I be? You're only trying to help."

I couldn't help but smile. This boy would never cease to amaze me.

The small candle burning on his nightstand was almost completely gone, but the last of the dying flame flickered in his blue eyes. I pushed him and we fell back onto his bed, and I rested my head on his strong chest and said, "Show me another equation."

Chapter 14

The city of Hewe was magnificent. It was like nothing I'd ever seen before. Mr. Monte took us on a tour, and the streets were so crowded, there was barely enough room for all of us to walk. My hand was interlocked with Flint's, and Charlotte was on my right, pointing out a chapel in the distance. Down from there a little further, there was a family of ducks at play in a lake with water as clear as crystal. And there was a shiny black fence surrounding the perimeter of the lake. The sun beat down on a clock tower that climbed high into the sky, making the little hand glimmer. *Bong, bong.* It rang loudest and longest when the big hand struck noon.

The group walked along the harbor where boats the sizes of buildings were docked. Men bustled back and forth on the deck, scrubbing the salt off the wooden planks. Merchants unloaded crates of supplies and put them in large piles on the loading dock. Further inland, women in dresses of assorted pastels walked around near tall brick buildings.

"Prostitutes," Charlotte said in a hushed voice while tracking my line of sight.

I had seen a few in Axminster. What a regretful way to spend your life, pleasing others without getting any pleasure in return. A man behind a wooden stand sold newspapers displaying a front-page article about our two performances in Hewe. I purchased one, finding my name among the list of performers. I thought it would be nice to hang in my room.

That evening, when the circus met in the dining area. Mr. Monte stood before the seated audience and exclaimed, "We are in the entertainment capital, which means we have to give a jaw-dropping performance. Monroe, Valetta, and I have created a show unlike any of our others—a show filled with lights, gems, and skin. A lot of skin," Mr. Monte said, and he looked at me.

And I gulped.

"It needs to represent wealth and fame. Facial expressions: confident! Poses: statuesque!"

All of the girls giggled while the men shifted awkwardly from foot to foot, possibly picturing the women in their revealing outfits.

"Every group leader has been given a checklist of tricks that need to be perfected for this performance. Get to it! You're dismissed."

The members dispersed into their individual groups and assembled an extensive list of moves and techniques. Unfortunately, I had no group to assign myself to. It was just me.

I sat down in front of Monroe, Valetta, and Mr. Monte, feeling as though I was being interrogated. "Usually, we would create something more universal, but I personally want Gisèle and Lionel to see you as our leading lady. I want them to know that the wealthy have joined our ranks. And beyond all, I want them to be mesmerized. When they see our performance, I want them to feel as though they've discovered magic for the first time."

The wealthy have joined our ranks...

Was that all they saw in me? The wealthy? I was human. I was alive. I was just like them.

Valetta leaned in close and the thick frame of her glasses slid down her slim nose. "I've designed an intricate ensemble for you. Does this look okay?"

"I don't think I have any real opinion here," I said, without even glancing at the charcoal sketch in her hands. "If it shows just how *wealthy* I am, then so be it."

Days passed and before I knew it, our performance was upon us. Black metal gates surrounded the entirety of the estate. We walked up a grand stone staircase toward a cathedral-like manor sitting at the top of a hill in the heart of Hewe. The Janvier home was known as the Broken Arrow Estate. It was divine, and perhaps too big that any two humans should live in it alone. Ivy crawled up the limestone walls, manicured hedges depicted men and women throughout history, and the staircase was adorned with small lights to illuminate the path to the entrance. As we approached the large double doors, Mr. Monte showed a guard dressed in a crimson red suit the invitation to Broken Arrow Estate. And without hesitation, the guard twisted the golden doorknob and allowed us into the home.

Once inside the mansion, Gisèle Janvier greeted us in the vast entryway from which you could see the rest of the home. The glassy marble tile made our shoes clack when we took each step, creating quite an echo to announce our arrival. Gisèle's hair was bright blond and tied up in tight ringlets, and her smile was lovely and bright. Her dress was huge and her waist, miniscule. She looked beautiful. Expensive. Fragile.

"Welcome, Circus! Thank you for so kindly coming to our home. We would love to serve you dinner before your performance. While it is being prepared, feel free to make yourself comfortable."

She welcomed us in and introduced us to the entourage of servants lining the long hallway. Dressed in black linens which did nothing for their frames, they reminded me of my servant, Kathryn, in Axminster. I hoped they all were being treated respectfully. I noticed the other performers scanning the expensive artifacts around the room, and Olive seemed troubled that there were so many servants. She must have thought it extremely unnatural to have so many servants in one home, but to me it was customary. Most wealthy families had at least one servant, and the number increased according to the size of your home. Suddenly I felt guilty.

I entered Broken Arrow Estate alongside Mr. Monte. The other performers were still stuck on the delicate oil paintings and glass vases littering the room. Apprehensive of entering such an expensive home, their steps were careful and their voices low—nothing like their normal raucous nature. There was such a stark difference in our attires. On one side of the room was Gisèle and her husband in the most expensive fabrics, and on the other was the circus, dressed in dirty poet's shirts and breeches. And I knew the others saw it as well. By the hesitation in their steps, I knew they felt out of place. How could they not? We'd come to the most expensive estate in the world to showcase our odd talents. We were not here to join them for tea or sit down for small talk. We were here to entertain them, and nothing less.

I felt as though this encounter might permanently change my friends. By bringing them here, I had put them into a situation they'd never known, or rather a situation that reminded them of what they'd never have. It must have been disappointing to them, and I hated myself for it. I wished for this to be over as soon as possible.

Gisèle joined her beau and led us into a room filled with floral sofas and settees. There were small tables lined in gold, with saucers and teacups enough for all of us, it seemed.

"I'm sure your journey has been long. Please drink to your enjoyment." Lionel Perrault spoke kindly, with his arm wrapped around his soon-to-be wife. He looked down at her lovingly, and my cheeks bloomed for the beautiful woman.

Just then, a coldness swept through the room and made my skin tickle.

"You did the right thing," Flint's confident voice sounded abruptly from behind me. His chest pressed against my back, and when he trailed his warm hand down my arm, I leaned into him.

I wished we could be alone. I wished I could tell him all that was on my mind at that moment. But he already seemed to know, and just his presence was reassuring to me. Sadly, when I turned to face him, he had stepped away to talk to Mr. Monte.

And in his place, was Cassius, holding a metal flask to his tea cup and pouring in a brown liquid. Every few minutes, he'd add more to the cup, and over time, I saw Cassius's eyes grow baggy and red. *Please, don't make this harder than it has to be*, I wanted to tell him.

As dinner was announced, Mr. Monte grabbed Cassius's arm roughly, bringing their faces close together.

I passed by them hurriedly and tried to catch their conversation without appearing nosy.

"If you don't stop, you won't be performing tonight. Understood?"

Cassius scoffed and took a guzzle from the flask, completely discarding his teacup. "You need me."

"That is where you're wrong." Mr. Monte walked away, leaving a stooped Cassius alone in the hallway.

I couldn't discern his expression. Betrayal? Pain? Possibly both. But when Cassius caught me staring, he rushed past me into the dining room, bumping my shoulder in his endeavor. I stumbled and the green tea I was holding spilled onto my tan dress. I was last to enter the dining room, and I sat quickly to cover the stain with a white napkin and tried to avoid Cassius's eyes. I'd talk to him later, but I couldn't let his rudeness ruin the night.

The feast was extravagant—honey drizzled lamb chops, steamed broccoli, roasted spinach and barley potatoes, chocolate dipped strawberries, green and orange melon, kale salad with pine nuts and vinegar, chicken coated in lemon cardamom sauce, roasted sausage, garlic butter bread, and crystal glasses filled with grape wine.

The array of performers with tattoos and piercings looked misplaced in such a fine setting. Not because they were abnormal, but because they were more free than anything so confining and pristine. The performers talked with one another, filling their stomachs to their hearts' content. The food on the train wasn't as divine as these delicacies, so this was a rare treat. Flint and Charlotte conversed with the rich couple extremely well, whereas Cassius didn't utter a single word and barely picked at the food on his plate.

When dinner concluded, I became more anxious for my performance, but I was greeted by Gisèle herself, which took my mind off my anxiety.

"It's nice to see you again." She smiled and hugged me tightly.

I squeezed her back and said, "It's been so long. You don't know how much this means to me. Thank you for allowing us to perform for you." Gisèle and I were childhood friends, but I hadn't seen her for years. My family would take trips to Hewe to see the Janvier family, but we stopped when her father became more involved with his business.

"I'd do anything for your family, Juniper. You must know that. I didn't know you were interested in drama and entertainment. I must say, when I opened your letter I was very surprised," she said as she laughed a little.

"I didn't know either." I pushed away the comment. "But it's the best thing that's ever happened to me."

"And your mother, I'm sure."

I laughed heartily. I hadn't given a thought to what my mother must think of me joining the circus. She was probably fuming.

"Performers, it's time we get ourselves ready," Mr. Monte exclaimed.

"I shall gather the crowd," Miss Janvier announced with a wink.

I followed the crowd out of the estate, around the property, and into the couple's large backyard where a tent had been positioned. Ready to begin, I untangled the tan dress I wore, revealing a lavish translucent costume underneath. The ensemble was completely see-through, but a slim trail of diamonds curved down around my hips and up around my décolletage. Pearls hung in long strands down my chest, a plume of white dove feathers was braided into my hair, and three-inch silver heels made me feel ten feet tall.

I lined up beside the dancers, who wore matching dresses made of shimmering grey fabric, with slits up their thighs. The crowd buzzed but the lights remained off until Mr. Monte dropped his hand, signaling for them to be turned on. At the request of the Janvier family, the circus had a special guest performer tonight. She was a small woman who was illuminated by a spotlight, gripping a thin pole with a microphone in her hand. Her short hair curled against her head and her eyes were dusted with glitter. She wore a silver dress that hugged her hips and touched the floor, and she began to sing a lovely melody to the crowd with a band of saxophones, guitars, and piccolos at her side.

"Strangers ride quickly through the moonlight..." Her voice was airy, filled with a resounding rasp. And between verses, she scatted a light rhythm and bopped her hip with the band.

The dancers lined up perfectly behind her, so when Charlotte waved her arm behind the singer's body, it looked as though she had a third arm. Charlotte flicked her wrist and her bracelet caught the light, and then she grasped the pearls hanging on the singer's forehead and shifted them slightly. The crowd giggled when the same hands trailed down to the singer's slim waist, making the woman gasp girlishly and bring a gloved hand to her mouth.

"If only to fall asleep..." the vibrato in her voice wavered beautifully.

Charlotte's hand covered the singer's mouth, causing her to fall to the floor in a dreamy sleep, and the crowd gasped when Charlotte's figure was revealed.

The band continued a smooth jazz rhythm as Charlotte beckoned her dancers forward. Just then, I stepped onto the platform, twenty feet above ground. A steel ring floated back and forth slightly, hanging from the ceiling, and as the drummer hit his bass drum, I leapt onto the ring, pulled myself into the hoop, and moved my bottom to one side and my shoulders to the other. I extended my feet away from the hoop and balanced one of my knees on the steel, arching my back so far toward the ceiling that my neck ached. The contraption slowly moved toward the floor, and the audience cheered when they saw my curved body in the ring. A foot away from the ground, I unwound myself and stepped onto the sand, then touched my fingertip to the singer's forehead causing her awaken magically.

She stood in confusion and began to sing again in a trance. "A wounded man follows his lover…"

I leapt toward the band where one of the performers—a flamethrower by the name of Cole—was disguised as a musician. I threw my leg onto his shoulder while he feigned surprise, even though his cheeks turned true red, and then I whipped my head back and fell off him into a back walkover. Turning to the crowd, I pushed my breasts together and shimmied my chest, causing them to laugh wildly. Wanting more from them, I kicked the dust once, then twice, and turned my bum toward them before lifting up my skirt. Just then, a musician chimed a triangle, and a high-pitched bell rang throughout the tent. This was my cue to raise my gloved hands to the sky, trail them down my body, and climb the platform quickly to step out onto the tightrope. I quickly flipped, landing on the bridges of my feet, then pirouetted once, twice, and thrice, causing the curls on my head to come loose from their pins. With my arms still high in the air, the woman stopped singing, and the room was left in silence.

Soon the crowd caught their breath and erupted in cheers.

I could almost guarantee that the wealthy would have an entirely different opinion of the circus after this.

After a successful performance, the couple welcomed us back into their estate for late-night drinks. Lucky for Cassius, there was plenty of alcohol to maintain his stupor. He held himself together well enough during his performance, but he was wobbly and careless, not his usual serious and precise self.

Gisèle and her partner congratulated me, and their praise made me bloom. Having a close friend approve of my talent with the circus made my doubts disappear. I was surrounded by good people, in the wealthiest kingdom known to man, sipping champagne from expensive china. And the circus seemed to finally be embraced by the elite. I was on top of the world.

I was deep in conversation with Lionel Perrault, when there was a large crash behind me, and I turned quickly to see Cassius stumble and fall. The alcohol in Hewe was rich and far more effective than the cheap ale we were accustomed to. Several porcelain plates were shattered to pieces at his feet, and I felt it my responsibility to apologize and clean up the mess since I'd brought us all there.

"I'm so sorry." I apologized to Lionel, and then rushed to be with Mr. Monte and the incoherent boy in the corner. His lips were glossy and he looked dangerous, yet breakable at the same time.

Mr. Monte grabbed him by his collar to shake some sense into him. The last thing we needed was for Cassius to get angry and continue his downward spiral. Our hosts needed to see us as a unified family, not divided and fighting.

I grabbed Mr. Monte's shoulder and said, "You address the mess. Apologize. Tell them it was a simple misunderstanding." I looked around the room warily at the appalled guests and added, "Thank them repeatedly and continue to have fun. I'll take care of this."

Mr. Monte's angry eyes darted between mine, but realizing my ability to repair the relationship, his expression changed. "I'm so sorry for the mess. It was a simple miscalculation. We vagabonds are not used to such fine wine." He laughed heartily as the servants rushed to clean up the mess.

I grabbed Cassius's arm and helped him to the door. His feet were heavy and it seemed to take forever to get him into an empty room, hidden from attention, as his boots dragged across the shiny tile floor. We reached a small sitting room, and I attempted to push him onto a couch to lay down, but he forced himself to remain upright.

"What is wrong with you?" I screamed in a hushed tone, although there was no one around to hear.

"Don't lecture me." Cassius pointed an accusing finger at me, as if I was the one to blame. "We came here to be part of the wealthy life, correct? That's exactly what I was doing. Taking it all in." He raised his long arms from his sides to preach to an invisible audience.

"That's not what this was about. This was about forming a connection with landowners that could help us promote our show. We were here to build a relationship with these people...not destroy their property!" I yelled.

"*Your people*," Cassius corrected me.

My nostrils flared as Cassius absent-mindedly reached into his black jacket and pulled out a flask and brought it to his mouth.

"You've had enough." I snatched the flask from him, splashing the brown liquid on his jacket in my haste.

His eyes turned dark and a flash of fear coursed through my body. I'd never been afraid of him before, but now that he was intoxicated and beyond reason, I wondered what he would do to me. Would he dare touch me?

He clenched his jaw and watched me for an uncomfortable amount of time. His silence frightened me as he thought carefully before asking me, "You did this, didn't you? You organized this meeting with Gisèle Janvier." He spoke her name harshly, stepping closer to me.

I shook my head in an attempt to avoid the question. He'd hate me more than before if he really knew the truth, so I looked to the floor to avoid his penetrating eyes.

"Answer the question." He wasn't too far away from me now.

I couldn't force myself to speak. My throat was dry and his closeness was suffocating.

"Your mother taught you that much, didn't she? To answer when you're spoken to? It's only manners. Answer the question Juniper. Did you organize this? Do you know the Janvier family?" He continued to raise his voice.

The room shrunk around me. I couldn't breathe. Every piece of furniture, sewn with lavish fabric and golden thread, closed in on me, and the dark oak walls had sharp teeth that wanted to take a bite out of me. I needed air.

Cassius took one more step before grabbing me and pushing me up against the wall. I gasped as his thumb and pointer finger neared my jugular, but his hand was so warm, and I believed that, even drunk, he wouldn't hurt me.

My flesh burned under his touch and my head throbbed. I grabbed at his hands and whispered, "Yes." I wondered why he was so angry. What had happened to him that made my allegiance with the wealthy such a threat to him?

His chest pumped and his eyes darted between mine, with disappointment and anger written on his face. Finally, he let go and my body dropped to the floor.

I rubbed the skin on my neck while tears streamed down my face. I wanted to yell at him and tell him not to ever speak to me again, but I couldn't form the words.

He stormed off, his black boots thudding on the shiny floor.

The sound echoed in my mind even after he slammed the door behind him.

Chapter 15

Today's local headline was bound to get the attention of the people in town, and it was sure to be received with mixed emotions.

Circus performs at Broken Arrow Estate for newly engaged Gisèle Janvier and Lionel Perrault
Our very own Juniper Rose astounds on the tightrope!

Colette…

My mother often sat across the table reading the local newspaper, officially known as The Axminster Publication. From the courtship of Duke Heming to Lady Petrova, to the fluctuation of the market on the bay, it was all the same to her. She enjoyed immersing herself in the economy and the society around her. It was admirable at times to see that she was so devoted to Axminster and our faith, but sometimes I wondered if it consumed her. I wondered if she had immersed herself in society so much that she looked in the mirror at the woman she would like to be instead of the one God created her to be.

But today was different from all the others. As soon as I returned from the chapel, she exploded, "Have you seen what's in the paper today?" She stomped her foot and shrieked, "I can't believe this! I can't believe she would embarrass me like this! Everyone in the entire city knows that my daughter has betrayed me!"

My mother's cheeks were red and her eyes were bloodshot. There were no tears and no real grief at the loss of my sister, just anger. She turned over the newspaper so I could read it, and sketched in bold ink was a picture of Juniper, front and center. Her cheeks were drawn back in a full smile, and she looked radiant and never happier. Also included in the article was a schedule for the circus's future performances.

My mother smiled and ran a hand down the thin sheet of paper, as if Juniper were standing there in front of her and she could feel her soft skin. "I know where she is."

I shook my head, unsure how to calm my mother down. This was truly a mess, and I didn't know if I could protect Juniper any longer.

"We are going to put an end to this family embarrassment once and for all," my mother sneered.

I was restless the whole night and awakened at random when I felt a hot fire spreading through my throat. I never expected Cassius to touch me so angrily. I still couldn't discern how to gain his trust. He was so enveloped in his past that he truly couldn't see the opportunity of expanding the circus's fame by forming this friendship with the wealthy. I had risked everything—security, a family, and a future—to be here. I had everything planned out for me in Axminster, and although I might have next to nothing now, I hadn't felt this fulfilled in years. Cassius was just a loose cannon. That was all I knew. He was prone to cracking at any moment, taking out everyone within a mile radius. The only option I had was to stay away from him.

In the days that followed, I managed to distance myself from him, but it was impossible to keep him out of my head. Tonight, when the sun had fallen and I had gone to bed, I felt my eyes darting back and forth. The crowd was cheering and throwing roses at my feet, and a little boy in the crowd reached for me and then smiled as I took his tiny hand in appreciation. But his grip hardened to the point where he pinched my skin, and when I looked down at his hand, I saw that it had shifted. His veins pulsed, his knuckles became larger, and his fingers extended toward my wrist. My chest pounded as I realized that the boy's face had morphed into Cassius's. His hand flew to my neck and his fingers pushed so deep into my skin that they created dark purple bruises. In my dream, I leaned into his touch and sank into his chest, and the dull ache of his heartbeat pounded in my head. He smiled at me, as if he had done nothing wrong, and I smiled back.

Suddenly I lurched forward in bed, clawing at my neck and gasping for air.

Flint had taken to staying late with me most nights. Noticing my ragged breaths, he hastily lit a candle and pushed the hair out of my face. "Are you okay?"

I nodded, trying to shake the image from my head. "Just a bad dream." He folded me in his arms, and I exhaled. I was not afraid of seeing Cassius's dark eyes or feeling his strong grip. I was afraid that I liked it. I anticipated the feel of his warm skin on my own. That's what scared me the most.

We had approximately one week before our next performance in Hewe, and Mr. Monte suggested I try something new, called Corde-lisse, which is an acrobatic performance on a vertically hanging rope. It requires a great deal of upper body strength, which is something I do not have.

Mr. Monte stepped into my tent with Monroe at his tail. "A fine morning it is, my rose. Monroe here has a friend who specializes in Corde-lisse, and he knows many of the techniques after studying her performances over the years."

Monroe never took his eyes off me, and after studying my body for an inappropriate length of time, he finally grabbed the fabric before him. "We will have to work on your upper body strength, but much of the work can be done with the strength in your legs and feet. This will always be referred to as silk," he explained as he ran his hands down the fabric. He seemed oddly knowledgeable about the subject—more than a person with a friend specializing in the skill would be.

For some reason, I made a mental note of that.

"Reach above your head with both arms, grab each silk, and jump."

Easy enough. Two heavy pieces of lavender silk hung down from the rafters of the tent, with plenty of extra length puddled in the sand. I grabbed the two pieces and jumped, but my arms quivered and my shoulders ached from trying to hold myself up, and I dropped down to the ground.

"Good. It's always tough to remain in one position for too long. That's why you want to always be moving." He smiled at me with slightly crooked teeth. "This time when you pull yourself up, bend your knees into your chest and just let your body fall backwards."

I jumped again and tucked my knees into my chest, and when I leaned back, the rope twisted easier than I thought it would.

"Very nice. In order to perform spins like an expert, you must get higher and twist the silk more. When you fall backwards, extend your legs into the air, twist to the left, and hook the crook of your knees into the fabric. This will create an invisible chair for you to sit in."

I did as I was told. I extended my toes to the sky, but my arms shook so violently, I feared I would fall on my head. I swung my body around both silks and pulled my knees over my head, and after I flipped over myself completely, the silk became tight across my waist and my bum sat nicely in the hold. I dangled in the air and asked, "What do I do now?"

Monroe stood below me and placed his hand on my calf. His skin was clammy and slightly moist. "Now that you're steady, just repeat the same process."

I held tight to the silk to ensure I remained in the same place before I unhooked my legs, and after repeating the same process, I was higher in the air than I had been before.

"Perfect. Now you are going to keep the silk close to your chest after you come out of the hold."

Just as I had been told, I unwound from the hold and pulled the two silks to my chest.

"Take your legs outside, then inside of the silk."

Outside. Inside. The rope twisted over my thighs.

"If you roll your feet and twist both of your ankles, the silk will attach across your ankle as well. And after you do so, bring your knees to your chest and the silk will untangle itself from your thighs, so the only thing holding you up is the hook across your feet."

I struggled thinking about the mechanics of it all. I tried to think about how Flint would do this and how the exact angles would pop into his head. The thought made me smile, and I maneuvered my ankles so I could stand tall. As the loop across my foot proved to hold me up, I decided this was far easier than walking on a tightrope. Once I was in this hold, I had no possibility of falling, whereas on the tightrope, I could lean too far one way or the other and fall off the side. Feeling accomplished, I swung back and forth happily in the silk with my legs spread wide.

When I returned to the ground, Mr. Monte's hands were folded behind his back—a position I had come to know as approval. "Very good job. Your body looked extremely limber."

"I've never seen anyone complete training for silk acrobatics so quickly," Monroe exclaimed approvingly. "I am impressed beyond measure."

"Thank you." I tipped my head at both of them, and they left to practice with the others. I spent hours repeating the sequence over and over—pull, tuck, roll, lift, pull, tuck, roll, lift. Once I was high enough, I hooked my feet around the silk and remained there as long as I could. My hands were raw by the time I was finished, but I felt stronger already.

It wasn't quite time for dinner, but I couldn't pull my body weight up on the silk anymore, so I waited in the dining room instead.

"Ale, Miss?" Wilman offered, standing behind the bar wiping the crystal glasses with a dirty white towel. A simple brown vest covered his chest, and his white sleeves were rolled up to his elbows.

"Water will be just fine." It wouldn't burn my throat or make my stomach bubble.

Wilman poured a glass of water to the brim but then stared at me with an arch in his brow. I studied the glass of water before sliding it down the bar and asking, "Who am I kidding?"

Wilman snickered and filled a mug of ale for me. "How ya gettin' along, Miss Rose?"

"Just fine, Wilman. Just fine."

"Just fine is somethin' never heard in da circus. Aren't you supposed to be havin' da time of ya life?"

"I am." I smiled to cover my fatigue. "I'm in love."

"Oh?" Wilman set down the glass he'd just cleaned and put his elbows on the counter to lean toward me. He waited expectantly for the details while curling the end of his mustache.

"In love with this circus," I clarified, laughing. "It's more than I ever expected. I always thought this was a place for dirty vagabonds who had no aspirations or motivation to get a real job."

Wilman's eyes sank, as if he was personally offended.

I tried to repair what I had just said. "My *mother* taught me to believe that. The whole country did. But now that I've witnessed it for myself, I realize the circus is a place for those who might feel they don't belong out there in the world." I caught the dying sun in the distance of an open train car. Its rays were golden yellow and orange, melting into the waving fields of wheat beyond. "The circus is a place for people who have an abundance of talent and imagination, and to watch them pour that into something special for others is really admirable to a person like me."

"A person like you?" Wilman rarely answered me with an opinion. He frequently asked questions, making me think more often than I'd like.

"Someone who's wealthy." I rolled my eyes. An image of Cassius exploded in my head. *Your people,* he would say.

"Now Rosey, that ain't nothin' you have to worry about. Here, everyone's welcome. I would be lyin' if I said we weren't all surprised to see someone of your status join our ranks, but you're not any less welcome 'cause of it. Look at all you've done."

Wilman didn't know me. He didn't understand the life I'd come from and how spoiled I was, but he didn't hesitate to welcome me. "Thank you, Wilman."

He nodded and cleared some invisible crumbs off the bar.

I grabbed an early dinner, eager to get to sleep. I was exhausted and ready to rest before tomorrow. When I got to my room, I took off my shoes and undressed, and then sat in front of my vanity and tied my hair away from my face.

I sang quietly to myself, "Take a chance, beat your fate, kick the dust."

I dressed in a simple nightgown and removed the covers from my bed and slipped inside. I hadn't seen Flint tonight, which made me a little sad. I felt so comfortable in his arms, but I needed to focus more on my upcoming performance than my own fleeting desires. As I prepared to blow out the candle on my bedside table, a small *woosh* echoed in the room, and an envelope with my name scrawled beautifully on the cover slid under my door. I stood warily to retrieve the letter and wondered who could be writing to me at this hour. And why? Why not knock on my door and tell me personally? Unless this letter didn't come from inside the circus...maybe it was my family. Once in a while mail came to the circus, but I didn't expect my mother to write to me. If she really knew where I was, she wouldn't try to contact me.

I slid my finger under the fold on the back of the envelope and tore it open. Pulling out the thin sheet of paper, my eyes raced over the messy penmanship. There were only four words scrawled on the parchment, and since we had been confined to the train to practice before our next performance in Hewe, this message most certainly came from inside the circus.

RUN WHILE YOU CAN.

Chapter 16

Run while you can?
My breathing was ragged and my hands shook, and I felt like I might throw up. What the hell was this?! Who would send this?

I ripped open my door, searching up and down the hall, but by now, whoever sent this was long gone. Why would someone threaten me after all I'd done to help the circus? It didn't make any sense.

Suddenly my mind turned to one person. Cassius. He was the only one who despised me enough to scare me half to death so I would leave. I raced down the hall toward his room at the end of the train, my hands shaking and my jaw trembling. When I spotted his small name plate, I ripped open the door.

Cassius was sprawled out in his bed. His chest was bare and one leg was strewn out of the sheets, with his arms resting behind his head as he looked up at the ceiling. He seemed startled at first, but then he sat up on his elbows and waited with amusement in his eyes.

"Why would you do this?" I yelled with tears streaming down my face. "Was it because I sent a letter to the Janvier family? Was it because I come from the wealthy side of Axminster?" In that moment, I could feel the suffocatingly warm texture of his hand on my throat again. Was he really intent on going to such lengths to threaten me?

"What on earth are you rambling on about?" He laid back down and threw his head against the pillow dramatically.

I shoved the paper in his face.

He looked at me like I was a lunatic, but when he took a second glance at the letter, his face shifted to seriousness. He hesitated and then whispered, "I didn't write this."

"Like hell you didn't," I huffed, although something told me he was telling the truth.

He looked almost as worried as I did. Almost. But if he didn't write it, then who did?

Run while you can.

My lungs throbbed, my nose stung, and tears welled in my eyes. My heart felt so heavy, and all I wanted to do was sink to the floor. But I couldn't. Not here. I ripped Cassius's door open and ran down the hallway as fast as I could. The person who wrote this was here somewhere, and I was afraid of what they might do next.

"Flint!" I screamed, banging on his door. I didn't hear anything on the other side. Only silence and emptiness. Most of the crew was still in the dining room, drinking themselves silly, which was probably where he was. But I couldn't go there in this state.

I sobbed into my hands. I needed him. I needed his warmth and I needed his help.

In the days that followed, I practiced ten hours a day, only taking a break for lunch and dinner. I avoided Cassius out of embarrassment, and when Flint knocked on my door, I ignored him too. I didn't know what to say. I felt like I was a burden to him. All I did was complain about my past and how the performers would never accept me, and now there was something else he had to hear about. I just couldn't bring myself to tell him. I belonged here. I knew that much. And I didn't need to worry him over a silly prank. That's all it was. A silly prank.

But of course, Flint knew where to find me, and he promptly barged into my tent and demanded, "Why won't you talk to me?"

I shook my head. "I need to practice. The show is tonight."

"Is something wrong? I know you're busy but you've barely spoken a word to me since I don't know when."

"I promise I'm okay." I pulled him close. "Just stressed is all. I'll see you after the show, yeah?"

He looked at the ground and pursed his lips, but nodded in agreement. I think he knew something was wrong, but he decided not to push me further.

I grabbed his jaw and pecked him on the lips. I just had to get this stupid letter out of my head, perform tonight and impress the crowd, and then everything could go back to normal.

When the sun fell, the circus headed to the rim of the city, where a large tent had been erected. I was happy to be performing on the silk today. It felt steadier than the tightrope.

Once everyone was settled, I walked to the center of the tent where the two sheets of silk hung. I took both fabrics into my hands and tucked my knees into my chest, and when the lights turned on, I extended my toes toward the ceiling, slowly and gracefully, just like Mr. Monte had taught me. The crowd watched intently as I pulled myself higher and higher. I twisted my legs inside and then outside of the silk, and the fabric tightened around my thighs. Then I rolled my ankles and the silks wrapped around the bridges of my feet so I could stand with stability. I slowly moved my feet away from one another and lowered myself into a split. Finally, I grabbed the silks above my head and pulled my legs back together. The air was mostly quiet, but in the faint cheering down below, I heard a strange sound.

I twisted my right leg over my left, and the silk wrapped around my thigh, helping me climb higher and higher. *Shlink.* There it was again. As I neared the top of the tent where the silk was attached, I looked carefully at the silk to find there was a small tear growing across the fabric. Terror coursed through me. If I backed out now, the crowd would be extremely disappointed. I had to finish this performance, so I tried to maintain a smile while I unhooked one of my legs completely from the bundle of silk and let my torso fall toward the ground. The crowd applauded as my body hung upside down, with only one leg holding me.

Shlink.

I clenched my jaw. Suddenly the silk jerked and my body fell, but only a short distance. And I managed to hide my terror.

The crowd clapped, thinking it was a part of my performance, so I looked out toward the sea of people and smiled brightly, pointing my arm above my head. My eyes darted between men and women of varying heights and sizes—a woman with dark skin and blinding white teeth, a man with a humongous forehead glaring down at his disobedient daughter, and a woman wearing a tight corset and the purest white gloves. It reminded me of the day my mother glided down the staircase and trailed her soft velvet gloves along the polished banister, a week after my father left. It was the first time we had seen her since the day he left. She was dressed in her most magnificent ball gown, and her hair was curled tightly. It was the same woman I stared at now. My throat caught, but I couldn't take my eyes off of her. My mother, in all her splendor, was here. She was standing in a dilapidated tent, with dirty sand at her dainty feet, and she stared back at me with a disapproving glare in her eyes.

The crowd had gone silent because of my inactivity. Remembering that so many people were counting on me, I hooked my right knee around the silk and pointed my left leg straight out. And as I did so, the last of the silk tore, my legs untangled from the silk, and my body spun violently toward the ground. I thrashed, trying to get ahold of the silk where it was still attached. My fingers caught it but I fell too quickly and it slipped out of my grasp. All of the air was taken from my lungs. There was no landing pad to catch me and no net to stop my momentum. I closed my eyes when the sand was inches away, and in a matter of seconds, my body hit the ground. I screamed, feeling my shoulder shatter. I could feel the bones rub together, and the burn on my skin was unexplainable. The world spun around me, tears poured down my cheeks, and I couldn't move an inch. I sank my head into the sand, and all thoughts of my performance were gone.

The crowd stood in worry while performers rushed out from behind the tent.

Mr. Monte sprinted over to me, but his figure faded in and out of focus. He yelled something I couldn't comprehend, and I couldn't help feeling like I had ruined all of the progress we'd made. Because of one mistake, I might never be able to restore people's image of me.

Someone's arm scooped under my knees and as they did so, my shoulder twisted limply to the side, causing me to wince in pain. The individual muscles in my arm moved every time I breathed, making my pain unbearable. *Hold it together,* I told myself. *Just for a moment longer.* I searched for my mother in the crowd. As much as I feared her arrival and her intentions, all I wished was that she would tell me everything would be okay. The pulsing inside my arm was excruciating, and the volume in the room made my head throb. Finally, the pain subsided when my eyes closed.

When I woke, I was surrounded by the thin wooden walls of the train, cushioned by layers of blankets and a pillow resting too high beneath my head, making my neck ache. I attempted to sit up by leaning slightly on my elbow, but the pain exploded in my shoulder.

All I remember is the sound of my shoulder hitting the floor before I blacked out. How would I walk on the tightrope now? Mr. Monte would be so disappointed. I had failed the circus for good this time.

I remember something else—a woman wearing a perfectly coiffed dress with a placid expression, and those small gloves folded on her lap. No concern. No curiosity. Just emptiness. My mother...

A nurse entered the room to give me a sedative, which made me woozy as I watched the needle pierce the skin on the front of my elbow.

After a few hours of medication, rest, and small doses of food, I felt a little bit better. My back was sore from lying down all day, so I got up and tried to take a few steps. I peeled away my loose breeches to find a deep purple bruise blooming along my right hip. I was surprised I didn't break that as well.

I exited the medical tent to walk along the corridor. I thought Mr. Monte would be by my side when I woke up, but he was nowhere to be found. After searching for him, I discovered a group of people in my tent. The two pieces of silk had been brought here from the city, and they were discussing what might have gone wrong with them. Still in shock over what had happened, I wasn't sure I was ready to hear any of this.

Mr. Monte's arm was folded at his waist, and the other arm rested on that one so his fingers could play with his lip.

When the room went silent due to my presence, Mr. Monte turned to see where the attention had shifted. His eyes were rimmed in red and the skin under them was a deep purple. He was losing sleep, but a fix for that would have to come later. Right now, he stood beside Monroe and spoke in a hushed tone while a few of the flame throwers wrapped up the bundle of silk.

"My rose, come." Mr. Monte beckoned me to his side.

I walked as quickly as I could, attempting to hide my pain, although Mr. Monte saw right through me.

"How do you feel?"

"It's manageable if I don't move." I tried to laugh to lighten the mood in the room and to ease my own worry, but I couldn't move my arm. And I couldn't walk on the tightrope or use the rings if I couldn't move my arm. There's no way Mr. Monte would keep me. He'd most likely dispose of me by the end of the week, realizing that I had nothing to offer him.

"I'm bringing in the best of our doctors. We'll get you healed in no time. I don't want you to worry about the performances. I'm making some...accommodations. We'll make this work." He nodded to reassure himself. This was a surprise. Why would he keep me here if I couldn't perform on the tightrope? I'd be a lame duck. "As for the stability of our company…" he continued.

"What do you mean?" I questioned, shifting my weight to my left leg to relieve the pressure on the right side of my body.

"Someone is threatening to sue the circus." He turned to face the silk again. "Children come to watch our show. Seeing a woman break her arm can be rather traumatizing!" He groaned into his hands. "I'm sorry, I don't mean to blame you."

I shook my head, trying to think of something to say to ease his worry.

Monroe spoke first, touching a loving hand to his friend's shoulder. "We'll figure something out."

Mr. Monte turned his back and walked away while the flamethrowers lifted up the silk to clear the floor.

"Stop," I commanded. I wasn't able to take my eyes off the white fabric. They all looked to me as I studied the shredded silk, noticing something out of place. The fabric looked like it was cut at odd angles, which would cause it to tear the rest of the way. This was no accident.

"I looked carefully at the silks before they were brought to the site of the performance, and again when we arrived to perform. They couldn't have been torn by accident."

Mr. Monte and Monroe stopped and turned to me.

I lifted up the end of the silk to show them. "This was cut unevenly. There is no way such heavy fabric could tear so easily without it being tampered with beforehand."

"Are you suggesting that someone cut the silk before the performance, planning to harm you?" Monroe stepped forward, inspecting the fabric in his own hands. This had the potential to be a more serious insinuation than the lawsuit that had been threatened against us.

"Yes, I am." The reality that someone might want to hurt me hit me hard. What could they have against me? What had I done wrong?

"That's impossible. Why would someone do that?" Monroe's large pupils darted between my eyes.

"I'm not sure, but I received a message last night from someone within the circus--"

Mr. Monte interrupted me before I could finish. "And you just thought to tell us this now? What did it say?"

I sighed, "Someone wrote *run while you can*. Before, I was worried that I didn't fit in here. Now, I'm worried I'm not safe." The letter was the first attempt to rattle me, cutting the silk was the second, and who knows what the third might be. Maybe it goes beyond me. Maybe they don't want to hurt me personally, but the circus as a whole." The words fell out of my mouth before I could even process them. "You said that someone is threatening to sue the circus. And in order to do that, they have to prove that it's dangerous for its members. And what better way to prove that to the world than by harming its newest, most celebrated member?"

Mr. Monte looked at the tent around him, wondering if it could be true. "Monroe, please follow me to my office. Juniper, you need to get some rest."

"But Mr. Monte, we have to do something. We have to figure out who did this." I tried to hop over to him, but he had already begun to walk away.

"We will," he promised. "We will, but you need to recover. I'll have a plan by the end of the day. Try not to worry."

Pestering him about it wouldn't do any good. He was right. I needed to recover as quickly as possible if I hoped to get back on the rope. On the way to my room, another pressing matter popped into my head. My mother was here last night. And she wouldn't have come if she didn't have something to say to me, which means she was somewhere in the city waiting for me. My mother hated traveling and she would do anything to avoid it. If she was here, then it must be important. Was Colette alright? Did something happen to our home? What if Colette was getting married?

Thinking of strange possibilities was only worrying me more. I had to see that dreadful woman and just get it over with. I could only think of one place she would go.

The tent from our performance last night was still set up in the middle of the city. I shivered with only a simple shawl around my shoulders. It was freezing outside, and thick clouds filled with precipitation were building above. Winter was approaching and if I didn't hurry, I'd be stuck walking back to the train in the dark. I pushed open the tent flaps with my good arm, while my injured arm rested in a sling. Maneuvering in the sling was very difficult but less painful than letting my arm hang by my side. Looking through the empty arena, I saw rows of plain wooden benches stacked high and a million footprints scattered in the sand—pieces of the hazy performance all coming together.

I spotted something out of place among the dirt and piss and manure. My mother sat with her hands folded on her lap and her knees pressed together tightly. She wore a lace hat with a coral flower accenting the teal silk ribbon around the brim, and white gloves with two blue buttons on the outside edge. She gestured to me with a tilt of her head instead of speaking.

I hated how perfect she looked. It was hard to believe I had been in her household and under her thumb for so long. A part of me pitied her. And a smaller part wished that she could escape as I had and experience the world. But I couldn't help her.

"How did you find me?" *Really Juniper, that's your question after seeing your mother for the first time in months?*

She moved her hand under her bum and retrieved a flimsy newspaper that she used to protect her dress from the dirt. On the front page was my face and my name in big bold print, as well as a list of all of our performances. How could I have been so stupid? I had led her right to me.

"My daughter's name, printed on the front page..." she looked down at the paper.

"Is that pride I hear?" I was tempted to run away and never see her again.

"You forget your place." My mother stood.

"My place?" I laughed. "My place is no longer with you. It is here." I waved my arms at the expanse of space around me. I was no longer afraid to speak my mind, and my mother couldn't control my life anymore.

"You know not of what you speak." She shook her head at me, making me feel like a child again.

I had never been able to please my mother, and I never would. But for the first time, I wasn't upset with myself for the life I was living. "There's no show at this time, so you are free to leave now."

She stepped off the risers, her face twisting in disgust and her heel digging into the dirty sand. "Young lady, I did not come here to watch you. I did not come to make sure you are having fun or excelling at what you do. It is already apparent that you are not." Her eyes turned to my bandaged shoulder, and I was stung by her words. "I've come to tell you some important news."

I wrung my hands together nervously. It didn't matter how important it was, and I didn't care what she had to say.

"You remember the Young family, don't you?"

My family used to spend every summer with the Young family before my father left. I was an infant then, and too young to remember.

"Mr. Young is the ambassador of dwellings in Axminster and Penketh. He is a very wealthy and influential man, and his son is equally as respectable. Our families plan to join together." She smiled brightly.

Oh no. "So, Colette has finally decided to sell her soul?" My sadness grew for my sister even more. Why would she agree to this? Was it just to please our mother? Did she love him?

"Oh, my little prune," she sighed. "Colette has yet to find a suitor. I've promised Joseph Young that he may have your hand."

The breath was knocked out of me. Me? Marry Joseph Young? His name barely rang a bell. I didn't even know what he looked like. "But mother--"

"Now it is up to us to plan an extravagant wedding. In Axminster of course," she added, as if I would accept this idea without hesitation. "You'll have to pack your bags immediately. I have a carriage waiting."

I wanted to hurt her. Really hurt her. My whole life I knew this was coming. I knew I would be forced to marry someone for their money. I was taught at church that men were created by God to protect women. And after my father broke his vow by leaving, my mother's only source of security was in protecting our futures. But I couldn't marry someone I didn't love, let alone someone I could barely recall. I wouldn't do it. "You can tell Joseph Young that I have declined his offer. Goodbye, Mother."

I turned around and briskly retreated from the tent. Once she was out of my sight, I ran as fast as I could. I sprang down the street, despite the pressure pounding through my broken body every time my feet hit the ground. I turned corner after corner, brick walls blending into one another until I had no idea where I was. The city was darkening by the minute as the sun disappeared behind the small businesses around me. Steam rolled out of chimneys and evaporated in the cold wind. Something tickled my nose and I stopped to see a light snow beginning to fall on my face and stick to my eyelashes.

I didn't recognize any of the businesses or shops, confirming that I hadn't been to this part of the city before. I passed an old antique shop called Edward's Collectibles and Miscellaneous Artifacts. I folded my hands under my armpits in an attempt to warm my frozen fingers while I kept moving. The temperature was dropping quickly and, before long, I couldn't feel my toes. After walking for a few miles, I asked a man with grotesquely yellow teeth for directions, but he was no help. Too tired to keep going, I sank into the wall and frost crawled through my shawl and into my shoulder blades. It suddenly frightened me that I didn't know how to get back home.

Marry Joseph Young? I could never. The idea was preposterous and my mother knew it. Her focus had been on marrying off Colette for years now, since she was the oldest. I knew the only reason she was marrying me off so quickly was to get me back home. But I had risked too much to return to Axminster now and allow her to make decisions for me any longer.

As I sat there in the alleyway, I tried to think of what Joseph might look like. Was he handsome? Was he tall? I envisioned him to be 5'9", with straight, clean teeth, and a nice smile. Nothing crooked or out of place. I bet he barely grew stubble on his chin, and when he did, he would probably shave it at first sight to appear fresh for every occasion. My thoughts turned to his wardrobe. He must have stacks on stacks of colored vests to choose from and patterned ties to match. I imagined the steam rolling off his pressed overcoat and him fashioning a top hat on his head.

My mind was growing weary and my bones shook. *I'll just rest for a moment*, I thought. *Just a minute and then I'll continue.*

As I drifted from consciousness, I saw Joseph's eyes staring into a mirror until I realized they were not looking at his own reflection, but gazing at me. I couldn't discern the color of his eyes, nor the shape. Were they blue and full like Flint's eyes, or brown and almond shaped like Cassius's? Was his heart warm like Charlotte's? Was he as devoted to his trade as Gus was? Was he as compassionate and encouraging as Mr. Monte?

I knew the answer to all of these questions without knowing him at all. If I were to marry him, he would want to tame me, and that was the worst thing I could imagine right now. I would not have a life of my own or a name of my own. The moment Joseph placed a dazzling ring on my finger, my virtue and my future would belong to him. My happiness would be subject to his whims, and my duties would be dictated by him alone. Juniper Young. The name made me gag.

In the bitter cold, when my stomach began to shake uncontrollably, I was unable to withhold the salty moisture in my mouth. I curled my head between my legs and emptied its contents. I tried to stifle the disgusting noise coming out of my throat, but I couldn't control the unstoppable fear of fate. *Fate.* Why must fate play a role in our lives at all? If I made it to heaven, that was one question I intended to ask God—Why must our lives be planned out in accordance with your will? Why must our free will be altered based on what you decided was right for us?

I leaned my head back on the brick wall and a single tear dripped down my cheek. I knew there would be nothing left of me if the circus was taken from me. Maybe a few twisted organs and a slowly beating heart, but there would be no joy, no purpose, and no passion. I had committed my all to the circus—something that seemed so far away now. I closed my eyes and the feeling in my legs faded away as the snow coated the ground. I shivered so hard that it took an act of God for my eyes to close. And when they did, I feared I might never wake up.

Chapter 17

The circus was in an uproar. With two weeks until the performance in Turnstead and a four-day journey ahead of us, we had to pack up and get on the road before any more time had passed. It was dark and all the performers worked late into the night. Mr. Monte stormed down the hallway before jumping outside in a fury where one tent stood alone—the tightrope walker's tent.

"Where is Juniper?" He yelled angrily. There was no time to waste.

Flint rushed through the throng of people that had gathered outside the tent. His cheeks were blooming in the cold wind, and his breath fogged in front of him when he spoke. "Sir-" Flint took a moment to breathe. "I've looked everywhere. Juniper's gone."

"What do you mean gone? She's probably just galivanting around the train," Cassius said, with a cynical laugh.

Flint whipped around to face Cassius. "I mean she's *missing*."

Suddenly Cassius's face moved from unfazed to concerned.

Mr. Monte wrung his hands through his hair, perplexed. "A group of you will head toward the city and find her. Did anyone see her leave?"

Evelyn raised her feeble hand, and the crowd pulled back so Mr. Monte could see her. "I saw her walking in the field. I think she went toward the city center." The woman pointed into the distance where the spire of a church jutted out above the other dwellings.

"I'll lead a group into the city!" Monroe volunteered, straying from his quiet demeanor. He gathered a few worthy souls, including Flint, Charlotte, a begrudging Cassius, Gus, Rosyln and Raelynn, and a few of the flamethrowers. While the others helped Mr. Monte load the final items onto the train, the rescue group set out toward the city.

Cassius...

"Juniper!" Charlotte yelled into the night. A storm was brewing and the snow was falling harder and harder. The temperature had to be close to zero. If she was out here, she would be in bad shape.

"Have you seen a woman with black curly hair?" Gus asked a vendor on the side of the street.

The man shook his head and returned to cooking thinly sliced pieces of meat over a fire. The performers separated, familiar with the city because of their previous visits.

I walked down the street with my hands tucked into my pockets. It was bloody freezing. Why the hell did Juniper have to get lost and put this burden on everyone else? I'm not entirely sure I believed Flint. Maybe she ran away? After that stunt she pulled with the Janvier Estate, I was sure she was halfway to Axminster by now.

The other voices grew faint as I traveled further from the heart of the city and into the outlying district. I rounded corner after corner, my pace hastening. This girl was stupid. She was stupid and reckless. But she couldn't help it. All privileged women were raised to let others think for them. That was why Juniper surprised me so much. She had her own beliefs and a strong will to follow her heart. She came to the circus on her own accord. Why, I couldn't quite understand.

I heard a small cough to my left, and when I looked at the dirty man lying in the cold, I wanted to throw up. I hated it here. I hated the memories of my past that resurfaced in my mind at the sight of him. I wanted to find Juniper as fast as I could and go home so I didn't have to look at another beggar as fragile as I once was. I began to jog through the winding alleyways. "Juniper!" I yelled, cupping my hands around my mouth so my voice would travel further. My face was already numb. If she was really out here, she would be frozen. I knew what it was like to be cold—the kind of cold that made your skin tingle so that you wanted to cut it right off to stop the pain. I shoved the memories back and focused on Juniper. I hoped to God she had found shelter inside somewhere.

"Juniper!" I yelled again. My voice broke and nearby, I heard a small scuttle. I whipped around nervously to find someone hunched over on the street. A man was kneeling on the ground and when he shifted slightly, I got a better view of him. His jaw was cleanly shaved and his hair was gelled. Behind the man's broad frame, I saw a pair of small legs. I approached him to find the woman was dressed in black leather pants and a thin blouse. Taking one step further, I saw her rosy cheeks and her black hair covered in a layer of snow.

As the man turned, I discovered it was Monroe. "Monroe! You found her!"

Finally noticing my presence, he jumped up like he'd been caught doing something he shouldn't have been. "I was just about to go and find some help. Thank God you're here!"

I bent down quickly to examine her state of consciousness. Her mouth was blue and her fingertips were the color of plums. She didn't shake as I expected her to. She was just numb. I gripped her shoulders and tried to shake her awake. "Juniper!" She didn't move an inch. "Juniper listen to me! You have to wake up!" She must have been out here for hours! Why would she travel so far without a companion?

Monroe jumped up to say, "I'll go tell the others!" And he wasted no time sprinting into the city to search for help.

I wondered if I should wait until someone arrived to help me. That could mean dealing with Mr. Smartass, Flint. What a prick. I'd rather not add another hopeless case to my list. But despite my anger toward that man, this was about Juniper's safety. And she wouldn't last another twenty minutes out here. I bent down and looped one arm under Juniper's knees and the other under the small of her back. I carried her for at least a mile, without seeing any of the other performers. They must have headed back to the train or further into the city. My arms ached, but after a little while, her body seemed to awaken with the warmth of my body. She began to shake and her teeth chattered. I tried to ignore the way her head nuzzled closer to my chest and the way she clung to my shirt.

I had to get her back to the train where it was warm. I jumped slightly to move her body higher in my arms, and suddenly the twin dancers ran around the corner with beet red noses.

Monroe hadn't returned, which made me doubt that he'd warned and of the other performers. "Tell the others I found her. Round 'em up and get everyone back to the train."

The twins nodded in unison and raced into the city in search of the other performers.

Those two terrified me sometimes. They acted in sync and talked in sync. It was like their brains were molded together. My breath was ragged and it was difficult to move my frozen legs. After many blind turns and dark alleys, the buildings faded away and I came out at a corn field on the outside of the city. I felt exhausted as I walked the final stretch toward the train in the distance. In our time away, Mr. Monte had dismantled Juniper's tent and packed the rest of the train.

Why would Juniper go into the city alone in the cold? Was she running away? And if she was, then what was I doing exhausting myself, carrying her back to a place she didn't want to be? I tried not to think too hard over the fact. I could be mistaken. She could have simply gotten lost. I had overheard Mr. Monte speak about someone intending to harm Juniper by cutting the silks before her performance. Maybe this was the culprit's way of trying to hurt her once more. Maybe they had led her out of town in an attempt to hurt her. The thought hit too close to home. This had happened before, many years ago. No one spoke of it anymore, not even I, but I could still recall the headlines in the newspaper: *Penelope Plume—star of the circus—tragically killed. Accident or volatile crime?* I knew it wasn't an accident, but I didn't have proof. And if the plot to harm the tightrope walker was recurring, I had to do something before it was too late. I had to find this menace. I had to keep Juniper safe, despite my disdain for her upbringing, as hard as it might be. I owed it to Penelope.

When I finally made it to the train, I was panting. Juniper's lips had grown less blue, which I was grateful for, but my irritation returned when Flint stumbled out of the train with hope in his eyes. When he spotted me holding her, his happiness waned and he approached me with his arms folded across his chest. God, I wanted to punch him in the face. What made him think he was so special? I can't believe Mr. Monte assigned him as captain of the riders. What a joke.

"This is one of the only good things you've ever done." Flint raised his eyebrows and opened his arms. "Hand her over."

Juniper's hands were ice cold on my chest, and as much as I yearned to taunt Flint even more, she needed help. I pulled her body away and offered her to Flint, and he eagerly accepted. For the next few seconds, I swore something spiritual stirred in me. I felt like Juniper's God had taken it upon himself to grant me permission to protect Juniper at all cost. Making Mr. Pretty Boy jealous was just an added bonus.

Flint spun sharply on his heel and carried her to his room.

I hopped on board, just as the steel wheels screeched on the metal tracks and the train began to pull away. Sparks ignited on the train tracks, signaling our departure from Hewe. Until next time...

I peeled my eyelids open in the darkness. It took a moment for me to piece together the events of last night. It felt like a dream that was missing most of the details. My mother traveled all the way to Hewe to inform me that she intended to give my hand to Joseph Young, without my consent—that I remembered. Suddenly my jaw shook and my teeth chattered, reminding me of my frozen endeavor into Hewe. I couldn't remember how I ended up in the city, but I was grateful to be safe.

Flint laid behind me with his arms wrapped around my body protectively. My body was warm against his, but my face was numb. I turned sharply and my shoulder ached for me to slow down, but I ignored it and buried my head in Flint's chest.

Flint finally stirred and grasped my head in his hands. "How are you feeling, J?" He gently brushed the static strands of hair out of my face.

Instead of answering, I posed another question, "What happened?" My mouth tasted faintly acidic.

He sat up on his elbow and rubbed slow circles on my lower back. "We found you. Cassius found you," he corrected himself. "In an alley about three miles inside the city."

Cassius...Cassius found me? Had he offered to help search or was he dragged into it?

"How did I get back here?"

"He brought you back. You were blue in the face, J. I thought you were--" his voice faded, but he regained his composure so as to not worry me further. "You're okay now, and that's all that matters. What made you travel into the city all by yourself after dark?"

How could I tell Flint that my mother demanded I return home to marry a man I'd scarcely met? I didn't want to worry him over something that was never going to happen. Besides, it was absurd. "I- I was thinking about getting my sister something. I miss her dearly and I wanted to send her a gift. I get lost very easily." I tried to laugh off my nervousness. I didn't want to lie to him, but I saw no other option. I really liked Flint.

He looked at me for a moment, weighing the truth of my account. But he smiled and said, "I'm glad we found you then. Half the circus was searching for you."

I squeezed my eyebrows together in surprise.

"You are more needed than you'll ever know." Flint kissed me gently on the lips.

Half of the circus had left the train and scoured the city in the snow to find me. My friends had risked their lives for me. I couldn't believe I had been so skeptical of that before. I rose from bed and dressed in wool pants and a fur coat.

"Where are you off to?" Flint asked in surprise at my quick recovery.

"To pay someone my respect." I shut the door before Flint could disagree with me, and wrapped myself tighter in my fur coat to keep my arms from shivering. All night I had been painfully cold, the kind of cold that could make your bones ache deep inside. I rapped my knuckles on Cassius's door, and I could hear his loud footsteps from outside. I was nervous for some reason.

When Cassius opened the door, I was taken by surprise. His nose was red and his eyes were droopy. He looked sickly. He raised his eyebrows at my appearance. I hated Cassius. And Cassius hated me. We were both aware of this. But it was because of him that I was standing here now.

"Thank you," I blurted out. "Flint told me it was you who found me last night, and I just wanted to thank you."

"I'm surprised Mr. Perfect decided to be so humble." Cassius ran a hand through his messy hair.

I rolled my eyes. "I don't know your history with him, but this is the part where you say 'you're welcome.'"

He nodded slowly, "Despite how badly I wanted to leave you in that storm, you're welcome."

The silence following that was deafening, and I shifted awkwardly from foot to foot, trying to pretend I didn't care.

Cassius spoke before I had to, "What led you into the city anyway?" He leaned on the doorframe of his room in disinterest.

"It's a long story." I avoided his eyes. I was embarrassed to tell him, knowing he would judge me because of my mother's offer. He would undoubtedly make a crack about the traditional values I grew up with.

But he surprised me by saying, "Tell me on the way." And he slammed his door and walked quickly down the hallway. Something had changed in him in the past twenty-four hours. He seemed calmer around me—as if he no longer felt the need to banter with me or make fun of me. Was it possible we had come to an agreement? *And to think, it only took weathering a storm and almost catching pneumonia.*

I stood there perplexed, but when he disappeared, I quickly ran to catch up and found him heading toward the front of the train.

In response to my question about where in the world we were going, he said, "It's a surprise, Princess. Better start talking."

When Cassius called me Princess, I nearly choked. I didn't think he'd ever stop degrading me for my past, but the nickname was actually more playful than rude. The thin walls pressed closer in on me. I had to get this off my chest and make sense of it. I had to tell someone, even if that someone was cocky, self-absorbed Cassius. A part of me wanted to tell Cassius because I knew he wouldn't refrain from being honest. "My mother was at the show."

He listened intently.

"My mother despises travel. She believes too much activity will wear out the softness of her heels, and that it's not a lady's place to do taxing things or travel long distances and tire herself." I gagged. "She was there for a reason. That's why I went into the city."

"Is this when you tell me your mother killed someone and is asking you to come back to help her bury the body so she isn't suspected by her creepy, churchy neighbors?" Cassius joked and looked back for a split second.

I snickered, "Worse."

"What's worse than religious fanatics?"

"Your mother forcing you to marry a man you hardly remember?" I suggested.

Cassius stopped abruptly in his tracks. I almost ran into him because of how quickly he turned on his heels. "She demanded you return to marry a nobleman?"

"The date is already being set without my permission." My head sank to the floor.

Cassius continued down the hall toward the back of the train. "You entitled preeners and your infatuation with marrying young will always confuse me."

I couldn't disagree with him on that. I had hated that custom ever since I came to know of it. My mother was obsessed with finding Colette someone to marry, only so she could produce more entitled brats and earn us a segment in the newspaper dedicated to our big, entitled family. It was quite shameful.

"Easy solution. Don't go back home. What's the worst your mother will do? Get her coiffure in a knot and come take you away?"

I laughed out loud. Despite my hatred for Cassius, he had a way of lightening the mood.

"We're here," he extended his arms toward an array of tall cages. "I want you to meet Mildred." The corners of his mouth tilted up into an appreciative smile. Not a smirk, but a full smile that stretched his cheeks apart and gave me a glimpse of his bright teeth.

"Mildred?" I questioned.

"She's our oldest giraffe, but a fine lady at that." He looked her up and down with wide eyes.

It was clear that he was truly passionate about his animals. The way he spoke of the eldest female giraffe made my heart warm, and I was eager to hear more about his affection for the animals. I wanted to understand why he did what he did. And I wondered what had led him down this path.

"Mildred." I stepped forward and greeted her by running my hand along her neck. Her head almost reached the top of the train.

"You helped me rescue her." Cassius rested his large palm on her chest.

That day seemed so long ago. I almost forgot his rudeness at my attempt to help. "Ah, I remember now."

"That was not one of my kindest moments." He ran a hand through his hair—a motion I'd come to realize was nervousness.

"You've never had a kind moment." My mind raced through every conversation between the two of us. I did remember when he looked at me proudly in the mirror after my performance and told me, *You didn't need me.* And although I may never hear the same words again, I would remember them. But I wouldn't give him the satisfaction of telling him that.

Cassius looked at me from under his brows, and his golden eyes shimmered shamefully.

Suddenly a sharp noise came from the end of the train, and we turned to find Mr. Monte poking his head through the open train door. "Just the two I was looking for! Come to the dining hall quickly!"

Cassius and I shared a worried glance before hustling to the busy room. Bodies filled every square inch of space, and we found ourselves between the twins. Cassius looked at them with worry and leaned down to whisper, "Don't touch that one. He might bite you."

I tried to hold my laugh, but it snuck out quietly. The twins were strange at times, but they seemed nice enough. "Give 'em a chance," I said as I pushed him lightly. Cassius was being more playful that normal, and it made me wring my hands together nervously. I didn't know if I could get used to us not making rude comments to one another. Was it even possible for us to be friends?

Mr. Monte leapt onto the stage and rubbed his hands together. He was usually easy to read. He tended to show his emotions on his face, but right now I couldn't discern whether he looked worried or excited.

"I know all of you must be wondering about our current predicament. With our new tightrope walker injured, she will not be able to perform on the rope for another six weeks at least."

My eyes bulged out of my head. "Six weeks?" That means my next performance would be in Eanverness, in December.

Mr. Monte looked at me as if to say, *you and I will discuss this later.* He faced the crowd and added, "But my colleagues and I have thought of an idea to make her useful. Juniper," he turned to me and smiled, "you will perform with the lion tamer for the next six weeks as his helpless victim." The look in his eyes was wicked.

Cassius's eyebrows were raised as high as the ceiling while my jaw fell to the floor. No. This was not a good idea. In fact, this was the worst idea! Cassius was impossible to work with and we never got along. We'd fight the whole time!

Mr. Monte continued, "The best investigators in Hewe helped me determine that the silk that Juniper fell from was indeed cut deliberately. I wanted to inform everyone of this so that we protect one another. We have not discovered who did this, whether it be an outside agitator, or heaven forbid, one of our own."

The crowd mumbled to one another and the room seemed to darken. I felt as though I was drifting outside of my own body, watching the room from a distance. The memory of my bone shattering under my skin was so vivid, and the prospect that someone inside the circus—one of my friends—could have done this, made me sick to my stomach. In my head, I made a mental list for the next six weeks:

1. Convince Mr. Monte to give me another role in the performance.
2. Find who was threatening the circus.
3. Heal faster.

I wasn't sure if I could accomplish the last task, but if it meant lying in bed for a straight week and never moving, I would do it.

"I will do everything in my power to stop whoever is threatening the lives of my performers. In the meantime, I want you all to protect each other and take precautions with where you're going so you can continue to be my wonderful muses. You're dismissed!"

The crowd dispersed immediately but continued to mumble about what had been said.

Cassius turned to me. "So, partner, are you ready to practice?" The right side of his mouth lifted into a smile.

I raised my eyebrows, appalled by the fact that he was okay with Mr. Monte's decision. I thought he hated me. Unless he had helped Mr. Monte with the idea in the first place. But that didn't make any sense. "This isn't happening," I concluded.

"You're my helpless victim. Even better, you're my student." He leaned closer to me. "You better get used to it."

I shook my head and whipped around to find Mr. Monte bustling past me and walking away in a rush. When I opened my mouth to speak he held up his finger to silence me. "You heard the boy. You've got a lot of work to do."

The train suddenly came to a screeching halt. Cassius threw open the entrance, where the sunlight burst through the opening and a slight breeze made his curly hair flutter. "Welcome to Turnstead, famous for its French cuisine." He closed his eyes and took a breath of the fresh, sweet air. "Il est temps pour vous de rencontrer notre chat."

Cassius's lips moved quickly and the R's rolled off his tongue eloquently. His voice was beautiful, almost romantic even, and I wanted to melt into its softness. Where had he learned French?

"What does that mean?" My voice sounded small.

He chuckled, "It is time for you to meet our cat, Mr. Abbas."

Chapter 18

I slammed my back against the wall in terror. The lion's gaze was penetrating, and from this close, I could see precisely how its large pink lips surrounded its even larger teeth.

"He's never going to trust you if you fear him." Cassius grabbed my elbow through the white sling, and I hissed as pain ricocheted into my shoulder.

"I'm never going to trust him if he continues to look at me like that."

"Is that what you say to all the suitors in Axminster?"

I scowled at him, not at all interested in practicing while he tormented me with inconsiderate comments. "I'll practice the rest of tonight on my own." I retreated to my bedroom and when I closed the door, I was finally able to give in to the pain in my shoulder. I took off the sling to determine if it was getting better or worse. Some days the bandage was too tight, and others it was too loose, but I was uncomfortable day in and day out. Resigned to my pain, I rewrapped the sling and made sure it was the right length this time. When a light knock sounded on my door, I opened it grudgingly, thinking it may be Cassius ready to fire something else stupid at me, but I found Gus waiting patiently instead.

"Hey Gus." I smiled. I'd been so busy I hadn't talked to him in quite some time.

"The post came in," he said as he handed me a small letter wrapped in brown parchment.

Curious, I grabbed it and flipped it over to find my mother's name on the front. My stomach dropped at the thought of what might be inside, but I ripped it open and read over it carefully.

```
Juniper,
    Mr. Young requests your appearance at his
family's annual winter banquet. I promised the
Young family you would attend, hoping that you and
```

Joseph can become better acquainted. I'll see you on December 26th, Prune.

Sincerely, Mother

"Miss Rose, is everything alright?" Gus hadn't moved an inch.

"You're a magician," I stated. "Which means you read the present and the future correctly?" My tone was clear.

"Yes," Gus said with equal clarity and then showed me to his room. The dark candlelight and miscellaneous scarves and jewels around the room were all too familiar. "Sit."

I sat across from him at a small wooden table. He uncovered a crystal ball and moved his hand around it in a slow rhythm. I watched him search through the foggy glass and wondered what he could see. All I could see was my own faint reflection. From a very young age, my mother taught me not to believe in the devil's work, which included black magic. But I didn't know what I believed anymore. I didn't know if black magic existed or what would happen if I took part in it, but I also thought I might never understand the true plans for my future if I didn't partake. A dabble with magic wouldn't negate any of the faith I had in God anyway.

"What would you like to know, Juniper?" Gus looked deep into my eyes while stroking the palm of my hand.

"My mother. Will she come after me?" I asked honestly. I couldn't stand seeing my mother in the crowd one more time or, even worse, having her take me away from this life by force.

"The image is cloudy. I don't think you'll see her unless it's of your own accord."

I nodded my head, and said, "Good." Because I had no intention of ever seeing that woman again. "And what about a man named Joseph Young. Is he honorable?"

"Yes," Gus answered quickly, without hesitation. "But there is mystery surrounding his upbringing." He opened his eyes suddenly. "I can see quick blasts of images from his past, but it's hard to garner information about people I don't know. It's more just a feeling I get."

I sat in silence. There was one more question weighing on my mind. "It wasn't an accident was it? Someone cut the silks on purpose...to hurt me. To kill me?"

Gus's head twisted to the side, as if the answer was difficult to find in the mess of information. "No, it was not. And those you trust are not too far from becoming your enemies."

The breath was taken from my lungs. "If this person is among us, then how do I find him?"

"That's not something I can answer for you. But do not separate from your friends because of this warning. Keep them closer. They're the only ones who can help you at this point." Gus leaned over the table to grasp both of my hands in his.

I refrained from coming out of my room to practice with Cassius for the next two days. I knew what would happen if I did. He would make fun of me, try to dominate me with his knowledge, and then make fun of me again. It was a waste of time. Pairing up the two people who resented each other most was the worst decision Mr. Monte could have made.

"Why are you not practicing?" Mr. Monte asked in a raised voice.

I sat down in front of him after being beckoned to his office. "Cassius and I hate each other. You really couldn't have picked anyone else for me to perform with?" I demanded to know.

"Maybe it is *because* you hate one another that I have paired you together," he boomed. "I know Cassius is hard to deal with, but he's more knowledgeable than you realize. Give him a chance."

"Like he's given me? Cassius hasn't given me the chance to prove myself, so I'm not going to waste my time on him." He actually had given me a chance once. He helped me. But I didn't want to take it for granted that he'd be a gentleman from here on out. Because he wouldn't.

Monroe suddenly walked into the room with a manilla folder in his hands.

"I've got better things to do," I said and stood to go.

"Like what, young lady? You didn't come to the circus to slack off, and if that's your intent, then you won't be staying. What is so important that you must miss rehearsal for it?"

"My mother. She's contacted me twice requesting that I return home. What am I to do?" I trusted Mr. Monte with this information and I needed his help. The situation was troubling me more than I realized.

"Maybe you can ask Cassius," he said as he dismissed me and turned to discuss the contents of the manilla folder with Monroe. I had the urge to curse Mr. Monte out until I was blue in the face, and when I found Cassius shirtless in the tent, my anger only increased.

"Finally decided to show up, huh?" Cassius pushed back his hair, wet with sweat.

"Let's just get this over with, shall we?" I rolled my eyes.

"I thought you were afraid." Cassius walked to the cages in the back.

"Not anymore," I said as I took off my coat and rolled up my sleeves. My arm brace would get in the way, but I would be permitted to take it off in a week, and I was determined to follow the doctor's instructions.

Cassius walked out with a small peacock, petting its beautiful plume. He said something in its ear and it shook its feathers in response. The two of them stopped a safe distance away and looked at me calmly. "This is Lady Pine," said Cassius. "She pecks ferociously, but she's a sweet girl once you get to know her." He unhooked the collar around the bird and let her walk around freely.

Her feathers were beautiful shades of turquoise and emerald green. I crouched low and reached out my hand for her to smell, but she snapped her head forward violently and pecked me with her beak. "Oh, my gosh!" I exclaimed, as I watched the blood roll off a cut in my palm, which I quickly brought to my mouth to soothe.

Cassius rubbed his fingers on his forehead, obviously annoyed, and said, "This is going to be one hell of a process."

I jumped off the stool, pulled it around in front of me, and held it with one arm. I'd grown stronger with my left arm from using it so frequently. Cassius smiled in appreciation. "Shall we try it with the tiger?"

Cassius and I had been practicing every single day for eight hours, and each time I returned to my room, I was sweating and exhausted. I had learned how to ward off the tiger as well as how to use facial expressions to appear dominant. But I had yet to tame the animal, and I was terrified every time I stood before her.

Despite that, I nodded my head, determined to try again.

When the tiger yawned and stretched its massive paws, Cassius laughed. "Me too girl, me too." He rubbed right behind the tiger's ear, causing her eyes to close and a purr to reverberate over her massive neck and mouth. "This is Toulouse."

Toulouse was a beautiful black and white striped Saber Tooth tiger—she was like nothing I'd ever seen before. Saber Tooth tigers were almost extinct, and it was incredible that the circus was able to keep one.

Cassius held out a hand in front of the tiger's eyes. "Place!" He instructed the tiger to stay where she was and came to stand behind me. He grabbed my palm softly in his, which made me flinch. Cassius had been so rough, loud, and obnoxious. I couldn't help remembering his hands on my throat, so this gentleness caught me off guard. "Reach out your hand very, very slowly. In this situation you are not the tamer. You are the victim. You wait for the tiger's lead. Never make the first move—that is rule number one!" Cassius traced his hand along my palm and led my hands up slowly toward the tiger's face.

My breathing quickened when the tiger's eyes grew wide. Her nostrils flared in and out, and her hot breath snaked down my arm. Cassius pressed his back against mine to stop me from moving, and suddenly Toulouse calmed. She blinked once, twice, and then took a step toward me. And when she opened her mouth, her hot breath blinded me this time.

I squealed and turned around so quickly that I ran straight into Cassius's chest. My balance was gone, and I grappled for anything to hold on to.

"Woah!" Cassius yelled as he fell back with my momentum. I landed on top of him, grabbing hold of the cloth on his chest. With a thud, Cassius groaned, and my eyes closed tightly, wondering where Toulouse was and if she was going to pounce on me. Cassius's chest moved up and down below me, and I opened my eyes to find the world spinning. *Oh god.* My heart was thundering in my chest. The sun shone through the flaps of the tent and caught Cassius's golden eyes perfectly, and I stared at them far too long.

Cassius's eyes darted around awkwardly, and he slowly removed his hands from my waist. He cleared his throat and said, "We can be done for the day. I think I've seen enough."

I jumped up and brushed the dust off my corset, thankful his voice filled the silence in the room. His awkward tone made me feel ashamed, but of what, I didn't know.

Late that night when the sun had fallen behind the vast mountains in the distance, I couldn't seem to enter the dark abyss of sleep. I laid restlessly in bed for an hour, imagining Toulouse's snarling teeth and her fierce claws. You would think she was a mere kitty cat, the way Cassius interacted with her, but she certainly wasn't. I couldn't stop thinking about the horrible things that beast could do to me. But I needed to push that aside if I was going to succeed. After my injury in Hewe, I had to please the crowd somehow until I could perform on my own.

I tore back the sheets on my bed, donned a night robe, and trudged quietly into the hall. I kept my weight on the tips of my toes, careful not to wake anyone. In the night, the circus was still and quiet and allowed space for thought. It was like the human body. All day, the body worked hard keeping the blood pumping, but at night, the heart slowed and all motion stopped. The wooden walls cracked and bent in the darkness, and there was no light except from the small candle in my hand. As the wax dripped down the silky shaft, I watched my shadow elongate on the opposite wall. I hurried down to exit the train, and when I pulled the doors open, a cold gust of wind hit my face. My eyes stung and began to water in the biting cold. I skipped across the field towards the snow-covered tent where the wind would be quieter from inside the canopy.

The tent appeared larger when Cassius wasn't occupying it. He seemed to take up all of the energy in the room—like my mother's new-fangled vacuum that sucked up everything in sight.

A deep grumble resonated in the back of the room where a black curtain partially covered the animals' cages. I took one step and the sound became louder. *Toulouse.* I grasped the heavy curtain with my fingertips and pulled it aside. Cages lined the wall, filled with animals of all shapes and sizes—a gentle koala sitting in the stillness of night, a lion pacing back and forth with quiet footsteps, and a giant snake coiled behind glass. And then my eyes met with Toulouse. Two rows of large canine teeth slammed down on the bars of the cage and bent the very metal. Her pink gums were slimy with mucous and her eyes were a bright grey color, fierce with her need to protect her territory. I jumped back, my heart pounding out of my chest.

I used to be afraid of the course my mother had set for my life, but I no longer was. Maybe I could use that same determination to turn this fear of Toulouse into something productive. I left my life in Axminster without looking back, so I did the same thing here...I took one step forward without even thinking. Toulouse didn't move an inch, and I closed my eyes and breathed, reminding myself that she might be just as afraid of me as I was of her. I pulled my arm up slowly like Cassius taught me and came in contact with something soft. I opened my eyes slowly so as not to scare her, and her large lips curled back as if to smile at me. A deep grumble echoed in Toulouse's throat as I reached my arm all the way through the bar. She licked my entire arm, which made me squeal and laugh at how rough and wet her tongue felt. I sighed in contentment and said to her quietly, "I think this might just work."

<hr>

Cassius...

I heard a low grumble echo in the field, which was odd. Toulouse was usually asleep by this hour. My irritation grew quickly. I had finished choosing the training barricades for the riders after they adjourned late to the dining hall, and all I wanted to do was lie down and sleep before another exhausting day with Juniper. That girl took more work than an angry gorilla. When I heard another grumble, I began to worry. The animals were never this noisy. What was going on in there?

I pulled back the tent flaps in a hurry, not expecting to find Juniper, of all people, with her hands stretched out toward Toulouse. The tiger smiled and purred at her touch. Toulouse was a difficult girl to tame, but Juniper had managed it all on her own.

"Atta girl," I whispered and folded my arms across my chest as I watched Juniper giggle when Toulouse licked her face.

Chapter 19

The perpetrator...
I've had many dreams in the past twenty years—dreams that most couldn't live with. Dreams where small girls broke their limbs. Dreams where blood spilled like ink on parchment paper. Dreams where the only sound was that of a loved one screaming. And I dreamed of her every night screaming for my help—yelling for anyone to save her. But no one did. Instead, they destroyed her. Every day until it became too much to bear. And that's when I lost her.

The hallway flooded with noise as jittery performers attempted to fit in more practice for the upcoming show in Turnstead. I folded my leather gloved hands on an empty piece of parchment, determined to write the perfect message. Something that would scare her before the big day, enough to make her mind reel. I knew that what I was doing was right. It would benefit all of us, but most importantly, the memory of my love.

I picked up my quill and touched the point to the paper. Black ink spilled across the surface, reminding me of that fateful day those twenty years ago when crimson spilled across the sand. It was the biggest performance of the year for the circus. And one of the most dangerous.

I folded the letter and placed it in an envelope before gently tucking in the flap. Now we would wait...

"Mr. Monte wanted us to depict a pair of similarly talented lion tamers. Your face tells me everything, Juniper." Cassius hung onto my name in a sing-song voice.

"Do it again," I groaned.

He rolled his eyes and locked up Abbas to give him a break. When it was time to run the routine again, I managed to not get my arm bitten off as Abbas lunged for me and I jumped out of the way. "This is impossible. Abbas hates me!" After last night I thought it would be easier, but no matter how comfortable I became, Abbas didn't trust me.

"That's because you don't trust *me*. Abbas is like my brother. He knows what's good for me and what isn't. He knows my friends as well as my enemies. He's smart, and he understands that when I unlock his cage, you fear for your life because you don't trust me."

"I do trust you," my voice wavered. Although I didn't think anyone on earth trusted Cassius. He was rude and inconsiderate, and he had belittled me from the day I arrived. So, no, I didn't actually trust him.

He rolled his eyes again and said, "Get on the rope."

"What? I can't. My arm isn't healed yet, and Mr. Monte will kill me." I tried to think of as many excuses as I could, but the truth was that I was afraid.

"Get. On. The. Rope." Cassius crossed his arms defiantly.

I didn't like it when Cassius was angry. I didn't like Cassius under any circumstance, but at least he was tolerable when he was trying to be fun and lighthearted. I climbed the ladder quickly with one hand, complaining the whole time. "Cassius, I don't want to do this," my voice shook as I worried my injured arm would throw off my balance.

"Just take one step. And if you fall, I'll catch you."

"Is this your plan to kill me? Because it's not funny," I yelled down to him.

"Like I said. You don't trust me." Cassius shrugged his shoulders.

To prove him wrong, I stepped onto the tightrope. My breathing got heavier and when I stepped again, I leaned too far to the left to compensate for my fear. I yelped and my legs sprang off the rope as I closed my eyes tightly, expecting to hit the pad below. If this injured me further, I would kill Cassius. But instead, I hit something much harder than the pad, and when I opened my eyes, Cassius's face was inches from my own.

"I caught you, didn't I?" He smiled.

I nearly punched him in the face, yelling, "Let me go!" As I jumped out of his arms, I faltered back and ran into Abbas. I expected to be mauled to death by the animal, but he only shook his long mane at me and then nuzzled his head into my stomach, making me fall backwards into Cassius, who barely caught me before we both fell to the ground. Abbas landed next to us and extended his paws to the sky while scratching his back in the sand, rolling around like a pig in mud. Cassius and I laughed and rubbed his belly, as if he were a house cat.

Cassius's head fell back and the whites of his teeth gleamed. This was the first time I'd heard him really laugh. It was low and full and I loved listening to it. Cassius was always so angry and stern. I didn't know what made him that way, but I did know these animals made him happy. The *circus* made him happy.

"Juniper!" I heard my name called across the room.

I lifted my head up and winced when my shoulder turned the wrong way.

Flint stood at the doorway with his hands by his side and an expression of jealousy and anger combined.

I stood quickly and brushed the sand off my shirt.

"You ready?"

I nodded quickly and grabbed my bag. I forgot that Flint and I were planning to have lunch together. Looking back once more at Cassius, who still sat on the floor with a hand on Abbas, I smiled, and he returned the gesture warmly.

"What was that about?" Flint asked harshly. Flint never raised his voice.

"What was what about?"

He raised an eyebrow and stopped in the middle of the field outside the tent, where a light snow was falling on his dark brown hair.

I brushed away the sparkling snow and smiled at him. "Mr. Monte requires us to work together. Nothing more. Now can we please get out of the cold?" I whined.

When we got to my room, Flint took off his coat and began to unpack the basket of food he brought when I spotted something on the floor. Beside my door was a light-colored letter, and the handwriting on the front looked familiar. My heart began to race when I recognized that this one was similar to the threatening letter I had received a few weeks ago. I quickly brushed the letter under my desk with my foot. Flint couldn't know about this.

When our lunch date ended, Flint returned to work and I rushed over to the mess hall in search of Cassius. I had looked in the training tent, but he wasn't there, and after weaving through tables full of my drunken comrades, I found him. I flicked my head toward the back of the room where it was quiet, hoping he'd follow. Normally I wouldn't confide in him, but I knew I could trust him with this. I wasn't sure why, but somehow he related to my fear.

Without a word he met me there. I pulled the letter out of my jacket and offered it to him.

He took it from me and read over the script.

I WARNED YOU. YOU DIDN'T FOLLOW MY INSTRUCTIONS, AND YOU WILL PAY THE PRICE. THE LION TAMER CAN'T SAVE YOU NOW.

Cassius flipped the paper over in his hand. "This is from someone in the circus."

"How do you know?" I pressed.

"Because no one else knows that you and I are performing together. It's supposed to be a surprise for the audience." Cassius walked down the hall and I followed him into his dimly lit room. The last time I was there, I hadn't had enough time to look around because I was too busy screaming at Cassius. His room was much bigger compared to the others. On the far end of the room, there was a large, king sized bed made of dark cherry wood, with a rumpled red duvet and a grey fur at the foot. A zebra pelt covered the floor, and a small window looked out into the field beyond. I wondered why Mr. Monte had offered him special accommodations.

"This is the second letter," I said, more worried than the last time.

"The perpetrator is inconsistent and is giving us more clues without even knowing it. When did you receive these letters?" Cassius looked serious.

This was why I came to Cassius. He was quick to take action to solve the problem instead of worrying and making me more anxious. "The first one appeared at night, and this one in the afternoon."

"Hmmm, that doesn't really tell us much." Cassius sighed in frustration. "Make sure you tell me if anything else happens, and I'll be watching for anything suspicious."

I stood there silently for a moment, not sure what to say. "Do you think something will happen at our next performance?" I imagined all sorts of terrible things. Would it be another equipment malfunction like with the silks? Would it involve the animals, just when I'd gained their trust? Would I be the main victim, or would the perpetrator go after Cassius, leaving me at the mercy of the tiger? I didn't want Cassius getting hurt because of me.

"Maybe," Cassius said without hesitation.

I looked up at him quickly. Part of me wanted him to lie to me, to tell me that nothing would go wrong. But I needed his honest answer.

"But I'll be there to help if something does," he reassured me.

I took one more glance at his cluttered room and the hair in his eyes, and walked away before I could say something stupid.

―――◆―――

The night of the performance...

I plucked a shimmering champagne leotard from Penelope's vast walk-in closet and pulled the long diamond-encrusted sleeves up my arms. It stretched high over my hips, and the neckline reached to where my collarbones met. I ran my hands over the sparkling fabric and moved to grab the matching bedazzled headband, when I heard a rustle behind me. I turned around, expecting to find Mr. Monte or Monroe ready to escort me to the city, when I spotted a head of black curly hair. His back was turned to me and his muscles flexed as he grappled with the wooden drawers in Penelope's old vanity.

"Cassius?" I said, realizing he hadn't noticed I was there.

He turned around so quickly that he almost knocked the vanity mirror over. He looked surprised to see me, and then in a flash, he was furious. Like the night at the Janvier Family Estate, he squeezed his fists together at his sides and clenched his jaw.

"What are you doing here?" he erupted, walking quickly toward me.

I stepped back and collided with the wall. "I-"

He glanced down at my leotard with a dark glare blazing in his eyes. "Take it off."

I couldn't move an inch, I was so scared. What was wrong? I was just borrowing a costume. Why was he so angry?

"Take it off!" he roared, and his entire face shook. His cheeks were red and his eyes were on fire.

I was frozen where I stood.

Cassius stepped back and ran a hand over his mouth. "Where did you get that? Who let you in here?"

"Mr. Monte. He suggested I wear Penelope's old costumes," I squeaked.

Cassius's eyes became softer and his mouth turned down to the floor. A sheen covered his eyes. It almost looked like he was crying. Without saying another word, he rubbed his hands over his cheeks and stormed out of the room.

I finally took a breath and clutched my fast-beating heart. What was so important about this room and Penelope's costume to evoke such emotion in Cassius?

Cassius...

I burst into Mr. Monte's office. He was in a rush, as always, before a performance.

"Cassius, would you gather the dancers? We're already late and they're busy primping," Mr. Monte huffed as he donned his top hat and gathered a handful of papers that would permit us to enter the city.

"What the hell is wrong with you?" My face trembled.

Mr. Monte looked up in confusion.

"Penelope's chambers are off limits, Edward. And you allowed Juniper in there so she could play dress up?!" I yelled as I approached his desk.

Mr. Monte gave me a look of warning. "Juniper is a tightrope walker, as was Penelope. I think it wise to allow her to use Penelope's old costumes," Mr. Monte snapped back, as he returned to flipping through the pages in his hands.

"That was not your call to make." My lips quivered and my eyes stung. I had known Mr. Monte since I was a child, and I expected he would understand my wishes. *Keep that door locked,* was what I told him five years ago. Mr. Monte was the closest thing I had to a father, and I trusted him. And he had gone behind my back and done the very thing I had asked him not to do.

"I'm sorry Cas, but right now I'm doing what's best for the circus." Mr. Monte tried to reassure me as he touched my shoulder lightly.

I brushed his hand away, unable to look him in the eyes. "You bastard." I shook my head and exited the room. Loosening the buttons of my shirt to give my burning throat some air, I rummaged for a bottle of ale in the dining hall. Throwing open the entrance to the train, I waded through the field of wheat and made my way toward the city while guzzling down half the bottle. Juniper didn't understand this world and she never would. She may have made some friends and worn some scanty clothing, but that didn't mean she wouldn't run back to her mommy when things got tough. And for that very reason, I intended to make things really tough for her.

I coated my lips in a sparkling gloss, brushed a shimmer along my high cheekbones, and pinned the hair on the right side of my head back so my face could be seen. As I approached the edge of the tent, my arms were shaking as I remembered there was someone here who wanted to hurt me. I looked to the right where Charlotte, Roselyn, and Gus were talking with the horse riders. And to my left, Flint and Josephine were having a rather heated argument over the reliability of horseshoes versus rim shoes. It could be any of them. I returned my gaze to the break in the tent where I saw the flamethrowers jumping through rings of fire while the twin jesters rode in circles on their unicycles.

I hadn't seen Cassius since he stormed out of the train, and our act was almost up. Where was he? He was clearly angry that I went into Penelope's chamber and used her things, and he could hate me forever if he wanted, but we had a performance to do.

As soon as the jesters rode behind the tent, Cassius appeared by my side with a glaze coating his eyes.

"Are you drunk?" I whispered angrily.

He looked forward and clenched his jaw, paying me no mind.

"Don't do anything rash," I told him, and stepped up to the opening.

"I wouldn't dare, *Prune*," Cassius spit.

I gasped. Where had he heard that name? That was something only my mother called me. My abdomen clenched and my heart pounded. He had no idea how much I resented that nickname. How dare he throw it around so carelessly?

"Juniper!" Mr. Monte yelled from across the tent. His mouth hung open and his arms were spread wide as if to say, *what are you doing? Get out there!*

The audience was silent while they watched an empty stage. I had to move, but I couldn't. *Prune*. Just take one step, *Prune*. I ignored the deafening silence and closed my eyes to clear my head. Fine. If that was how Cassius wanted to play, then I'd play.

As the audience watched intently, I placed my good hand on the fabric above my head and the other hand on my hip, while looking into the blinding light. The audience gasped to see me performing so soon after my fall. Every newspaper in every kingdom had my face on the front page with the woeful tale of the plotted vengeance to kill me. Everyone had come to know of the atrocities that happened to performers in the circus, and it was clear that no one expected me to be performing at this point. I walked to the center of the sand circle and smiled at the crowd. When I extended my hand toward the opposite side of the tent, Cassius emerged with a long silver rod in his hand. He was dressed in a black leather vest, and his arms were bare and looked dangerously tan under this light.

Three pedestals of different heights were positioned in the ring. At the back of the tent, the cages were opened and three lions emerged from the darkness and stalked toward us like the predators they were. My heart was beating so fast I thought I might throw up; meanwhile, Cassius was calm like a slow-moving river. The lions approached us quickly, and I flashed a black sheet in front of them to divert their attention to the pedestals.

"Up!" Cassius flicked the rod at the animals, and one by one they jumped onto the pedestals. They faced the audience and sat on their hind legs obediently, and the crowd clapped in approval. It was my job at that point to reach into a bucket and throw each of them a dripping piece of meat, which they caught effortlessly with a snap of their teeth. Cassius attached a piece of meat to the end of the rod as I walked closer to the lions. Placing the rod a foot in front of my face, he waved Abbas over to us, while I closed my eyes and took in a deep breath. The air seemed to be sucked from the room all at once. My hands were shaking but I tried to remain still, and when I heard another snap, I opened my eyes to find Abbas even closer to my face. He stared at me with golden eyes while the audience roared.

To the amazement of the crowd, I grasped his jaw and rubbed my nose against his lovingly.

Cassius watched with disdain before leading the lions into the back, out of view.

Next, I took center stage, where a single steel ring hung. The audience watched with anticipation as I grasped the ring with my left hand and jumped as high as I could. I gripped the steel and wrapped my ankles around it to pull my weight up with my left arm, while keeping my right arm by my side as much as possible to prevent it from swinging.

Suddenly the sound of screeching metal echoed in the vast room, and the audience turned their attention to a large cage rolling into the tent. It was covered in black fabric, preventing anyone from seeing what was inside. The cage stopped right below my feet, and I locked my knees around the bar before slowly lowering myself so my head dangled right above it.

Cassius ripped away the covering to reveal a colossal tiger, just in time for it to rear its head and roar so loudly the earth shook. I knew this tiger as Toulouse, the cat I had befriended, but the audience only saw her as a man-eating beast. When she opened her mouth, two ten-inch fangs extended to the sky. The audience was visibly shaken and awed by the beautiful black and white cat. She spotted me swaying above her head and moved to climb on the bars to stick her head out and snap at me, but I pulled myself up, narrowly avoiding getting my head taken off. In my haste, the beautiful jewels around my neck fell into the cage, and I gasped and tried to reach for them, but it was too late.

Cassius whistled and pulled a piece of meat from his satchel to wave it in front of the tiger's nose. Then he continued to whistle to keep her focused so I could quietly slip off the ring and onto the top of the cage. I grappled with the lock on the cage, and when it clicked, the tiger faced me once again, and my heart leapt out of my chest.

Just then, Cassius threw the meat into the cage, and the tiger tore it apart within seconds.

Finally, I got the top lock undone and slipped inside, being careful not to land too hard on my heels and alert the tiger. I successfully grabbed the jewels and slipped around the preoccupied cat to the back of the cage, where there was another door I planned to escape through. The lock was simple—slide left and then up. It took a good amount of strength, but it wasn't complicated. So, I slid it slowly to the left and yanked up on the bar, but the metal clanged and rang the steel walls of the cage. The tiger slowly turned her head toward me, her nostrils dripping with snot and her eyes completely black, with no variation between the pupils and the irises. I pushed the door, thinking it would slide open easily, but it didn't move.

We practiced this yesterday and the door opened just fine, so I rammed my shoulder against it once more, but it didn't budge. I looked to Cassius with wide eyes and a thundering heart. Despite his hatred toward me, he made a promise to keep me safe. Surely, he wouldn't go back on his word.

He threw two pieces of meat into the cage and let the bucket spill blood all over the floor to distract the tiger before rushing to my side. He yanked at the door with both arms, but still nothing. Hair fell in his eyes and sweat dripped down his cheek as he pulled on the lock frantically.

Behind me, the audience was silent, unable to differentiate between what was an act and what was real. The tiger stopped smacking her lips and turned to face me. Snarling, she showed her teeth dripping with the blood she had licked up, and bent her head low, preparing to charge me.

"Cassius!" I screamed, with tears forming in my eyes.

His mouth hung open and he looked like he had no idea what to do, but before I knew it, he had reached into the cage and slammed his fist on the lever. His knuckles split open and blood dripped down his fingers, and just as the tiger lunged for me, something clicked and the door sprang open. I jumped out of the cage and slammed the door closed behind me, and then fell into Cassius as he collided with the floor. Sucking air in short little gasps and unable to take a full breath, my whole body shook on Cassius's chest.

"Get up," he whispered. "Put on a big smile."

At this moment, acting for the audience seemed beyond what I was capable of. I never wanted to do this again. I didn't want to let go of Cassius, and I didn't want to stand for another moment. I just wanted to stay there, right there in the sand. But everyone was watching me, counting on me. So, I rolled off him and he grabbed my hand to help me up, and then he lifted my arm to the sky so we could bow together. The audience erupted with cheers, and bodies of all shapes and sizes stood, drowning the room in applause. We had fooled them yet again, and I maintained a big smile for the crowd, wondering when it would all be over.

Cassius's warm fingers grasped the diamonds in my hand. I had gripped them so hard that when he took them from me, their shape was inscribed into my palm. He clasped the diamonds around my neck, and then trailed his fingers down my arm, while I shivered under his touch. The women in the crowd went crazy, cheering with jealous smiles.

The horse riders pushed the cage into the back of the tent, and the Saber Tooth tiger growled again, slamming her body against the cage to try to escape. When the animal was finally contained, we made our final bow and exited the stage. My fellow performers surrounded me, and the room was so chaotic and loud that I couldn't take my eyes off the floor.

"You did amazing, Juniper! Your acting was so believable!" One of the dancers shouted.

"It wasn't an act, you dimwits. Someone find Mr. Monte immediately," Cassius boomed.

"No." I grasped Cassius's arm to stop him, startling him with the gesture. The other performers looked at me worriedly, but I didn't want to ruin their acts. And our act still deserved to be tonight's showstopper, and it wouldn't be if everyone was preoccupied over the mishap with the cage. "We'll deal with that tomorrow."

During the closing ceremony, we all lined up in a single-file line and Cassius watched me like a dog. Once the ceremony was over, I gathered my equipment to make my way back to the train. We all walked together, leaving the maintenance crew and Mr. Monte to tear down the tent. I just wanted to be by myself so I could close my eyes and forget this had ever happened. All I could see was the tiger's long teeth extending toward me and her black eyes swallowing me whole.

Finally, we arrived at the train, and I made a move toward my train car, but the thought of being alone to think about the events of tonight sounded almost worse than being in a crowded room. Just then, I spotted Cassius's hand dripping blood on the floor. It was split from one end to the other and looked bruised around the edges.

I didn't know why he was angry with me, and I didn't need to know. But I needed to thank him for helping me tonight. Without thinking, I grabbed Cassius's free hand and pulled him to his chamber, then slammed the door behind us and pushed him onto the sofa in the corner. I found a bottle of liquor on top of his dresser and a white shirt in his closet.

"What are you doing?" He asked when I popped the bottle cap off with my teeth. "Juniper, wait!"

I poured the liquid over his hand and he groaned, attempting to push me away. His face shook and he clenched his teeth, making it very clear how much pain he was in. I quickly took a seat beside him and tore the shirt in half to wrap it tightly around his hand.

Sighing heavily, he laid his head back on the soft cushion. "That was a perfectly good shirt."

I took a large swig of the amber liquid before Cassius eagerly snatched it from me to guzzle it down. The moonlight shone in through the small window, illuminating his strong jaw and the little freckles across his nose. Suddenly the image of black and white fur flashed in my head, causing my eyes to slam shut. We would figure out what happened in the morning, but right now I just wanted to forget. And then another image entered my mind—the soft touch of Cassius's fingers on my neck.

I opened my eyes then, to see him looking at me in a way I didn't recognize. He had just been so frustrated with me, and now he looked at me so tenderly, like he needed me.

He placed his hand gently on my knee, and I couldn't take my eyes off it. The bones and the veins under his skin made his hand look large and strong. And it was warm. This was different than anything I had ever experienced with Cassius. He had always hidden behind sarcasm and anger, but now it seemed he was letting down his guard.

His touch made me really nervous. What was he doing?

He answered my question when he lifted my chin. His eyes were soft and flicked between mine, once and then twice, as he considered what he was about to do.

My chest rose and fell quickly, and my heart felt like it would pound out of my chest. I shouldn't have wanted this, but I did, and it seemed Cassius did too.

He leaned closer to me and crashed his lips against mine, as my stomach fluttered with a million butterflies and I melted into his touch. He cupped my cheek and warmth spread through my face as his mouth moved slowly, not rough like I would have guessed. He knew exactly what to do, and his lips were so soft and tasted like rum, bitter and cool.

Suddenly I was overcome with guilt. Despite how good it felt kissing Cassius and how much I wanted it, I was seeing Flint. He was probably waiting for me, and I should be loyal to him. Flint had been trustworthy and kind and steady, and Cassius had been none of those things. What was I thinking? I broke away quickly and stood. "This was a mistake," I said as I turned to leave. I glanced back once more to see the sincerity in Cassius's eyes, and my desire and my guilt were replaced with total confusion.

Chapter 20

My stomach growled and my head pounded, but I was so warm I didn't want to move. I'd finally been able to get a few hours rest after being awake most of the night. I couldn't stop thinking about Cassius. Why did he kiss me? Why did I *let* him? Flint would be furious if he ever found out, and I didn't want to hurt him. He meant the world to me. The longer I laid there, tossing and turning, the more I knew I had to do something. I couldn't let what happened last night happen again, and I sure as hell didn't want it to be awkward between me and Cassius. Despite my nerves and the lightheaded feeling that came when I remembered Cassius's lips, I marched down the hallway to Cassius's room. I knocked quickly then opened the door, and he was lying in bed with his arms crossed behind his head.

When he realized it was me, he looked nervous and sat up straight.

I spit out what I wanted to say, figuring honesty was the only option if we wanted to maintain a good working relationship. "I'm worried about what happened last night, and it can't happen again. I'm in a relationship with Flint and you and I are partners. We should be professional."

"Don't even worry about it. It didn't mean anything." Cassius shrugged his bare shoulders and his tan muscles pulled tight. "Besides, I was drunk. I've kissed almost every girl here. Well, except for Josephine and that one girl...I think her name's Denise," he said proudly.

My jaw practically hit the floor. Was he kidding? One, I know he wasn't drunk. The alcohol had long worn off by that point. And two, he had sunk lower than I ever thought possible. Bragging about how many girls he'd kissed made him look like an ass. But rather than stoop to his level, I said, "Perfect. I'm late to meet Flint, so I'll see you at practice later."

Cassius scoffed, "Yeah, have fun with Captain Wonderful," he said as he rolled his eyes and laid back down.

What a perfect response from someone who'd been demoted.

Suddenly someone yelled from down the hall, "Cassius!" Mr. Monte's footsteps grew impatient before he barged in and shouted, "Cassius! I've been looking for Juniper all morning, but I can't-" His eyes bounced between Cassius and me, and a smile spread across his face. "I didn't think you could do it, my boy. Fifteen right? I'll get you the money later." Mr. Monte laughed heartily with a hand over his stomach.

"Excuse me?" I turned around to face Mr. Monte. "Is this some sort of bet about how many women Cassius can sleep with?" I erupted in fury. It was disgusting. Another pitiful thing about Cassius among so many others. "And I didn't even sleep with him!"

"Mmhmm, sure, Miss Rose. It's okay to admit it. Cassius is quite the lady's man." Mr. Monte pulled the covers off Cassius to expose him in nothing but his underpants, riding low on his abdomen and revealing the muscled planes of his torso. "Get up Cassius, I need to talk to you and Juniper immediately."

Cassius rolled over to face Mr. Monte. "Why should I listen to anything you have to say?"

Mr. Monte pinched the bridge of his nose between his thumb and forefinger, "Because this is important, and due to your current position, I think you might want to hear what I have to say. Please, we'll talk about your frustration with me later." Mr. Monte motioned for us to follow him again.

I turned to do so, and Cassius stopped me abruptly to say, "Oh, and another thing...if I ever see you in that room again, I won't hesitate to do everything in my power to run you away from the circus."

"If I'm not wrong, that's what you've been trying to do for months?" I answered, with a great deal of conviction.

"Guilty." Cassius pulled on his pants, and it seemed he had said his piece. But he grabbed my arm harshly and added, "I have the power to make sure it happens."

Memories of last night resurfaced. How could he have been so kind only hours before, and then so awful? But before I could say anything, he brushed past me to lead the way to Mr. Monte's office.

I feared running into Flint, but fortunately I didn't see him. I had no idea what I was going to tell him. I wanted to be truthful about what had happened, but I didn't want to lose him. *That's why you shouldn't have kissed Cassius in the first place,* my mind yelled at me.

"Juniper, did you hear me?" Mr. Monte asked.

"Hmm?" I said as I lifted my head.

"The cage was tampered with shortly before the performance. You see these marks here?" Mr. Monte pointed to a series of light scratches along the dark metal around the lock.

I examined the lock carefully, and I saw them clearly.

Cassius remained still beside me. "How could this have happened?

"I don't know. This person is very sneaky. I instructed Monroe and Valetta to watch your equipment carefully, and according to them, they didn't see anyone approach the cage." Mr. Monte sighed heavily.

I stood and cleared my throat. "I could have died. There has to be something we can do to stop this. Has anything like this ever happened before?"

Mr. Monte looked quickly at Cassius before returning his eyes to me. And Cassius fumbled with his hands, thinking I didn't notice their little exchange. What was this about? Were they hiding something from me?

"No. This is the first incidence. I would try thinking about agitators from Axminster. Maybe someone is angry with you for leaving such a fortunate life and joining a vagabond crowd that dishonors your god and your people?" Cassius quipped.

I nodded, but no one came to mind.

"I have another matter I'd like to discuss. Despite the danger of last night's mishap, you two put on an exquisite show. People are touting your performance as the most unlikely romance of the year. "'Lovers from different sides of the tracks.' That's what the papers are calling you." Mr. Monte spread his arms wide in celebration. "Cassius, the way you put the necklace around Juniper's neck made the public think of you two as quite the item. I want to use this to our advantage, and I will create new performance plans accordingly. Is that clear?" Mr. Monte looked between us.

I glanced at Cassius and responded, "Mr. Monte, I don't think that's a good-"

"Good. Everything is settled then."

When Mr. Monte disappeared from the tent, I looked to the floor. This was a disaster.

Cassius began to walk away without saying a word. "Hey! We're not going to talk about any of this?" I yelled.

He turned around and glared at me, "We're not lovers, Juniper. I'll play into the world's fantasy about you and I. But we? We are not even friends. Is *that* clear?"

I looked at him in disbelief. I didn't want to talk about last night. I wanted to talk about our current predicament and about the person trying to harm me. I thought he would want to help me figure out who was doing this. But it was clear that he was just as spiteful as I thought. I wouldn't be needing his help in the future. "Crystal," I said as I brushed past him.

I found Flint immediately. If Cassius wasn't going to help me, then I needed to tell someone else. I informed Flint of everything that had happened—the letters, the tampering with my equipment, all of it. He listened intently and took everything exceptionally well, despite the fact that I had been withholding it from him. And when I was finished, I sat quietly and waited for him to say something.

He responded with, "I think you should be careful. If this person is inside the circus, then you're not safe anywhere. And until we find who it is, I think it would be better if you avoid going out and making yourself vulnerable."

"But Flint, I can't just put everything on hold. This person hasn't tried to harm me except on the night of a performance. I need to practice!"

"And you will. I'll escort you to practice and to dinner from here on out. But otherwise, you shouldn't be roaming the halls to meet with anyone." Flint stood, closing our conversation.

This was not how I expected him to react. I didn't want this perpetrator to make me feel trapped. I didn't want to have to fear him and hide away. That was exactly what the killer wanted. "But Flint-"

"Juniper. This is the best way I know to protect you."

I sighed. Cassius wouldn't do this. He'd let me wander through a dark forest all by myself. He'd enjoy the thought of me being mauled by a bear, most likely. God, I hated him. But why was I thinking about him now? I came to stand behind Flint and wrapped my arms around him. "I know I've been a little distant lately," I said, as I turned him around and kissed him passionately.

He returned the gesture and placed his hands around my waist. "Where's this coming from?"

"I just missed you, that's all."

Flint smiled and kissed me slowly, but I didn't feel the same fire as when I kissed Cassius. I pushed that thought out of my mind, but I realized that keeping this secret might be harder than I thought.

Mr. Monte...

Juniper's question racked my brain and made me think so long that my hot tea got cold. *Has anything like this ever happened before?* Her voice was stuck in my head as I focused on the portrait of a young woman with flaming red hair. She was dressed in a sparkling blue leotard with green and turquoise feathers extending behind her like a throne. Penelope Plume, the star tightrope walker. Years ago, a similar danger had afflicted the circus. It was never reported in the news and never told to the general public for fear that it would lead to the destruction of the circus. It remained a secret until it destroyed Miss Plume—until it turned the beautiful woman inside out and gnawed at her until she couldn't fathom the idea of living with it any longer.

That's what secrets do. They eat you from the inside out.

Cassius entered the room just then with a bottle of amber liquid, waking me from my thoughts. "I figured you could use something stronger," he said.

"Thank you." I discarded my cup of tea and replaced it with ale. A large sip would help me settle my mind. "I'm sorry I didn't ask you before allowing Juniper to use Penelope's costumes. I know how much Penelope means to you."

Cassius nodded silently, refraining from speaking.

"I don't know what to do," I admitted. "It's happening all over again. Someone is targeting another tightrope walker. But why?" I looked at Cassius for help as he took a seat across from me.

He had entered his own daze, sipping at his drink slowly, "Maybe that's it. Tightrope walkers are being targeted. Since that night five years ago, no one else has been harmed or threatened-"

"Until Juniper Rose arrived," I finished.

The room was silent until Cassius cleared his throat. "I liked seeing Penelope's costume on Juniper. Does that make me a horrible person?"

I looked at Cassius, seeing a young boy instead of the grown man he had become. The boy's legs dangled off the chair, not yet hitting the floor, and his hair was so long that it curled around his ears. When he first sat across from me as a child, that was what I noticed. I told myself we would cut his hair the moment he had settled in, but he refused. Only when he grew to be a teen and the girls started noticing, did he consider cutting it shorter. He was the youngest performer I had ever accepted—six years old to be exact. He was extremely timid and kept to himself, always drawing in a small red journal he kept with him. He never spoke to anyone except me and the horses. I would find him in the stables late at night, having all types of conversations with them. So, he joined the riding team at six, after becoming accustomed to the way of life with the circus. He made friends with all of the boys and became a confident young man, asking often when he could have his first glass of ale. But when I finally let him, he spit it out on the floor.

I smiled, thinking about those times. "Of course not, my boy. It makes you human. It was a fond reminder for all of us to see her costume worn again."

Cassius nodded to himself.

I changed the subject so he wouldn't blame himself anymore. "It could be anyone—someone who is upset about Penelope's demise and wants to ruin the circus by proving it harmful to the performers, or someone who just thinks Juniper deserves it."

"It's bigger than that though," Cassius blurted out. "I think you're right to assume that this person wants to end the circus, once and for all, but because of something personal. They could kill any performer and the circus would be damaged, but they chose Juniper for a reason. It's someone with a personal vendetta against tightrope walkers," Cassius explained. "And we never found the man that hurt Penelope."

Cassius wrung his hands together nervously, and his eyes shifted to the ceiling. My heart broke for this boy I had watched grow up. He used to be so lighthearted and carefree. But ever since Penelope's death, he had been different. He had become angry and turned to alcohol to avoid his problems. And he pushed people away. I couldn't blame him, given the situation, but if there was any chance of getting that exuberant boy back, I would do everything in my power to make it possible. "You think it's the same man?"

"He must have the same motives. And he's using the same threats. I'm sure of it." His voice sounded truly positive for the first time in months. Something had changed in his eyes. He looked determined, even hopeful at that moment. Finding the person that caused Penelope's death could give him the closure he had been needing.

I nodded in affirmation, "Then I'll help you find him."

Cassius smiled. "Here's to finding that bastard and protecting our family."

"I'll toast to that," I agreed, and clanked my glass against his.

Colette...

"I've met someone, mother. Someone kind and honorable," I said softly.

My mother sat on the plush red sofa with her knitting needles in hand and stared out the crystal window in the living room.

"And who is this person you speak of?" My mother didn't take her eyes off the empty yard and spoke with contempt.

"His name is William Lloyd-"

Before I got a chance to explain, my mother interfered. "The police officer?" She laughed heartily, as if she thought I was joking. She would only allow me to marry someone wealthy and that made me furious. William was kind and loving, and although he didn't make very much money, I could say more of him than any of the suitors she had introduced me to.

"Yes. He is very kind, and he has a noble job, don't you think?" I asked her hopefully, folding my hands in my lap. I planned to see him either way, but I wanted her to approve of him.

"I agree. But that doesn't mean he is worthy of your hand. He is middle class, Colette, and you are worth more than that."

"I decide what I'm worth. And William treats me just as well as any nobleman would!" I shouted as tears welled in my eyes. I hadn't felt this way about anyone before. For years, I had been pressured into relationships and engagements by my mother. And for the first time I had chosen someone I was fond of—someone I thought of every night when I closed my eyes and every morning when I opened them. It was exciting, and I was not at all surprised that my mother was doing nothing to support me. For once I just wanted her to be proud of me. I wanted her to allow me to make my own choice, just once!

She put down her needles grudgingly. "Colette, my mind will never change. My parents wed me to a wealthy man, and I was very fortunate to enjoy a life of ease. And I'll do the same for you because I love you. I'm only trying to ensure your future."

"And look where that got you." My mother's eyes met mine and her cheeks turned a hot red. "Where is Father? Where is he? Did he love you enough to stay?"

"That is enough." My mother looked me dead in the eyes.

I had never talked of their relationship because I knew it would upset her, but right now I was grasping to convince her that William was the best thing for me. "I'm an adult. And I appreciate your input, but I will be the one to decide what makes me happy from now on. And if that means marrying a man who doesn't have buckets of money, and living a modest life, then that's what I will do." I walked away before she could argue. Juniper was right to set out on her own. And it was time I did the same.

Flint grabbed my hand tightly and walked beside me all the way to the tent. He kept his eyes peeled and moved rather quickly, and when we entered the tent, he looked around as if something would jump out at any moment, before determining that I was safe. A bit unnecessary, if you asked me.

Cassius popped out of the back after cleaning up a pile of manure in the giraffe cage. He wiped his hands on his dirt-stained breeches and looked at us oddly. "You've got a professional escort now?"

"Call me what you want—it's just for her protection." Flint puffed out his chest and wrapped his arm around my waist to pull me close.

"I was thinking of maybe calling in an entourage of rhinos to escort her from dinner to bed. What do you think?" Cassius's face remained straight, despite his joke.

"Very funny, Cassius." Flint turned his attention to me and pecked me lightly on the cheek. "I'll see you at six."

"Bye," I whispered and kissed him back quickly before walking over to Cassius in shame. It was embarrassing that I had to be escorted everywhere. I felt helpless. But I was eager to practice, so I pulled off my coat to reveal the plain tan leotard I had chosen for today.

"All queens have entourages—don't be embarrassed," Cassius laughed.

"Stop it." I shook my head, but smiled nonetheless. It was hard to look at Cassius the same way after what had happened last night. My anger toward him was the same, if not increased, but my mind quickly shifted to the memory of his hand on my cheek rather than the harshness of his words.

Cassius secured a bucket of feed in the koala cage before turning to me. "I spoke with Mr. Monte. We think the person threatening was also involved in Penelope's death."

"The same man?" I asked with curiosity. Stopping this menace would take a great weight off my shoulders.

"We don't know. We never found the man that hurt Penelope." He looked to the floor worriedly. I think Cassius had a deep connection to Penelope. He had fervently helped me with the killer's letters, and then he erupted in anger over my appearance in Penelope's chamber. She must have meant a great deal to him. Maybe she had been his lover? The thought made me more jealous than I wanted to admit. Did he still think of her often?

"What do you mean hurt? Wasn't she murdered?" I stepped closer and looked under his brows.

"Not exactly," he mumbled, while his eyes darted around the room.

"Then what happened?" I pushed.

"It's not important. What matters is that the same man might be at it again," he said, attempting to change the subject.

Why was he keeping this from me? I felt like I was always on the outside when it came to the history of the circus. Although I hadn't been there to experience it, I still deserved to know what happened. "Cassius, it is important. I need to know what happened to her if I am to understand the perpetrator's motives," I argued. Disagreement was a constant with Cassius, and the back and forth was exhausting.

"Just let it go, Juniper. You wouldn't understand," Cassius said in a demeaning way, shaking his head.

"Why? Is it because I'm not from *your* world?" I fired my anger from that morning and the night before at him. First, Cassius was furious that I wore Penelope's costume, and then he decided to kiss me but promised we would never be friends. And now this? I didn't understand.

"That's exactly why!" He screamed. "You weren't here when it happened, Juniper. You act like you're a part of our world, but you know nothing of what we all had to go through to get here." His eyes looked sad, as if pleading with me to finally let this go.

I bit the inside of my cheek. "Then tell me! All I want to do is understand. I want to be a part of your world, but you're not allowing me to, Cassius. Help me understand."

All of the sadness drained out of his face, and what remained was a cocky, self-pretentiousness. I could hear his thoughts and I imagined he was thinking something like, *you don't deserve my help.*

My blood boiled. He couldn't get angry at me for not understanding their lives if he wouldn't help me to. "You're a selfish bastard, you know that? And you do nothing for anyone but yourself. It's pitiful. At least I was daring enough to come here on my own, knowing full well that I would be treated differently. Coming from a hard background must have been difficult, but-"

"Don't assume you know what it's like to be me, Juniper. I had to work hard to find my way in this world. It wasn't served to me on a silver platter," he hissed, waving an arm at me emphatically.

"I'm not my family, Cassius. I ran away from that world to come here. I've risked everything!"

"You should listen to your mother, *Prune*."

I'd only heard that name from my mother's mouth, and every time she said it, it dug deeper into my heart. I hated that name and I never wanted to hear it again. It reminded me of the indulgence of the wealthy. But from Cassius, it hurt ten times worse. I wanted to cry and slap him, but I couldn't move. I just stood there and listened to him insult me.

"You are an attraction in Axminster. The famous darling of the church, rising in the ranks of the Rose family. I've done my research." He squinted at me in disdain. "What could be better than that?"

My lips quivered. "Don't assume you know what it's like to be me." I snatched my coat off the bench and trudged toward the door. I couldn't do this today. I couldn't even stand to look at him.

On the verge of tears, I had one last question for him. I turned around slowly and spoke with a quivering voice, "Where did you hear that name?"

"Mr. Monte wanted clues from the first threatening letter, so he asked me to retrieve it. While I was doing so, I found that lovely letter from your mother. I have no idea what Prune means, but I have to admit, it's kind of catchy." He laughed like it meant nothing. "How interesting that you keep in touch with her."

A tear fell down my cheek, and I took in short gasps of air before turning to go. I wanted to lash out at him and make him take back all the hurtful things he had said, but instead I turned around and spat, "I feel sorry for you, Cassius. I don't know what happened five years ago, and I don't know how you got here. But I think you were right."

He squinted in confusion and his leg jerked, like he wanted to take a step forward. I almost thought he might apologize.

But rather than wait and see, I finished, "It's better if we're not friends."

I sipped slowly on a glass of sweet plum wine. I think if I were to return home to a cup of my mother's famous lemon tea, I would hate it. It would be flavorless now. I laid on the floor across from Charlotte, with her blonde curls splayed next to my head. She almost passed out, she was so tired. All of us had been working extremely hard. Having performances back to back, week after week, was exhausting. Our next performance in Eanverness was in a few weeks, which gave us more downtime than usual. But the most pressing matter on my mind was the mystery of Penelope Plume. My first night here, I spotted Charlotte on Cassius's lap. Maybe she knew more about what had happened to Penelope.

"You know Cassius pretty well, right?" I asked quietly.

"If you mean I slept with him, then yes," she retorted.

Her smile was kind and bright, and it lit up the entire room. If I had to pair Cassius with anyone, it would be her. She was beautiful and the two of them were both equally rowdy. "Are you two-"

"God, no." She hiccupped, which made her laugh. "He's a fine man, but I don't commit myself to anyone and neither does he. Cassius has slept with practically every girl here. I guess we all share a part of the lion tamer."

I tried not to think about any of the innocent young dancers with such a vile boy. I wasn't surprised because I knew this to be true from the beginning, but a part of me wished it wasn't.

To change the conversation to something less vulgar, I asked, "What happened to Penelope?"

The air in the room shifted, and the light was dimmer. Charlotte's face fell and her eyes became sad. And the walls and the floors stopped creaking, as if they were waiting for an answer to my question as well.

Charlotte sat up and picked at her fingernails before she answered quietly, "Well, you know Penelope is Cassius's sister, right?"

All of the wind was knocked out of my lungs. His sister? I had no idea they were related. If I ever lost Colette, I don't know how I would go on. She's everything to me, and without her I would be lost.

"See, Cassius was six when he arrived at the circus—the youngest ever to be taken in. And his sister was only a few years older. She cared for him as a boy and brought him here, and after years of training, they became stars. Cassius was shy around the other performers for a long while, and he stuck close to her side. They did everything together, and when they grew older, Cassius was appointed as lion tamer and Penelope was asked to be the tightrope walker." Charlotte paused to look over to me.

I almost yelled at her to continue because I was so eager to hear about what happened. Cassius was only six? What had happened to his parents? His schooling? Where had he lived?

Charlotte continued, "Penelope was the most famous woman in the land. She was beautiful beyond measure—bright red hair, glistening blue eyes, and the skin of an angel. She was perfect. And she was determined. On the night of the biggest performance of her life, when a showman named Abelard Chevis came to watch her in hopes of recruiting her for Culchester's renowned theater, she fell. The world thought it was an accident, but we knew better. Penelope was flawless on the tightrope, and if she occasionally wobbled, she always knew just how to correct herself. And as you know, a tightrope walker can't fall perfectly. But Penelope did. She fell at exactly the right time, in exactly the right position. Her neck hit the floor and it snapped, and she died within seconds." Charlotte's eyes welled with tears, and I wondered if they had been close friends.

I couldn't imagine witnessing something so horrific, and I hoped nothing that terrible would ever happen to me.

"Her neck was mangled, and when her body was examined in the morgue, the diener found something strange—marks along her hips and on her inner thighs. They expected it was from a sexual assault." Her blue eyes brightened and turned red. "Penelope had been raped, and because of that dreadful thing, we believe she fell on purpose. We had all noticed her being different in the weeks before her last performance. She was distant, almost unresponsive. And she looked sick, like a ghost, but we had no idea how serious it really was. So, on the night of her death, we were all shocked."

I took a moment to process the information. "I'm so sorry." I looked away as tears fell down Charlotte's face. I had been so selfish to think of myself this whole time and not acknowledge that something truly terrible had happened to all of my friends.

"She was a close friend of mine. Everyone in the circus mourned her for months," Charlotte said, as she ran a hand across her nose. "Cassius was a disaster. Watching his sister die was too much for him to handle, so he turned to the rum and the sex. He grew mean and distant and spent the days practicing in his tent and wasted the nights with girls of all kinds. Girls in the circus, girls he found in the city, it didn't matter. He used them to cope. But after many months, and almost killing himself from being so miserably drunk, he finally started putting himself together for the sake of Penelope's memory. He drank less and distanced himself from all the girls. He busied himself making the circus a safe place, and spent endless hours with Mr. Monte planning exciting performances. But now that the menace is back, I'm worried what will become of him. Either he'll choose to help you and the future of our show, or he'll give into fear and return to his old ways."

There were so many things I wished I had done differently. I wished I hadn't been so hard on Cassius. I wished I had considered the circus's past rather than being so eager to fit in. The circus had memories, good and bad, that I might never understand. "Thank you Charlotte. There's nothing I can say, except I'm sorry this happened to such a wonderful lady, and I'm sorry it caused you all such pain. Now, if you'll excuse me, there's something I need to do."

Charlotte nodded her head and dried her eyes.

I retreated from the room and rushed toward the tent. I was overcome with sadness and guilt about Cassius, and I needed to see him. I quickly apologized when I brushed past some bystanders in the hall before jumping off the train. It was so cold, but I had to get rid of this overwhelming ache in my body. When I made it into the tent, Cassius was nowhere to be found.

I searched all over, and finally he came out from behind the cages. He wore a frown on his face, and he was messing with a metal contraption to fix around the tigers' paws for clipping their claws. His dark circles, the permanent furrow in his brow, and the slow blink of his eyes all added to my sadness for him. He chucked the thing to the floor angrily and ran his hands through his hair, until his eyes moved around the room to meet mine.

I walked over to him and it looked as though he was going to say something, but I silenced him by wrapping my arms tightly around his neck and nuzzling my head between his shoulder and his neck.

His warmth radiated into my cheek and the closeness of our bodies made my stomach jump. He didn't move or say a thing, and his arms were secured at his sides.

"I'm sorry," I whispered, as I found my voice. "Charlotte told me what happened to Penelope, and I'm so sorry."

Cassius pulled me away and gripped my shoulders tightly. His eyes were stern and his lips were pinched, and he shook his head profusely and said, "Don't pity me."

He became mean and distant. Charlotte's words replayed in my head. He was trying to push me away, and I couldn't let him do that. He needed to know that he was important. "What I feel for you is far from pity. I *appreciate* you, Cassius." I smiled lightly.

His brows furrowed even further, but as much as he tried to hide it, a small smile lifted at the corners of his mouth.

"You were right." I tipped my head forward to glance at my feet, having a particularly hard time acknowledging the fact. "I didn't appreciate the work you all did to get here and the challenges you faced. You? This group of people? You are the strongest people I've ever known."

Cassius looked deep into my eyes and his smile grew. He leaned his head from right to left and rolled his eyes. "You were right as well. As much as I detest you, I'm-" Cassius paused to clear his throat. "I'm jealous. Not of the overprotective mother you have or the religion you were forced into, or of that pretty boy of yours. But of the fortune you were given. I won't lecture you on my past, but I wish I could have had even a fraction of what you had. A home. A warm plate of food on the table. Shoes on my feet." Cassius sighed.

I watched the toughness seep back into him as the seconds passed. I wanted him to learn that it was okay to be vulnerable sometimes. It didn't make him any less strong. I was proud of him because I knew it took great strength for him to talk about this, let alone admit he was wrong.

"That is not an excuse for the way I treated you, and I apologize."

"Thank you." After a moment of silence during which the tension between us grew, I reached over and ruffled his hair.

"Don't think we're friends now," he said, as he pointed an accusing finger at me.

"I wouldn't dare," I answered, as I stripped my coat off. "Let's get to work."

Chapter 21

"No!" Mr. Monte erupted. "Where is the tension? Where is the desire? Run it again!" He threw his arms into the air emphatically.

Cassius lifted my back after performing a dip and stars danced in my vision. I was tired and I didn't want to repeat the same thing over and over. I couldn't do what Mr. Monte was asking me. Cassius was a decently attractive human being, I'd give him that. He was determined, wild, and unchangingly stubborn. When we argued, he somehow pulled me back in with his harsh words and cocky attitude. I hated it, but it could be addicting sometimes. But now that we were on good terms with one another, we were afraid to fight or do anything reckless that we'd regret. That made this practice completely useless because we wanted this performance to be full of desire, but we were barely able to look each other in the eyes.

We ran the set again and I tried to portray a woman in love. I grabbed Cassius's shirt hard in my hands and pulled him closer to me, but it was strange with his lips so close to mine.

"Stop! Stop!" Mr. Monte yelled. He threw his script down and walked over to us. "Cassius, you look disinterested. Juniper, you look bored." He looked quickly around the room, weighing his options, before unbuttoning his vest and rolling up his sleeves. "May I use you as an example, Juniper?"

I nodded, despite my nervousness. This close, I feared that Mr. Monte would notice my struggle to perform even the smallest task because of my injury. He grabbed my right hand, and the first scene began with a gentle waltz. I winced when Mr. Monte lifted my right arm too high, but he didn't seem to notice. I swung out toward the audience, and he pulled me back into his chest, then grabbed my knee and lifted it up to his waist. Being this close to him was rather uncomfortable, but I reminded myself that it was only for teaching purposes.

"Cassius, it is all about you two knowing one another. You both need to learn each other's bodies so you can use that knowledge in the performance. Watch yourselves in a mirror, and know how close you can get...where it feels most comfortable. Touch, grab, and look like you're having fun." Mr. Monte flicked his wrist to the corner of the tent where Wilman was stationed.

Wilman quickly dragged over a large mirror on wheels, positioning it in front of us.

"Mr. Monte, don't you think it's a little unprofessional to-" I stuttered with my words, before adding, "learn each other's bodies in the way you suggest?"

"Everyone can see the attraction between you two," Mr. Monte said, while Wilman nodded along.

I raised my eyebrows, surprised by his candor.

Cassius cleared his throat and clapped his hand on Mr. Monte's back. "We'll get right on it, Sir."

Mr. Monte disappeared to watch the performers in another tent.

I looked at myself in the mirror, dressed in a black diamond leotard with an A-line skirt. One side of the skirt dipped to my calf and the other barely reached past my hip. Cassius was dressed in a dashing black vest that fit well over his abdomen, and a simple cream colored poet's shirt rolled up to his elbows, accentuating the veins in his strong forearms. He stepped behind me and grabbed my waist lightly, as I took a deep breath and raised my left arm to caress his face. Drawing my hand down his jaw, I turned my head gently to the side, as his curls tickled my forehead and made me smile. I stepped forward and let him guide me through an elegant dance taught to us by the dancers. He brought my arm over my head to twirl me, and I spun three times, as I watched my short curls bounce just above my shoulders in the mirror.

He grabbed my waist tighter this time to stop my momentum, and I aligned my body beside his and jumped. As I bent my knees, Cassius kneeled slightly to lift me onto his hip, and I grabbed his hair between my fingers while he slowly lowered me in front of him.

The dancers had taught us a flip called the Tunnel Inversion. Cassius stood behind me and reached around to grab my stomach, as I prepared to tuck my knees and kick into the air so he could lift me over his head. I slid down his shoulder, and he spun me around and around until I was so dizzy I couldn't see. When we finally stopped spinning, I gripped his head in both of my hands, and the only sound in the room was our breathing, rough and quick. A glimpse of us in the mirror showed Cassius's face turned to mine with his mouth at my throat, and his hand gripping the bottom of my skirt and dragging it up to my hip.

"Juniper!"

My name came from across the tent, and I turned quickly to see who it was.

"It's time to go." Flint stood at the other end of the tent with his hand tucked tightly into his breeches. I had a feeling we would be talking about this tonight.

Cassius stepped back quickly and ran his hands through his hair while I gathered my things.

The whole night Flint lectured me on how what Mr. Monte was making me do was unethical and inappropriate. I sat across from Flint, thinking back to the image of Cassius and me in the mirror, and I wished I was there now, practicing into the late hours of the night. I was touched by his story, and everything about him seemed to make a little more sense now. Maybe that's why I had this strange new desire to be around him.

"Did you hear what I said?" Flint asked angrily.

I turned to him with my mouth agape. "No. I don't like talking about this, quite honestly. Let's grab a drink instead." I grabbed his hand, not giving him the option, and he complained all the way to the dining hall. I snatched us several ales, and after his third drink, he was more relaxed. We mingled with the flamethrowers for about an hour, but all of my attention turned to Cassius when he walked into the room. He unbuttoned his vest and threw it on an empty seat at the bar, and I slipped away when Flint started to argue with a man named Spruce, knowing he wouldn't notice my absence.

I took a seat next to Cassius while he took a sip from a wooden mug of ale.

He turned to me abruptly and asked, "Is he always going to be like this?" Cassius flicked his head toward Flint who had stood up to Spruce, pushing back his shoulders.

"He's just trying to protect me," I answered in embarrassment.

"That wasn't the question I asked."

I met Cassius's hard eyes and continued with more confidence. "Yes. Unless I find a way to convince him that I'm safe." Cassius stared at me for an uncomfortable amount of time, which gave me a chance to voice something that had been confusing me. "Why does the perpetrator only attack in public? He's had ample opportunity to kill me otherwise."

Cassius popped a peanut into his mouth and spoke while he crunched down on the hard shell. "Because I think he wants everyone to see it happen. He wants the spectators to know what it feels like to lose someone. This is personal for him and I'm guessing he lost someone in a similar way. Maybe he wants the crowd to see what he saw and feel what he felt." Cassius looked down at his hands.

I trusted Cassius because he had thought for years about the man who killed his sister and how to stop it from happening again.

"So, he's not going to strike in the train, or in the dining hall, or out in the field?" I questioned.

"Not unless there's a crowd watching."

His words made my stomach drop. When everyone was watching—when the stakes were highest—I would be in the most danger. How could I perform with confidence knowing that? I was comforted by Cassius's honesty, but I did wish he would say something to make the situation less terrifying. But that was stupid. Cassius wasn't going to tell me half the truth.

That night when I informed Flint of Cassius's hypothesis, he fired back at me by saying, "Cassius doesn't know what he's even talking about."

"I think Cassius knows the most about what he's talking about!" I yelled, frustrated with Flint's belligerence. "This is my life we're talking about, and I'm choosing to trust Cassius. I can't live in fear, Flint. That's what this man wants. And I can't continue to be coddled every day."

"Well, you'll have to live with it as long as I'm in your life. I'm just trying to help you-"

"I know," I cut him off.

Flint scooped me into a hug, not knowing I didn't have the desire to be close to him at this moment. "I'll see you in the morning," he said, and left without delay, sensing I didn't want him to stay.

I lied awake in bed all night, flustered with my decisions. Flint was kind and he was only trying to protect me. But every time I saw him standing at my door, or at the opening of the tent, I was reminded that I was being watched. And that gave me as much anxiety as knowing there was a killer wandering in my midst. I believed I wouldn't be harmed in the practice settings because that didn't fit the killer's agenda. But on the other hand, I felt guilty, like I had to allow Flint to do this because I kissed Cassius. And that wasn't fair to either of us.

I was so conflicted, but the sun rose before I had time to make a decision about what would be best, so I got dressed quickly, anticipating a full day of training.

I had decided not to be angry with Flint when he arrived at my door. He slung his warm arm around me, and I melted into his side. Flint was good for me. He was.

The perpetrator…

I rushed down the hall, sharing smiles with the many performers. I had an idea—one that would bring all of this to an end. Despite my influence with this establishment, I would need help from an outside source. So, I wrote to her.

> **MADAME DIANA,**
> **CONTACT YOUR SOURCE. IF YOU REALLY WANT TO END THE CIRCUS, YOU HAVE THE POWER TO DO SO. WE CAN BOTH GET WHAT WE WANT. I'LL SEE YOU ON THE 3rd OF FEBRUARY IN AXMINSTER. IT WILL ALL BE OVER BY THEN IF YOU COME PREPARED.**
> **SINCERELY,**
> **YOUR FRIEND**

At the next performance, I intended to accomplish the demise of Juniper Rose. But if I didn't manage that, then my affiliate could help me destroy the circus once and for all in Axminster.

Cassius puffed out his cheeks and his face turned red, as I tightened my core and extended my arms, attempting to make my body as straight as a board. He lifted me above his head, but his arms shook and he let go, sending me to the floor. I landed in front of him, but he held out a hand for me to grab so I didn't hurt myself.

"Keep your core tight, Cas!" Charlotte yelled with her arms clenched nervously in front of her chest.

Cassius groaned and shook out his arms. We had been practicing for two hours, and we were exhausted. We couldn't do this much longer without hurting one another, and as Cassius lifted me again, his elbow snapped.

I yelped and fell right over his head, attempting to turn my body so I would land on my left side, but instead falling on my injured shoulder.

"J, are you okay?" Cassius kneeled by my side at once. "I'm sorry, I tried to hold it, but I couldn't."

I rolled over and grasped my arm, while I bit the inside of my cheek in pain.

"Get me the doctor!" Mr. Monte shouted, running over to the group of dancers.

This was so embarrassing. "It's fine!" I yelled. "I'm fine. This was bound to happen." I stood up despite the fogginess in my head and the urge to throw up my breakfast.

"Cassius, maybe you can go over it again with the dancers. I think it's time we get this arm checked out." Mr. Monte grabbed my elbow and led me to the exit, despite my protesting. There's no way I was getting out of this, but I was afraid of the results.

And, as I expected, when the doctor examined my shoulder, his face sank. "The good news is that the bones in your shoulder are healing, despite your unwillingness to wear your sling." He raised a disappointing eyebrow at me, and I wanted to sink into the velvet sofa.

Monroe entered the room then, tying up his tousled hair. "Sorry I'm late. Continue." He nodded his head at the doctor. Monroe was a part of every important meeting Mr. Monte attended because he was in charge of the finances for the circus.

"But you're overworking yourself and that's causing the ligaments around the bone to tear. "The glenohumeral ligaments are the main source of stability for your shoulder. And since you're overworking your arm, they've been damaged. If you hope to get back on the tightrope, then you need to stop moving your arm completely for the next two weeks."

Mr. Monte spoke for me, "Doctor, we have a performance in two weeks. She needs to practice. Is there any device that will hold her arm in place so she can do that?"

"We can put her in another sling and tape it so it's more secure. But Juniper, you have to promise to be wise with your body. If you're not, it will put you at risk for permanent damage."

I nodded my head vigorously, like a small child. "I promise, Sir. I'll be careful."

He marked something on my chart before securing a white bandage around my shoulder and forearm. This sling was much tighter than the previous one, and my right hand now rested on top of my left shoulder, securing my right arm tight to my chest. It would be impossible to practice in, but it was better than being condemned to the medical wing for a week so they could watch my every move.

"Thank you." I exited into the hall with Mr. Monte and Monroe. Sighing, I said, "That was easy."

"There's a cost for everything, Miss Rose," Mr. Monte said, in an exhausted tone.

"What do you mean?"

"Our income is in short supply. It's already troublesome enough to pay for our arenas, and the tears in our ropes or the cracks in our cages, but now I have to figure out a way to pay the doctor as well."

I didn't realize, but of course the doctor would need to be paid. "I'm so sorry I was careless before. I'll take a week off and rest if that's what we need." The last thing I wanted was to make this job harder for Mr. Monte. He was under enough stress as it was, trying to create a show-stopping theme to finish our last four performances.

"Thank you, my dear. I appreciate that," Mr. Monte said, but his smile didn't reach his eyes, which made me sad.

"I'll be in my office working out the cost. Maybe you'd like to help, Miss Rose?" Monroe gestured to me as he opened the door to his office.

"Sure," I agreed. If I could learn more about the circus's finances, maybe I could make Mr. Monte's job less stressful. Monroe's office was tidy to say the least. His desk was cleared of any stray papers, every surface looked like it had been wiped clean, and every pen and pencil was straightened to perfection.

When he noticed that I was staring, he laughed and said, "I'm a bit obsessive." He took a seat in his large leather chair and riffled through the drawers in his desk. "You can start by looking through this stack of papers."

Monroe slammed the large stack on the desk, making me jump. "What exactly am I looking for?"

"This stack includes finance sheets for every expense we've had recently. I need help organizing them so I can figure our total expenses for this month. And while we're at it, we need to find the one that details the equipment we used shortly after your fall."

"Okay." I flipped through page after page of expenses with too many numbers to make sense of, but I was glad to be of some help. I flipped through several pages listing costs associated with the importation of ale and food, and suddenly I came upon a $500 receipt. This receipt stuck out to me because it was a large amount of money, with no detail, except that it was a direct check to account #18980345 from account #5178402. There were no names provided, so perhaps those involved in this transaction wanted to remain anonymous. Looking again at the date, I realized that it was the day before I fell from the silks.

"What's this?" I asked as I showed the paper to Monroe, and he quickly snatched it away.

"Oh, that's nothing. It's just from one of our regular supporters."

That check was sent *to* someone outside the circus. And by the red heat in Monroe's face, I had a feeling he wasn't telling the truth. I decided to let it go for now and continue to help him get organized.

"Thank you," he said as he began calculating the totals. His ability to work well with numbers reminded me of Flint, and I smiled. I looked forward to watching him scrawl down numbers on a page again. We hadn't had the time for that in weeks.

"How does all of this work?" I asked curiously, taking a seat across from Monroe.

His tongue darted out of his mouth, and he licked his lips incessantly while he scribbled numbers in the log.

He took a break from his calculating to answer me. "There are five categories the circus's finances are divided into: NOURISHMENT covers food and drink for the performers and the animals; ATTIRE covers all costumes and grooming; TRANSPORT covers the cost of coal to fuel our train; SPACE covers the cost of the performance arenas in each kingdom; and PERSONAL covers the salaries paid to the performers."

"Wait," I said as I held up my hand to silence him. "We get paid?" The thought hadn't crossed my mind.

"Yes. A very small amount, but enough to provide something for your future if you decide to leave the circus," Monroe answered as he flicked a pencil between his fingers.

"I never knew how much work it took to make everything go to plan," I admitted, standing near where he had set the stack of papers. I spotted the corner of that mysterious receipt poking out.

"People rarely do," he smiled. "That's something I hope to be recognized for one day—the work it takes to even finance this band of vagabonds, as the rich call us. But it's nothing compared to the dangers the performers face every day." Monroe's eyes suddenly turned dark. "They risk their lives performing in the circus. They give up everything, only to please a crowd of uppity noblemen."

He was beginning to sound like Cassius.

While he stared at the finance log in front of him, deep in thought, I slipped my hand into the stack of papers to grab the receipt and tuck it under my sling.

At that moment, Monroe shook his head. "Sorry for my morose attitude. A lot of work goes into making this show happen, and that's not even to mention the hard work you all do every day. Don't push yourself too hard, for all of our sakes."

I nodded my thanks. The room became unbearably hot as he continued to stare at me. Monroe was an odd man. He rarely noticed personal space or social cues, but I don't believe he meant to make people uncomfortable.

I took the end of his comments as my cue to exit the room, and my heart was beating quickly thinking about what I'd just done. I closed the door and bounded toward my room. I had no idea what this receipt meant or why I thought it was important, but something told me that it was.

Chapter 22

Eanverness—December 19th—L'Acre du Grand Ours...
When the dancers kicked their legs, they sent a plume of sand into the air. A herd of horses trotted into the arena with a male horse rider squatting on top of them. While the horse ran at a slow pace, the man stood to his full height atop the lead stag and opened his arms to the crowd, and a surge of voices cried out their approval. The group of horses, led by Flint, filed into a V-formation at the front of the stage. They sat like guards while three flamethrowers descended from the ceiling on long ropes, landing lightly on their toes with their arms stretched out wide to steady themselves. They all ran to grab a log of wood from the fire pit in the center of the room, while a team of young boys emerged from behind the tent with snare drums strapped around their necks. They beat a slow rhythm with their faces turned toward the floor and hoods covering their eyes. The flamethrowers launched swords of fire into the air, mesmerizing the crowd, before catching them in sync at the very moment the light vanished from the room.

Curious voices whispered in the crowd, and all that remained were three torches in a sea of darkness. As the flamethrowers brought the tip of the flame to their mouths, they spat out a plume of fire aimed at the fire pit in the middle of the tent. The blaze erupted immediately and the flames danced in their eyes as the crowd awaited my entrance.

I took Cassius's hand and breathed deeply. Sometime during this performance, my life would be threatened. Fire danced in the sand, hooves beat dramatically, and ropes hung from the sky. Which method would he choose tonight? A trip wire? A trap door?

"Look at me," Cassius said softly while the sound of the drums diminished.

The silence in the room grew to the point that I felt I would drown in it, and I could barely see Cassius in the dark, except for his glistening caramel eyes.

He squeezed my hand. "You're going to be fine."

His words sent hope to my heart, but I wondered if he really believed that. Whether or not he spoke the truth, I didn't have time to question the fate of this evening. He pulled the veil over my eyes and gave a small nod.

I swallowed my fear when he tore away the folds of the tent. I sauntered to the platform in the middle of the room to stand before a tall man in a fine suit, and the fire surged as the crowd witnessed me join him in an elegant evening gown. It was covered with golden flowers and bright yellow lace, and it had short frilly sleeves and a tight corset that made it hard to breathe. The gentleman across from me, formerly known as Gus, the magician, now played the role of my suitor in a rich kingdom. He wore a black suit with a gold vest and matching cravat, and the gold buttons traveling down his waistcoat glimmered in the fire before him.

The man kneeled gently on his knee, displaying a small leather box containing a ring with a diamond the size of a coin. I brought my hand to my mouth to feign surprise, just as the audience gasped when another character entered the scene—Cassius, dressed in black leather with a silver cane and a suede top hat. His hair curled devilishly in front of his eyes, which were lined with black charcoal and purple eyeshadow to make him look sick and threatening. He looked sunken and dark, and his approach was confident and strong. I turned away from my suitor toward the rebel approaching us, as he stopped in his tracks and removed his top hat, placing it over his heart solemnly. The darkness over his eyes faded and was replaced by a sense of understanding.

I took a step forward and reached out toward the rebel, causing my suitor to grab me by the waist and pull me back.

The audience leaned closer, wondering which man I would choose.

Using my good arm, I elbowed my suitor in the stomach and he fell to the ground. The crowd cheered when I ran to Cassius, but as soon as it appeared I was safe, my suitor reached up from the ground and grasped the side of my dress. A false seam gave way and my dress ripped from my armpit to the floor. It was designed to tear easily, and the crowd roared when I stepped out of the expensive fabric in a black leather leotard. The shiny texture ran high on my hips and dipped low in front to accentuate my chest. Now, I matched my rebel.

This story had special meaning to me because it represented a girl who was trapped by modesty in her old life and destined to marry a man she didn't love. By running away with someone she truly cared about, she left her wealth behind, but it was replaced by hope for her future. When I ran away to the circus, I discovered who I was truly meant to be. I was never meant to live in Axminster in a large house with fancy curtains and rugs made of golden fabric. I was never meant to have servants obey my every command. I was meant for more than that, and despite the proposal my mother had arranged for me, I had made my decision.

I ran into Cassius's arms and he held me tightly to his chest. I breathed in his strong scent, and when I turned to the crowd, there was a new fire in my eyes. Looking down at Gus, I knew I would never stoop so low as to accept Joseph Young's hand.

After a quick intermission, the story of Cassius and I resumed, this time with more heat. A slow song played with the constant beat of a bass drum, as Cassius grabbed my hips and spun me toward the crowd. I lifted my arm to the sky, and he reached up to grip my fingertips and spin me around. Suddenly, my body sank into the splits, and I pushed my left leg back so I could lay on my stomach, and then kicked my legs like a little girl and rested my head on my hand. I had to be extra careful with my arm in a sling, paying close attention to not put too much pressure on my injury. When I rolled onto my back, Cassius's face appeared above me. He reached out to pull me up, and he smiled when I grabbed his hand, but instead of standing, I pulled him down with me. The women giggled and I spotted a man prod his wife's side playfully, letting us know our story was understood.

Cassius's face was close now, and his eyes darted between mine as we wiggled in the sand, sinking lower. We rolled over and I sat up and trailed my hands down his chest, all the way to his belt. He bucked his hips and his eyes went wide when he looked at the crowd. We received a *hoot* from a man in the audience, and I giggled and rolled off of Cassius to grab a prop that laid nearby.

The drum beat faster and I turned toward the crowd with an umbrella in hand, spinning it as I moved my hips toward Cassius. He grabbed my waist and turned me around to tangle his hands in my hair. The longer my back was turned to him, the more the audience protested, eager to see if the "lovers from different worlds" would finally kiss. Finally, he spun me back around to face him and trailed his hands down further, and the very moment he grasped my bum, I popped up my umbrella to hide his hands. By this point, the crowd had become furious, and I giggled when Cassius took the umbrella from my hands so the crowd could see, and their fury gave way to applause.

The song grew faster and faster, and when Cassius grabbed my waist, I hooked my good arm around his neck, bent my knees, and turned my legs to the side while jumping up. He bounced me from hip to hip and I tried to use my momentum to help him.

He set me down and spun me dramatically. With the arches of my feet firmly together, I spun as quickly as I could with my arm tucked into my chest. As I approached the fire pit in the middle of the tent, and I stopped moving and the room stopped spinning, I realized how close I was to the fire. Just then, the flames shot out at me. It looked like there was liquid falling from the ceiling and I wondered if this could be gasoline, used by the killer to make the fire surge. I jumped back and clenched my arm in pain when I realized I had been burned.

At that moment, one of the sandbags used to weigh down the ropes dropped from the sky and landed with a thud behind me, almost crushing me. As I moved to avoid it, I jumped toward the fire and the flames singed me again. When I pulled my arm in to examine it, there were long red burns reaching halfway up my forearm. The room had become so hot, and I tried to put on a smile and keep going, but the stinging in my arm was excruciating.

Finally, Cassius ran over to me and pulled me away from the pit.

"We have to finish this early," I whispered in Cassius's ear when he pulled me close. I hooked my calf around his knee, and he dipped me in a low bow.

His eyes scanned the room as he quickly tried to determine a jaw-dropping end to our performance. He turned me to the crowd and when I spun back into his chest, he dipped me low, and his mouth was an inch from my own.

Suddenly he asked, "Do you trust me?"

Despite being somewhat unsure if I did, I whispered, "yes."

And before I knew it, he had crashed his lips on mine. And the crowd went wild. The pain in my arm subsided when we kissed, and I grabbed onto his shoulders tightly, memorizing the feeling of his warm hands around my waist. The sound in the room diminished when I felt his smooth lips, and we stayed in that moment for what seemed like an hour, almost forgetting there was a crowd at all. When he pulled me up, I smiled and reminded myself it was almost over. Together we bowed and the room tilted, and I knew if I didn't get out of here, I would fall over where I stood.

Finally, Cassius grabbed my hand and ushered me to the exit quickly. Once we were out of sight, he started yelling at one of the doctors standing by, "She needs ice and a towel!"

I grabbed onto Cassius's arm and held on for dear life, as he positioned me on the chair and laid my head down gently. When a nurse placed a cool cloth on my arm, I clenched my teeth together and blew out sharply to keep from cursing. I closed my eyes as the nausea built, and a familiar voice rose so loudly it made my head pound.

"That wasn't part of the script!" Flint screamed, as he surged forward, his face red with rage.

When I opened my eyes I spotted Cassius about to throttle him. I grabbed Cassius's arm lightly and he stopped to look at me. In that moment, I knew that either I could lie to Flint and tell him that Mr. Monte made us convince the crowd of our love, or I could tell him the truth and put an end to this terrible guilt I felt. If I told Flint the truth, I wouldn't have to be walked like a dog on a leash to every practice. I wouldn't have to be coddled like a child anymore. But the images of that boy in my room, eagerly scrawling equations down on yellow parchment, flashed in my mind. And then there was Cassius, the boy who made rash decisions and pushed others away constantly. But he was also passionate and I loved that about him. I didn't know if he'd ever love again after losing his sister, but in this moment, I wanted to help him. Looking at Cassius, my eyes jumped to those lips that just kissed me minutes ago. And I realized that those were the lips I wanted to kiss, time and time again, if he'd let me.

"You're right. It wasn't." I looked up at Flint.

He faltered back at my response and glared at me.

I never meant to hurt Flint. I never wanted things between us to end this way, but it had all happened so fast. And Cassius...Cassius was wild and daring. He had snuck into my heart without me even knowing it. He didn't care if he hurt those around him, and that should have made me nervous, but it excited me.

"I'm sorry, Flint. I-"

"It was my idea." Cassius spoke over me, standing to his full height. "Mr. Monte came to me before the performance started, worried that the audience would be preoccupied with the danger surrounding the tightrope walker and miss the *love* between us." Cassius rolled his eyes like it was some joke. "It was a stupid idea, but it was mine. I just kissed her to please the crowd, nothing more."

Flint stared down Cassius like he was going to kill him, but the darkness in Cassius's eyes was more determined, making Flint appear small next to him. "Is this true?" Flint asked me.

I laid there, sweat beading on my forehead. I didn't know why Cassius was protecting me, especially because he knew I hated how Flint was so protective. Why did he choose to help him now? But despite that, Cassius had made it clear where he stood. "Yes, it is. I had no idea Cassius was going to kiss me."

Flint kneeled before me, "Can we talk about this more later?"

"The final bow is about to start." I stood up and my head spun. Flint meant a lot to me, but right now I didn't have the energy to argue with him. He'd just make me feel even more guilty, and quite frankly I'd spent my whole life feeling guilty, and I didn't want to feel that way anymore.

In front of the crowd, I put on a fake smile and bowed my head, while a fire surged in my arm. I looked to my right and Cassius smiled at the crowd, but when he looked at me, he licked his lips and winked. As soon as the final bow was over and the crowd had gone, we grabbed our things and headed back to the train. Thankfully, Eanverness offered us an arena that was in close proximity to the train instead of in the center of the city.

I headed straight for Cassius's room and barged right in. "Why did you do that?" I demanded.

"Do what?" He acted innocent, puckering his lips into a frown.

I laughed and turned on my heel. "Don't play with me, Cassius."

"I thought you liked that." His heavy boots thudded on the floor as he approached me.

I turned around quickly to find Cassius right in front of me. "Did you kiss me to please the crowd?"

"I kissed you because I wanted to."

I huffed out a laugh and ran my hand through my hair.

"What?" Cassius asked sarcastically, stepping closer, pressing me against the wall. "Would you like me to tell Flint that I enjoyed it? Even more, that you enjoyed it?"

My back hit his door and I lifted my head so I could look him in the eyes. "It would have made this a hell of a lot easier."

"I'm sure it would have." He dipped his head closer and I could feel his breath on my cheek. "But I'm not the good guy, Juniper. If I had grown up in a stable home with a nice family, maybe I would be, but I'm not. You have to know that."

"Oh I do," my voice was slow as I tried to escape the spell of his irresistible eyes. I leaned forward and kissed him gently. What did this mean? Was Cassius someone who could actually care for me? And was I willing to give up kind, loving Flint, for him? I couldn't avoid him anymore, I knew that much. Cassius had a rough past—one that had made him distant and harsh. But he could also be caring and protective. And when I was alone or with Flint, I found myself wanting to be with Cassius. I looked for him in everywhere I went without even realizing it. And now that I knew about his past, I only wanted to make him feel better. I didn't want him to be so angry all the time. I wanted to make him happy.

"You sure you don't want Mr. Nice Guy out there?" Cassius motioned to the door.

"Positive." I pressed my lips into his and enjoyed the fresh taste of his mouth again. I ran my hands through his curly hair, wondering how it had ever come to this. How had I—Juniper Rose—caught the eye of the lion tamer?

Cassius looked to the floor, almost in embarrassment, and then surprised me by saying, "Will you stay awhile?"

I nodded innocently, not realizing how much I'd wanted him to ask me that. I sat down across from him on his bed and asked, "Would you tell me about the circus, before I arrived? What was it like?"

Time passed quickly as he told me story after story. He told me about when Hugh arrived and commenced drinking so much he blacked out and was hungover for two days straight, and about the time Gabe and Gretta started acting too much like their pet snake and decided to bite another one of the performers.

I laughed and said, "I knew the twins were strange, but I guess I didn't know the half of it!"

"And get this." Cassius pointed a finger at me while a wide smile spread across his face. "Once before boarding the train to head for our show in Dangarnon, Mr. Monte exclaimed that he was finished. Juniper, he quit the circus!"

"What do you mean?" I asked emphatically. Mr. Monte quit? There's no way!

"It had been a particularly stressful season, and he just said that he was finished. He stayed in Islebury for a month, gained a few pounds, grew a mustache, and then came back. That was that, and nothing's been said about it since."

"He grew a mustache?" I whispered, as if Mr. Monte was listening.

Cassius nodded before we both burst into laughter.

After all his stories, there was a lull when neither of us spoke, but just looked at one another. There had been something on my mind that I wanted to share with him, so I blurted it out, figuring there was no easy way around it. "I'm going home."

Cassius's eyebrows furrowed in confusion. "What? Why?"

I tried not to look at him, because I knew he'd change my mind if I did. "The Young family—the family of the boy I'm supposed to marry—is having a dinner party. My mother requested I go, and at first I was against it, but I think I have to."

He remained silent.

"Joseph's father is a very wealthy businessman. He owns land in many kingdoms."

"And why is that important?" Cassius snapped.

I knew he would react this way. After such a lovely evening spent getting to know him better, I hoped this wouldn't ruin it. "Because his father can help us. I have a plan," I promised him. "All I'm asking is that you trust me."

Cassius's eyes moved from my eyes to my lips. "And you're not running away to marry him because you're scared?" He asked.

"Cassius-" I reached out to grab his arm. "I'm not going to marry Joseph. I would like to see my mother and sister and find out if Mr. Young will help the circus. And then I'll return."

He laid his back on the bed harshly.

"Why would you care anyway?" I folded my hands on his chest and rested my head on them.

"I wouldn't. But you'd be missing out. He's definitely not as dashing as I am." Cassius flipped his hair dramatically.

I swatted at him and instantly regretted it when the burns on my arm raked across his bare skin.

Cassius begrudgingly pushed himself up and I watched the muscles in his torso shift. "Come on, let's get you some bandages."

I couldn't figure out how to tell Flint about my plan to leave until the day before I left. I sat down before him in his bedroom, gazing at the littered pieces of paper on the floor. "I'm going to visit my family for the holidays. Please don't fight me on this," I blurted out, figuring the bare truth would be easiest for him to comprehend.

Flint shook his head, "It's not safe, Juniper. The perpetrator could follow you there. What better time to harm you than when you're traveling and unprotected?"

"Flint, that's ridiculous. The perpetrator isn't going to harm me on this trip. We've already determined he wants to make a spectacle out of me for all the circus goers to see. This isn't debatable." I tried to sound strong. I just wanted Flint to agree with me for once.

"This isn't smart and you know it. You should stay here for the holidays until the danger has passed."

"When will it have passed?" I exclaimed. "The circus never found the man that killed Penelope. And what if we never find him? It's unreasonable for you to deny me my freedom, because this may never be solved."

"Unreasonable? I'm only trying to keep you safe."

"Just stop!" I said emphatically. "It's suffocating. I can't practice on my own. I can't walk anywhere on my own. What's next? Soon I won't be allowed to breathe on my own without you by my side?"

Flint scoffed in anger.

I wished Flint was more like Cassius. More understanding, more real. And I shouldn't be thinking that, but he gave me no choice. "Look, I think you're the smartest boy I've ever met. And you're kind. Too kind. But I can't be with you if you don't give me some freedom."

"Juniper, I can't just let you wander around here when there's a killer on the loose-"

"Then this isn't going to work between us, I'm afraid." Just yesterday, Cassius had encouraged me stay with Flint. Maybe because of his own insecurity, or maybe because he thought Flint would be better for me. And I knew Flint would be, but I couldn't stop thinking about Cassius. I stood and opened Flint's door, feeling so regretful. This was all my fault. Yes, Flint was smothering me, but I could have dealt with that had I not fallen for Cassius.

"Juniper-"

"I'm sorry, Flint." I really was. I wished this could have worked. I wished Cassius had never kissed me. I could have fallen in love with Flint. I could have made a life with him, and I hated myself for not wanting that because of some rough, dark boy who didn't really care for me, and whose life was full of trauma that left him damaged. I was confused, but I knew I couldn't continue to be so unfair to Flint.

I informed Mr. Monte and Monroe that I would be going home for the holidays. They were not put back by the idea, but they suggested I be back in time to practice for our performance in February. That wouldn't be a problem as I didn't plan to stay a day later than I had to.

The end of December rounded the corner sooner than I would have liked, and it saddened me that I wouldn't be spending Christmas with the circus, but there would always be next year. *Next year.* That sounded nice.

I hopped off the train, eager to get this visit over with. Since the rest of the circus wouldn't travel to Axminster for weeks, I had to make the journey on my own, but the two-hour train ride wasn't bad. I began to walk through the nearby field, when I heard a rustle behind me. Turning around quickly, I spotted Cassius leaning against the train with his hands in his pockets.

He tried to look disinterested, but a smile broke the adamant look on his face. "Don't come back a posh princess, okay? I might hate you even more than I already do."

I rolled my eyes and blew him a sarcastic kiss before turning my back. A small suitcase swung by my thigh as I passed bare fields where corn and wildflowers had been harvested months before, and entered the bustling city. Bouncing carriages rolled by on the cobblestone streets, while horsemen whipped their horses into obedience. After seeing how the circus treated its animals so kindly, this world I used to be a part of seemed so cruel. I noticed the local newsstand was selling a paper advertising the circus's recent performances. It was incredible to watch people stand in line to buy a story about the show I'd worked so hard on. It almost didn't seem real. Could these last few months have been a dream?

The train whistle blew and steam rose high over the city. It was time I went to say hello to Mother Dearest.

Chapter 23

I walked up the stone path, surrounded by a small wooden fence on either side. Yellow wildflowers swayed in a light breeze, and the sweet cinnamon air wafting from the city brought back distant memories. This was not my home anymore, and I couldn't believe I had attended chapel here every Sunday or the famous Cornell Family banquet every year. It seemed sad to have been a part of something so dull, so individualized. Wrapping my palm around the brass doorknob of my childhood home, I reminded myself of one thing: *Mr. Young's support is where your attention lies, Juniper. Do not get distracted.*

I walked into the foyer and set my bag on the floor. I found my mother in her usual place in the parlor. She spotted me instantly and lowered the newspaper she was reading onto her lap. "Juniper-" she half gasped, half whispered.

"Hello, Mother," I sighed.

She uncrossed her legs and jumped up to greet me, "Oh my, I'm so glad you've come. I didn't hear back from you." She wrapped me in a tight hug that almost sent me to the floor. Coming back to her senses, she let go and gently swatted my chin. "What the devil is wrong with you, running away like that?"

"I-" I began, but found myself cut off before I could explain.

"No matter." My mother pushed her hair out of her face and clasped her hands together, as if her plan had finally come to fruition. "This family will not have to worry about you any longer. I'm glad you've returned...for good."

I smiled at my mother's glare. "No, Mother, I have not. I will be returning to the circus after the Youngs' banquet."

"My dear, once you meet Joseph, I'm sure you'll change your mind." My mother pulled me into the sunroom in the back of the house, where Colette sipped on a cup of tea with two lemon slices. Her favorite. I always remembered her chastising my mother for not putting enough sugar in it. I laughed lightly, and as soon as Colette heard the sound, she jumped up and wrapped me in a suffocating hug.

"Oh J, I missed you," Colette whimpered in my ear.

"I missed you too," I said in a muffled way, my mouth still pressed into Colette's neck. I did wish I could see my sister more, but I couldn't forsake my life with the circus. Why did we have to be apart to be happy? I wished Mother would just see that none of us was meant for this life. Then instead of feeling ashamed of my new life, I would be able to see them whenever I liked. But I'd learned not to expect too much, believing if I became greedy, then the things that mattered would begin to fade.

"Come now, Prune. Colette and I picked out a gown for you. Miss Gwen did an extremely fine job making this dress. The craftsmanship is impeccable." My mother took me to my old room where an extravagant gown laid on my four-poster bed. The open windows, white-washed walls, and pea green furniture seemed completely out of place. It was too open. Where was the privacy?

"It's lovely," I said, despite my disinterest. The gown was made of the deepest blue silk, depicting the color of the midnight sky. It was covered with glittering stars, and had a golden band looped around the waist. The heels weren't too tall, but it would take some effort to break them in. In the past months, I'd gotten used to walking barefoot or in boots that were worn thin.

My mother pulled me away from my thoughts suddenly by saying, "I'm so glad you've arrived early enough that we can have a nice dinner and still have plenty of time to open presents."

Presents. In all the fuss, presents were the last thing on my mind. But I was grateful to acknowledge Christmas with my family, and I couldn't help but feel a small surge of excitement at the thought of getting something new and shiny.

"Feel free to unpack and settle in before coming downstairs," she said, closing my bedroom door on her way out.

I didn't dare take the clothes out of my bag. The less I moved in, the easier it would be to leave.

Realizing I hadn't eaten anything since that morning, I came downstairs prepared to dive in, when my mother cleared her throat, and said, "Have you forgotten that we bless the food before eating it in this house?"

I set my spoon back down and bowed my head. My mother thanked the Lord for my safe return and kindly asked that he convince me to stay in Axminster. It seemed she was attempting to wash the dirt off me with her words.

I scarfed down my dinner, as we were accustomed to doing in the circus, and my mother was horrified. She must have thought I was ruined forever, but I had better things to do than be proper and waste time picking at my food.

Finally, my mother and sister rose from the table and we all gathered around the Christmas tree. Looking at Colette's smile made me feel like we were little girls again, excited to tear open our presents. I hadn't expected my mother to buy me anything this year, and when I looked at her in surprise, her eyes said, *I knew you'd be back.*

The gifts labeled for me revealed a new satchel decked in finely stitched flowers, a new pair of orange and white saddle shoes, and an expensive pair of earrings that shimmered under the golden lights of the tree. I thanked my mother, but my heart was conflicted.

Suddenly I was struck that my friends were probably not opening gifts like I was, and I wasn't in need of any of these new things. And as much as I was touched by my mother's gifts, there were things I had longed for from her my whole life—acceptance, affirmation, freedom—that I would never get. It was another reminder of the contrast between the life I left and the one I gained.

I retired early but my eyes stayed wide open as I anticipated tomorrow's plan. The house was colder than usual, reminding me of my room on the train. There was always a draft in that room. I smiled and stuffed my hands into my pockets to warm them up, coming in contact with a piece of crumpled paper. I pulled it out quickly and examined the loopy handwriting. I had almost forgotten I had this with me—the odd receipt from Monroe's office. I ran through what I would say to Mr. Young, and when I had tediously rehearsed the words to the point of exhaustion, my eyes finally closed with the piece of paper clenched tightly in my hand.

Late the next day as the sun sank over the horizon, I pulled on the midnight blue dress. The stiff sleeves itched, and the fabric was too heavy; nothing like the loose, frilly attire at the circus. I took one more look behind me, catching a glimpse of the receipt sitting on my nightstand. I wouldn't need it. There would be no one to answer that question tonight. But another part of me thought I should keep it close at all times, so I grabbed it as a precaution.

The Young Family home was much larger than our own and was lined with colossal pillars along an extensive staircase at the front entrance. The courtyard in the front was surrounded by small lights, illuminating a water fountain in the center.

"Juniper Rose, we are so glad you could make it," Mr. Young said, as he moved toward me. "I'm positive your mother mentioned it, but our Joseph is very excited about the opportunity to take your hand."

I had the urge to spit out something vile about my mother to turn Joseph and his family against us. But then my mother would do everything in her power to forbid me from speaking any further with Mr. Young, so instead I responded kindly, "Yes, she did."

Joseph finally stepped forward and lightly kissed the back of my hand. "It's nice to finally meet you." He was rather tall with golden blonde hair, gelled to perfection and flat against his head.

I smiled warmly at him and his eyes widened at my appearance. Surely, he wasn't prepared for what to expect in me—a rebellious girl who had escaped to the circus and returned a different woman.

"We've got a delightful spread. Let's eat in celebration of the holidays!" Mr. Young's wife, a petite woman with bright skin, led us into an adjoining room. Delicious smells wafted through the air and made me salivate. Dinner consisted of an enormous roast, cooked to perfection, with bright green asparagus, and warm bread with delicious honey butter dollops. Napkins were folded into quaint roses and set delicately on three china plates at each place setting.

Really? Three? Isn't that a bit excessive? Oh dear, I was starting to sound like Cassius.

I shook my head at any remembrance of him and pushed my way through the heavy feast. I was not used to eating this much, and as soon as I finished, I felt queasy. Champagne was served, and we all adjourned to the sitting area to engage in small talk. I left my sister's side for a moment, coming to stand in front of Mr. Young. He was rather intimidating due to the permanent glare of his fierce, gray eyes. "Sir, may I have a word with you?"

When the man agreed, I nudged him away from his son.

"I know my son can be a little reticent, but he means well. He is very fond of you," he told me, and then took a long draw from his crystal glass.

Looking back at the boy's wandering stare, I wasn't sure that he was, but I agreed nonetheless. "No, Sir, your son is very kind. But I was actually hoping to speak on a different topic...an economic proposal."

"Oh?" Mr. Young's bushy eyebrows peaked.

"My mother informed me that you hold a considerable amount of land in this region?" I posed the phrase as a question to make sure I was not mistaken.

"That is correct."

"I apologize for my candor, but I'm also assuming that land has made you a great deal of money, and I was wondering if you would be interested in the option of investing in something more exciting?" I weighed his reaction. He seemed interested, but I was worried that as soon as I mentioned the circus, he'd think I was crazy. I swallowed carefully, "The circus is a growing establishment. This year, it performed at the Janvier Estate in celebration of the Gisèle Janvier's engagement, it traveled as far as Eanverness to perform in one of the most extravagant opera houses to ever exist, L'Acre du Grand Ours, and it graced the famous theatre district in Sprionnamp. You may not be aware that the circus holds half of all the income in the entertainment industry. I believe it would be a very prosperous investment for you."

"Miss Rose, I appreciate your passion, but I must stop you there." Mr. Young held up a thick hand. "I will not invest in such an unsteady establishment. The circus does receive a superfluous amount of attention, but that does not mean it is a prosperous investment. I look for businesses that can give me something in return. And all of the money the circus makes is used to fund their survival. I would be supporting a group of homeless people, not making a good business decision."

His inconsideration made my skin crawl. "If you were to invest in the circus, supporting it in a way no one ever has, the profit made from our increased success would come to you. In a few years, the circus would be wildly successful, and so would your pocketbook!"

"My mind is made up, Juniper. I suggest you keep your sights set on the real role of a woman—marriage." Mr. Young excused himself to gather his wife into his arms, and then immersed himself in a heated discussion about coal mining in the outskirts of the city and whether it was profitable to invest in such a dangerous operation.

I glanced at Joseph and he walked over to me and smiled warmly, looking toward our families. I saw the same judgement in his eyes, although slightly more reserved. He had more patience than I ever would. "I can't stand when he talks business. It's all about money, money, money. It's never about personal enjoyment." This was the only thing Joseph had said to me since my arrival.

"What do you mean?" I inquired.

"He does business to improve the status of his name and his home. He would rather buy luxurious things and accumulate land than focus on his family. It's discouraging for all of us," Joseph admitted, finally taking his eyes off his father to look at me.

His eyes were breathtakingly blue. Maybe Joseph and I were more similar than I thought. He didn't seem as uppity to me as he did an hour ago. "I thought you would be just another entitled nobleman, but I am relieved to say I was wrong."

Joseph smiled, revealing his beautiful white teeth—the most perfect I had ever seen, to be honest.

It looked like was going to speak, but he was interrupted by a loud knock on the door. I didn't think we were expecting any more guests.

Colette eagerly hopped off the loveseat she was lounging on and skipped toward the foyer. She pulled the large double doors open to reveal a tall man with light ginger stubble on his chin. He was dashing, but his attire did not fit the high-class crowd tonight. I would guess he was rather common, and when she kissed him on the cheek, my mouth dropped. My sister, Colette, was dating a lower-class man. I wondered how that conversation between my mother and sister had gone. I giggled, watching from a distance as the pair gallivanted into the living room. Her beau seemed rather quiet and uncomfortable.

"Welcome," Mr. Young announced, handing him a glass of champagne.

Was my mother okay with this? Was my sister given the freedom to marry the man of her choosing, while I was stuck in this predicament with Joseph? How was that possible?

The man whose name I have yet to learn, turned to whisper something in Colette's ear, and that was when I saw the golden badge in his pocket, identifying him as an Axminster policeman. I had considered tonight a total waste after Mr. Young refused to help me, but it seemed there was hope for the evening after all. My eyes widened and I practically ran to introduce myself. "My name is Juniper Rose. And who might you be?"

"My name is William Lloyd." The tall man extended his hand warmly and I shook it vigorously, despite the scolding my mother might give me.

I tried to think of a way to get him alone, but my sister dragged him along to meet my mother and the rest of the family. My mother was spiteful at first, but I think she actually liked the boy. For a moment, I wondered if she would like Cassius. Surely she would judge him for his brutal honesty and vulgar comments. Flint, on the other hand, she would adore. I groaned and snatched another glass of champagne off the nearest servant's silver platter.

"Thank you," I told her, dipping into a short curtsey.

She was taken aback by my kindness, and she bowed deeply in front of me as a way of saying thank you. None of the servants were ever spoken to kindly. The woman had beautiful brown skin and light green eyes, and I thought to myself that she would look divine in the circus.

As the night drew to an end and my mother gathered her coat, I finally took my chance to speak with Mr. Lloyd.

"How was it, dining with the esteemed class?" I joked.

"Intimidating to say the least," he said, his laugh lines appearing around his jolly smile.

I knew he was fond of my sister just by the way he looked at her. I wished I hadn't had to turn the conversation to something serious, but the timing was dire. "There's something really important I need to ask you. And I'm sorry to bring this up in the middle of the merriment, but it's crucial."

"By all means." William set down his glass and motioned for me to continue.

I reached my hand into my dress and shoved the paper into his hand. "You're a police officer, correct?"

"Yes ma'am," he clarified while examining the parchment.

"Then you must run analysis on people frequently and deal with fraud, right? With this information, would you be able to find out who belongs to bank account #18980345? And also account #5178402?"

"Yes." He nodded his head sharply. "My men and I can go to the bank personally and request access to this information. What is this about, if I might ask?" He flipped the paper over in his hand before tucking it into his vest.

"It's fraud. Someone paid someone else to lie about something in order to take down an establishment. That doesn't make a lot of sense, I'm afraid," I said, and laughed nervously.

William stared at me, searching my intentions. When I didn't elaborate, he changed the subject rather quickly, "Your sister told me you returned from the circus?"

"Yes, Sir," I said, and nodded respectfully.

He smiled a crooked smile and said, "Then, no more questions. I'll get right on it."

William was a fine gentleman. He might not be rich or have a grand home, but he seemed kind and hard working. I was so relieved to know that someone was finally willing to help me. And William barely knew me. I was proud of my sister for finding such a great man. And I was even more proud to be making progress with the issue involving the circus. If I could make sense of this fraudulent transaction, made the day before my fall, maybe it would uncover a connection to the perpetrator.

"If you figure anything out, just give the information to my sister." I found my coat and hurried to the door where my family waited. "I enjoyed meeting you," I told Joseph in a rush.

He smiled and brought his lips to my cheek as he responded, "And I, you. I do hope to see you again."

I nodded without answering him and closed the elaborate door behind me. Did I want to see Joseph again? I was surprised by our similarities, but there was no way I could leave the circus. And my heart didn't belong to him. I wished it did, truly. I wished I could make my mother proud—happy even. But the truth is that she hadn't been happy since the day my father left, and it would not cure her sadness to see me marry a man who was just as susceptible to leaving.

I slung my bag over my shoulder and grasped Colette close to my chest. "I'm sorry I have to leave so soon."

"It's alright. I know it's important to you." She sniffled and wiped the tears from her eyes. I hoped she wasn't too lonely here. Having William by her side, I'm sure my mother was easier to tolerate.

My mother remained seated without sparing me even a look. "Goodbye, Mother," I said flatly, as I picked up my bag.

"You'll be back. I noticed you got along with Joseph quite well last night. I'll be setting a date for this summer."

"You can inform him that I will not be attending. I do not love him, Mother."

"And whom do you love? Who will provide for you when the circus drops you on your ass with no money?"

It was the first time I'd ever heard my mother curse. The word sounded so strange coming out of her mouth. "The circus is my life now. I love nothing but the circus. And it's time you see that, just like you see Colette's love for William." My voice was shaky but I held back my tears. My mother would chastise me if I cried.

Her face was stern and unchanging.

I wished only one thing in this world, and it was that she would see me the way she saw money. With respect. With love. But my mother would never respect me until I made the same decisions for my life as she had. And that fact saddened me. It made me want to curl up in a ball and cry. I tried to muster a confident smile, but I ended up walking out in silence.

I didn't waste time milling about the city, afraid I would remember too much of my childhood, but headed straight back to the train instead.

When the circus train came into view, my heart leapt with joy. My shoulder ached from holding my bag all the way from the city, but a burst of energy prompted me to run toward the train. The cold wind numbed my face, but I didn't care. I was elated to be back where I knew I belonged. I wanted to see my friends. I wanted to drink an ale. And I wanted to see Cassius most of all. I wanted to tell him how much I hated being in the same room with my mother, and that it meant the world to me to be accepted into this new family.

I burst onto the train, greeted by many familiar faces.

"Welcome back, Juniper!"

"Happy Holidays!"

I smiled and hugged Charlotte before hurrying to the dining hall, where I expected Cassius to be. When I bounded into the room, everyone cheered at my return, and I tried to acknowledge their kindness, but I was really preoccupied with finding him. Through a sea of miscellaneous eyes that were less important to me, a golden pair met mine, and I pushed through the crowd toward the smile on Cassius's face.

When I reached him, I grasped his collar and crawled onto his lap, pressing my lips against his. I didn't care who was watching. I didn't care if Flint saw. I only cared that Cassius knew I was back and that I never wanted to leave again.

He faltered back on his stool in surprise, but he kissed me back with just as much conviction.

I pressed both of my palms on his cheeks, feeling his warmth spread into my fingertips.

He raised his eyebrows, and said, "I'm guessing you're not a married woman?"

I shook my head and bit my lip, and then spun on Cassius's lap to sit between his legs and shouted, "Can we get something stronger than ale?"

The room erupted into cheer, and before I knew it, Wilman had filled twenty mugs to the brim with rum.

◆────────◆

The following morning, everyone packed up and we were off to Axminster. I was nervous to be performing in my own kingdom and anxious to be returning so soon. I might see people I knew—people whose respect I risked losing. And if my family came to the show, their respect for me would be gone for good. But at least I could give them a show they'd never forget.

I rapped on Mr. Monte's office door.

"Come in," he yelled behind the door.

I entered and folded my hands across my lap. "I want this performance to be special, like nothing people have ever seen before. I think I'm ready, Sir."

Mr. Monte huffed out a laugh, "For the rope? No way."

"It's been six weeks, Sir, if not more! I can do it. I have to."

He searched my eyes, as if he was searching for every secret I held close. What he found, I don't know, but something in his eyes changed. "I'm bringing Monroe and the medical staff to watch you closely. And so help me, God, if you don't do everything I say, you will not be allowed to perform on the rope in this show. Do you understand?"

"Yes, Sir, but I have an idea I'd like to share-" I was cut off by Mr. Monte pointing his finger toward the door. "Right." I hustled out the door and ran to my room to find my leotard. I spent the two-hour train ride walking through the motions of my routine in my room. I was nervous to walk the tightrope again—terrified actually—but I needed to. I had to impress the crowd, and as much as they adored seeing the story unfold between Cassius and me, it wasn't enough. I worried they would get bored, and I wasn't going to wait for that to happen.

Finally, the train came to a stop, and I ran into the field to help set up the equipment.

On the way, Cassius spotted me rushing and asked, "Where are you off to?"

"The rope. They're letting me get on the rope!" I exclaimed in excitement.

His face fell into worry. "Is that a good idea?"

I shrugged and answered, "I've had ample time to heal. It'll be fine." I helped the crew set up my tent, and then I quickly bandaged my heels and the bridges of my feet and chalked my hands. When Mr. Monte's team arrived, I was nervous and shaking.

"We'll start with the low rope. I just want you to make it across. Then we'll try some flips," Mr. Monte said, as he folded his arms across his chest.

I climbed the ladder onto the pedestal. Balancing was a little foreign after not doing it for so long, but it felt good to be walking on the rope again. The grooves meshed with the arches of my feet and my arms felt loose by my side. Making it to the other side was a great start, and when I finished, I looked to those below me with a relieved smile.

Mr. Monte spoke with Monroe for a moment, and then said to me, "Let's try a handstand to see if your shoulder can support your body weight, yeah?"

I nodded and kicked my right foot back and pushed into a handstand. Using my shoulder for the first time was painful, but bearable.

"A roundoff," Mr. Monte declared with a furrowed brow.

I jumped into the air, placing both my hands on the rope, then twisted my body, making sure both my feet landed at the same time.

"Front handspring," Monroe shouted.

I performed it with some difficulty, but that skill would come back in time.

"Double turn out," Mr. Monte demanded, as he watched to measure my reach.

I raised my arms in front of my chest, pointed my left foot into my knee, and completed a double spin.

Mr. Monte brought his fingers to his lips, contemplating. I breathed hard, waiting for him to say something, anything. "Keep working."

"I told you I was ready!" I shouted down to him in excitement. I couldn't believe I had actually done it. When the doctor said it would take six weeks to get back on the rope, it sounded like an eternity, but I still worried that would be too soon. I was so relieved the doctor was right. For our next performance, the crowd would be delighted to have their tightrope walker back.

"That you did," Mr. Monte finally said to me as he left the room, discussing my progress with the doctors.

For the rest of the evening, I tested my limits. I jumped and flipped like it was my first time. I was renewed by the sense of floating above the world, and I felt like nothing could touch me.

"Juniper!" Someone shouted below.

I turned on my heel, almost falling off the rope, and looked down to find Cassius gazing up at me with his hands tucked in his pockets.

"It's getting late!" He wore a smile on his face, making his cheeks nice and round. I loved when his eyes crinkled just slightly. "You've been up there for hours. The rope will be there in the morning."

I wanted to keep practicing, but he was right. I needed to take a break. I hopped down next to him, and we walked back to the train together. When we reached his room, I pulled open the door and groaned, realizing the pain in my shoulder was agonizing. I shouldn't have pushed myself so hard this afternoon.

"Sit," Cassius commanded.

I followed his order and sat on the edge of his bed.

Cassius crawled across the bed to kneel behind me. He kissed the back of my neck gently, which made me shiver, then his warm hands moved to my shoulders, rubbing gently. I hissed in pain at first, but the discomfort was replaced with relief. I sighed as his rough fingers dug into my tense skin, and as he grabbed my recovered shoulder and gently rotated it in a circle.

"Cassius-" I yelped, realizing my shoulder wouldn't move the same way it had before.

"Trust me," he shushed.

Slowly, my pain resolved and my shoulder felt better, even after such a vigorous day of work. "Thank you, Dr. C.," I laughed.

He pressed his fingers in a little deeper, making me squirm, and whispered in my ear, "Don't call me that."

I couldn't help but laugh, but then we heard some commotion in the hallway and perked up to listen.

"Mail's here!" I heard someone say.

I jumped up quickly and straightened my hair. When I turned around, Cassius was still sprawled lazily across the bed, his body taking up the entire length of it.

"You coming?" I offered him my hand.

He shook his head and said, "You go." He attempted a smile, but I could tell there was something wrong.

Did Cassius get mail from any of his loved ones? Or even friends? I reminded myself to ask him later. Running into the hallway, I found Wilman with a load of small envelopes in his hands. I waited in line with the other performers, and suddenly Charlotte grasped my arm.

Locking elbows with me, she asked, "Did I just see you come out of Cassius's room?"

"I know. I'm a bore and no one thought it possible," I said, and laughed off her comment.

"Oh, I knew it was possible," she said as she nestled closer to me. "Just don't get hurt. He's had one-night stands with women for years. He'll throw you out before midnight."

"I know about Cassius's past. But I'm not sleeping with him."

I knew Cassius toyed with women, but for some reason he hadn't even asked me to stay the night. Why was he keeping me around? Why hadn't he just shooed me off like the rest of those women?

She raised her eyebrows, "You and Cassius didn't sleep together?" She asked the question as if it was impossible to believe.

"Yeah," I said, and I winced in embarrassment. I knew Cassius must be acquainted with every woman here, but I felt like he was different when he was around me. That might not be the best thing to trust, but I had nothing else at the moment. "We've kissed, but nothing more. He usually asks me to stay, and we end up just talking."

"Wait, rewind," Charlotte said, and she closed her eyes. "You kiss, and then he asks you to stay to just talk?"

"Yeah?" Why wouldn't he?

Charlotte huffed out a laugh, appearing slightly jealous when her eyes sank to the floor. "Cassius never allows *anyone* to spend time in his room. *Ever.*"

I was the first person to actually spend time with him? Why me? Could it be that I might get to know Cassius like no one else had? I looked to the floor to watch my feet shuffle forward. "From Colette Rose?" I asked when I reached the front of the line.

Wilman shuffled through the letters, suddenly stopping. "Here we are."

I snatched the letter quickly, bid my goodbye to Charlotte, and retreated back into Cassius's room. I couldn't wait to rip open the letter and search for any information from William Lloyd.

Cassius sat up attentively. "What is it?" I held up a finger, flicking through the lines of his primitive note.

```
Dear Miss Juniper,
My men and I have investigated the
transaction at Axminster's primary bank.
It seems account 18980345 belongs to a
man named Monroe Béringer, and the
$500.00 went to account 5178402, which
belongs to Diana Rose.
            Sincerely, William Lloyd
```

My heart dropped, and I rested my fingers over my mouth to cover my shaky gasps. My mother? Why would Monroe be paying my mother?

"What's wrong?" Cassius crawled off the bed and moved to stand in front of me.

I handed him the letter and rested my head in my hands, trying to prevent myself from crying. It could be nothing. Was my paycheck going to my mother because I was still under her guardianship? Or maybe my family was being given money as a thank you for my contribution to the circus. But the circus was low on funds and they couldn't afford that. Plus, many performers didn't have families. Was I trying to make sense of something that just didn't make sense?

Cassius's eyebrows furrowed as he asked, "What is this?"

"I don't know," I said, as I sniffled and wiped my nose across my sleeve.

Cassius stood awkwardly, not knowing how to help me. "Look, it's late. I'm sure it's nothing. We'll speak to Monroe tomorrow and figure things out, okay?"

I nodded. He was right. He was always right. This was probably nothing. But deep in my heart, I felt like it was something. I wanted to confront Monroe right then, but I knew Cassius would follow me there, and for some reason I was afraid of what Cassius might hear. Would he hate my mother even more if something suspicious was happening? Would he hate me?

He took my hands in his and we stood in silence for a moment. To take my mind off William's letter, I asked, "Do you ever get mail?"

"No," he answered dryly.

"What about your family?" I inquired. I only knew that Cassius had a sister, nothing more about his mother or father.

"I don't want to talk about this," he said angrily.

"Why not?" I asked. I wanted to know more about him, and I couldn't imagine what harm would there be if he told me a little about his past.

"We're not having this conversation." He raised his eyebrows, practically asking me to challenge him.

I bit my cheek, wishing he would let me in, but I understood. Pasts were hard. And I shouldn't expect him to talk to me about his. That was unfair.

I retreated back to my room for the night and read over the letter again and again, unable to get it out of my head. After another half hour, I couldn't take it anymore. I had to know what this meant.

I slid out of my covers and marched toward Monroe's office. The circus was wide awake, and laughter escaped from behind closed doors. When I first arrived here, I thought it was preposterous how late the performers stayed up, but now it felt normal. Monroe was sure to be up along with the others.

I rapped on his door with impatience.

"Juniper, what can I help you with at this hour?" He responded with an awkward smile.

"What is this?" I demanded, pulling out the receipt I took from his office.

He lowered his eyes in anger, and his neck grew red. "You stole this from me."

"Borrowed." I backed him into his office. "And I know you paid my mother $500 dollars. Why?"

He rubbed his eyebrows with his middle finger and thumb. I think he understood there was no escaping this, so he sighed and explained, "Your mother wanted you to return to Axminster. She contacted Mr. Monte and me personally, requesting that we return you immediately. And since you had become an irreplaceable part of the circus, Mr. Monte and I declined. After hearing this, and after seeing you fall in Hewe, of course, she threatened to sue the circus."

"She was the unknown spectator that threatened to end our establishment?" I asked furiously. I knew my mother was vicious, but trying to end the one thing I loved? I would have put that past even her. But I was wrong. She was determined to destroy everything that was important to me in order to get what she wanted—me, safe back home, married to a wealthy man. I couldn't believe she would go as far as trying to completely dismantle the circus. And if I didn't show up to wed Joseph Young this summer, what would she do then? Would she reduce the circus to rubble?

"Yes, she was," Monroe finally answered. "So, to appease her, I offered her money. She took it willingly, but refused to give up. And since she's continued to threaten us, Mr. Monte and I have money put aside to give her every month." He sighed in distress. "It was the only thing we could think to do."

The circus couldn't afford that. We'd be broke in a matter of months. And why would my mother be quieted by money? She had enough of her own. This still didn't make sense. But despite my confusion, I was no longer eager to blame Monroe for everything. "What do we do?"

He shook his head, "The question is what do *you* do? You have done exceptionally well, but given that the perpetrator is still after you, and that your mother is still threatening the circus, do you really think it's worth it to stay? Your mother could destroy us, Juniper. It's your decision. Do you want to save the circus, or do you want to cause its demise?"

Seconds ago Monroe admitted that I was irreplaceable, and now he was willing to give me up. There was so much pressure on my shoulders, I felt like I might crumble. My body began to shake and my head spun. I had enough answers for now. "Thank you," I said, and before he could respond, I shut the door behind me. Were it not for the people drifting in the hallway, I would have sunken to the floor. My legs felt like gelatin as they led me down the hall, but I didn't want to be alone, so I turned toward Cassius's room. I just wanted to feel him near and know that he was there for me.

I hesitated as I tried to decide whether to wake him up or just leave him to rest. I ended up laying down next to him as he laid there on his back, and resting my head on his chest with my arm around his waist.

He stirred, rubbing his hand gently along my back.

I tried not to cry, but a few tears slid down my cheeks and landed on his bare skin. Cassius gathered me into his arms, and I nuzzled my head into his neck, as his soft breathing and the steady *thump* of his heart lulled me to sleep.

Chapter 24

Diana Rose...

"Louis Young," I lowered my voice so Colette couldn't overhear from the other room. "I've made a deal with someone. I love my daughter too much to let her continue in such a dangerous activity. She deserves better. And I need your help to convince her to come back home." I cleared my throat. "I need you to come to the performance in Axminster because of your position. You are a profitable, well-known businessman who holds land across Hewe and Eanverness. And with such a monopoly, I believe you could destroy any establishment you deem unfit in favor of more valuable ones, am I correct?"

Louis looked deep into my eyes, "You know, your daughter asked me to help fund the circus. And now you are asking me to help destroy it?"

My eyes sunk. I had no idea Juniper had spoken to Louis about this matter. Of course, that must have been why she came. My daughter was too stubborn to do anything that didn't produce a result. She wasn't coming to the Young Family dinner to meet Joseph. She was coming to ask for Louis's help. "And pray, what did you tell her?"

"I told her no," he stated as a matter of fact. "Investing in the circus would be akin to investing in a farm. It is unreasonable and unprofitable. I wouldn't do such a silly thing." He waved his hand to add emphasis.

"Then for your son's sake, will you help me?"

Louis tilted his head to the right. "This is quite the idea you have. I must hand it to you. You've got more gumption than I knew." He paused to smile and added, "I'd love to help."

I'd been awake for about an hour, but I was too apprehensive to wake Cassius. He looked so peaceful, which was so different from his normal volatile personality. Cassius had been through a great deal in his life. I didn't know the details, but I knew his past was a source of great distress for him. So these moments of calm, I did not wish to disrupt. His eyes fluttered lightly and I feared my thoughts may have somehow disturbed his sleep, but he continued to breathe slowly.

My eyes welled up at the indecision that was tearing me apart. I wanted to stay with the circus. I'd never felt like I belonged more in my entire life. I'd never felt more at home. And I didn't want to give up the amazing friendships I'd made. But that was selfish of me. The circus would be at risk if Mr. Monte and Monroe continued to pay off my mother. And despite the injustice of the situation, it was up to me to save the circus. Because of where I came from, it was practically a crime to run away to such a shameful life, so I had put all of my friends in danger. And I cared more for the people than the actual activity itself. For the sake of my circus family, I had to give my mother what she wanted.

Without any help, I knew the decision I had to make. But would I be able to go through with it? Would I be able to return to Axminster and live in my mother's home like none of this had ever happened? I couldn't imagine forgetting this life. Would I be able to marry Joseph? What about the relationship I had started to build with Cassius? I couldn't forget him and his constant pestering, or the way he had helped me, time and time again.

Suddenly Cassius shuffled next to me and slowly opened his eyes. They were glazed over and dreary, but deeply concerned when he saw my worry. "What's wrong?" he asked, sitting up to brush a tear off my cheek.

"Nothing." I smiled lightly. Cassius was a determined soul. He was more passionate than anyone I'd ever met, and if I told him about the distress the circus was in, he would say *Screw your mother. She can come here if she wants to ruin us. I'll be buried in the ground before I let someone touch our tents.* And he would. He would do anything for the circus.

"I've got terrible cramps. I'm bleeding early," I lied.

"Oh, say no more!" he said, meaning it most literally.

I laughed at how childlike he could be.

Cassius rubbed his eyes tiredly and yawned. The dark circles under his eyes were growing lighter day by day, which made me smile. I tried to think about what he may have looked like as a young boy. He must have had tousled black hair, glistening eyes, and chubby cheeks. And he was probably very small and skinny, which prompted me to ask, "Why did you come to the circus?" I leaned onto my elbow to face him.

He looked away quickly and said, "Like everyone else, I had nowhere else to go." He shrugged and slipped on a shirt.

"But why? Where were your parents?" I tried to compel him to answer me, but I could tell he was slipping further and further away.

"Look, just because we're getting closer doesn't mean I'll tell you everything about my past," he scoffed.

His honesty was like a shot to the heart. I admitted, I did want to know more about him. I wanted to know the little things that made him angry, or why he picked at the skin around his thumb when he was nervous, or why he blinked incessantly—far more than the average human. I wanted to know why the animals he worked with made him smile. And if I left, I'd never know these things. I'd never be able to walk on the tightrope again. And I would never be able to drink and laugh with the people who had become so dear to me.

Looking at the stubborn boy across from me, I questioned my decision more and more. I had to find Monroe and think of an alternative to save the circus. I couldn't just leave this behind. I needed to stand up to my mother, once and for all. So, I rose from the bed and opened the door.

I wasn't angry with Cassius. I was angry with my situation. And as irksome as Cassius could be, he was someone I wanted to understand. And I couldn't do that if I was hundreds of miles away.

When I entered Monroe's office, he was surprised to see me. "I must say, I've seen you more than any of the other performers over the last three days," Monroe said with a laugh.

I chuckled and wrung my hands together, realizing they had begun to sweat. "I can't abandon the circus. I just can't. Will you help me think of a way to turn my mother around?"

Monroe pinched his mouth together, thinking over my decision. "Of course. Come sit." He motioned to the empty chair next to him. "Just let me finish this last calculation."

I took a seat and watched him scrawl down a bunch of numbers. Monthly expenditures, I presumed. He folded the paper and inserted it into an envelope, sealing it with his tongue. Picking up his pen, he scrawled the name of a business on the outside—*THE BANK OF HEWE*.

The way he wrote his E's was quite odd. They looked like a backwards three, loopy and unrefined. But I recognized it from somewhere. Suddenly I remembered that I'd seen it in the letter I received from the perpetrator months ago. Written inside were the words *RUN WHILE YOU CAN*, and the penmanship looked identical to this.

Suddenly, I panicked. I could be wrong. Hundreds of people probably wrote their E's like that. I looked up slowly and my eyes met Monroe's, igniting his dull grey eyes, as if he knew the reason for my concern, but, how could he?

The fear of being in the same room as this man made me jump up out of my chair.

"Is everything alright?" Monroe asked in concern.

"Yes. I- I have to go," I stuttered. My blood raced and my hands shook. "I forgot Mr. Monte wanted to discuss the next performance with me." I ran from the room and sprinted toward Cassius's room, and when I pounded my fist on the dark oak door, he opened it in haste. I just shook my head while trying to form the right words. How could I say this? How could I divulge that Monroe—one of the most respected men in the circus, could be a killer. The one who killed Penelope, Cassius's own sister! "Monroe- Monroe's handwriting." My eyes darted around the room before I grabbed Cassius's hand and pulled him toward my room. I needed to give him a visual. I shuffled through the paperwork in my desk to find the letter for him to read. "Monroe's handwriting is the same as the handwriting on this page. I'm sure of it."

Cassius scanned the letter, remembering the night I had received it. He must have looked over it ten more times before finally managing a response. "That's not possible. Monroe is one of the managers. It couldn't be him."

I rested my hands on my hips and paced around my room in a circle. "But the way he loops his E's—that's exactly how they're written in that letter."

"It could be anyone's handwriting," Cassius urged, as he gripped my shoulders.

I nodded slowly, "You're right. I'm jumping to conclusions." I was so eager to catch the killer that I was picking out people at random.

"You have a right to." He tilted my head up so I could look him in the eyes. "I would do the same thing if I were being threatened. But I've known Monroe for years, and he is an exceptionally honorable man. He would never do anything to harm anyone."

I nodded my head, trying to convince myself that Cassius was right.

***

The perpetrator...

She was getting closer day by day. And I couldn't have her knowing who I was before the big night. That would ruin the grand spectacle. To keep her quiet, there was one last thing I had to do before show night.

***

The show in Axminster was only a few days away, and it was designed to have an underwater theme. Cassius would continue as my lover—a prince coming to rescue a maiden who was trapped by the king of the sea. I was to be graceful and helpless, as all women ought to be. But another element would make this show a bit tougher—Cassius would have to learn the tightrope.

I stood below him, watching with giddiness as our roles were reversed.

"Edward, this is ridiculous!" Cassius shouted from the tightrope. He'd been standing there for five minutes and refused to take a step. Once in a while he'd lurch, as if he was about to try, but he would always bring himself back.

"No, this is genius. If you can do this, the crowd will love you." Mr. Monte encouraged him.

"They already do," Cassius argued, as his forehead beaded with sweat. "I joined the circus to ride and train animals. That is my specialty, not walking a tightrope."

"If you are unwilling to try something new, then you obviously aren't meant for the circus. The young boy that came to me years ago was willing to do anything-"

"Fine! Okay!" Cassius screamed, as he shook his head and placed both arms out to his side.

He fell at least a hundred times. He would take one step, but as soon as he transferred his weight to the other foot, he would fall off the side. After landing forcefully on the landing pad so many times, he stormed off and shouted, "This isn't going to work!"

Mr. Monte sighed and pinched his eyebrows together.

He began to walk toward Cassius before I stopped him to say, "Let me talk to him." Any criticism from his mentor—the one who'd been with him since he was a young boy—might make him feel defeated. It would be better coming from me.

I sat next to him on one of the wooden beams and studied the way his knees were pressed together, with his hands inserted between his legs like a little boy. "You know, it took me weeks to take two steps, and it was the happiest day of my life when I finally managed to do it."

Cassius scoffed, "We don't have that kind of time."

I didn't mind that he was taking his anger out on me. I could take it. He'd always given me the truth, and now it was time I returned the favor. "You're right. We don't. But no matter how hard I practiced, it's because of two people that I managed to make it across the rope."

Cassius focused on his hands.

"Mr. Monte and you," I declared.

He suddenly looked up at me in surprise.

I smiled and looked deep into his golden eyes. "Do you remember what you told me?" When his eyebrows drew together, I knew he didn't. "You told me that I was afraid and that I needed to think less. You said get on the rope and jump," I snickered at the memory. "It seemed impossible, and I asked you, 'What if I fall?'"

"Then you try again," Cassius finished for me, and his eyes grew bigger.

"I couldn't be angry with you after that, although it peeved me that such a rude, conceited ass was right."

"Ass?" Cassius laughed a true laugh.

"Now get out there. Don't think about falling, just feel the rope under your feet, okay?"

He nodded and before he jumped up, I grabbed his arm and gave him one last piece of advice. "Oh, and don't look down."

He clenched his jaw before bounding onto the podium. He shook his nervous hands and breathed out before taking a step, then steadily switched from the right foot to the left, only wobbling slightly.

Cassius glanced down, and not a second later, Mr. Monte screamed at him to stop doing so, and Cassius immediately lifted his head up to regain his balance.

I folded my hands in front of my chest, praying that Cassius would make it across.

His upper body jerked to the right, but he managed to keep his balance all the way across. Just before the end, he placed his heel on the rope by accident, which caused the rope to jerk and him to fall. He braced himself for impact, and when he landed, he was not defeated. "Did you see that?" He ran over to me and picked me up by my waist to swing me in a circle.

I laughed and grasped tightly around his neck while the room spun.

"Excellent, my boy." Mr. Monte slapped him on the back. "If you can make it across and learn some tricks on the ring for the next performance, you'll steal the spotlight from Miss Rose." Mr. Monte winked at me.

I just shook my head, "He's not *that* talented."

"Oh you don't think so? I'm going to practice all night. You better be ready for the crowd to shower me with white roses," Cassius said, and he nudged my shoulder.

I pushed him back playfully before grabbing my things. "I told Charlotte I'd spend the night with the dancers. I'll catch you in the morning."

I took one look back and spotted Mr. Monte's arm slung around Cassius's shoulder. Mr. Monte looked young and excited again. I felt relief as I let the tent flaps go and the two of them faded from view.

The stars were brighter tonight, and I couldn't wipe the smile off my face, thinking about Cassius's success on the rope. It was funny to think about how I'd been so against the idea of Cassius and I becoming *lovers from across the tracks*. But Mr. Monte was right. Cassius and I worked well together, and I must say our chemistry inspired great adoration from the crowd. I slung my bag higher on my shoulder and took in a breath so cold that it burned my lungs. There were five tents strung up in Axminster. One for the tightrope walker, one for the dancers, one for the flamethrowers, one for the lion tamer, and the last for the riders. We each had our own talent to practice and our own space to do so.

When I passed the second tent, I heard a soft rustling behind me and turned quickly to find a tumbleweed brushing up against the leather exterior of the tent. I continued on my way but not long after, I heard it again, and louder this time. When I turned around there was no sign of the tumbleweed, and no animal skipping across the way. *Huh.* I was only a few minutes away from the train, but I quickened my steps nonetheless.

It's not safe out there on your own. He's lurking around, just waiting to snap. I heard Flint's voice in my head, warning me...

I wasn't sure if I should turn back and confide in Cassius and Mr. Monte just to be safe, or if I should get over my worry and press on for the train. I could do it myself. I wasn't some little girl who needed help across the street.

But he's out there, my subconscious warned me.

I shook the thought from my mind. The perpetrator wouldn't attack me in the middle of the night, with no crowd watching. It didn't fit his agenda. *But who's to say a killer's agenda can't change?*

Suddenly I heard the sound again, although it resembled something closer to the crunch of boots on gravel. I whipped my head around and there stood a hulking man, dressed from head to toe in black. A mask covered his whole face and there were no cut-outs for his eyes or his mouth. I screamed and jumped back, and my ankle caught a branch, sending me sprawling to the ground.

He was large...larger than most of the performers at the circus. My mind was racing and my heart was pounding, yet I couldn't move. I couldn't determine who was under the mask. I couldn't even think about how to scream, I was so scared.

"Who are you?" my voice shook.

"You don't know my name, but I know yours," he cooed, and his voice was high in the silence of the night.

All I could hear was the replay of his shrill voice and the rapid beating of my own heart. I dug my hands into the earth and tried to get up, but as hard as I tried, I couldn't move. And I surely couldn't get away.

"Juniper, you've been very stubborn the past few months," he laughed lightly. Was this a game to him? Did he enjoy seeing me in pain, shattering my shoulder and burning my arms?

"Why do you want to hurt me?" I began to cry, looking for something around me to stop him, or at least slow him down until I could get to safety.

"Because you deserve it, darling."

I shivered when he leaned down to caress my cheek.

"As did Miss Penelope Plume."

It was clear now. This man killed Penelope Plume five years ago, and now he was back to kill me.

"You deserve to feel what *she* felt," he spat at me. "What they both felt!"

"They?" I asked, dumbfounded, frozen on the ground before him. Who was he talking about? This was all so confusing.

"Katriane!" he roared. His voice became louder and his face shook from side to side. Where were his eyes? I wanted to look in his eyes to determine who he was. But instead, he was just a black hole, ready to swallow me.

Tears rolled down my cheeks. Who was Katriane? I'd never heard of her before.

He sighed and regained his composure. "That's okay, my dear. All that matters is that you stay quiet about who I am," he snickered to himself.

My jaw trembled. "I don't know who you are, I promise," I cried.

He stood to his full height above me. Suddenly he began to unbutton the golden buckle on his breeches. "Good. Maybe this will make you rethink your position at the circus."

His words reminded me of Monroe's when he asked me to decide if it was safer to stay or return home. My eyes opened wide when I realized what was coming, and I clawed at the dirt and mustered the strength to stand. "Cassius!" I screamed as loudly as I could.

The man grabbed me by the waist, spun me around, and slapped me across the face.

I screamed and grabbed my face to ease the pain. "Please, stop!" I cried, trying to wrestle out of his grasp. I felt completely powerless.

Penelope was raped, Charlotte's voice repeated this phrase over and over in my mind until I couldn't hear anything else.

He managed to pull his pants down to his knees while still keeping hold of me, and secured his hand over my mouth to silence my screams. I continued to struggle, bucking my hips and moving my waist as much as I could, but his hands still managed to slip under my dress.

I bit down on his fingers as hard as I could and he jumped back, clutching his hand.

"Somebody help me!" I screamed at the top of my lungs.

The man elbowed me in the stomach and pushed me to the ground to climb on top of me. "You bitch!" He sneered as he tied a gag around my mouth. I tried to scream through the gag, but the sound was muffled beyond coherence. I cried until my throat was dry and hoarse, flapping my arms in the dirt, but of course, my strength was nothing compared to his.

The man pushed my skirt above my waist and tried to force himself on me. I screamed as loudly as I could through the gag. I felt so utterly helpless and overpowered. There was nothing I could do to get out of this, no one near enough to hear me. My hands were bound by his sweaty hands behind my back, and as much as I squirmed, he still managed to keep a hold of me. I thought of everything my mother had told me.

Never walk in the dark by yourself. Never wear revealing clothing to arouse men. And never speak to them as if they are more powerful.

And although her words seemed so unimportant at the time, they made me rethink my decisions. Did I do this to myself? Did I portray myself to be a woman of desire and beauty to the point of being reckless? What was I thinking, putting myself in so much danger while there was a killer about? I should have listened to Flint when I had the chance. I should have protected myself. But instead of being careful, I gave up everything I once was to chase the dream of finding a home here. I abandoned the old Juniper and remade her into a girl of immodesty, stupidity, and frivolity. And now I was going to be punished for it. My virtue would be taken as a price for my childish actions.

"I'm sorry," I cried, although I didn't know to whom. Maybe to my mother, maybe to Flint. I wished I could apologize to both of them for not listening before now.

I dug my nails into the earth and tried to wriggle my arms free. This man on top of me felt so vile, so wrong, I thought I might throw up.

He pushed my chest into the floor, making it difficult to breath. I began to choke and a black tunnel slowly began to invade my vision, until everything faded out of view.

Cassius...

I unwrapped the tape from the balls of my feet to reveal badly calloused skin. They had not split open, which was a gift from heaven. I remembered when I came to Mr. Monte in tears after riding for hours in my younger days. The palms of my hands had become calloused from gripping the reins so tightly, and often they would split open and become infected.

I looked up at Mr. Monte now and remembered the man who had consoled me, wiped my tears, and cleaned my wounds. A soft breeze traveled into the tent, making my hot skin scream with relief. I couldn't stop smiling. Finding a new talent and becoming successful at it was the most invigorating feeling. Of course, I was good at taming lions, but this was an altogether new kind of excitement.

Mr. Monte laughed out of nowhere and the lines beside his eyes crinkled. "I remember when you were a stubborn teen. You had just become captain of the riding team," he began his story.

I remembered that day well too. My parents had left me when I was young, so I never even knew my own birth date. Upon arriving at the circus, Mr. Monte assigned me a new birthday—December 10. And two days after my fifteenth birthday, as a gift, I received a simple gold medal that designated me as the captain of the riding team.

"Captains had to be able to perform all skills to perfection. You had been struggling on one in particular." Mr. Monte turned to me and squinted, his memory faltering.

"The Wimborne Twist." I nodded. For this skill, the rider had to dismount his horse while holding the reins and performing a 360-degree twist. The hard part was that the rider then had to hook his heel into the foothold of the saddle on the other side of the horse. Essentially, the rider twisted off the horse and kicked his legs under the horse's belly until his foot was securely hooked in the foothold. It required a lot of upper body strength, and I struggled to get my foot in the hold, which put me at risk of being trampled by the horse.

"You came to me in a tantrum, your face beet red," Mr. Monte laughed. "I tried to settle you down, but you were too stubborn to listen." Suddenly Mr. Monte's big smile turned more sincere, and his eyes dropped to the specks of sand at his feet. "I'm glad you have someone like Juniper to see past your anger and help you," he said, and he looked up at me.

What was that expression on his face? Pride? I wouldn't know what a father's approval looked like, but I assumed it would be something like this. Suddenly the corners of my mouth lifted and the back of my throat constricted. I wasn't very good at physical touch, unless it was with women, but I tried my best at giving Mr. Monte's neck a little squeeze. "I couldn't have asked for a better dad," I told him sincerely.

I heard him take in a large breath, and then he hesitated for a moment before slapping me on the back. "I am no good at fatherly advice, but I will say this," he pointed, daring me to listen closely. "Keep her around."

Without any other information, I knew he was talking about Juniper. I thought of her suddenly—her unruly black curls and the spiritedness that ran deep in her blood. Most of the women who came to me were needy and desperate and just wanted to hop into my bed. And Juniper was hard to understand and even harder to communicate with, but she had aspirations, which was something I liked. I despised her months ago. Literally. I was so fixated on making her leave. But she stayed. She fought back, and it opened my mind about the wealthy and the way the world operated. She challenged me, and although I wanted to throw her across the room sometimes, I was grateful that she was so committed to her own beliefs. She was more than just my next conquest. I wanted to know her deeply, and I wanted her to know me that way too.

"After eighteen years of knowing you, I have not seen a change this drastic in you. It makes me happy." Mr. Monte smiled kindly.

I didn't realize I'd changed. I hadn't felt this good in a long time, and a small part of me knew it was because of her. "I know I'm stubborn, but thank you for always supporting me. You never gave up on me." My eyes welled with tears. I hadn't ever confessed my gratitude to Mr. Monte. How could I have gone eighteen years without saying this? It saddened me to think of all of the work he'd done and how diligent he'd been with me. I was glad to finally tell him how much it meant to me.

Mr. Monte opened his mouth to speak, just as a high-pitched scream echoed throughout the tent. It sounded far away, but I stood quickly to poke my head out of the tent and survey the area. The dancers were usually a rowdy group, but it didn't sound like a girls' pillow fight kind of scream.

The scream rang out again, more scary and desperate this time. "CASSIUS!!" I heard my name called, and before I knew what I was doing, I was sprinting through the field. That was Juniper's voice, I knew it. She screamed again, this time much louder. I was getting closer. Clearing the stacks of wheat, with my legs moving as quickly as they would move, I pushed the dread from my mind. I stopped for a moment to search through the darkness, but my eyes were slow to adjust. I saw a flash of something ahead and whipped my head to find the white floral day dress Juniper tended to slip over her leotard while commuting to practice. I took off at a run when I spotted a giant man next to her pushing her stomach to the ground. He was barely noticeable because of the black clothing covering every inch of his body.

This is him. This is your chance, my subconscious said to me. If I didn't stop him soon, he'd kill her. But when I spotted him grab at her skirt, my heart stopped. I'd had nightmares about this nearly every night for the last five years. *Penelope Plume, brutally sexually assaulted in the compound of the circus.* I couldn't forget the headlines. My limbs were frozen. My own sister had been raped five years ago, and now the same thing was happening to Juniper. Sweet

Juniper, who never deserved any of this. This was the same killer. I knew that to be true now. He had some sick need to end the tightrope walkers and pleasure himself in the process. It was disgusting. I couldn't let him defile Juniper. It would destroy her. Thinking of Penelope and how this man led her to kill herself, I surged forward with my blood pumping. I couldn't help Penelope, but I could save Juniper.

I collided with the man and slammed him into the dirt. His arms flailed wildly, but I managed to get my hands around his throat and push his head into the ground. I pressed my lips together and my face shook with my hate for this man. I had five years of anger built up in me, and all of it was meant for him.

He was much bigger than me, and before I knew it, he slammed his hand into my elbow, forcing me to break my grip. He launched his fist into my face, making my head spin violently and my mouth gush with blood. My vision went black, giving him the chance to push me off him and run in the opposite direction, into the tree line.

I shook my head to restore my vision, but when I searched the distance, there was nothing to be seen. The man had blended into the darkness like he was never there.

I slid over to unhook the gag from Juniper's mouth, and she coughed and sputtered beside me, trying to take the air back into her lungs. "Go after him-" she tried to say. By the second, I could see her strength fading and horror setting in. "Go after him!" She screamed with tears dripping down her face.

I weighed my options, knowing I should attempt to find him, but I was afraid it was hopeless. The man was gone. I was so angry. How could I have let him escape? At this moment, all I could do was try and put Juniper back together.

Her jaw quivered and she looked up at the sky and blinked to keep from crying. Her hands were gripped together so tightly, her skin turned white, and they began to shake. I kneeled next to her and tried to fix her skirt. She looked so scared. I couldn't bear to think of how my sister must have felt. There was no one there for her. She must have cried out until she couldn't anymore, and no one came. I couldn't save her.

Tears welled in my eyes. I wished I could've been there. I wished I could have beaten the life out of that man. I wanted him dead for what he did to both of them, and I felt sick with shame at my inability to stop him. I was full of vengeance, but that was nothing compared to the despair Juniper must have felt. She just laid there on the ground, sobbing, her arms wrapped tightly around her legs, and when I reached out to touch her, she jumped back.

"Don't touch me!" she screamed.

I held up my hands in an attempt to ease her worry. I didn't know what to do but I wanted to comfort her, to say something, anything, to make this better. I wanted to hold her and tell her that everything would be okay. I didn't want her to be afraid of me, but she had nearly been raped, and I understood she couldn't bear to be touched now. I couldn't just leave her out here, so I approached her slowly and said, "I'm going to get you back to your room, okay?"

She looked at the ground, trembling, and remained silent while I grabbed under her legs and around her lower back. She thrashed in my arms, and as I walked her back to the train, she continued to punch at my chest, pleading with me to put her down. I sniffed to hold back my tears and looked forward to avoid her eyes. She could take her anger out on me all she wanted, but I was still going to protect her.

I had to stop this man. He didn't deserve justice. He deserved death. And that was what I was going to give him.

Chapter 25

I spent hours trying to fall asleep, watching the flames from the candle on my bedside table flicker on the wall. The moment my eyes closed, an image of the man dressed in black invaded my mind, and my eyes flew open again. My chest hurt, my lungs hurt, my whole body hurt. I had never felt so small. I couldn't remember anything other than the blackness of him. His eyes were empty sockets and his frame blended into the dark abyss of my dreams. I spent the night drifting in and out of sleep. And when morning came, there was a thick film of sweat on my brow and my whole body was shaking.

At noon, someone came to check on me, but I couldn't meet their eyes. A small part of me hoped it would be Cassius who walked through that door, but it was only a nurse. She brought a tray of food, but I was too sick to eat.

I was sure everyone in the circus had heard what happened, which only made the situation worse. It was hard to accept the fact myself, and now I would have to worry about how everyone else would treat me because of it.

I got up for the first time at two o'clock to dress in more comfortable clothing. Last night I hadn't had the energy to take off my day dress and leotard. And seeing myself in the mirror, nothing looked different. But everything *felt* different. I looked down at my legs and memories of the attack surged back to me. The feeling of the fabric of my dress being pushed over my bottom; the feeling of my stinging skin when he slapped me across the face. Realizing there were tears sliding slowly down my cheeks, I grabbed the top sheet from my bed and covered the mirror at once. When my image faded, my heart settled a bit.

Suddenly a knock sounded at my door. I didn't want to speak to anyone. They would look at me like an injured animal or barely speak to me for fear their words would break me—and they might. I just wanted it to be quiet.

But the voice that spoke through the door was soft and gentle. "Juniper?"

Cassius. My heart warmed. I thought of him every time that vile man entered my mind. I thought of his confusion when he considered chasing the man last night. But the deep sadness in his eyes made me realize he wasn't concerned just for me. His sister. I completely forgot that this had happened to Penelope five years ago. Was he there? Did he see it happen? And if not, did Penelope ever tell him about the atrocity before she took her life? *Cassius.* I began to sob for him and my heart wrenched. I couldn't imagine the pain he had experienced, losing his sister. If anything like that were to happen to Colette, I would never be the same.

The pain I felt now was so intense, I didn't know if I would survive it. How could I ever feel good again? How could I ever let someone touch me without being terrified? I buried my head in my hands. Why did this have to happen?

"Juniper," Cassius said, and then he paused before continuing. "Mr. Monte has gotten the police involved. They'll be on guard throughout the train in case the perpetrator tries something before the performance. And they'll be posted in the tent on performance night. We're going to find this man."

Cassius always knew what to say. I didn't want to be coddled, comforted, or touched. I just wanted to know that all of this would be over. And that's exactly what he told me. I slowly got up and walked to the door, swallowed the lump in my throat, and pulled the door open.

Seeing Cassius brought tears to my eyes. The softness of his face reminded me of something important—something I'd almost forgotten. My circus family was always going to be there for me. Cassius kept me alive last night. And Gus, Charlotte, Olive, Flint— they would do the same. Any of them would risk their lives for me. It would be foolish to think that the next few weeks and months wouldn't be painful, because they would be. But I had something great here, and I couldn't give up on that because of a deranged killer whose only pleasure came from hurting others.

I nodded slowly, a small motion that took a great amount of effort.

Cassius looked at me tenderly and said, "Take today off, but we should practice tomorrow if we hope to make the show spectacular."

I nodded, but the idea of resting all day, being forced to think about the night before, sounded worse than wearing my body out on the rope. Cassius began to walk away before I could utter, "Cassius-"

He spun around quickly.

"Where is Mr. Monte?" I asked.

"In his office," he answered patiently.

"Thank you." I donned a coat and tied up my boots, preparing to take my mind off the perpetrator. I knocked lightly on Mr. Monte's door and heard a faint sound from within, beckoning me to enter.

"Juniper!" Mr. Monte stood abruptly, surprised by my appearance. "How are you, darling?"

"Fine." I swallowed heavily. I couldn't talk about what had happened yet. "I wanted to ask you about our next performance," I said, and I took a seat without being invited to do so.

He waved his arm welcomingly, "Go right ahead." His voice was calm and his motions were stiff, telling me he was worried about how I might react. But he didn't press me for details, maybe sensing that it wasn't the right time.

"Axminster is my hometown, and I know almost every esteemed family, from the chapel all the way to the mountains on the outskirts. They'll be expecting something extraordinary, something they've never seen before. And as one of their own, they will expect even more from me."

Mr. Monte listened intently and nodded his head along with my words.

"I want to do something different. I want to create a story they will never forget. Imagine the magicians erupting in smoke, the dancers doing triple spins, and the jesters rolling all the way into the crowd on their unicycles-"

When I took a breath, I watched Mr. Monte carefully. His silence made me nervous. He sat with his hands folded in front of his lips while his eyes flicked between mine eagerly. And then he sighed and sat straighter in his chair as he said, "I love it."

Those words gave me the reassurance to continue, "When I first arrived at the circus, people were wary of accepting me, thinking I was nothing more than the money in my pocket. And I'm sure the wealthy crowd's opinion of me has changed as well. I want to create a connection between the rich and the outcasts of our world to show everyone that success isn't defined by family name. I want the setting to be glistening in diamonds, and when the main character—the wealthy daughter of a noble family—leaves to begin her life as a circus performer, the setting will shift to a dirty, rusty one. I think this will set the stage for the pursuit of free will and the triumph of the human spirit. We need lively music, mesmerizing costumes-"

"And of course, a love story," Mr. Monte interrupted me briefly.

I smiled at the thought of Cassius and I performing together and said, "Yes, a love story. But we also need to engage the men in the crowd. What about fighting and disagreement?"

Mr. Monte nodded more eagerly. "Yes. The wealthy will resent the fame the circus is achieving and feel their status in society slipping, and a brawl will commence at the climax of the story." He grabbed a piece of paper and began to sketch some ideas for the scenes and costumes. When he looked up at me, he said, "It seems we have some solid ideas in the works."

I smiled and said, "It seems we do indeed."

"I should go talk to Valetta about costume designs. I'll stop by your room later to discuss the plan for your part in the performance." He jumped out of his seat in excitement.

"I'll be in the tent," I announced spontaneously. I needed to get back on the rope. "The only thing holding me together is the tightrope, and I owe it to everyone to do well in the performance."

"I'm glad to hear that," Mr. Monte said.

I rose from my chair and walked to the door. When I reached for the door handle, Mr. Monte's voice sounded faint behind me.

"I'm proud of you," he continued. "I know I don't say that enough, but I couldn't have asked for a better tightrope walker to join our crew."

I couldn't speak, but I turned to give him a look of gratitude.

"I'm so sorry for what happened to you and that I couldn't protect you from it, but for some reason, I think it's going to be okay." He swallowed nervously. "I think you're very different from our Penelope Plume. I think you'll stay with us." His voice was gentle and hopeful.

"I'm planning on it, Sir." I dipped my head to the floor.

As he opened the door to go, he said, "Will you come to Valetta's office with me to talk about the costumes for the performance? I could use your help."

I'd offered my help countless times before, but I was touched that this time Mr. Monte was asking me for my help.

Valetta shuffled her small feet feverishly, gathering fabrics of all colors and textures—white fur, silk and satin, wide wale corduroy, heaps of tule, and pinstriped knits of different sizes and colors. She gathered fabric until she couldn't carry any more, threw it all on a wide table, pushed her falling glasses up onto the bridge of her nose, and untangled a measuring tape from around her neck to begin.

I began sketching rough designs as she advised on how the looks would come together.

"I have this beautiful corduroy, but what on earth could we use it for?" Valetta asked.

My finger popped up signaling a brilliant idea, and I spouted, "Trousers."

"That's perfect! With suspenders and bowties, sure to impress the wealthiest spectators."

Valetta hopped in front of her sewing machine, and her foot began bobbing rhythmically on the pedal. She wasted no time in getting started on what was sure to be our most elaborate costumes yet.

Meanwhile, Mr. Monte and I continued to talk through different ideas as they came to mind. My hands were stained with charcoal, and by the end of the night I felt like a bona fide costume designer, as I worked alongside Valetta. Mr. Monte watched proudly, giving his insight on the men's costumes, and the excitement never left his eyes.

Being a part of this process made me believe I could be more a part of the circus than just being a performer. I came here thinking I might not even succeed as a performer, but I had begun to see the possibility of leading the circus into the future.

I felt renewed by having worked with Valetta and Mr. Monte the night before, and I awoke planning to practice hard. As I pulled my tight, tan leotard over my hips, I tried not to imagine his hands on my waist, pushing me into the ground. I pulled the straps over my shoulders and had to physically shake my head to get rid of the feeling of his hands on my throat. I felt nauseous, so I ripped open my door and walked into the light corridor, where the blinding sun forced me to raise my arms to cover my eyes. I walked quickly down the hallway until I reached the exit of the train. As I stood there at the door, I took in the crisp and serene air of the open fields, but I had the overwhelming feeling that I couldn't go out there alone.

"Charlotte-" I stopped her when she walked in front of me.

She whipped her head around and her eyes immediately brightened. "Juniper!" She wrapped her arms around my neck. "I'm so glad to see you. How are you doing?"

"Will you walk me out?" I asked abruptly.

A low voice spoke from behind me, "Allow me ma'am."

I turned to find Gus offering me his arm, and I accepted. We walked slowly through the fields, and I kept my head down while trying to enjoy the breeze waving through my hair. Despite my fear, Gus's presence by my side made me feel safe. Gus was a rather large man—six foot, four inches was my guess. When we reached the tent, he walked me safely inside.

Cassius turned around quickly when he heard the flaps of the tent shift, and his face lit up when he saw me. "Thank you, Gus. Most appreciated," Cassius said, and eagerly shook his hand.

Gus looked like a giant next to Cassius. That was not to say that Cassius was small, but Gus was hulking compared to him.

Cassius's eyes caught mine for a fraction of a second before they darted away nervously, and I stood there awkwardly, wondering what to do. Cassius usually took the reins in situations like these, but he just stood there with his hands folded in front of his waist. I tapped my foot on the floor, trying to think of what to say, when Mr. Monte sprang into the tent.

"My beauties, my stars, I have an idea!" He spread his arms like he was introducing himself. Noticing our lack of emotion, his face fell. "Try to appear more enthusiastic, will you?" He rolled his eyes and scoffed, deciding to continue despite our blank expressions. "For many years, we have showcased the tightrope walker, primarily on the tightrope and the steel ring. But this year, to celebrate our wonderful addition," Mr. Monte looked at me and winked, which slightly lifted my spirits, "I want to try something a little different." He paused dramatically and allowed us to soak it in.

"And what is that?" Cassius asked harshly.

"The trapeze!" Mr. Monte's eyes widened in excitement. "It requires the same strength and the same flexibility, so it will be no problem for you, my dear Rose."

I interrupted him quickly before he could travel too far down this road. "But Mr. Monte, the trapeze requires two participants."

His smile only grew bigger, as he agreed, "Precisely, Juniper."

Mr. Monte looked to Cassius, who immediately ran his hands over his eyes and turned away. "Oh God," he said, as if it was the end of the world. The trapeze took a more developed kind of trust, which I was sure Cassius and I had. Plus, he had done astoundingly well on the tightrope.

"My boy, you will be amazing! The trapeze equipment will arrive tomorrow, and in the meantime, I want you two to spend some time stretching. I'm looking at you, Cas!" And with that, Mr. Monte turned on his heel and stalked out of the tent.

The silence in the room was deafening. Instead of nudging Cassius to do anything, I took a seat on the floor and brought my toes together in a butterfly stretch.

Cassius slowly took a seat across from me, and he kept his eyes on his toes, not sparing me a glance.

"Is there something wrong?" I asked him, more harshly than I intended to.

"No," he spoke softly. When he brought his toes together, his knees rose high into the air and his back hunched awkwardly. He was doing it all wrong.

"If you straighten your lower back, you'll have more chance of actually stretching your muscles," I advised him.

He lengthened his back and groaned. "This hurts," he whined like a child.

"That means it's working."

The next two hours were spent in complete silence, other than the one moment Cassius accidentally touched my hand and apologized quietly, like he was in trouble. I knew last night was terrifying for both of us, but I didn't want him to remind me of what happened. I wanted him to make me forget. When the sun fell, I couldn't find the courage to talk to him about it, so instead I retreated to Mr. Monte's office for a cup of tea and some advice. Mr. Monte had seen how Penelope suffered; maybe he could help me too.

He poured me a cup of boiling blueberry tea, adding a dash of rum to his china cup. Mr. Monte had a few small knick-knacks around the room that appeared to hold value, such as his china tea set and the crystal wine glasses in his curio cabinet. The rest of the room was rather plain, not decorated in crystal or fancy furniture, but that was what made these items stand out.

Mr. Monte spoke up in response to my wondering expression. "I know, the trapeze seems a little far-fetched." He bobbed his head to a silent rhythm.

"No, I love it," I said truthfully. "During my third year of ballet, there was a moment in our performance when the smallest girl would be lifted in the center of the group of dancers. I had practiced for months, hoping that I would be selected, but I wasn't small enough. So, I was on the outside and I watched as someone else got the spotlight. But now, if all goes to plan," I said excitedly, "I'll get to be the high flyer!" But after months of having the lights on me and the crowd watching me, I didn't know if I felt the same way. Now that I had become a young woman, I realized that I didn't need to be in the spotlight to feel like I was seen. I had been seen for months by the circus.

Mr. Monte smiled. "Cassius may resist it for a day or two, but in time, he'll put aside his pride and realize just how fun this could be."

"That's actually what I wanted to ask you about," I told him. I thought about Cassius avoiding my eyes and the constant furrow in his brows—the look of concern, not anger. And before we moved forward in our performance, I needed to understand why. "Do you know why Cassius is acting so strangely? I know that his sister was sexually assaulted, even more than I was, but-"

"She was raped. It's okay to say it, Miss Rose." Mr. Monte folded his hands on his desk and sighed heavily, like the words were taking a toll on him. "Of course, what happened to you is a terrifying reminder for him. He never knew what happened to his sister until the coroner's report came back. She never told him. And he blames himself for not being there to save her, every single day. And although he was able to save you last night, his concern runs deeper than that." Mr. Monte paused to think. "Cassius and Penelope were abandoned as children. Their mother and father left them when

Cassius turned two. I guess they just decided they couldn't handle two children with no money. So, they left the children in their aunt's care in Dangarnon."

"I never knew that," I whispered in disbelief.

"Their aunt died a year later." Mr. Monte's eyes were glued to his desk. "Cassius was only three years old."

"They were completely alone?"

He nodded and continued. "They drifted from orphanage to orphanage but were never adopted. Penelope was growing too old for the orphanage, so three days before she was officially discharged to take care of herself, she grabbed her brother's hand with a plan in mind, and they left. They crossed the border and ran all the way to Penketh, where we were performing. Cassius was six when we took him into the circus."

I couldn't even imagine being on my own in an orphanage for three years, surrounded by strangers, let alone being abandoned by my own parents. Was he hungry? Was he cold? I was disappointed in myself again for being so entitled. As dull as my life in Axminster was, I was extremely fortunate to have grown up in a stable family. I had three meals a day and warm clothes on my back. I had activities that excited me, like baking and ballet. And Cassius had none of that, until he found the circus. It had been too easy for me to forget that no one here had come from the privileged life I had.

"What happened last night reminded him of his sister, but it also reminded him of when he was a child. He's afraid, Juniper. Afraid of being abandoned. And as much as he tries to push you and his friends away, all of you mean more to him than he'll ever admit." Mr. Monte chugged the last of his tea, leaving only the dark flakes at the bottom of his cup.

"Thank you for telling me. He might never have told me himself." In that moment, I was finally able to stop thinking about what had happened to me last night and think of someone else. I thought of Penelope and the events that drove her mad, of Cassius and his overwhelming fear of being alone, and of Mr. Monte and the way he loved Penelope and Cassius and gave them a home and a family.

"I don't know." Mr. Monte smiled lightly and met my eyes for the first time since I had sat down. "I think he might eventually. He is fonder of you than you know."

Just hearing those words made every doubt I had about Cassius and the circus blow away, like dust on a book I'd been reluctant to read, not knowing how the story would end.

"Thank you, again."

"There are guards lining the hallway and one positioned outside of your room," he reassured me.

I closed his door behind me, dreading the thought of going back to my room, despite the guard outside. I still doubted my safety. What if the perpetrator were to kill the guard? Then I might be locked in my room, alone with him, caged in like an animal. Thinking of Cassius and his story, as well as my own fear, I thought I might be able to kill two birds with one stone.

I knocked lightly on Cassius's bedroom door, and his steps were quick, which made me feel such relief. I spotted a guard not fifteen feet away, but I didn't feel safe lingering around.

"Juniper!" His face was full of delight when he saw me.

Thank God. I couldn't stand it if I had to be with him in awkward silence a moment longer. That just wasn't how Cassius and I operated. We communicated with harsh words, insults, and sometimes meaningful sentiments. "I, um, was wondering if I could stay a while?"

He may not have been able to be there for his sister, but he could be here for me, and that made him smile and open the door wide.

I walked inside as if it was the first time I'd been there. The black sheets looked darker, more consuming. I ran my hand over the red duvet, and the soft velvet felt so warm and inviting, like standing over the oven in winter after playing in the snow. I closed my eyes before pulling back the duvet to lay down. Cassius moved toward me and gently pulled the covers over my chest. My mother always used to tuck the blankets so tightly around my sides, it felt like I couldn't breathe. But Cassius's sheets were loose around me, allowing me to move.

He laid down next to me, keeping his distance.

I laid my hands on my chest and looked up at the ceiling. The soft moonlight shone onto the floor in small rays of dripping silver. I wondered if I touched them, if they would spread across my skin like liquid or if they would dissipate like dust. I shifted my attention to the lamp on the bedside table and the golden atmosphere hovering around the shade. But in the shadow at the edge of the room was a man in a black mask, and for the first time I could see his eyes. They were illuminated by moonlight and had extremely dark centers, expanding to silver gray. I looked away immediately.

Cassius pretended not to notice, but I knew he did. So instead of looking back into the darkness, I focused my attention on him. His back was turned to me, and he put his hands gently under his head. I wished I could snap a picture and capture that moment forever—the look of his legs slightly bent and the curl of the hair on his neck. How could someone so brave and talented also seem so small? I tried to imagine what it would have been like to be him. Would my hair be longer? Ratty and unkempt? Would my stomach hurt from hunger? I'd never been hungry before, not once, so it was hard to imagine. I wondered if he ever tried to imagine what it would have been like to be me. Had he tried to imagine what it would feel like to be full or content? Suddenly I got angry at the thought that he might long for a different life, because then he wouldn't have ended up here.

I reached across the spacious bed and touched him without thinking. My fingers caught fire when they came in contact with his sharp shoulder blades.

Cassius slowly turned around to face me and his eyes were soft— so soft I think I could have melted into them.

"Thank you," I said sincerely.

He continued to look at me, remaining silent.

When tears welled in my eyes, he inched closer and took my face in his hands, bringing my head into the crook of his neck. I breathed in his rusty smell and felt the warmth of his neck on my forehead. I took the first calm breath I'd taken all day, and when my nose stopped quivering and my eyes stopped stinging, I found the courage to say what was on my mind. I deeply hoped it would reassure Cassius.

"If it weren't for you, I would have been seriously hurt last night. I might even be dead. But I want you to know that I'm not going to leave because of what happened."

He remained silent before inhaling sharply and saying with a shaky voice, "Good."

I wrapped my arms around him and my heart felt full. This was where I was meant to be. Not in Axminster, not with my mother, and not pretending to fit in with the wealthy. Here. At the circus. And in Cassius's arms. I didn't know what our future would look like together, but he was the bravest, most talented man in Mr. Monte's circus, and I wanted him to know he had changed me in every way possible...for the better.

"Good! Right there, that's perfect!" Mr. Monte held a pen between his lips which made his voice slightly muffled and incoherent. The equipment for the trapeze had arrived in large trucks right outside my practice tent, and Mr. Monte came with notes in hand, making sure everything we needed was there. Once the deliverers helped us set it up, it was time to attempt our first trapeze swing.

Getting onto the trapeze was similar to getting onto the tightrope. There was a tall platform for me to stand on, and on the other side of the tent, Cassius stood on a similar platform. Right in front of my head was a bar to grab onto, connected by two long ropes running up to the rafters of the tent.

"Alright, you two. There is a net right below you, so if you fall, you'll land safely. After you grab onto the bar and step off the platform, you need to swing your body as hard as you can to gain momentum. When you swing back, kick your ankles up and pull yourself up so your waist rests on the bar."

That seemed easy enough, I reassured myself.

"Are you sure we won't collide with one another?" Cassius shouted down to Mr. Monte.

"You'd have to be swinging a lot more to hit one another, so don't worry about that."

I grabbed the bar and Cassius followed. I shifted my hands around, hoping they would stick and thought, *God, please don't let me fall.* I felt light at first, but gravity quickly pulled my weight toward the ground. Soaring through the air was exhilarating. I kicked my legs forward, then back to produce the momentum Mr. Monte talked about, and then kicked extra hard and bucked my hips to force my ankles to the bar. When my ankles touched the bar, I used all the strength in my arms to pull myself up. And without too much trouble, my hips settled onto the bar, and I hung there.

I wanted to scream, I was so happy. That was so much easier than balancing on the tightrope.

Looking across the room, I saw that Cassius had completed the sequence as well. "What now?" he asked.

"You fall." Mr. Monte said, as if it was common knowledge.

"What?" I yelled. I didn't know why the idea of falling still surprised me so much. What did I think would happen? The bar would magically lower to the ground? A harness would bring me back to the platform? No, the only way was down.

Mr. Monte bent over his knees and laughed.

I took a steadying breath and pulled my hips off the bar so I was hanging limply by my arms, and without a second thought, I fell. My heart plummeted into my stomach while I kept my hands securely over my chest, and after a few seconds, my back hit the net and I sprang up into the air. It took a few more bounces to finally settle my weight, but when I stopped, I began to laugh, a deep laugh full of excitement and terror. When Cassius finally let go, the weight of his body helped him settle much faster, and hearing my giddy laughter made him laugh too. What was so invigorating about the feeling of falling? Maybe it had to do with the adrenaline rush, or maybe it was not knowing if we would land in one piece.

Chapter 26

For the past week, I'd been training non-stop with the thought that my family might see me perform. Part of me doubted they'd dare to enter the muck pit of this common life, but part of me knew they'd be curious enough to want to see me in action.

Cassius remained my constant, and performing on the trapeze together gave me great comfort. We had learned a few more tricks, slowly, and we were getting better. And even a taste of what we could do would bring the audience to their knees. I was sure of it.

"What are we doing today, Sir?" I asked.

"Stop calling me Sir. It makes me feel too old," Mr. Monte said, and he shivered grotesquely.

"Sorry," I quickly added.

"Today, I want to perfect a trick for the performance coming up."

Suddenly it hit me that one week from today, I could be looking into the eyes of my family. One week from today, they could be deciding my worth as a circus performer.

"This will take a lot of strength on your part," Mr. Monte said, pointing to Cassius. "And a lot of attention to detail on yours," he said to me. "It's called a Catch! The flyer (Juniper), and the catcher (Cassius), will meet in midair. The catcher will grab the flyer's hands when she leaves her bar. There are many different ways we can do this, but I want to start with a single backflip."

My eyes widened at the thought. If Cassius and I were swinging from opposite sides and at different speeds, how would he catch me?

Mr. Monte continued to explain, "You will complete a leg lift or rather, a kip, bringing your ankles up and hooking your knees to the bar, before swinging back and forth. When you've built your momentum and you swing back to the middle, you will let go, arching your back and completing a backflip, just before grasping Cassius's hands. The most important thing about this exercise is timing, and you will fall a hundred times before you get it right. But soon enough, you'll learn to count and listen to each other, and you'll land the trick."

I nodded my head in agreement.

"When you flip backwards, do not take your eyes off Cassius and his outstretched arms. Now Cassius, you will start in a standing position, swinging back and forth. When Juniper mounts her bar, you will turn around, sit and then fall back and be hanging upside down on a double bar, where your knees hook around one bar and your feet hook under the other. This will take a lot of strength, and you will need to adjust your momentum, so that when Juniper is prepared to let go and flip, you are aligned and ready to catch her."

"This all sounds exciting but rather difficult," Cassius admitted. "I don't fully understand it."

I'd rarely heard Cassius admit to confusion. He seemed to know everything, and even if he was short on knowledge, he wouldn't admit it.

"I know, but this is a simplified version of this trick due to the number of acts we're trying to fit into one show. And this is the last skill you need to master, so if we can get this down, you'll be set for the show."

I sighed heavily and said, "Let's give it a go then."

Mr. Monte switched the standard bar to the double bar and showed Cassius what he had to do. "Remember to face front, turn around, sit, fall back and let your knees catch, and then at the climax of your swing be reaching and ready to catch Juniper. Do you understand?"

"I think so," Cassius responded. He shook his arms before stepping onto the bar and bending his knees to swing back and forth. The first time he attempted the move, he swung high enough but hesitated in his turn and fell off of the bar completely.

"You're waiting too long!" Mr. Monte shouted. "I'll count you off. Do it again!" Mr. Monte's impatience was growing by the second. He was eager to prove to the world how great the circus was, especially in light of the recent scandals involving its performers. But his eagerness gave way to impulsive anger.

Cassius tried again and made it through all the steps this time, and when his bar climaxed near the top of the tent, Mr. Monte yelled, "Now!"

In a fit of nervousness, Cassius dropped off the bar suddenly.

Mr. Monte took a steadying breath. "Do it again. You cannot let fear control you. You will need to trust yourself and your partner."

Cassius nodded, but frustration was growing in his eyes. He attempted it again, and despite Mr. Monte's yelling, his timing was still not quite right. I was grateful for the earlier warning that we would fall a hundred times before landing this trick, but I could tell both Cassius and Mr. Monte wanted to skip that part.

Cassius groaned and rubbed at his skull as Mr. Monte approached.

"You must listen, Cassius! You aren't listening-"

"I am listening, Edward! With all of your screaming, it's hard not to. But I can't focus!" Cassius lashed out, pushing himself over the side of the net and lowering himself into a sitting position.

This moment seemed too personal for me to be listening, and I didn't know if I should stay or leave. But Mr. Monte could often get ahead of himself, and right now, Cassius needed to be left alone to go over his mistakes and determine how to fix them. I knew this because Cassius's mind worked similarly to mine.

"Mr. Monte," I said, as I gently touched his shoulder. "I will work on it with him. Give him time."

Mr. Monte looked sad, and he opened his mouth, preparing to say something, before closing it abruptly. I know he didn't mean to push Cassius. We all get angry with those we hold closest.

"I know. It's okay."

Mr. Monte's head was down as he walked out of the tent.

I carefully made my way over to Cassius. He was like a child, unable to forgive himself for not doing things perfectly, and I didn't want to upset him further.

His eyes were fixed on his palms and he licked his lips feverishly as I sat down next to him. "I shouldn't be angry with him. He's only trying to help," Cassius said, before I could say anything.

I prepared to listen while he shook his head and started to speak. I had been learning that just listening was sometimes more valuable than trying to fix the problem.

"Edward has always been there for me, but because of that, I think he expects more of me than what's reasonable."

I nodded my head and said, "I see that."

He sighed and continued, "How can I not get angry when he treats me like I'm some special case who can deliver things no one else can?"

I didn't entirely understand their relationship, but I think I knew enough to piece together something that might make sense to Cassius. "Mr. Monte watched you grow, and he understands your talent more than you do because he was the one to teach it to you. But that's not to say you can't get angry with him or feel it's unfair of him to expect so much from you."

Cassius nodded in agreement.

I grabbed his hand gently and smiled to comfort him. "It's okay to be frustrated. Mr. Monte pushes you because of a deep concern for your future and because he believes you are always capable of more. You've made him proud ever since you arrived here. That's why he works you so hard."

A wave of jealousy crashed over me when I said this. I wished my mother had pushed me to do the things I loved because she knew I was capable of them. But I'd grown to accept that she didn't, realizing sometimes life doesn't hand you what you want.

I rubbed the pad of my finger over the calluses on his hand, and his fingers wrapped around mine.

"Let's try again," I said softly and stood with his hand still intertwined in mine.

We worked through the timing slowly, even while he fell over and over again. With his knees hooked on the bar and his upper body hanging limply, his face turned red with all the blood rushing to his head, and I laughed when he wiggled like a worm. All of his motion finally stopped, and he curled up and grabbed the bar with his hands so he could unhook his legs.

I was in a daze watching his biceps flex and barely heard him when he said, "How am I supposed to be able to catch you when I'm upside down?"

"Let's figure that out tomorrow," I snickered.

I raised my hand in the air and he slapped it in agreement. Now it was my turn.

I hung on the bar and swung back and forth. And like Mr. Monte instructed, I kipped my body and brought my ankles to the bar, but as soon as I did, I froze. The world was moving too quickly, and I could see the platform moving when I tilted my head back. My heart began to race, and I let go. Long before it was time to complete the backflip, I had plummeted straight down and bounced in the net a few times as I gazed at the bar slowly swinging above my head.

"Not very easy, is it?" Cassius said, with his head upside down when he stood over me.

I pushed him away and climbed the ladder, jumping onto the bar before I could stop to think. I swung back and forth and brought my ankles to the bar again, and then released earlier this time so as not to give fear a chance to set in. I managed to complete the flip in mid-air before landing on my side on the net, and looked up at Cassius with a beaming smile. He had his arms crossed and an angry look on his face.

"Don't pout now," I said, puckering my bottom lip.

"That's not fair," he said, curling his fists at his waist.

"How is it not fair?" I asked lightheartedly, as I jumped out of the net and grabbed my shawl.

"Well, you- you just-"

"I'm just more talented?" I said jokingly, but Cassius didn't take it that way.

"That's it!" He bent too quickly for me to realize what he was doing, and in a flash, he had thrown me over his shoulder.

"Cassius put me down!" I yelled, but I couldn't stop laughing.

"Not a chance, Princess." He laughed, deep and low.

I groaned at the name, but giggled all the same.

Cassius walked over to the exit of the tent, throwing his coat over me, and I laughed as I tried to get the dark fabric out of my face. Below the cover of his jacket, I watched his long strides, but everything else was dark. And for a moment, I stayed there. I let my body relax and memorize the rhythm of his shoulder shifting every time he took a step. I tried to commit the sound of his boots crunching on the gravel to memory. I wanted to remember this night.

But suddenly he lurched and stopped completely, then turned abruptly, walking much faster than before. Something was wrong. Maybe he had just forgotten something. I ripped the coat off my head to find that he'd entered the tent once more, and I heard faint whispers in the distance.

Cassius lowered me to the ground.

"What's going on?" I asked.

He pushed his back against the tent and brought me to his side. "There are guards at the flamethrowers' tent." Cassius spoke quietly, afraid of being heard. He slyly peaked his head out and said, "It looks like they're searching in every tent. Maybe someone spotted the killer. We're going to stay here until they say it's safe," Cassius said without giving it another thought.

My breathing started to quicken. I had just begun to take my mind off the killer, and this commotion brought it up again. "This will never be over, will it?" I asked quietly, almost to myself.

At a loss for what to say, Cassius just cradled my head in his chest and swayed from side to side.

Was he out there? The guards wouldn't be checking every tent if someone hadn't tipped them off. What if he were to hurt Cassius? What if he finally got to me before I could perform in front of my family? I wanted them to be proud of me for once. I wanted them to clap and smile like they'd never seen anything so wonderful.

Out of nowhere, I said, "My mother never came to my dance recitals."

"Hmm?" Cassius pulled my face away, but I couldn't look him in the eyes.

I stared at the small grains of sand on the ground, glittering when the setting sun hit them just right. "I took ballet lessons for ten years, and she never came to my recitals. Not once. Why didn't she want to see me?" Tears welled in my eyes. This was something I had never mentioned to anyone. I barely realized it myself. It was something I had pushed into the deep parts of my mind. I was four years old when I started ballet, and I was heartbroken when I didn't see her in the front row of the auditorium for my first recital. My dance coach had to walk me home that night, my bag slung over my shoulder with my pink tutu and ballet slippers inside. My mother was entertaining a group of diplomats when I arrived home, and I couldn't bear to look her in the eyes. By my final evaluation for qualifying to dance en-pointe, I had long since given up on my mother.

"What about your father? Or your sister?" Cassius asked intently.

"My father left when I was born. My sister came to some of my performances, but she was older than I was, and very much committed to my mother's affairs." I turned my head away and clenched my jaw, as tears spilled onto my cheeks. No one came to watch me, and as a little girl, I was devastated. Since then I've never expected anyone to stick around to watch me do the things I love, until I came to the circus. And if I die before this performance, my family might never see me do anything meaningful.

Cassius grabbed the side of my face, his caramel eyes wide and full of compassion. He'd never looked at me this way before. "I'm watching you."

I trembled when he said those words to me—words I had needed to hear for years. I'd never felt this special to anyone before. I closed my eyes and put my forehead against his, and somehow, he knew not to let go. It was then I decided I didn't want to go a single day without this boy.

Suddenly the flaps of the tent opened and four guards entered.

"Hello officers, is everything okay?" Cassius spoke up for me, keeping me at his side.

"Everything is fine. Have you seen anything suspicious? Your dancers thought they saw a man exit the train with a mask on," one of the officers said, surveying the area.

"We haven't seen anything here," Cassius informed him kindly.

"Alright. Just doing some precautionary checks. I suggest you return to your rooms for the night just to be safe."

Cassius nodded his head and placed a hand on my lower back to lead me out of the tent. I looked back to catch the guards checking behind our equipment and in the dressing rooms. *They're going to find him one day*, I reassured myself. *They have to.*

In the days that followed, I stuck to a schedule. I woke up in the morning, grabbed breakfast with the dancers and others who wished to join us, and practiced until five o'clock when the sun began to go down. I didn't like to be out after dark, so each day at five, I would go back to Cassius's room where we'd enjoy a round of Écarté—an old French card game where two players are dealt five cards and must determine the trump suit as they turn over one card at a time. Our laughter filled the dank halls of the train until the early morning, and it was just what I needed to take my mind off things. Being with Cassius had become the thing I looked forward to most each day.

Sometimes I thought about Flint, especially when we passed one another in the hall or interacted on show night. There were plenty of awkward glances, but not much was said. I wondered if he was still working on equations and shoving that pencil between his teeth, or if he was still worrying about me like he used to. I hoped he wasn't, and I hoped he didn't hate me for being with Cassius. I didn't even know if I was *with* Cassius in that respect. What were we? We hadn't defined ourselves as being in a relationship, and I didn't know if we ever would, but it was easier to get to know Cassius this way. Maybe after performance season I would ask more about our relationship status.

The night before the show, Cassius and I dragged Mr. Monte into the tent. "This better be worth it," he said. "I'm supposed to be in a meeting with Valetta to make sure the costumes are all ready for tomorrow," he added in an irritated tone.

Cassius winked at me and we both stripped off our coats, showing off my bedazzled red leotard and his extravagant suede suitcoat and crimson tights.

Mr. Monte's eyes widened in surprise. "What is this?"

"We want to show you our progress," I said, and we quickly climbed the ladder in anticipation.

Cassius and I jumped onto the bars at the same time and swung in unison. I waited for Cassius to push his bar to the top of the tent, and from that distance, I could faintly spot his lips counting to eight. This was what we had practices for endless hours. He leaned back and let his body fall, which was my cue to increase my momentum before I kipped my body forward. I arched my back and tilted my head to the floor, flipping over while I kept my legs tight. When I flipped around, I searched for Cassius's hands and reached out far as my injured shoulder would allow me. Cassius looked rather close—like I may hit him—when suddenly our bodies jolted and I realized he had caught me safely.

Mr. Monte clapped like crazy from the ground. "Bravo, bravo! My stars, you will be adored tomorrow! Now stop working and go celebrate with the rest of the crew," he urged, as he patted both of us on the back.

"Okay, okay, we're going!" Cassius grabbed my hand after Mr. Monte pushed us out of the tent. We raced through the dark field with the stars glittering above, and into the train to the sound of blaring music and shouts of jubilee.

"Juniper!" Charlotte yelled as she skipped over to me and wrapped her arms around my neck. "Cassius," she muttered as she dipped her head solemnly in his direction.

Cassius looked between us awkwardly.

I'd be lying if I said I didn't get jealous knowing that Cassius had slept with nearly every girl in the room, but I was also glad he had chosen to stick with me. He was growing as a person, and I was the one who had helped him do it, which made me proud.

"I'll be at the bar," Cassius announced as he stalked away.

Charlotte tugged me into the throng of people, where hands were raised high in the air and bodies danced wildly without a care in the world. I snatched a drink from a table nearby, not knowing who it belonged to, and within a few minutes, I began to feel light enough to join the crowd. The musicians in the corner played a lively beat on a guitar and a small drum set, inspiring Olive to clap along excitedly. She skipped around and around until Beckett grabbed her small hands and led her in a vigorous waltz. She knew every step by heart, and when the song ended, Beckett grabbed under her arms and tossed her into the air, which made for quite a grand finale. And just when we thought she was done, she pushed him to the side and skipped out a tough rhythm, like she owned the night. Evelyn gently tugged Olive back to sit on her lap, and the little girl began to whine, questioning why she couldn't dance with everyone. I thought I heard Evelyn say, "you'll have to wait to dance with a bunch of drunken idiots until you're older," but I couldn't be sure.

I found Charlotte slow dancing with a tattooed flamethrower, and since she was taken, I danced alone. Feeling awkward, I found my way back to the bar and grabbed a strong whiskey to sip on. As I watched the laughing performers at each table, I decided this was my favorite place. Finally free of the pressure of performing for a crowd, we got to be ourselves, in all our wild glory. In this room, no one had to put on a show. We didn't have to smile for the crowd, just for one another. This was the circus.

I spotted Cassius at the end of the bar, intently listening to Bruce, an older jester who made a joke out of everything. Cassius's eyes were slightly glazed over, his smile was sloppy, and that small dimple had formed in his right cheek. His teeth were slightly crooked, but not enough to look gangly; they were perfectly imperfect, and I loved them. When he pushed back his hair, that same small curl fell into his eyes, and I had the urge to run my hands through it. He looked really handsome when he had a few drinks in him.

"Won't you dance with me?" I asked, my words dragging. I couldn't seem to stop one word and start the next properly.

"I think you've had too much to drink," Cassius laughed and pushed me back after I stumbled into him.

I wanted him to touch me like he used to. After the attempted rape, he had treated me like I couldn't be touched.

"Come on. Come dance with me," I leaned down to whisper in his ear.

He stood abruptly and pushed my shoulders back to hide my cleavage. "Sorry boys," Cassius apologized. "I have to follow orders."

The men's laughter faded behind me as I tugged Cassius to the dance floor. We became entangled with the other dancers, and he twirled me around but kept his distance. Feeling such freedom, I tilted my head to the sky and smiled at the shadows dancing on the ceiling. My forehead was sweating and I felt sticky, but was I enjoying it when, suddenly, Cassius gripped my waist and pulled me in close.

"Your dress is too revealing," he whispered in my ear.

"I was taught to be modest my entire life. Let me live a little," I whispered back at him.

"Not when everyone's watching you," he said, his tone serious this time.

I pulled away from him, curious if he was mad.

"You're mine, Juniper. And if you keep dancing like that, people will see what only I should see."

You're mine. This boy drove me crazy. I didn't like feeling controlled, but I wasn't suffocated by his claim. It felt like he wanted me all to himself, and I liked the feeling of belonging to someone completely.

"Okay," I whispered, unsure of what else to say. What he had just said meant a lot to me. I'd never loved anyone before. After all, I'd never found anyone as individualistic, passionate, and self-driven as me, until I met Cassius. He knew how to push me to be better, and he knew how to comfort me. And I wasn't sure what it felt like to be in love, but I was beginning to wonder if this was it.

Cassius...

The way she moved her hips and looked up at the sky made me feel lightheaded. This girl was amazing. When I first met her, I thought she was uptight and controlling, but seeing her now, with sweat on her brow, all that had changed. In the candlelight, her skin looked warm and soft, and I wanted to touch her more, and kiss her. God, I wanted to kiss her until I couldn't feel my lips anymore. And I'll admit, I wanted a hell of a lot more than her lips on mine, but Juniper was more than just a body to fill my bed. She was important to me. And nobody had meant this much to me since my sister. Juniper made me want to be a better man. She made me want to stop drinking and enjoy life as it came. She made me want to stay, not just sleep with her and move on the next day, like I had done so many times before. She challenged me, and as much as I wanted her, I wanted to wait even more. And then when we did share ourselves with each other, it would be better than anything before, because I would know her, and she would know me.

Chapter 27

A harsh breeze rumbled over the city when the clock tower rang to awaken the citizens. The streets were bustling with people, rushing to their errands and odd jobs. Venders stood on street corners, shouting out prices for their various goods. The sun was beating down on the windows of brick buildings, freshly cleaned, thanks to a man in white and blue striped overalls who took his job very seriously. A carriage rolled by on the dusty cobblestone street, carrying a woman in a light blue day dress with a gray pinafore and silver buttons descending down the front of her chest. The fabric along her shoulders was padded, and the small hat on her head held a white veil in front of her eyes. She sat with her head high, attempting to impress those outside the carriage walls. Steam rolled from a dirty grey chimney in the center of the city, where the wind blew it into the outskirts, among the tall houses resting in the middle of the open fields. Out here, people were untouched by the outside world—they lived in their own little bubble of wealth. Past the fields was a dense forest of tall oak trees. And past that were the train tracks.

 I looked at myself in the mirror and my skin was golden, like it had been kissed by the sun. My eyes were bright and filled with wonder. My face was plain, not overdone with makeup or red from the pinch of my mother's fingers on my cheeks. I dressed in the only ensemble I had brought from Axminster—an ornate dress and a corset with many loops of string to tighten it, as well as a pair of white heels. I turned my head back and forth to examine my image. This was a girl playing dress up. But I wasn't the girl from Axminster who used to spend her afternoons in the tall chapels of the church. I was a girl transformed by the circus, and it didn't feel right dressing this way. So, I stripped off the dress and watched it drop to the floor, falling easily like a feather, and pulled on a pair of black breeches, a plain white shirt, and a pair of brown boots with two-inch heels. I pulled my hair out of the small bun on top of my head and let it fall freely across my shoulders. Much better.

Before closing the door, I looked back into the small space of my room. I remembered walking down these halls for the first time, feeling cramped, and then feeling a sense of relief when Wilman opened the door to my bedroom. I didn't have to watch the beggars starve to death through my crystal window, from my four-poster bed with the custom rose canopy. I didn't have to feel ashamed for the expensive clothes on my back because now I had none. I was just like everyone else, and the plain wooden walls, the small bed in the corner, and the tainted mirror atop the tiny desk had never felt so right. At that moment I knew I was home. I smiled, closing the door softly behind me.

"Hey there," Cassius sidled up next to me with a cup of ale in hand.

"Isn't it a little early?" I giggled.

He poked his head out of the train to take a look at the sky. "Nine o'clock…not at all," he laughed.

I laughed along with him. I wished I could stay here with him all day, but there was something I had to do before the performance tonight. "Cassius, I'm going into town," I told him. But maybe there was a way for us to spend the day together after all. "Would you like to come with me?" I asked without thinking.

He stopped in his tracks, looking at my arm in his. "You want me to go with you?"

I'd lived in Axminster for twenty years, but it couldn't seem any more foreign to me. I finally knew what it was like to live in the real world, outside the confines my mother had set for me. I knew what it was like to jump on a train, stay out late at a bar and sing jolly songs, and walk a wavering tightrope high above a crowd in awe. And I had to admit, I was worried I wouldn't know how to act anymore among civility. It would help immensely to have Cassius by my side. "Yes, I would like that."

He nodded and led me out of the train. When we reached the city, the streets seemed unfamiliar. The sun stood behind the steeple of the church, casting it in shadow, and I turned to Cassius to see his mouth open wide. It was beautiful, I had to admit. Perhaps he had never seen anything quite so magnificent.

"So, this is your home?" He turned to me and asked.

"A home, no. Just a city," I remarked regretfully.

"It has to hold some meaning to you," he said, as he stepped around the corner to look down the alleyway.

"The circus has more meaning to me than this place ever will." Cassius's face twisted in confusion, but I didn't want to dampen the mood, so I said, "Never mind...I'll show you some of my favorite places."

I pulled him behind me, running through the streets, past men in top hats and waistcoats with briefcases in hand. He laughed, begging me to slow down, but I only ran faster. Finally, I stopped abruptly and he ran into me, his breath ragged in my ear. "This is Barnaby's Bakery, famous for its raspberry pastries and lemon pie." A rough barking pierced my ears and I turned to find a dog jumping on a poor man and his bagel. "Captain, you come here and leave that man alone!" I yelled at the dog. Instinctively, the dirty dog ran over to me and jumped up on my legs, and I bent down to ruffle his long hair before pointing an accusing finger at him. "You run along home now and find Mr. Marbury. He's probably worried sick."

I took Cassius past the chapel, the ballet studio, and the school I attended growing up. All the while, Cassius looked meaningfully at the city, as if he appreciated getting a glimpse of the life I used to live. The sun shone on his golden skin and made his eyes glow more than usual.

"There's one more place I want to show you."

Winding down the long streets, I found myself just on the outskirts of the city. Three houses were lined up perfectly in front of me—a soft rose-colored house, with a white picket fence surrounding a lush garden; a daisy yellow house, which would have blended in with the sunflowers if not for the brown trim on the outside; and a tan home with red shutters lining its bay windows. The roof on the last house was steep and a lengthy pathway led to the door, running through the garden which was hemmed in with a white fence. Beautiful flower pots lined the entrance to this home. *My home.* It looked exactly like I remembered it—the soft cream curtains fluttering inside, and the grand arrangement of lounge chairs on either side of the brown double doors, perfect for afternoon tea. Part of me expected it to be different, so I was struck that it looked the same as it always had. It confirmed for me that if I were to stay here, I would be trapped by the traditions of my mother and of this city, and I knew that I had made the right choice.

"This was my house," I told Cassius, who had remained silent beside me.

He looked at my home dreamily, like it was something famous. He had never had a home of his own, where meals were regular, and where family gathered around tea and biscuits. But I didn't want him to think of this place as something he didn't deserve himself. I brought him here to show him that despite its grand appearance, it couldn't compare to the far more meaningful home Mr. Monte had created. The one *we* had created at the circus!

"I thought if you could visualize it, it might be easier to understand my point of view." I turned to face Cassius, still gazing at my home. "I know we have our differences. I know we don't always agree, and I know you once hated me because of where I came from. But this place isn't extraordinary." I paused, and he looked at me, as if to say *continue*. "Every morning I would wake up at eight o'clock and have tea with my mother and sister in the dining room. My mother often spoke about politics or about the tendencies of those who were beneath us. And at nine o'clock, before school, I would go to say my daily prayer at the chapel, where I would confess my wrongs and ask forgiveness. And then after school, I would pick up groceries at the local market for dinner. Most nights were spent with a neighboring family or with ostentatious men who were vying for my sister's hand. We did not laugh or make pleasant conversation, and we did not eat for pleasure. It was always business."

Cassius listened intently, watching my mouth move, and once in a while he would look back as if to say, *I can't believe all that you're telling me.*

"Can you understand now, that I love the circus with everything that I am? There's nothing here for me, Cassius." I sighed and held out my hands to my previous home. "And I know I was meant to live a different life, and so were you. Maybe that's why we both responded to the train's call."

He looked at me differently—more closely—as I was saying this, and locked his fingers around my waist while keeping his eyes on me. "It's not that pretty." He wrinkled his nose and nodded his head toward my house.

"It's pretty gross," I joked.

"Disgusting actually," he gagged.

We laughed together for a moment before his face became solemn. "I'm sorry." He looked at our feet pointed toward one another. "For treating you that way."

I slung my arm through his and started to say, "You don't have to apologize-"

"Yes, I do," he interrupted me, looking deep into my eyes. "Like you said, we have different pasts, and it was rude of me to assume that you were entitled and proper, like all the other noblemen and women here. You never once spoke about my rank, and I am sorry for doing that to you."

I brought my chest closer to his and hugged him tightly.

"So much I once thought was true has been proven false because of you, J." He pulled me away, closed his eyes, and gently brought his lips to mine.

I closed my lips softly around his and melted under his touch. When my nose brushed along his cheek, he tilted his head to the left to kiss me deeper. Each time I kissed him, I felt a little closer to him. I smiled and lead him toward the city, saying, "Let's get ready to blow the crowd away."

Colette...

I donned a floral headband and straightened the simple brown dress over my chest, picking at an invisible piece of lint. William was accompanying me to the circus tonight, and I couldn't wait to see my sister perform. I had been so worried about the separation that might result if Juniper decided not to marry Joseph Young, but I didn't see how she could marry him after being away with the circus. I knew she was fond of the activity and that she wouldn't leave easily. And that got me thinking about why my mother was so persistent in marrying Juniper off. Why couldn't she just let her daughter go?

"Come, Colette! We're going to be late!" My mother shouted up the long staircase.

"Coming!" The sun had just begun to fall. We were going to take a carriage to Upper North Rafad, just past the center of the city.

While descending the stairs, I heard my mother talking faintly to Mr. Young, and I pressed my back against the wall, even though I felt I shouldn't be hearing this conversation.

"Don't forget what we're doing this for. This is for your son and my daughter," she whispered harshly.

What was she talking about? What was she planning? When I heard my mother's heels clacking on the floor, coming to scold me again, I took the opportunity to go downstairs and join the group at the front door. Whatever she was scheming, I feared it was too late to interfere. I couldn't warn Juniper now, so instead I whispered a little prayer that tonight would go smoothly.

Globes of golden light illuminated my face as I watched performers bustling behind me, bedecked in their finest colors—costumes in hues of blue and green and brown. The dancers chalked their feet and the jesters put on vibrant makeup, accentuating their cheeks with red rouge and contouring their jaws with white face paint. Animals roared and squeaked in their cages as the lights turned on in the tent, and the red and white fabric rustled in the wind while the crowd surged in. The day I left Axminster, I knew I was headed to where I belonged. A year ago, looking in that dirty storefront window at animals of all shapes and sizes, and sun kissed people filled with glee, I thought I saw a future image of myself. And now, in unbelievable likeness, here I am with a crown of black feathers on my head, bejeweled wristbands snaking up my arms, and scarlet tights stretching over my thighs. A dream come true, a wish fulfilled, and now, it was time to put on a show.

Mr. Monte...

"Ladies and gentlemen! Welcome to the circus, where all things are possible! Tonight, I promise you will be intrigued by all that is natural and unnatural!" I smirked at the crowd and tipped my cane to the front row, making the audience smile in wonder. "My name is

Mr. Monte and I founded this circus thirty years ago, when I was a young man. It has been my pride and joy to train these wonderful people to perform for each one of you, young and old!"

As I introduced myself to the audience, something dropped from overhead and hit my shoulder. I tried to be professional, but I was distracted by what felt like a drop of water. It was odd. Was it raining outside? Was there a hole in the tent? I was determined to check it out as soon as I had the chance, but when I touched the spot on my shoulder, it didn't feel like water. It was stickier and heavier—like oil. And as I looked more closely to determine where it had come from, I felt another drop on my cheek. My eyes moved to where the tightrope hung high in the sky, and I could see the rope glistening slightly on every side.

Had he oiled the tightrope?

I was worried the killer would strike again tonight, and I needed to warn Juniper. I turned back to the audience, hoping they wouldn't notice my inattention, and continued my announcement. "From jesters to lion tamers to tightrope walkers, we have quite a spectacle in store for you tonight. So, hold onto your hats and enjoy the show."

The crowd cheered wildly, which was my cue to exit the ring and slip behind the curtain of the tent. "Juniper!" I called out to my star. "Juniper!"

"I'm right here!" she squealed, trotting up to me in alarm. "What is it?"

"You can't perform on the tightrope!" I spat out.

Her eyes sunk in confusion. This was her act, and to be deprived of that would be like being deprived of the show entirely. People came to see her on the tightrope, and I could almost taste how disappointed the audience would be, but I had to keep her safe. "The killer has oiled the tightrope and if you walk, you will fall. It's too dangerous!"

"But Mr. Monte, the tightrope is my act! The crowd will be so disappointed. *I* will be disappointed! What about all the hard work I've done?" She tried to urge me to let her go ahead.

"I know, dear, but this is his last attempt to hurt you and we can't risk it!" If the killer wanted her dead, he was going to have to try much harder than this. And as heartbroken as she was, I knew Juniper was smart enough to follow my command.

"We'll start with the trapeze. Prepare Cassius to get on the bar," she instructed me, and ran to find her tape and chalk.

When I informed Cassius of the situation, he sighed and said, "Thank God you discovered that before she was hurt," and he jumped to change into his costume for the trapeze.

I turned around briefly to find all the performers waiting for my instruction. I hadn't hoped to start the night in a nervous frenzy, but I had to make due under the circumstances. "Send out the jesters!" I yelled, and before I knew it, they had boarded their unicycles and were set to go.

The crowd had been waiting patiently for the show to begin while whispering quietly amongst themselves, and finally, the lights dimmed and the guests turned around in anticipation to find the jesters rolling down the aisles on their unicycles. They juggled balls in their hands while looking merrily at the crowd, and then rolled down the ramps to enter the rings and welcome the dancers.

Next it was the dancers that entered the ring in a V-formation, leaping, skipping, and throwing their arms up as they pointed their toes to their knees and pirouetted. Autumn kicked her leg high in the air before lowering herself to the ground and rolling from hip to hip, flipping her hair sensually. Every dancer took their moment to shine, and then Olive and Piper, the smallest of the group, threw their arms out wide as four stags galloped into the arena, with fur as white as snow, glistening under the candlelight. The stags trotted in sync and came to stand behind the dancers.

In grand fashion, Charlotte stepped out and sashayed toward Raelynn and Raegan, who lifted her up into the air and rested her bum on their shoulders, where she sat high and mighty, reaching her hands to the sky as if trying to touch the heavens.

Just then, I descended from the sky on a steel ring, the only thing holding my body up being my neck. It was a difficult skill that took immense strength, requiring me to bend my head toward the sky so the fold in my neck would secure me, while holding the sides of the ring with my arms and allowing my legs to dangle. For dramatic effect, but more for stability, my legs pedaled back and forth smoothly while the ring lowered to the ground.

All of the dancers wore golden dresses with tinsels that swayed back and forth as they danced, and paired with my ruby and diamond costume, we portrayed the essence of wealth. The dancers gathered near the twins to build a pyramid around me as I continued to lower myself on the ring, and when I was close enough, Charlotte grabbed my calves and gently set my feet on her shoulders, making me the crowning jewel. When Charlotte nodded, I let go of the ring, keeping my body as stiff as I could.

The crowd erupted in cheer and I beamed at their praise while searching the crowd for my mother. I spotted Colette sitting next to William and my mother, beside Mr. Young and Joseph in the fifth row. I didn't expect the Young family to attend, so I was even more determined to make a lasting impression. While maintaining eye contact with them, I bent my knees and Charlotte grabbed the bottom of my feet. She lifted me with all of her strength and I tucked my knees to my chest, flipped over the pyramid, and landed on my feet, giving the crowd reason to cheer again.

But suddenly the light dimmed, and a low, dark rhythm began to play from the band behind the tent. We all looked around in fear when a group of men dressed in the finest suits emerged and stalked up to us, shouting things like, "Go back to your train!" and "You belong to the streets!"

The separation between the wealthy and the dregs of society was clear to the crowd, but by their intrigued expressions, I couldn't tell which side they were cheering for. The men's shouting urged us to flee from the tent and the scene went dark, but not long after, the lights came back on and little Olive sat in the middle of the ring with her arms wrapped around her legs. She had on a wig and boy's clothing, and dirt across her cheeks, as she portrayed an unfortunate boy in poverty, turning to the circus for a better life. She stood when the lights turned on, looking around at the world in wonder.

Just then, Mr. Monte emerged from the back, in a bold new move. He had never acted in the show before, but he approached Olive, who was playing the measly boy, and offered her his hand. "Are you hungry?" He asked.

She nodded sadly while gripping her stomach in pain.

"What is your name?"

"Cassius," Olive whispered.

"You look nimble, 'eh?" He bent down to her level and the crowd leaned closer with him. "I think you would be a fine rider in my circus. What do you say?"

The little boy smiled brightly when Mr. Monte pulled out an apple from his suit. Taking it gently, the little boy followed him back into darkness, and the crowd clapped warmly, moved by the idea. Moments later, the real Cassius returned by Mr. Monte's side, all grown up. He was no longer a timid boy. He had become a star.

But suddenly, the rowdy group of men emerged, threatening Cassius with torches and pitchforks in an attempt to burn the tent to the ground.

"You don't understand! The circus is my home, my family! I won't let you tear it down!" Cassius was clearly no longer the lost little boy he once was.

But before Cassius could finish reprimanding them, the men threw their torches at him and the ground erupted in flames. He ran to avoid the fire, but it spread into a circle, surrounding him.

The crowd erupted angrily, shouting something like, "They can't destroy the circus!"

Clearly, we had won over the crowd, but Cassius was still in peril, as the flames threatened to engulf him inside the ring of fire, and the angry men threatened to overtake him if he escaped. In desperation, he jumped over the flames, singing the bare skin on his upper body as he did. And then, realizing his predicament, he backed down and surrendered, and the men, realizing their victory, left the scene.

Within minutes, the fire had died down and the crowd's attention was turned to Cassius and I sitting on a platform high above, ready to begin the act we hoped would be the highlight of the evening.

I locked my fingers in Cassius's hand and rested my head on his shoulder, in a sweet moment that left the crowd wanting more.

To appease them, Cassius leaned forward slowly. His breath tickled my lips and made me shiver, and even in the heat of our performance, with my family watching us, I wanted him to kiss me. But what would Joseph think? Surely, he would know it was an act, and why did I care? I hadn't told my family of my feelings for Cassius because they would be furious if they knew the reason I wouldn't leave the circus to marry Joseph was because of this boy. But I couldn't worry about that right now. I had a crowd to please.

"Kiss her already!" A man shouted down below.

Cassius snickered before pressing his lips to mine deeply. He grabbed my cheeks and pulled me closer to him, kissing me harder than he ever had before. Maybe it was the people watching that made this moment so spontaneous for him.

Delighted with ourselves, we ran to opposite platforms and prepared to swing. I grabbed my bar, and when he took to his bar and swung back and forth, I leapt, and we proceeded to follow the timing and sequence, just the way we had practiced. Cassius's distance worried me, and I wondered if he had swung too far back, but before I could question it too long, I let go and arched my back. I watched the crowd cheer wildly below me as I searched for Cassius's hands, and when they came into view, I reached out and grabbed them, and he held on tight. Cassius swung his body, and when he had built up enough momentum, I quickly switched my hands and spun my body around, ready to catch my bar again.

Cassius threw me forward, and I caught my bar securely, then wrapped my hands around the bar and pulled my body up so my hips rested steadily in place. My arms were beginning to tire, but I pushed my body back and forth, and this time when I released, I lifted my toes high in the air so I could flip twice. After completing a beautiful double back handspring, Cassius grasped my ankles, and we continued to fly through the air. As our bodies rebounded, I looked down to the audience and waved, and just then, Cassius swung me hard enough to throw me up onto his bar. This was so difficult because my feet had to land outside his knees as they hung on the bar, so he could lift himself into a sitting position and push his head through my legs. Using the ropes to lift myself, I put my feet on his shoulders, and he stood up. This was the trick we had worked tirelessly to perfect, and it was amazing!

He bent his knees to increase our momentum, and then I jumped onto my own bar once last time. I fell backwards and hooked my knees, then spun around my bar until I was dizzy before letting go. Finally, I tucked my knees tight and flipped three times before extending my body to fall into the net.

Just then, Cassius fell in one swift motion, landing next to me. We somersaulted off the net, and he pulled me in by my lower back for a kiss, making the ladies swoon and the men cheer.

But amid the heat of our performance and the awe of the crowd, there was another uproar as this army of protesters surged forward to approach the couple in love.

Cassius and I feigned fear and began to run from them, and when the music turned lively, the whole circus emerged and created a barrier around the two of us, prepared to fight. The flamethrowers blew hot red flames at the men, while the tigers slashed their claws, the elephants reared on their heels, and the dancers lunged forward in rhythm to push back the men.

"Up!" Cassius commanded a lion in the center of the circle, having quickly changed out of his trapeze outfit into fitted breeches and a poet's shirt, under the cover of the performers. Abbas jumped onto a platform, reared his head, and roared so deafeningly the crowd had to cover their ears. We stood tall against the protesters, lifting our heads high while the lion's jaw trembled and his authority shook the tent. And the crowd went absolutely silent, wondering how the story would turn.

Cassius lifted his hand high and pointed toward the men, and the lion followed his instruction, leaping over all of us. The lion's golden fur billowed above our heads, his limbs stretched far, and his claws protruded from his paws before he landed, making the ground tremble. Everything had begun to progress in slow motion, it seemed. And in one last attempt to rid the circus of the wealthy, the lion lashed at the men's clothes, tearing them off their bodies to reveal nothing but plain scraps underneath. The wealthy had dressed themselves in fine silks and diamonds, but when they were stripped of their money and their hearts were exposed, it was revealed that they were just like us. Finally, the protesters put out their torches in the sand and ran back into the streets.

The crowd stood and clapped, and their hollers reverberated throughout the room.

"Let's hear it for our amazing performers!" Mr. Monte emerged from the back to acknowledge everyone to the crowd. "Cassius, our lion tamer, turned trapeze artist!"

Cassius bowed his head and rested his hand on his heart, signaling his deep love for the circus.

"Young Cassius, played by our very own Olive!" The little girl ran up next to Mr. Monte and threw off her wig, making the crowd fall even more in love with her.

I laughed with a sense of deep joy, watching my friends in the spotlight.

"Charlotte, our star dancer!"

"Woohoo!" I cupped my hands around my mouth and shouted for her. And I shouted again when Gus and Flint were introduced.

"And last, but certainly not least...Juniper, our one and only tightrope walker, ring acrobat, and trapeze artist!"

I stood next to Mr. Monte and he took my hand and raised it in the air, as I smiled and gazed over pleased faces until I found my family. My sister was clapping and speaking wildly to William, but my mother's face was placid and hard. For once, I thought she would be proud. I thought she would be on her feet, cheering for her daughter because she had missed the chance so many times before. But I was wrong.

I turned away quickly to avoid further disappointment. My mother may not be happy, but this was our best performance of the year, and I was proud of myself and my friends. Our dedication had made this an unforgettable night.

Out of nowhere, Gus and Cassius grabbed my waist and lifted me into the air, and the rest of the performers surged forward and enveloped me, chanting my name.

When they set me down, Mr. Monte wrapped me in a hug and whispered, "This is all because of you."

This night was more than I could have even hoped for, and I didn't want it to end.

"Thank you all for coming tonight! It was our pleasure entertaining you. We hope you'll tell your friends and family what a stupendous show this was, and that you'll come back and see us again soon!"

The crowd clapped once more and we all waved goodbye, and I realized a huge weight had been lifted from my shoulders. I had finally performed in front of my family. I had finally shown them, and the rest of Axminster, what I was capable of. And that meant everything to me.

We packed our things quickly and took them to the field behind the tent so we could celebrate. "Ho! Hey! The circus has arrived!" Derrick, one of the magicians, shouted.

"It's late now, come and play outside!" The rest of the circus joined in. "You'll never know...how far you'll go!"

"Take a chance, beat your fate, kick the dust, clap your hands, say your name out loud!" All the riders screamed, pumping their fists into the air.

Our voices rose into the night, for all the city to hear. "Here comes the crowd...The circus has arrived!"

We laughed in chorus and jumped in circles with one another. But as we skipped through the field, with its flowers growing back after the winter months, someone shouted from a distance, "Juniper!"

I turned around quickly, wondering who could be calling my name. Squinting through the darkness, I found a group of five, with my mother and Mr. Young standing at the front. I wondered if they were coming to say congratulations. It couldn't be. I walked forward to meet them, and for some reason, the rest of the circus waited close behind, listening in on the wealthy man's words.

"I would say congratulations, but sadly, it was not the performance of the year for me. I've been to a few opera showings that were absolutely stupendous!" Mr. Young said in a loud voice, for all of my friends to hear.

I couldn't believe he was talking down to all of us when we'd worked so hard. And I wouldn't stand for it. I would not allow our night to be ruined by my inconsiderate family, and a practical stranger!

"I'm sorry, but I'm going to have to ask you to leave," I told him, with as much respect as I could muster. Oh, the damage I'd do if I had the guts to punch him right in that snobby face of his.

"I wasn't finished," he declared loudly, taking a stronger stance before me.

I raised my eyebrows in irritation. Who the hell did he think he was, talking that way to an accomplished group like ours? And my mother...I couldn't believe her. She stood behind Mr. Young like a little sheep, letting him do her dirty work. It was so like her to let a man take charge instead of standing up for herself.

Mr. Young continued, "You see, before coming to your performance, I did a bit of research. I think this is a conversation for everyone, don't you?" He asked my mother and she nodded her head, as if she was just an innocent bystander. I bet whatever was going on was her plan all along. "Listen up everyone."

"What's going on here?" Mr. Monte walked out of the tent and moved to stand next to the other performers.

"Oh perfect—the master of the circus." Mr. Young announced. "I've got something very important to say."

"Get to it, Mr. Shiny Shoes," Cassius spoke up, stepping to the front of the crowd.

God bless him, I thought. But my heart wrenched at the same time. I didn't like where this was going.

"I am a businessman and a landholder, which means I sell land to investors who seek to expand. And as part of my job, I have to make friends with all of the businessmen and entrepreneurs in a kingdom in order to earn their trust. I have befriended the men who own the most famous entertainment arenas in the land. And with one letter, I could make things very difficult for you." Mr. Young smiled as if it was funny to him to ruin the only home these people had—the only family.

"Luckily for us, we have connections as well, Sir." Mr. Monte stalked forward and held his head high, and with his cane and fitted suit, he almost looked wealthier than Mr. Young.

Mr. Young pressed on to say, "But these connections are allowing you the space to perform, am I correct? And if I were to tell them that the circus's own tightrope walker has been hurt, due to weathered, unkempt equipment, and that the previous tightrope walker was killed due to a fault in the tightrope, they would not hesitate to take you down."

The performers gasped, whispering amongst themselves.

"If you had legitimately researched like you proclaimed to do, you would understand that Penelope Plume did not die because of a fault in the tightrope. She committed suicide." Mr. Monte cleared his throat.

Cassius's face was twisted with grief. How could I fix this? How could I reassure my friends that everything would be okay and convince Mr. Young that he couldn't do this? Deep down, I knew it was too late. My mother had planted this seed in his mind long ago, and there was no way I could change it now.

"Regardless, I have allies far and wide, and many of them have no use for the circus." Mr. Young said proudly, as his face turned serious and his eyes were almost completely hidden under his evil brows. "The circus would be reduced to ashes in a month if I were to contact my associates. But, I do have a solution." He pointed a finger into the air, as if he was our savior. "See, my son is very wealthy and he deserves someone with passion and beauty, such as your star tightrope walker." Turning to me, he continued, "For many months, your mother has been intent on giving your hand to my son, Joseph."

When Joseph heard his name, he ducked his head. I doubt he saw this coming at all.

"If you accept his hand in marriage, I will allow the circus to continue. All of your friends will have a home, a family, and warm food to fill their bellies. They will continue to do what they love—pretending, acting, and faking for a crowd only looking for light amusement."

So he understood what he'd be taking from them if I said no! He knew it and he didn't care! My mind was screaming, *do something*, but I couldn't move or speak. All I could do was listen and hope this was a bad dream. I wished that I could wake up to find none of this was happening. How could life shift so quickly? One moment I was laughing and singing with my friends, and the next I was being asked to leave everything behind.

"If you want to protect this motley crew, come back to Axminster and marry my son. He will give you more than anything this life ever could!" he exclaimed.

"And what could he give me?" I asked, finally finding the will to speak. "Money? A nice dress? An expensive home to dine in? What about happiness? And love?"

"Money *can* provide happiness, my child."

"Do not call me your child. You are not my father and you never will be." I pulled back my shoulders, looking my mother dead in the eyes. She couldn't take this away from me.

"Then I guess you'll have to watch all of your friends be torn from the only thing that has given their life meaning. I'll send out the letters to all of my associates tomorrow demanding they break ties with the circus." Mr. Young turned to my family and attempted to lead them away.

What about the killer who led Penelope Plume to her death? If I left the circus, it wouldn't stop the killer. He would continue to threaten the next tightrope walker just like he did me. But if I stayed, the circus would cease to exist altogether because of Mr. Young's threat. I didn't know what to do.

"Wait!" I yelled. I needed time to make the right choice, but time was something I didn't have.

"Juniper-" Cassius began, but I held up a hand to stop him.

Mr. Monte's breathing was ragged behind me. He'd spent his whole life making the circus what it was today—a crew of performers, yes, but a family more importantly. And I couldn't take his pride and joy away from him just to secure my own happiness. I turned over my shoulder to look at my friends. The whole crew looked horrified. Charlotte's eyes were wet with tears. She'd have nowhere to go. I found Olive's small face in the crowd as she latched onto Evelyn's legs with tears in her eyes. She was only a girl and she would have to survive on her own in the world for the first time. Flint looked regretful at being unaware of the predicament with my family. I began thinking, if the circus was reduced to rubble, would he try to go back to school? Could he find a job and earn enough money to even afford it? But for some reason, I couldn't possibly see him at a desk, working on equations. His talent for the circus far outweighed his talent for math. This was where he really belonged. Gus gazed at me with wide eyes, pleading for me to make the right choice. But what was the right choice? If I left all of my friends after everything we'd been through, they might assume I was running back home like they always thought I would. How would they know I was leaving to protect them? And more than anything, I wanted to stay.

But when I looked at Cassius, I knew. The boy with caramel eyes and unruly black hair. The boy who stood up for what he believed in against all odds. The boy who changed my view of the world entirely, which I will forever be grateful for. The boy who despised me but came to understand *my* world. We had changed for the better because of one another.

An image of a small, measly boy, hungry and scared, flashed through my mind. Penelope Plume had taken his hand and brought him to the circus where Mr. Monte accepted him. And I knew I had to leave to ensure that he remained here where he belonged. Because I loved him. And I wished with all my heart that I could tell him that. I loved the way he brushed back his hair when he was frustrated or nervous. I loved the dedication he put into his work every single day. I loved his perseverance and his passion. He could have given up, but he didn't. All of these performers could have, but they didn't. And now I must make the same decision to not give up on *them*.

I looked once more at Cassius, knowing it may be for the very last time, and memorized his slightly crooked teeth, the dimple in his cheek, and his golden eyes. I hoped he understood that I was doing this out of love for the circus and for all of my friends, and for him. My jaw trembled and a tear slid down my cheek.

He stepped forward, about to say something before I turned my back on him. "Okay." I could barely speak. I couldn't believe I was agreeing to this. After months of happiness, in a single moment, it was all ripped away. I'd be back home by nightfall, as if none of this had ever happened. "I'll come with you as long as you promise to ensure the circus's future for the rest of time." My voice cracked and I didn't think I could stand for much longer. I just wanted Cassius to hold me. I wanted to feel his warmth, and the thought of never being able to again broke my heart.

I hated this. I hated it so much. I wished I could refuse Mr. Young's offer. But that was not how the world worked. Sometimes you had to sacrifice what was most important to you to make others happy.

"Until the day I die, I promise. That is the most I can do," Mr. Young offered, placing a hand over his heart.

I took one more breath and my lungs shook. *Don't turn around*, I told myself. *It will make saying goodbye so much harder.* But I couldn't stop myself. I turned around to look at each of my friends and wished them the best. They were meant for greatness.

"Thank you. For making me feel like I finally belonged. This will always be my home," I told Mr. Monte as tears ran down my face.

He dipped his head solemnly. Monroe was nowhere to be seen, but I wished I could thank him as well. And finally, I turned to Cassius. Tears were brimming in his eyes. *Don't cry*, I wanted to tell him. *This is where you are meant to be.* I didn't want him to think I was abandoning him, because if I had the choice to stay, I would in a heartbeat. I knew that nothing would ease the situation, so instead I took one step forward, and gripped his face in both of my hands.

His eyes closed and his lips trembled. "Please-,"

This was the last time I would feel the warmth of his skin, and that thought nearly killed me. But before he could continue, I turned to leave.

To the circus, I owed my life. I would never forget the moments I shared with each performer. I would never forget the sound of the crowd when I stepped on stage. I would never forget being a part of something bigger than myself. And as much as I would miss it, I couldn't wait to see how far the circus would go in the years that followed.

I came to stand next to my mother, feeling like I was standing next to a stranger. Walking back to Axminster, and away from the train, I felt as though I was leaving behind the only thing that had ever mattered to me. I heard nothing—even the wind made no sound. I was moving in step with my mother and sister, but I couldn't feel a thing. My vision blurred and a dark tunnel engulfed me, until I turned to Colette, and I saw in her eyes what I felt deep in my soul. Despair. She had no idea this was going to happen. I couldn't blame her. None of us did.

The End.

Epilogue

Mr. Monte...
 I gazed at the large tent, now empty, with no crowd to inhabit its seats. The sand was still, and the air was silent without cheers to fill its space. The only sound in the room was that of the tent flapping lightly in the wind.

I'd lost my star attraction. After five years of searching to the ends of the earth for a woman to live up to the standards of Penelope Plume, I had finally found her. Juniper Rose—the star of the circus. And I was only able to give her one year. It was my fault for not protecting her or ensuring her more time. I had failed her. Since I was twenty-two, I had sought to make life easier for those who had been handed the worst—the poor, the orphaned, the alone. I wanted to give them a place where they could be the star of the show. But I couldn't give Juniper a home as I had everyone else. She was flawless, jaw dropping, and crowd pleasing. She was perfect. And now she was gone.

I walked around the ring and surveyed the array of footprints in the sand while trying to visualize the dancers and the horses around me now. I tucked my hands into the pockets of my waistcoat and looked up at the vast ceiling of the tent. Small candles littered the room, casting a warm glow on the twisting hemp of the tightrope. It still glistened with oil, appearing smooth and soft to the touch. In the midst of all of this uncertainty, I knew one thing to be true. The killer was still out there. And he wasn't going to give up until he got what he wanted—Juniper Rose.

I wouldn't stop until I found him. This wasn't over yet.

Acknowledgements

This page cannot cover how thankful I am to everyone who helped me on the journey of writing and publishing this book, but I will try my best.

First, I want to thank my mom. You not only helped me edit with near perfection in mind, but you were and are as invested in the story as I am, and you helped develop some of the best ideas I've ever written.

And Dad, thank you for being so generous with your best plot twists (I think you're better at them than I am). More importantly, you never turn down an adventure and that has inspired my imagination and so many of my stories. I love that you are so wild at heart.

To my sisters—Olivia, Rebekah, Hannah, and Meghan—thank you for always believing in me. You all encouraged me to push through the difficult times and pursue what I love. It was with you that I discovered my curiosity for all things magical.

Aunt Paige, you were the one who got me started on the path to being published, and I cannot thank you enough.

A special thank you to New Book Authors for being interested in my novel and taking the time to drizzle some magic over its pages. It was my dream to become a published author, and you made that dream come true.

To all the readers of this novel, your support means the world to me. I hope you fall in love with these characters and become part of their world like I have. Thank you for taking a chance on me and the circus.

And to all the writers, artists, and creators who made me fall in love with the misfits, a huge thank you. Walking a Tightrope is about a group of vagabonds who are rejected by society but understand better than most what it means to belong. Juniper Rose took a risk to find happiness among those who are profoundly different. And there is courage in all of us to do the same.

About the Author

Emma Gilman was born and raised in sunny Colorado Springs, Colorado. She spends much of her time in pursuit of her professional writing and communication degree but continues to write for pleasure as time allows. When Emma is not writing, she is most likely watching Lord of the Rings—dreaming of being a hobbit on her own dangerous adventure, or being part of any one of the great stories that have been or are yet to be told. When not living vicariously through fictional characters, she enjoys spending time in the mountains or at home with her family.

Walking a Tightrope is Emma's debut novel.